Minding Molly

Books by Leslie Gould

THE COURTSHIPS OF LANCASTER COUNTY

Courting Cate
Adoring Addie
Minding Molly
Becoming Bea

Minding Molly

LESLIE GOULD

BETHANYHOUSE

a division of Baker Publishing Group
Minneapolis, Minnesota

Published by Bethany House Publishers
11400 Hampshire Avenue South
Bloomington, Minnesota 55438
www.bethanyhouse.com

Bethany House Publishers is a division of
Baker Publishing Group, Grand Rapids, Michigan

Printed in the United States of America

Library of Congress Cataloging-in-Publication Data
Gould, Leslie.
    Minding Molly / Leslie Gould.
        pages   cm. — (The courtships of Lancaster County ; 3)
        Summary: "In this contemporary Amish romance, Molly Zook's latest attempt to control her fate backfires. Will she finally learn to trust God with her life—and with her future groom?"— Provided by publisher.
        ISBN 978-0-7642-1033-4 (pbk.)
        1. Amish—Fiction. 2. Lancaster County (Pa.)—Fiction. I. Title.
    PS3607.O89M56 2014
    813'.6—dc23   2013032720

Scripture quotations are from the King James Version of the Bible.

Cover design by Jennifer Parker

Cover photography by Mike Habermann Photography, LLC

Author represented by MacGregor Literary, Inc.

For Taylor

Youngest son of mine,
a man of creativity,
strength, and humor

"Love one another."

John 13:34

"The course of true love never did run smooth."

William Shakespeare, *A Midsummer Night's Dream*, 1.1.134

CHAPTER

1

My *Dat* had been a small man. And thin. No one would have guessed he'd have a heart attack. But he did.

I buried my face in his forest-green shirt, pressing the soft fabric against my eyes. It had been my favorite of all his shirts. My morning task was to go through his clothes and decide what to give away, but I couldn't bear to part with his shirts—not a single one.

I'd use all of them to make a quilt for my sister Beatrice.

Not now—but during the winter months, when the work on our flower farm slowed.

I placed the shirt on top of the others and closed the box.

My parents' room looked the same as it had before Dat died— a double bed, one bureau, a straight-back chair—but now it felt so empty. My gaze moved to the small table against the window. Dat's Bible was on it, just like always, but there was a small sky-blue notebook there too, one I hadn't seen before. I stepped closer, reaching for it, but a knock on the door startled me.

"Molly? Do you need some help?" It was my half sister, Edna.

"No," I answered, stepping away from the table. "I'll be down in a minute."

She and Ivan, the oldest in my Dat's first family, had come

to help us today. I was plenty able to handle what needed to be done, but it was a comfort to have them with us.

I should have boxed things up right after Dat's passing, but we'd been in such a state of shock I couldn't bear to tackle it then. None of us could—especially not my sweet *Mamm*. But now enough time had passed since that fateful day.

It was the first week of June. The sun shone again. The days had turned warm, for good.

Dat would want us to move on. He'd want us to keep living.

Besides, tomorrow was the first day of the *Youngie* farmers' market I'd started a few years back. At the time it was all young people, but last summer I'd opened it to older vendors too. It had brought in extra income for our family, and we needed it now more than ever. It was time for me to buckle down and put business first again.

I glanced around the room one more time. I didn't know how Mamm stood sleeping in it alone. Beatrice had moved into my room the night Dat died, and the truth was, if she hadn't come into mine, I would have moved into hers. We were grown, me more so at twenty-two than she was at nineteen, but we'd both adored our Dat. Even though he was seventy-two, we'd expected him to live at least another decade. Hopefully two.

My eyes fell on the notebook again. It was none of my business.

I picked up the box of shirts from the bed and headed to the door.

As I started down the hallway, the light from the window fell across the worn wood floors. Our home was old and shabby, but it was ours. I was very thankful for it.

I stopped at the end of the landing and pressed my forehead against the cool glass of the window. Our fields were far from shabby. They brimmed with shrubs and trees, annuals and perennials, ground covers and decorative grasses. Nearly every shade of green leaves imaginable, with hints of gold from the late-morning sun, shimmered in the breeze. Splashes of color—including purple irises, pink peonies, and yellow roses—complemented the green.

We lived a few miles from the village of Paradise, but our land was truly paradise to me. There was nowhere on earth I'd rather be.

I hurried down the stairs and into the living room, where Mamm and Ivan sat side by side at the desk with a pile of bills. Ivan hid Mamm from my view as I hurried through. Dat had been thin and short, but Ivan was big and tall. My half siblings took after their mother, not the father we shared.

Even though Ivan had never married, he wore a beard and had for as long as I could remember. He'd been in his midtwenties by the time I was born and seemed much more like an uncle than a brother to me.

He had his own accounting business. The fact that Mamm had asked him to take a look at our finances meant things were worse than I'd feared. She'd always been involved in the day-to-day operation of the farm, but Dat had always seen to the books.

Dat hadn't shared our financial situation with me either, but I didn't remember him spending hours at his desk, looking worried, until a few years ago, after the economy had soured.

Seven years ago we'd had a thriving business, providing trees, shrubs, and plants to landscapers throughout the area, including those affiliated with commercial builders. As the business grew, so did our overhead, and Dat took out a mortgage to pay for the new greenhouse, office, and irrigation system. It had been a wise business decision—at the time. But then the financial downturn meant less development, which meant less landscaping, which meant fewer sales, which meant we had to scrape to meet each payment.

It had been my idea to add crops of *Blumms* and *Rauda-shtokk*. But the flowers and herbs didn't bring in the income that the nursery stock did.

I needed to figure out more ways, besides the farmers' market, to ease Mamm's worries.

I'd reached the hallway when she called out my name. "*Jah.*"

"Come here," she said.

"Just a minute." I continued to the sewing room and put the box—not wanting Mamm to see it—on the floor and returned to the living room.

She sat with her reading glasses on top of a closed manila file, her small hands folded in her lap. A few stray hairs had escaped her gray bun and trailed down her neck alongside the ties of her *Kapp*. "I forgot to tell Mervin to water the dogwood trees," she said.

"I'll tell him," I answered.

Ivan pushed his chair away from the desk. "Anna," he said, addressing my mother by her first name, the way he always had, "I don't see how you can keep the Mosier boy on. Not with the way your finances are."

I didn't see how we could afford not to, but I didn't say it out loud.

It seemed Mamm didn't hear, or didn't register, what Ivan had said. She continued talking to me, "And tell Mervin to repot the geraniums. It's getting late in the season for those, but it would be good to sell as many as we can."

I nodded my head. "Jah." We'd talked about it the day before. I planned to try to sell some tomorrow at the market. It had been a cool spring—I imagined not everyone had all their potted plants out yet. "Anything else?" I asked.

She shook her head and smiled, slightly. More wrinkles lined her face than had a few months before.

Ivan cleared his throat, as if he was readying himself to say something, but Mamm put her hand on his, and my half brother remained silent.

"I'll go give Mervin the instructions," I said.

"Denki." Mamm picked up her glasses and opened the file.

She'd clearly communicated that I should leave, but I stayed for a long moment, staring at her as she bowed her head over the papers.

She'd worked as a teacher in Ohio before marrying Dat. Although she didn't know much about business, she was organized and efficient, two skills that she'd passed down to me. And she had liked working alongside Dat. They'd complemented each other well in both their personal relationship and their work together. Plus after teaching for so many years, she was used to doing more than just housework and said she found the family business a satisfying endeavor.

Thankfully Beatrice enjoyed running the house, at least more than doing outside chores, and once she was out of school she'd taken on more and more of those responsibilities.

Although I could handle managing the house just fine, I too enjoyed working outside. Where I most differed from both my parents was in personality. They were quiet and didn't socialize much, except with people in our district, but I was outgoing and had friends from across Pennsylvania, and in neighboring states too.

Beatrice, however, took after my parents when it came to social needs—except she didn't seem to have any at all.

Edna already had a chicken roasting in the oven, potatoes boiling on the stove, and sticky buns cooling on the counter, but she wasn't in the kitchen. I headed out the back door to find her. My half sister was eighteen years older than I and left home to marry soon after I was born, but she'd always doted on Beatrice and me. She hadn't been blessed with children, and then four years ago her husband, Frank, had been gravely injured in a buggy accident and died months later.

She'd taken Dat's death hard too—more so, I guessed, than if Frank had been alive.

Our house sat on a hill. An arbor Dat had built, covered with clematis leaves, stood at the top of the path. I couldn't remember the baby pink clematis flowers blooming last month, although I'm sure they had. Nor could I remember the flowers of the dogwood trees or the lilac bushes. I'd lost all of that to my grief.

I exhaled. I wasn't going to lose any more.

The weatherman had predicted a high of eighty-five. The hottest day of the year so far.

I took another step toward the path that led to the pasture below.

The highway bordered the pasture where we held the farmers' market, and our driveway curved up the hill and along our property line. To the west our flower fields would soon bloom with lilies, lisianthus, and dahlias. To the south, behind the house, our huge white barn towered above everything else, including our greenhouse next to it. To the east was our garden, surrounded by a fence.

Edna stood at the garden gate, her back to me, while Beatrice stooped over in the first row, her bare feet half covered by the dark soil.

I couldn't tell what my older sister said, but Beatrice answered, "Denki," as she straightened up. Beatrice was beautiful—far more than I—with an untamed look and dark, intense eyes. She seemed oblivious to her good looks though. She tucked a strand of her chestnut hair under her Kapp. "I could use a break," she added. When she caught sight of me, she waved. "Come into the house," she called out. "Edna has a snack ready."

"I'll be in shortly," I answered.

I hurried on toward the greenhouse, along the stone pathway Dat had put in a couple of years before. Our land had served him the same way a canvas did an artist. I had often expected one of the bishops to accuse Dat of being too fancy. He'd added whimsical touches all over our farm. Besides the arbor covered with clematis, he'd built trellises and archways and placed slate pathways and rock gardens all over the property.

I stepped into the greenhouse, expecting to find Mervin. He wasn't there, but the geraniums were—all repotted. Perhaps he'd read Mamm's mind.

Mervin's parents had the farm next to ours, although their house was on the far side of their property, as far away from ours as possible. But still we'd grown up together—gone to the same school, the same singings, the same parties. He was like a brother to me.

My best friend, Hannah Lapp, and Mervin had been courting. But around the time my Dat passed, they stopped spending time together. Usually I would know what was going on, but for the first time since I was six and she was five, I hadn't kept up with Hannah. I hoped she understood.

Standing beside the greenhouse, I searched the field of nursery stock. Hydrangea, forsythia, and azalea spread out in front of me. I walked along, peering down each row. Next came cherry, myrtle, and plum trees.

A flash of yellow made me smile.

"Here, Love!" I called out to our lab.

She darted out from between the trees and rushed toward me. She'd been Dat's dog, and he had named her Love, he said, because God had blessed him with a life of love.

I thought it a ridiculous name at first, especially when Dat called, "Here, Love!" but it grew on us in time. And it turned out to be the perfect name for her. All dogs loved unconditionally—but Love would have won the first-place prize if one existed.

She'd refused to leave Dat's side when he'd fallen, and now she'd wait beside the back door at night, as if still believing he would come home.

With Dat gone, she tended to follow Mervin around when he was working. Otherwise she held Mamm and me in equal esteem, but Beatrice had never bonded with the dog much.

As Love reached me, I spotted Mervin by the dogwood trees, a black hose in his hand, his straw hat riding back on his head, his aviator sunglasses perched on his long nose. Wondering how he'd known what Mamm wanted him to do, I made my way down the row of trees, my flip-flop-clad feet sinking into the soft soil, Love at my side.

"Have you learned to read minds?" I called out to Mervin.

He pushed his glasses up on the bridge of his nose to where the tops were level with his sandy-colored bangs, met my gaze, and pursed his lips.

"How did you know what you were supposed to do?" I asked.

Mervin shook his head. "Your Mamm told me—yesterday at quitting time."

Mamm had been forgetful lately, but I'd chalked it up to Dat's death. All her energy had gone into coping—how could we expect her to keep track of mundane details?

But her giving Mervin instructions and then entirely forgetting she'd done so was something new. And she was only sixty-three. It had to be stress related—not age.

"Did she tell you to repot the geraniums too?" I stepped closer to Mervin, reaching down to pet Love as I did.

"Jah. In fact she told me more than once."

I shoved my hands into the pocket of my apron. "How many times?"

14

"Four. Maybe five."

"Oh dear," I whispered. Then in a normal voice, I said, "Denki for all your hard work. I don't know what we would have done without you these last months."

I turned to go but had only made it a step when Mervin said, "I wanted to ask you something."

"Jah." I stumbled on a rock, stubbing my toe, as I turned back around.

Love pressed her body against my leg as Mervin steadied me.

"Denki," I said, pulling away, aware of his hand on my arm.

"I was wondering," he said, his voice deep and strained, "if you'd go to the singing with me."

I tilted my head. So things had come to an end between him and Hannah. Most likely months ago. I hadn't been to a singing since Dat died. "Could I let you know tomorrow?"

"Sure," he said, but his voice sounded down.

"I'll see you after dinner."

He nodded in response. Even though workers often ate the noon meal with their Amish employers, we'd worked out the routine of him going to his house for dinner. His Mamm always fixed a big meal, and that way if Mamm, Beatrice, and I just wanted to eat leftovers we didn't feel pressured to do a lot of cooking. All three of us had lost our appetites—except for when Edna visited.

Love stepped back to Mervin's side.

"Is she bothering you?" I asked.

"Of course not."

I patted the dog's head and made my way back to the end of the row. When I reached it, I kicked my flip-flops off, shook the dirt off of them, and dragged my bare feet along the grass. As I came around the side of the greenhouse, movement across the highway caught my attention.

A man driving a team of mules was cutting alfalfa. Certain it was Phillip Eicher and not wanting him to see me, I hurried toward the house. We'd dated—briefly—but he'd broken it off, much to my chagrin. I told people it didn't work out; he told people I wasn't the right girl for him—which was obviously true. Still, it had hurt my feelings and, to be honest, also my pride, even though I knew that was wrong.

Hannah had laughed when she found out Phillip had broken up with me. That hurt too. "Oh, Molly," she'd said, "it's only funny because this is the first time in your life you didn't get what you wanted."

I guess Dat dying was the second.

Now Phillip was courting a seventeen-year-old girl from across the county. I'd heard she was a beauty.

When I reached the house, the screen door slipped from my hands and banged. No one was in the kitchen.

"Molly? Is that you?" It was Mamm again.

"Jah," I answered.

"Could you come here?"

I sped through the kitchen, stopping at the living room doorway. She sat at the desk alone.

"Where is everyone?" I asked.

"Beatrice convinced Ivan and Edna to go see the new kittens in the barn."

That sounded like Beatrice. And like my older siblings to give in to her *kindish* ways.

"What do you need?" I asked Mamm, pointing to her cup. "More coffee?"

"No." She pulled her glasses from her face. "I've been thinking about ways to try to get our profits up." She put her glasses down on the desk again.

I smiled, pleased she was thinking about our profits too.

"And that got me thinking. I've noticed Mervin looking at you, following you around. I think he's sweet on you."

I couldn't imagine what Mervin's feelings toward me had to do with our profits.

"I didn't tell Ivan this," she said, placing her hand on the side of her head. "There's no point yet, but a wholesaler left a message, asking if there was any way we could increase our production. He said if we could, he'd be willing to buy from us."

I hadn't noticed it before, but as I stared at her—in disbelief— I noted that her hair had grown whiter in the last couple of months.

"It would make me so happy to have you marry and settle down," she said. "What could be better than to join our two families? We've been good friends all these years."

My mouth fell open, but I couldn't manage to form a sound.

"Our farms are side by side," she continued. "You and Mervin would be able to provide for yourselves and for me in my old age. And for your sister."

"Mamm . . ." I finally managed to say. She and Dat had never meddled in my life before.

"Think about it," Mamm said, putting her glasses back on her face. "And in the meantime, I forgot to tell Mervin to water the dogwood trees. Could you tell him?"

"Mamm, you—"

"And to repot the geraniums."

"No, you already did." My voice wavered. "It's all done."

She looked up at me. "Are you sure?"

I nodded, a sick feeling settling in the pit of my stomach.

She lowered her voice. "Molly . . ." She took a deep breath. "I'm worried."

Jah, I thought. *Me too.*

"It's your father." She stopped again and stared at the closed folder.

"Ach, Mamm. I know it's hard . . ."

"He's been gone so long," she said, turning her head to me, tears filling her eyes.

I nodded. It had only been a couple of months, but it seemed much longer.

"When is he coming back?" she asked.

"Mamm?"

"I thought it would only be for a short time." Her eyes held a longing in them I hadn't seen before. Was it grief that had her confused? Or was something horribly wrong?

"He's gone," I said. "Remember he . . ." I didn't want to think of Dat lying on the front lawn, let alone speak of it. "He passed, Mamm. We had the funeral. In April. Now it's June."

She shook her head.

Maybe it was just grief. But what if Mamm was having a stroke? I had no way of knowing. What I did know was I couldn't lose another parent.

"Stay right here," I said to her.

Before Dat died, I'd always left my cell phone in the greenhouse office, but since he'd passed, I kept it in my apron pocket—just in case. I pulled it out as I sped through the back door, heading toward the barn. I keyed in our doctor's number as I ran and yelled, "Beatrice! Ivan! Edna! Come quick!" I shouted again as a voice on the other end of my cell said hello.

Beatrice appeared at the barn door first, leaving it wide open. I motioned toward the house. "It's Mamm," I called out. "Something's wrong."

She took off running, her hands holding her dress above her knees, the ties of her Kapp trailing over her shoulder. Ivan and Edna followed.

18

Somehow, all the way in the field, Love sensed something was wrong and came bounding to my side. I put my hand on top of her head to calm her as I explained the situation to the nurse.

"Can you bring your mother in?" she asked.

"I'm thinking I should call an ambulance," I said. That's what we should have done with Dat.

Edna kept going toward the house, but Ivan stopped beside me, saying, "That would cost quite a sum of money."

The nurse asked, "Is her speech slurred?"

Ignoring Ivan, I answered, "No."

"Face droopy?"

I would have noticed that. "No," I answered.

"Arm weak?"

"I don't think so." I started for the back door, with Love still beside me and Ivan right behind.

"Are her words making sense?" the nurse asked.

"Jah," I said, "except she was asking about my father as if he is alive, but he passed two months ago. It seemed she didn't remember that."

"How about her vision?"

"I think it's fine. . . ."

"Any headaches?"

"Some, just lately, but she said they're from stress . . ."

"How old is she?"

"Sixty-three."

"Any other signs of dementia?"

"Dementia?"

"You know—forgetfulness, confusion."

"She has been forgetful. . . ." I told Love to stay and stepped into the kitchen with Ivan right behind me. "Should I call for an ambulance?" I asked the nurse.

"Can you bring her in?"

19

"I'll call our driver and see." If she wasn't available I'd call 9-1-1.

"Oh, you're Amish," the nurse said. "I remember now, about your father . . ."

"Jah," I answered.

Her voice overflowed with compassion. "I'll tell the doctor to expect you."

"Thank you." After I said good-bye, I ended the call.

Edna stood to the side of Mamm. Beatrice had planted herself behind them, a confused look on her face. She mouthed, "She says she's fine."

"Mamm, do either of your arms feel weak?" I asked.

She shook her head.

"Can you see all right? Does your head ache?"

"Molly, I'm fine."

Ivan was right, calling an ambulance would cost a fortune, and it would worry Mamm. I stepped back into the kitchen and called our driver, Doris. She said she'd be at our place in half an hour.

Edna served up dinner in a hurry, and I waited until the driver arrived to tell Mamm I was taking her to the doctor.

"Oh, that's not necessary," she said. "I'll just go take a nap."

Before I could say anything, Ivan jumped in and said, "Anna, we're concerned about you is all. Humor us."

She glanced from Ivan to me and then touched the side of her head. At last she said, "Oh, all right."

Edna said she would stay with Beatrice. I shouldn't have been surprised when Ivan followed me and Mamm out to the car, but I was.

Mamm sat on the examination table while I stood beside her and Ivan sat in the chair. We'd been at the clinic for a couple of hours. The doctor had done an exam, the lab tech had drawn blood, and the preliminary tests had already been completed. The doctor had ruled out both a vitamin deficiency and a stroke, but he was concerned about Mamm's headaches, which were worse than she'd been letting on. She managed to be honest with the doctor, although she claimed they were grief related. The doctor conceded that grief—and stress—could cause physical symptoms, but he didn't think that was the case with her.

The doctor sat on the spinning stool. "I want you to get a CT scan. At the hospital." He took out a pad of paper from his coat pocket and wrote down a number. He started to hand it to Ivan, but I intercepted it.

Ivan didn't seem to mind. "What are you looking for?" he asked.

"Any abnormalities," the doctor answered.

When I asked about dementia, the doctor answered that it could be a concern too.

Ivan asked if there was any reason not to have the CT scan.

"If Mrs. Zook wants to know what she's up against, she should have it. Hopefully it's nothing, and that would be good to know too."

"What will be will be," Mamm said.

"Granted," the doctor said kindly. "There are some people who, once their children are all raised and perhaps after a spouse has passed, decide not to go ahead with tests and such." It seemed he was choosing his words carefully. "But, Mrs. Zook, you have two daughters in your care." He'd been our doctor for years, since Beatrice and I were babies. "And you're still relatively young."

Relatively? She could live for another thirty years, easily.

"Jah, Mamm," I said. "You're very young." All my life, I had thought my parents old—until today.

The doctor said to call him if we had any questions but to make the appointment for the CT scan as soon as possible. I said I'd make it immediately, unfolding the piece of paper with the number on it and taking my cell from my pocket as he told us good-bye and left the room.

As I keyed in the numbers, Ivan said, "Goodness, Molly. Couldn't you wait until we got outside?"

I shook my head as I patted Mamm's arm.

My call went through, and I took the first available appointment—on a Tuesday, a week and a half away.

When I told Mamm when the appointment was, she said, "See, I'm fine. If they really thought there was a problem, they would have gotten me in sooner." She scooted off the table. "In fact, call back and cancel."

I slipped my phone into my apron pocket. I wasn't raised to disobey. So I pretended I hadn't heard.

As we left the doctor's office, Mamm sighed and said, "Now I have another bill to figure out how to pay." She padded down the carpet of the hallway in her soft-soled shoes, me on one side of her and Ivan on the other. "And then another for that test you didn't cancel."

"You've paid into the church fund all these years," I responded. "There will be plenty to cover your costs." Members from every district put aside money each month in a health-care fund that we pooled to pay medical expenses. We'd used some when Dat died, but not that much.

"When it's my time, it's my time," Mamm said. I decided to ignore that too.

"The Lord knows the number of my days," she added as we reached the door.

"Mamm . . ." I pushed it open, stepping out into the afternoon heat. "You're life isn't all that's at stake here. Beatrice and I need you. We're not ready to be orphans."

The driver had parked her car on the edge of the lot, in the shade, and Mamm stepped off the curb, leading the way, as I grabbed her elbow.

Ivan stepped quickly to Mamm's side. "Anna, I was serious about buying the—"

She put her hand up, swinging her purse around. He stopped.

I stopped cold, even as the heat swirled up from the pavement. "What?" I blurted out as I glared at my half brother.

"It's not right for three women to be living alone."

I shook my head. "What are you talking about?" I asked. "We're doing fine."

Mamm continued on toward the car.

Ivan's face reddened. "After paying off the mortgage, there'd still be enough money from the sale for you to buy a house in town, maybe on a double lot."

"But you don't even like to farm," I said.

Ivan's face grew redder.

The farm was my home. For as long as I could remember, I'd hoped the man I'd someday marry would want to farm it with me. I took off marching, biting my tongue from saying more, gaining on Mamm. But then she stopped abruptly, and I bumped into her.

"Sorry," I said.

Ivan stopped behind me.

Mamm turned toward us. "I just want both of you to know," she said, her voice firm and clear, "I know your Dat passed. Maybe I had a moment of wishful thinking, but I don't have dementia. I'm sure of it."

"Of course you don't." I took her hand and squeezed it. "It's far more likely there's a physical explanation for all of this. That's why you should have the scan done."

She started walking again, and when we reached the car,

Mamm and I climbed in the back seat, leaving the front for Ivan. Doris asked how things were.

"I'm fine," Mamm said. "I'd know if there was something wrong."

"She needs more tests," I clarified.

"Oh, well, I'm sure everything *is* fine," Doris said. "But, Mrs. Zook, for the sake of your girls, you're doing the right thing."

Mamm crossed her arms, an uncharacteristic gesture for her, and I gave Doris an apologetic nod. She smiled at me and mouthed, *"No worries."*

Ivan stared straight ahead.

I'd been my Dat's girl. The one who worked alongside him outside. The one he told his plans to. The one to whom he'd rattle off the Latin names—that I could never remember—of plants and flowers.

But he and Mamm had been best friends, holding hands in the privacy of our home. Stealing kisses in the hallway. Sharing their love of nature. I could only hope I'd have a marriage as dear as theirs someday.

As much as I missed and mourned Dat, I couldn't imagine how much Mamm missed him—I couldn't fathom how her inner world had shifted. Perhaps today's incident *had* been caused by stress.

Doris pointed out the wild flowers alongside the road and then a colt romping in a field. Then she commented on the beautiful weather, saying she and her husband planned to barbecue for dinner. Usually, I would have kept the conversation going, but I couldn't seem to hold up my end, and the car fell silent.

When we reached our farm, Mamm started to pay the driver, but Ivan said he would, which was generous for him. He paid quickly and then climbed from the car and headed toward the house. After telling Doris good-bye, Mamm took off for the house too, followed by Love, who had been patiently waiting.

24

"She needs to have a CT scan done week after next—that Tuesday morning," I said to Doris. "But she doesn't want to do it."

"Give her a day or two," she said. "I'll put it on my calendar."

"Denki." I gave her the time and said a quick good-bye.

As I neared the house, I heard men's voices on the porch. One was Mervin's. I couldn't place the second one, but it wasn't Ivan's.

Instead of going through the back door, I headed around front with Love following me. Too late, just as my head popped above the railing, I realized the second voice was Phillip's.

I quickly retreated while Love headed for Mervin. If either Phillip or Mervin saw me, they didn't call out my name. Ivan stepped onto the porch from the front door, saying hello to both, and Mamm followed, asking everyone if they'd like lemonade. It should have been me being hospitable, instead of my poor mother, but I simply didn't feel up to it.

I headed to the back door and into the house, finding Beatrice in the sewing room, kneeling on the floor next to the box I'd left. My little sister looked up, her face streaked with tears. "How's Mamm?" She clung to Dat's green shirt.

"She's okay. It's probably nothing." I knelt beside my sister. "It wasn't a stroke, but she needs to have another test—to rule other things out."

Beatrice put her head in her hands and said, "What will happen to us if she dies?"

I could barely hear her and leaned closer. "What do you mean?"

"Where will we go to live?"

I took a deep breath. "We'll stay here."

Beatrice shook her head. "Ivan will want to sell the place. He won't want us to keep it."

"No, that's not true," I said, even though I wasn't at all sure what Ivan would do. He didn't think it was right for the *three* of us to be living alone. He'd think it even worse for just the two of us. "Our home has been in the family for over a hundred years. We wouldn't sell it to strangers."

"That's not what Mervin was just telling Phillip." She swiped at a tear. I was certain the farm meant far more to me than my sister, but still this was home to her too. "He said we're bound to lose the farm no matter what."

"Bea," I said, "you shouldn't be eavesdropping." The last thing I wanted was for Bea to know how dire our situation was.

"That's not all they said." She held Dat's shirt to her face. I could barely hear her words. "Mervin said if you marry soon, maybe your husband could save the farm."

"He said that in front of Phillip?"

She nodded.

"Oh goodness," I said. "That's ridiculous."

"Mervin didn't seem to think so." Beatrice dropped the shirt to her lap.

I lowered my voice. "Did he say anything else?" I feared there was more.

"No, that's all I heard. I came in here after that . . . and then found this." She placed her hand on the box of shirts.

I'd intended the quilt as a surprise, but sometimes there was comfort in anticipating a gift. "I'm going to make a quilt for you out of Dat's shirts."

Tears filled her eyes again. "Denki," she said.

I heard someone in the kitchen. "Where's Edna?" I asked, hoping maybe she was going to serve the front porch gang her famous sticky buns.

"Resting, but she's going to stay here tonight and tomorrow night too. She said we need some extra love."

I was relieved to hear that. It would be a blessing to have

her cook while I worked the market the next day, and for her to help keep an eye on Mamm too. Our district had cared for us well during the weeks after Dat's death—helping with the chores, bringing meals, chopping wood, and cleaning. But that had come to an end, as it should have.

Bea swiped at her tears.

"Enough of that now," I said. "Pull yourself together and go help Mamm."

Beatrice leaned back, away from me. "Don't be so bossy," she said.

"We have a porch full of men to serve a snack to." And I didn't want to be the one to offer Phillip a glass of lemonade.

"You were bossy enough before Dat died, but now you're nearly intolerable."

I stood. "Bea, I—"

"You always have to be in charge," she said without looking at me as she refolded the shirt and put it back in the box.

"Well, jah," I said. "Someone has to be."

She rose to her knees and looked out the window, toward the barn and greenhouse, and then sniffled again. She was sensitive, even more than usual since Dat died. And with good reason. She'd lost her father, and now she was afraid of losing her childhood home.

I stood and followed her to the window. "Nothing's going to happen to the farm. This is our place. This is where we're going to stay." I could only hope my words were true.

CHAPTER

2

I placed a large bucket of snapdragons in front of my table at the market, and then arranged smaller buckets of lavender, rosemary, and lemon thyme around it.

At the beginning Dat had opposed the Youngie farmers' market, saying he didn't think it would bring in much money, but he allowed me to give it a try. It wasn't long until he supported my efforts completely, although he never did get used to the traffic and crowds on market day. Neither did Mamm and Beatrice.

But I loved it.

I was in my element, meaning combining the two things I enjoyed most—flowers and people.

Nell Yoder, who was my friend Hannah's aunt and sharing my booth, stepped to my side. "Oh, look at those snapdragons," she said. She pointed to one of her potholders, made from a red-and-yellow print, and then pointed at my blooms, saying, "They match."

That made me smile. She had to be in her early forties or so but she seemed younger, maybe because she'd never had the stress of having her own family. "Those blooms won't last once the weather turns hot though," she added.

"Jah," I said. "That's why I need to sell as many as possible this morning."

She lowered her voice. "It's nice to have Jonathan and Addie back with us." The two stood at his booth, talking with an *Englisch* couple.

I nodded. Addie was Nell's niece, along with being Hannah's cousin. She and Jonathan had been selling at markets far more upscale than mine, as far away as Maryland. I was thankful they'd booked with me for our opening day, but next week they'd be off somewhere else.

I headed toward Jonathan's booth. Several Englisch people were examining his woodwork—mantels, hope chests, and bookcases, along with smaller items, including trivets and bookends.

Addie waved to me, and I said hello and picked up a trivet with a daisy carved on the top. If I had any extra money, I'd buy it for Mamm. I put it back down. "Where will you two be next Saturday?" I asked Addie.

"New Jersey," she answered. "It's an especially busy market."

I'd heard that.

Addie stepped closer to me and said, quietly, "I heard Phillip is courting Jessie Berg."

I nodded as a lump lodged in my throat. I didn't want to talk about Phillip Eicher, not even with Addie.

"Are you okay with that?"

"Of course," I managed to squeak. Addie and Phillip had courted before she fell for Jonathan. Phillip had been hurt and still talked about being jilted by Addie when he and I briefly courted. He more than talked, actually. He obsessed.

Addie shielded her eyes from the sun. "You and Phillip came to an understanding, then?"

I nodded.

She smiled at me, her eyes crinkling around the corners. "Oh good. Because I truly think that's what's best for you," Addie said.

I tilted my head, wondering what she meant.

When she didn't elaborate I asked, "How's that?"

She stepped even closer. She really wasn't one to gossip, not like her Aenti Nell, so I knew to listen to what she said. "Phillip, at least when he courted me, mostly cared about himself. I was worried about you."

Nell's shrill voice interrupted us. "Molly!"

She stood in front of our booth, waving at me and pointing to an Englisch woman who was holding a large bunch of snapdragons in her hands.

I turned back to Addie. "Customer. Gotta go," I said as I stepped backward, away from her. "Denki for your concern." I waved as I spun around and hurried back down to my booth, thankful to have escaped any further discussion of Phillip Eicher. He had been self-absorbed when we'd been seeing each other, but I'd thought it was due to the fact that Addie had hurt him so badly, that he was still licking his wounds—and his pride.

After I took the Englisch woman's money and she'd headed toward Jonathan's hope chests, a movement on the knoll caught my attention. Beatrice, with Love by her side, was unpinning the wash from the clothesline, her image framed by our white house directly behind her.

I'd asked her just that morning to leave it up until at least noon.

"I'll be right back," I said to Nell.

I grabbed the hem of my dress, lifted it to my knees, and began jogging through the back of the pasture and then up the slope toward the yard. "Bea," I called out.

She turned toward me, squinting. Love did too, although her brown eyes lit up and her tongue fell out of her mouth.

"What are you doing?"

"The laundry."

"I told you to leave it. Remember?"

She turned her back to me, reaching back up to the line, plucking another wooden pin. "I'm not waiting to do my chores to please the Englisch."

"But they like looking at our wash."

She'd made a face and said, "Which is exactly why I want to get it down." She could be awfully black and white in her thinking.

I used my kindest tone and said, "Just leave it for a few more hours. Please."

She spoke around the pin in her mouth. "It's already nine. The morning is half gone." She held another pin in one hand and Mamm's dress in the other.

"Just another hour." I stepped closer to her. "It might help save the farm."

That was a stretch on my part, but it seemed to give Beatrice pause.

"Instead, could you help Mervin cut more flowers before it gets too hot?"

She held up the dress, as if asking what to do with it.

I nodded toward the line.

Instead of obeying, she tossed it at me, followed by one pin. Then the other. Both of which I managed to catch. And then off she marched toward the flower field. Love turned and gave me a sorrowful look. She hated it when any of us had a spat. "Go with her," I said. Love wasn't allowed down at the market.

The dog took off at a run and in a minute was far ahead of Beatrice, dashing toward Mervin.

I repinned the dress. Beatrice had been all over the map as far as her emotions since Dat had died. Yesterday she'd been tearful. Today she seemed angry. I couldn't blame her. My emotions had been off-kilter too.

I took a step backward, taking in the clothesline. Our laundry was a sure sign that the farmers' market below was authentically Amish, but I couldn't help but mourn that Dat's shirts weren't flying alongside our dresses.

I sighed, encouraging myself to look on the bright side. Dat had lived a long life, and we still had our memories of him and our time together.

Dat had always complimented me on my optimism. He used to call me Sunny, both for my disposition and blond hair when I was young. I wasn't going to let him down now.

I headed back down the path, taking in the sight below me. Thirty booths filled the front part of the pasture. Cars filled the makeshift parking lot, along with the buggies. Below, a mix of Englisch and Plain people ambled down the aisles between the booths. Besides Jonathan's woodwork and my flowers and herbs, the vendors sold quilts, potholders, yard art, soaps, candles, preserves, produce, and ready-to-eat food.

The savory scent of sausage grilling wafted up the slope toward me as I navigated the path.

"Molly!"

Startled, I stopped, my white tennis shoes stirring up a mini cloud of dirt, and turned toward the voice.

Mervin bobbled toward me, across our lawn, a bucket of sweet peas in each hand. Water sloshed over the edge of one onto his boot. He jerked his foot away and kept on coming. Even though it was still morning he had his aviator sunglasses on while his straw hat rode back on his head.

"Wait," he called out.

"I need to get back," I answered, turning to go.

"Take these," he said. "And I'll go back for the herbs."

Reluctantly I agreed, hurrying back up the trail and then balancing the buckets as best I could, but still water sloshed over the side onto my right shoe, turning the dust to mud. I poured half the water out of each and then hurried on down the path.

When I reached my booth, Nell said I'd missed a customer. "She said she'd come back," Nell said, settling back down into her chair and taking up a potholder she'd been quilting.

I had a spurt of sales, mostly snapdragons and herbs, but a few peonies too. They were my favorite. I turned toward the slope to the field, searching for Mervin. He was descending slowly, holding two more buckets out at arms' length. Behind him walked my mother.

A movement on the lawn pulled my attention upward. Beatrice was back at the clothesline taking off the wash after all, folding it into the basket she had left behind. It was useless for me to plead a second time.

"Molly," Nell said, pulling me away from spying on my sister, "I'm going to take a walk. Would you keep an eye on my things?"

I assured her I would. She stretched her plump arms and then wandered over to Joseph Koller's booth, picking up a wooden buggy as if she might be interested in buying it. She must have complimented his work, because above his long gray beard his cheeks grew pink.

Joseph had been a widower for several years and had seemed interested in courting younger women. Nell was, at least, within a decade of him in age. I didn't want to start any rumors, but I thought the two were sweet on each other. Nell deserved some happiness after devoting her life to Addie's family, the Cramers, for years.

Focusing back on my herbs, I combined them into one container by the time Mervin and Mamm reached me. After Mervin lowered the new buckets, I gave him the empty ones.

But then Mamm said, "Mervin, watch the booth for a few minutes." Then to me she said, "Come walk with me."

"Now? Are you feeling all right?"

"There's nothing wrong," Mamm said. "I just want to have a chat with you."

I followed Mamm to the end of the field, to where the creek ran between our property and the Mosiers'. The way she clipped along, I began to believe there was nothing wrong with her. Across the fence Mervin's twin, Martin, who also wore aviator sunglasses, was dragging their pasture. He waved. I returned the gesture. Mamm smiled. She'd always been fond of the Mosier twins.

When we reached the fence, Mamm turned right and started walking the property line up the hill. "This was your Dat's land, and his father's, and his grandfather's," she said. "More than anything I want to keep it for you and Beatrice. If it's not God's will, I'll accept that, but I plan to do everything I possibly can first."

I nodded. I felt the same way.

"I don't want what happened to Edna to happen to us," Mamm said.

I couldn't agree more. After the accident, Frank had been in the hospital for three months. Edna finally sold their farm—to Ivan. He kept it for a few months and then ended up selling it at a profit. Thankfully Edna had enough money, after paying the bills the church couldn't cover, to rent a little house in Paradise. She didn't keep a horse and buggy—she got rides to church from others in her district and hired a driver when needed. She seemed resigned to her lot. I couldn't comprehend Ivan buying her place and so quickly selling it for his own profit, but Edna never seemed to hold it against him. And Dat made it clear it wasn't any of my business.

Still I understood what Mamm meant. I didn't want us to have to live on someone else's property. Or even on our own place but someplace new, say in a house in town. I wanted to live on our farm. True, Mamm hadn't lived here much longer than I, but it was the only home she had left. Her parents had passed away years ago, as had most of her siblings. She had no desire to return to Ohio. She loved our land nearly as much as I did.

We continued on in silence. She must have wanted someone to walk the property line with her, as if to gain courage for the challenge ahead. But by the time we neared the top of the hill, she was struggling.

Finally she slowed and, putting her hand to her chest, said, "I don't know when I got so out of shape."

"It's a steep climb," I said. "Plus it's getting hot."

Ahead was the flower field, where Beatrice was now working. Mamm stopped and leaned against a fence post.

"Maybe we should go over to the shade," I said.

"This is a fine place," she said. "No one can hear."

"You need a glass of water," I said. "We should go to the house."

She shook her head. "We need to talk about our farm." She squinted at me. "The more I think about it, the more I like the idea of you marrying Mervin."

I stepped backward, bumping against the top rail of the fence. "Mamm." I'd thought she was done with that nonsense.

"Now hear me out. There's no reason for you to wait to get married as long as I did." She'd been forty. And I agreed with her. I planned to marry within the next couple of years, God willing.

The truth was, I'd expected to be married by now. I'd always had lots of boys for friends, from my school days on. And I knew Amish young men from all over—as far away as Indiana.

I'd had a few interested in me from other places, but I didn't want to leave Lancaster County.

"You've known Mervin your whole life," Mamm said. "He's good and kind, to Beatrice and me too. He'd make a good husband. And he likes this business—I'm sure he'd expand it over to his farm too."

I knew his parents hoped to retire soon.

Mamm smiled, her eyes lighting up. "And he's smitten with you."

My face grew warm. "But I don't love him."

"That will come." Mamm took a deep breath and then exhaled slowly. "I've never told anyone this. Not even your father. But I didn't love him when I married him."

"Mamm—"

She put her finger to her lips. "Don't tell a soul, but it's true. I liked him, jah, and I knew he was a good man, so it wasn't as if I took a risk. But I didn't know him well enough to love him."

I shook my head. "How could you marry someone you didn't love?"

"I wanted children," she said. "I knew I wouldn't likely have another chance."

I crossed my arms. "I don't believe you didn't love Dat."

"That's because I came to love him." Tears filled her eyes. "More deeply than I ever dreamed."

"And you think that would happen with Mervin and me?"
She nodded.

"But I'm not sure Hannah doesn't still care for him. I'd never do that to her."

"Ask her," Mamm said. "Mervin said he hasn't seen her in weeks. Perhaps she's courting someone else already."

I pursed my lips together. I doubted that. Maybe she wouldn't mention she'd stopped seeing Mervin, but I certainly hoped she'd let me know if she'd started courting someone new. My stomach sank. I'd neglected her these last couple of months—and all my other friends, except for Mervin.

A concerned expression settled on Mamm's face. "I'm afraid maybe you've gotten false ideas from all your running around—expecting lightning to strike with the appearance of some sort of Mr. Right. The truth is you could probably make a future with any of the men you already know, as long as he loves the Lord."

I wasn't sure if that was true. "Well, I'm not a *Maidel* . . . yet," I said, trying to make light of the moment.

There was no doubt I'd make a good wife and mother. There wasn't a Youngie woman in all of Lancaster County who worked harder than I did or who was more organized. Plus I had a head for business. And I could manage a home just fine too, if I put my mind to it.

Mamm turned toward the Mosier farm. It wasn't like her to meddle. Usually she was as mild as a barn mouse. "More than anything, I want to know that you and Beatrice are cared for. I hope Ivan would help out someday, if needed . . ."

"I'm sure he would," I said. "And I know Edna would help."

"Her resources are limited. . . ." She turned back toward me, her expression weary. "Think about it," she said. "And pray."

I nodded, swallowing hard as I did.

"I'm going to go get that drink of water."

Mamm started toward the house but then turned back around, slowly, her eyes as serious as I'd ever seen them. "I've been debating whether to tell you this or not. . . . Don't tell Beatrice . . . but Ivan did a preliminary run-through of our books and said they're as red as"—she glanced down to the market below—"those geraniums we're trying to sell."

Now I struggled for breath. "Ivan knows books, right? Not business. We should get some help to turn things around. Right away—and not just from Mervin," I said. "How about Bob Miller?" He was my friend Cate's father and one of the most successful businessmen in the area.

"Good idea," Mamm said. "And in the meantime, think about Mervin." She turned back toward the house again, calling over her shoulder, "Tell Mervin to spend the rest of the day helping you with the market. Try to sell all you can. . . ." Her voice trailed off as she shuffled along. Love waited for her on the edge of the lawn.

I watched my Mamm, my breathing ragged. I never would have imagined her pressuring me to marry.

Nor that we might lose our farm.

I half listened as Nell told me about the quilt she was making, watching as Mervin stood along the highway, waving a bunch of flowers to attract business. It really wasn't our way, but Mervin could pull it off with his sunglasses and goofy grin. He was a people person, like me.

And unlike Bea. She wasn't shy one-on-one, but she definitely didn't like crowds. Nor did she like the market. "All those strangers," she'd say, "tramping around our property."

I saw the activity as money to pay the bills. She saw it as an intrusion.

If we couldn't save the farm, what would happen to Bea? And where would I host my farmers' market? And where would Mamm live out the rest of her life?

Sweat trickled down the back of my knees. Mervin enjoyed the work of raising flowers, trees, and shrubs, plus he really was good at selling.

I pulled the white cloth of my apron up to my face, blocking the sun for a moment, dabbing at my forehead, as Nell prattled on about the shadow design she'd modified for the quilt she'd just started. When I put my apron down, an Englisch couple with three young children, all boys, approached our booth. The youngest one, around three, began to cry, and the father scooped him up, jostling him around. The boy smiled for a moment but then began to fuss again.

"Have you seen the handmade toys?" I asked the father as his wife looked at Nell's potholders. "Right over there?" I pointed to Joseph Koller's booth. The two older boys tore across the aisle at the word *toys*.

The father turned.

The youngest son pointed at the booth and squealed. The father headed that way, and the mother let out a sigh of relief and then bought a pot of geraniums.

As she turned to leave, Mervin headed back toward me, his hands empty, except for the money in his fist.

"Denki," I said, as he came near, his hand extended. I took the money. "You should go eat."

Mervin smiled broadly. "After you. I'll stay here with Nell."

Her eyes lit up.

"You can tell me the latest," he said to her.

"Well, well, well," she said, standing. "You won't be sorry. I'll leave you in anticipation for a bit though. Be back in a minute."

A mock expression of surprise passed over Mervin's face, but then he smiled as Nell headed over to Joseph's booth.

In that moment, marrying Mervin didn't seem like such a sacrifice to me. After all, he was probably on my list of the top five men I could marry—now way above Phillip Eicher, but still below the man I hoped was still out there, that I had yet to meet. The one who, as Mamm would say, would arrive like a bolt of lightning. How'd she know that's what I'd set my sights on once things had fallen through with Phillip?

Jah, Mervin was right up there. I knew I could do a whole lot worse.

Mervin tilted his head. "What are you thinking?"

Actually, Mervin might be at the top of the list. If Mervin was interested in me, who was I to say I couldn't be interested in him?

"Molly?" Mervin stepped closer to me, taking his sunglasses off. His hazel eyes shone bright and clear.

I grabbed for his glasses, thinking I'd wear them for a while.

He laughed and ducked away, but I still got a hold of them—probably because he let me. Mervin grinned and his eyes danced, but then, in a split second, they fell flat, as if he'd been reprimanded.

I slipped the glasses onto my face anyway, hoping to make him laugh again. "What do you think?"

From behind me a voice—Hannah's to be exact—said, "Not your style."

I spun around. Hannah stood with her hands on her hips. I removed the glasses and handed them back to Mervin. He positioned them on his face and stepped away, over to Joseph's booth.

"Hi," I said to Hannah, hoping my voice conveyed how happy I was to see her.

"I thought you were in mourning," she said, a note of sympathy—and concern—in her voice, but also a hint of disapproval.

I nodded. I definitely still was.

"It didn't look like it."

"We were joking around," I said, taking a deep breath. It seemed Hannah still liked Mervin. How foolish I'd been to think otherwise.

"I was going to call . . . but decided to come by instead."

"I'm glad you did," I said. "I've been missing you."

She smiled then, clearly pleased. We were opposites in several ways. I was fair with blue eyes. She had dark hair and brown eyes. I had a pale, heart-shaped face. She had an amazing olive complexion and dimples. I was thin. She had curves. I was the optimist. She could be a little pessimistic, at times. I was responsible. She was lackadaisical.

"We have so much to talk about," she said.

"Jah . . ." I agreed, expecting her to say something about Mervin.

But she said, "Like the camping trip."

We had talked about a trip—it wasn't unusual for a group of Youngie to go camping for a few days. In fact I'd suggested it after church a few weeks ago, thinking it might take my mind off my Dat, but I hadn't given it much thought since then, except to mention it to Mamm, in passing. In her usual supportive way, she'd agreed it was a good idea, as long as I took Beatrice along.

But Hannah and I hadn't talked about who else would go. "Molly?"

"Jah," I said again. "Let's talk about it soon."

"Like this evening? Can you spend the night?"

"Maybe." I couldn't ignore my feeling of apprehension though. I shouldn't be going anywhere—not even to Hannah's—if Mamm was ill.

A hurt expression—one I knew too well—passed over Hannah's face.

I whispered, "Mamm hasn't been well."

Hannah pointed behind me. "She looks fine."

I spun around again. Mamm was standing with a small bucket of rosemary in her hand. "Go," she said. "I'm fine. And Edna will be here tonight."

I took the bucket from her.

She glanced toward Mervin. He must have said something funny because Nell and Joseph were laughing.

"Go to Hannah's," Mamm said. "It will give you two a chance to talk."

"I should stay," I said.

"No. It's good timing," she answered.

There was no church service the next day. We used to visit friends and relatives in other districts on our off Sundays, but we hadn't since Dat died. Mamm turned to Hannah. "She'll be over before supper."

Hannah smiled.

"I'll see you then," I said.

I expected her to seek out Mervin next, but she didn't. Instead she started toward Addie and Jonathan's booth.

Mamm headed back to the house, and Mervin joined me again, taking the rest of the snapdragons to try to sell along the road. And then, a few minutes later, Hannah headed toward her buggy without talking to Mervin at all.

CHAPTER

3

We closed the market at four. Mervin stayed and helped me—picking up trash, putting away our tarp and tables, carrying our buckets back up to the barn, and helping vendors carry their unsold wares to their buggies. I appreciated how I hardly had to boss Mervin around at all. He seemed to know what needed to be done and took the initiative to do it.

As I interacted with each individual, I asked how he or she'd done that day. Jonathan and Addie did the best—but his hope chests and fireplace mantels were high-end, and each one sold for more than all of my herbs, flowers, and plants put together.

Nell did well too, and so did Joseph. Everyone, except Jonathan and Addie, said they'd see me next Saturday as they paid their rental fee for the market. By the time Mervin and I hauled everything up to the greenhouse, I was sticky from the heat. Mamm soon joined us.

"Go ahead and get cleaned up," she said to me. "And be on your way to Hannah's. She'll be expecting you. Mervin and I can finish up."

After I handed Mamm the money I'd taken in, and then turned to leave the greenhouse, Mervin followed me. "There's a party tonight," he said. "At Timothy's. Are you two going?"

"Probably not," I answered. "Hannah didn't mention it." The last thing I wanted to do was go to a party with Hannah—if she was still interested in Mervin. She could be fickle—and moody. She was definitely better than she'd been a couple of years ago when she ended up spending a few nights in a clinic and then got some much-needed counseling. Still, she had her moments. Perhaps she'd been unsure about her interest in Mervin, but she seemed focused on him today at the market.

I cleaned up quickly and hitched our gentle horse, Daisy, to the buggy. Mervin waved, with Love at his side, as I started down our lane toward the highway. I waved back, hoping I appeared enthusiastic. I really did need to speak to Hannah, even though I dreaded it.

As Daisy trotted along the pavement at a reasonable speed, my staccato thoughts matched the pounding of her hooves. Hannah didn't have to worry about saving her family farm. Many years ago the Lapps had turned an old dairy into a successful equestrian business. The family boarded, raised, and trained horses. Their seventy acres included a system of corrals, a huge barn, pastures, and a wooded area.

They'd stayed humble, but it was obvious they had more income than most, especially my family. Their house was fairly new. Hannah had her own buggy and horse, plus a Thoroughbred of her own. She'd been riding since she was five and was good at it. It wasn't the norm for an Amish girl to ride horses, but it wasn't totally unheard of either.

At their sign for Paradise Stables, I turned down the poplar-lined lane. Through the trees, in the first pasture, three knobby-kneed colts frolicked close to their mothers. One, with a star on his forehead, stopped and watched me pass by. It was cute, I had to admit, but I'd never been horse crazy like some girls.

Next was the first corral. A man had a palomino on a long

lead, running it in a circle around him. The figure was too lanky to be Hannah's Dat.

An early evening breeze danced through the tops of the poplars. I leaned toward the side of the buggy, hoping to get a better view through the trees. The man didn't have a beard, and he wore a funny hat and jeans, but his suspenders and shirt were definitely Amish.

I slowed the buggy.

He called out to the horse, which trotted to the middle of the ring. Then the man looked up, straight at me.

Embarrassed, I urged Daisy on again, stealing one more glance at the stranger. He stared at me but didn't wave. I hurried on.

Hannah met me at the barn to help me unhitch Daisy.

"Who is that?" I asked, nodding my head in the direction of the stranger.

Hannah gave me a puzzled look.

"Training the horse. In the first corral."

"Oh, him." Hannah patted Daisy's neck. "Some new guy Dat hired."

"Is he as handsome up close as from a distance?"

Hannah shrugged. "I haven't met him yet. He just arrived today."

"Where's he from?"

"Montana."

"Montana?" I knew there were Amish settlements out that way, but I'd never met anyone from there. "What's his name?"

"Leon," Hannah answered, tilting her head. "I don't think Dat told me his last name."

"How did he end up out here?"

"Dat put an advertisement for an experienced trainer in *The Connection*. Leon responded, so Dat's giving him a try."

"Don't they train horses differently in Montana than here?" After all, it was the Wild West. I imagined Indian ponies, not Thoroughbreds or quarter horses.

Hannah laughed. "I'm sure it's pretty much the same. His father grew up in Lancaster County and used to train horses. He probably taught Leon."

She led Daisy to their red barn and into one of the many stalls. Our barn was big, but the Lapps' was humongous. We used to play in it as girls, setting up whole settlements with our dolls, and then playing house with Hannah's little sisters when we were older.

"I'll get the brush," I said, heading toward the tack room. It had been one of our favorite places to play when we were young.

I opened the door, breathing in the scent of leather and soap and oil. Dozens of saddles rested on wall trees, and a few more were slung over the half wall that separated the room from a storage area. Bridles, harnesses, collars, and ropes hung from pegs. I grabbed a brush from the lower shelf and then turned toward the storage room, where we used to set up our pretend house.

"Don't go in there," Hannah said from the doorway.

"Why not?"

"That's where Leon is staying."

"In the storage room?"

She nodded. "It was his idea. I think he thought it improper to stay in the house with all of us girls." She giggled. "At least that's what I guessed from what my Dat said. Doesn't that seem a little backward? Like something a country hick would think."

I wasn't sure. I stood on my tiptoes, looking over the half wall. In the dim light I made out a cot with a sleeping bag and a table with a Bible, some sort of other leather book with a pencil box beside it, and a lantern.

"Come on," Hannah said, nodding to the brush in my hand.

I followed her back to Daisy's stall and sat on the railing while Hannah took care of the horse.

"There's a party tonight," she said.

"So I heard."

Hannah slipped to the other side of Daisy. The horse was in hog heaven. "Timothy left a message saying he'd give us a ride."

Timothy was Hannah's cousin, and also Addie's brother. He was a bit on the wild side.

"Mervin said he was going." I stepped to where I could see Hannah's reaction.

Her face brightened as she brushed Daisy's flank. "I was hoping he would be."

"So, you *are* still interested in him."

"Jah, of course." Her voice faltered. "Why wouldn't I be?"

"You didn't talk to him today."

"He's been distant. So I've been playing hard to get."

"Oh," I said, my heart twisting inside my chest. "We hadn't talked about it for a while. I wasn't sure . . ."

"Well, you haven't been very available," she said, bending down as she massaged Daisy's leg, and then added, "for good reason."

Then she gasped and her head popped back up, the brush in midair, a look of horror on her face. "Why do you ask? Is Mervin courting someone else?"

"No," I answered. "At least I don't think so." My face grew warm. I could only hope I wasn't blushing and giving myself away. "We should go help with supper," I said quickly.

"Jah, Mammi Gladys has been a handful lately." That was Hannah's grandmother. "Mamm's been overwhelmed with her since Tinker was born." Tinker was the nickname the girls called their little brother—the first boy after seven girls—claiming he wanted to tinker with everything. At a year and a half, he was into everything. He was named Owen after his Dat, but Tinker seemed to work well for him.

I took the brush from Hannah and returned it to the tack room, glancing again toward Leon's sleeping quarters. I'd read about bunkhouses in the West. Perhaps that was what he'd had in mind. Thinking of him made me think of Pete, my friend Cate's husband. Because of my contacts with Youngie in Ohio, he'd stayed with us and slept in our barn when he first came to Lancaster County. But then he'd married Cate, and after a short time in New York, where he was from, he and Cate moved into her Dat's house.

I doubted Leon would marry anyone from Lancaster. If he did, the woman would have to give up her family and move to Montana. I shuddered. Who would want to do that? Surely, he was just here for a short time, probably to learn what he could from Owen. It was a pity he was so handsome yet so unavailable.

"Come on," Hannah called out from the barn door.

I grabbed my overnight bag from the buggy, and we headed toward the house. "You seem quiet," Hannah said. "Is something wrong? You know, besides . . ."

"Not really," I said. "Except . . ." I took a deep breath. "Mamm had some kind of spell yesterday. Ivan and I took her to the doctor. She needs to have another test." Before Hannah could respond, I said, "Plus she's worried about the farm—about the finances." I couldn't say any more than that.

"Oh," Hannah answered. "Well, you're certainly doing what you can. With the market and all."

"Jah," I answered, suddenly feeling weepy. I'd never cried in front of Hannah, not even when I'd broken my arm when we were girls. I swallowed hard.

"It will all work out. You'll see," Hannah said. "Your Mamm's smart."

I nodded. "Jah, I know," I answered, biting my tongue from revealing her only plan so far was for me to marry Mervin. And that I could actually see her point—if it weren't for Hannah.

"We don't have to go out tonight," Hannah said. "I can see Mervin some other time."

"Denki," I said, relieved.

No matter how compatible Mamm thought Mervin and I might be, I couldn't do that to Hannah, not even to save our farm. I'd tell Mamm as soon as I got home.

I'd been friends with Hannah since she started school, when I was in my second year. I wasn't going to throw that away for Mervin or for my Mamm and . . . I stopped.

But what if it meant we would lose the farm?

We walked in silence for a few minutes, me fretting about my dilemma, Hannah most likely fretting about Mervin. Finally she said, "Let's talk about the camping trip."

"We should go help with dinner," I said.

"We can clean up—since we're not going out." She stopped at the edge of the grove. "Whom shall we invite?"

I didn't want to invite anyone. I didn't want to go.

"We'll need chaperones," she said. "What about Bob Miller and Nan?"

"They're getting married in a few weeks."

"What about Cate and Pete?"

"They'll be helping get ready for the wedding."

Her voice grew tense. "Addie and Jonathan?"

"It's his busiest time of the year."

She stopped. "Then let's talk about whom to invite. Mervin, of course," she said.

"I don't know if he can get the time off work."

Her eyes grew wide. "Honestly, Molly. It doesn't sound as if you want us to go."

51

"I'm just trying to be realistic."

"But it's not like you to be pessimistic."

A dog barked in the distance. "I'm not," I said. "Just practical." The dog barked again, this time louder.

Hannah narrowed her eyes and shook her head, but then her gaze moved past me, to something in the distance. I registered the beat of hooves behind me. Then the frightened snort of a horse.

Hannah stepped backward. I froze.

A deep voice yelled, "Watch out!"

I stepped toward Hannah and turned at the same time, just as the palomino horse and Leon, I was sure, whizzed by.

He pulled up on the reins and then jerked them to the side.

I gasped and, trying to cover my fear, said to Hannah, "I'm okay."

She put her arm around me, probably trying to swallow her laughter.

Leon turned the horse around and came back toward us at a pace too fast for my liking. "Sorry," he called out.

"It's all right," I said, trying my best to smile. "It's a horse farm, after all."

His hat, which mostly covered his dark hair, looked like something a country western singer would wear. Underneath the brim, his big eyes—the color of forget-me-nots—shone as he dismounted quickly, holding on to the reins. He towered over me—he was well over six feet, probably by a couple of inches. "I'm so sorry," he said. "Are you Hannah?"

My friend laughed behind me. "No, I am."

He extended his hand. "Nice to meet you." He sounded hesitant. I couldn't imagine anyone so handsome being shy, but perhaps he was. "You're the horsewoman?" he asked as he let go of her hand.

"Jah," Hannah said, "I like to ride."

Next he turned to me and extended his hand again. "I'm Leon Fisher." He smiled quickly, his white teeth a contrast to his tanned face.

"I'm Molly Zook. Hannah's friend."

He shook my hand. "Pleased to meet you, Miss Molly."

I couldn't help but smile. No one had ever called me that before.

"I am awfully sorry I scared you." He let go of my hand. "Lightning's a great horse, just not around dogs, it seems." He pulled the mare closer. She snorted and sidestepped. "Want to pet her?"

I shook my head.

"If you don't, she might associate you with her fear," he said. I was pretty sure he'd made that up, on the spot.

"Molly had a bad experience with a horse when we were girls," Hannah chimed in.

I took a deep breath, wondering why Hannah felt the need to be so forthright about my failing. It was something I tried to keep quiet.

"All the more reason to make up to one now," he said. This time he grinned, his eyes dancing. Perhaps he was shy, but he also had a bit of spark to him. I liked that.

I stepped toward him and the horse, putting my hand on Lightning's neck. The horse started to shy away, but Leon pulled on the bridle firmly, pulling her head down.

I stroked the palomino, feeling her muscles tighten under the weight of my hand, wanting to say, *Nice horsey*, but stopping myself from going that far. I didn't think she liked me any more than I liked her.

"See, she's not so bad," Leon said.

I looked up into his blue eyes. He grinned again. My knees weakened. Why did he have to be from Montana?

But then he nodded toward Hannah and grinned at her. "I was introduced to your horse earlier. He's a beauty."

Hannah smiled back, and I'd braced myself for a conversation about horses when the screen door to the porch banged.

"Hannah!" her Mamm, Pauline, yelled. "Do you want to finish up supper or get Mammi?"

"Supper!" Hannah responded.

Pauline started down the back steps. "Oh, Molly! You're here. *Gut!* The potatoes need to be mashed, the table set, and the roast carved. The girls are in the kitchen. Just tell them what to do."

Tinker let out a cry and Pauline hurried back up the steps.

I grabbed Hannah's arm and called out to Leon, "See you soon." I guessed he was eating with us—it's not like there was a kitchen out in the tack room.

"Sounds like I'd better get Lightning in the barn," Leon said, "or I'll be late." He tipped his hat at Hannah and then to me, pulled Lightning around, and then somehow managed—did he leap?—to land himself on the horse's back in one graceful motion. I watched until he reached the barn, my heart galloping along with him, until Hannah nudged me.

"Oh." I giggled. "Was I staring?"

"I don't know what at," she said.

"You're kidding, right?" I looked my friend in the eyes.

She nodded, a slight smile on her face.

"What do you mean? He's tall, dark, and handsome. And those eyes—I've never seen anything like them." I wasn't going to admit he'd actually made me weak-kneed. A little breathless, I inhaled deeply.

"Ach," Hannah said. "He's all right, but nothing like the boys around here."

CHAPTER
4

Pauline passed Tinker off to Hannah on her way out the back door, leaving me entirely in charge of getting dinner on the table, which I didn't mind at all. I rallied Hannah's sisters, asking them to set the table while I mashed the potatoes, and then to pour the water and fill the serving dishes while I carved the meat.

When Leon came in through the back door, the younger girls all grew shy.

"Owen's in the living room," I said to him because Hannah was too busy bouncing her crying brother on her hip to notice Leon. "Go visit with him."

He strode across the kitchen, his boots clomping on the hardwood floor, but stopped at the hallway.

"Go on," I said to him.

He smiled hesitantly and headed down the hall.

"Go tell your Mammi to hurry," I told Deborah. "Tell her I can't wait to see her."

If Pauline and Gladys didn't arrive soon, the food would begin to cool. Just as I put the platter of meat on the table, Gladys yoo-hooed me as she came through the back door. "Molly!" she called out. "What a nice surprise."

Pauline and Deborah followed behind her.

"You're just in time," I said to the old woman. "If you hurry, you can sit by our guest." For a moment I felt awkward that I'd said *our*, but no else seemed to notice. I stepped into the hall. "Come on, Owen and Leon. Time to eat."

By the time supper began, I wasn't the only one interested in Leon. Mammi Gladys, who was usually as cranky as could be, did sit by him and kept inching closer and closer. She smiled as she passed him the mashed potatoes and then said, "I know how hard you've been working today, running that horse back and forth in front of my little house."

"I hope I didn't disturb you, ma'am."

She waved her hand. "Of course not." If it had been Hannah running a horse her grandmother would have been more than disturbed. But it was nice to see her being so gracious with someone besides me.

I kept my eye on Leon as he passed little Maggie the roast, serving her first and then himself. Tinker squealed halfway through dinner, a loud, piercing scream that had me on the edge of my seat, but Leon grinned widely at the baby. The little guy laughed. Leon winked. The baby laughed again.

I wasn't one of those girls who got all gaga over a baby, but I couldn't help smiling as I watched. Leon seemed to be as gifted with children as with horses.

Maggie said something, but her sisters were all talking over her.

"Girls, girls," Pauline said. "Don't all talk at once."

Deborah and Sarah both started again.

Mammi Gladys exclaimed, "Pipe down," just as four-year-old Maggie tried to say something too. Perhaps it had been out of fear, or maybe just surprise at her grandmother's bark, but

Maggie bumped her glass, spilling her milk across the table. As it flowed toward him, Leon righted the glass. I stood, grabbed a dish towel from the counter, and tossed it at him. He quickly mopped up what he could.

"Denki," Pauline said as she came around to finish the job with the dishcloth.

Maggie began to cry, but Leon whispered something in her ear. Her chin quivered but then she broke out into a smile.

He seemed a gentle soul but certainly not a pushover, considering the way he handled the horse. And the fact that he was a little shy was actually endearing.

After dinner, Leon helped clear the table as Hannah and I started the dishes. "I thought you two would be off to a party tonight," he said.

"Why do you say that?" I asked.

"Ach, reports of Lancaster Youngie travel far and wide," he answered. "As far as Montana, to be sure."

"And what do those reports include?" I submerged a glass into the dishwater.

"Parties every Friday and Saturday night. Youngie coming from states away." He paused.

"What else?"

"Ach." He blushed. "I feel as if I'm gossiping."

I smiled. "Some reports are exaggerated." *Some.* I'd expected him to make a comment about the drinking that went on too.

"Want to go with us? There's one tonight," Hannah said.

I flinched at the thought. I'd much rather visit with Leon here, away from the throngs of other girls.

Leon put the platter on the counter. "Jah," he said. "I would."

Hannah gave me a look. I shifted my feet. If Leon wanted to go, the least I could do was be hospitable. I nodded to my friend and then turned to Leon.

"So you haven't joined the church yet?" I asked.

He shook his head. "I will though," he said, "when I go home."

"Molly and I were going to take classes this spring, but—"

"We will soon. Maybe this fall?" I took a deep breath and turned toward Hannah.

She nodded, pointing to my apron. She wanted my phone, to call Timothy. I turned so she could retrieve it from my pocket herself.

As she left, I focused on the bubbles in the sink, suddenly aware of how weary I was of thinking about Mervin and speculating on how to save the farm. Going to a party might be a good idea after all. I'd pull Mervin off to the side and tell him Hannah still liked him, that I could never court him and hurt my friend.

"What do you see in those bubbles?" Leon asked, stepping closer.

I laughed. "Certainly not my future." Not that I believed in anything like that. "Tell me about Montana," I said to Leon as Hannah's Dat came through the back door.

"Could you come on out?" he asked Leon. "I want to introduce you to someone." Leon complied immediately.

As I continued washing the dishes, I looked out the window over the sink. An Englisch woman was walking between Owen and Leon toward the barn.

Hannah returned, slipped my phone back into my pocket, and nudged me over. "She boards a couple of horses here."

"Oh," I answered.

"He is pretty nice." Hannah pulled some glasses from the rinse water and put them in the rack. She sighed. "But he's not Mervin."

I wanted to laugh but instead bit my tongue. I couldn't imagine who, as much as I adored Mervin, would choose him over Leon. "What did Timothy say?" I asked.

"He'll be here in half an hour.

"Let's get these dishes done." I began scrubbing a plate as Hannah's Mamm came into the kitchen with Tinker on her hip. He squealed when he saw Hannah.

"Take him for a minute," Pauline said. Hannah reached for her brother, and he fell into her arms.

Hannah's grandmother tottered into the kitchen next. "How long is that young man staying?"

"I don't know," Pauline answered, taking her mother's arm.

Gladys shuffled toward the door, leaning against Pauline. "Hannah should court him, don't you think?"

"Heavens, no," Pauline answered, shooting her daughter a grin. "There's quite a selection around here. We wouldn't want her to end up in Montana."

Hannah agreed and then kissed her brother on the forehead. He squealed again. "*You* should court Leon," Hannah said to me.

I exhaled, blowing my breath up to my forehead. The heat from the dishwater was cooking my face.

"I'm serious. It's been ages since you've been out with anyone. Since Phillip, right?"

I blew out my breath a second time.

"We're not getting any younger," Hannah said. "And if I'm going to get married soon, I want you to too."

Through the window I watched Pauline and Gladys shuffle along, pretending to be intent on what I was seeing so I wouldn't have to answer Hannah. Leon had nothing to offer me except wobbly knees and a racing heart. Things I'd honestly never experienced before. Things I found both exhilarating and frightening.

But there was no way I'd ever move to Montana. If I left, we'd lose the farm for sure.

⁓

As dusk fell, Hannah and I sat on her porch until Timothy's bright yellow Bronco hummed up the driveway.

"Where is he?" I asked, swinging my cape over my shoulders against the growing chill.

"Timothy?" Hannah teased.

I smiled but didn't respond. There was no need. As we headed down the front steps, Leon came around the driveway from the barn. He wore a regular straw hat and normal shoes. He'd also changed into trousers and a clean shirt.

Just the sight of him lifted my spirits, putting a bounce in my step as I followed Hannah to Timothy's vehicle.

Hannah climbed into the front seat and I opened the back door behind her. Leon strode over to the driver's side, introduced himself to Timothy, and then climbed into the back too.

I fastened my seat belt as Timothy took off, and Leon followed my example, smiling at me as he clicked it into place. There was a full seat between the two of us, but it felt as if we were nearly touching.

Timothy listed the people he expected to be at the party.

When he'd finished, Hannah added, "Mervin and Martin are going."

Timothy shook his head. "I called Martin—he said they're not. Something about Mervin being too tired."

Immediately Hannah's mood changed, and she slumped against her seat.

I reached forward and patted her shoulder. "Maybe they'll change their minds." Two years ago, Timothy had been out to get Mervin and Martin, but thankfully they'd worked it all out. Now it wasn't as if they were the best of friends, but they all got along.

Many in our group had joined the church in the last year or two. More and more of the partygoers were younger. We were definitely aging out of our *Rumschpringe*.

"When are you going to join the church?" I asked Timothy.

"Maybe never. Samuel . . ." He glanced in his rearview mirror at Leon. "That's my older brother. We've been talking about going down to Florida. Or maybe somewhere else. It'd be nice to see another part of the world." Timothy glanced in the mirror again at Leon. "Hannah said you're from Montana. Did you hire a driver to get out here?"

"No." Leon leaned forward. "I took the train. It's a good way to see the country."

Timothy asked Leon about Chicago.

"Jah, it's a big place," Leon said. "I imagine there's lots of opportunity—and lots of other stuff too."

That sounded like a pretty diplomatic answer to me.

"I can't imagine ever living in a city." Leon nodded out the window into the coming darkness. "Lancaster County is as urban a place as I ever want to live."

Timothy laughed. "What's it like in Montana?"

"Wide open spaces. Mountains. Endless sky. Lots of snow in the winter. Rivers to fish in the summer."

"But not many people?" Timothy asked.

"Yep," Leon said. "We definitely have more cattle than people."

That was hard for me to imagine. In Lancaster County we had lots of dairy cows, true, but I was certain we had more people.

"How many Plain folks in Montana?" Timothy asked as he turned off toward the trailer he and Samuel shared.

"Oh, I'd say a few hundred."

Timothy chuckled. "And it's a big state, huh?"

"Yep," Leon said again.

We had more than fifty thousand Plain folks in Lancaster County, let alone in the rest of Pennsylvania.

Timothy slowed the car on the rutted road. "What are some of the biggest differences between here and there?"

"Our school is made of logs, and so is our house and barn."

Timothy glanced over his shoulder as if Leon was kidding him. "Little cabins?" he asked, shifting his attention back to the road.

Leon shook his head. "Our house is big enough. So is our barn. It's not nearly as big as Hannah's family's . . . but it's a good size." I had the feeling Leon was being modest.

Ahead the trailer windows shone with electric lights, and several of the cars parked around it had their headlights on. "What else is different?" Timothy asked.

"We ride horses a lot."

I exhaled. Montana was definitely out as a possibility for me.

"To herd cattle, right?" Timothy asked.

"Yep, for that. But we'd ride our horses to go to school too."

"Even the little ones?" I asked.

"Yep. We're put in the saddle almost before we can walk. It's second nature. My youngest sister often rode in front of me, but only because she wanted to."

"How many sisters do you have?"

"Six," he answered.

"Ach, you poor thing." Timothy snorted. "I only have one, and she was nearly the end of me."

I shook my head. Addie was the sweetest sister anyone could have. Timothy had been the problem. I turned to Leon. "Where are you in the birth order?"

"The oldest."

"Really." No wonder he seemed such a gentle soul. "Your sisters must really be missing you."

He nodded, his face sad. The desire to reach over and take his hand overwhelmed me, but of course I didn't. Timothy swung the Bronco up along the trailer, and we came to a stop.

"We may not want to stay long," Hannah said.

"Just let me know when you're ready to go," Timothy answered.

I couldn't help but ask, although nicely, "So you won't be drinking tonight?"

"That's right," he said. "I've given that up." I wasn't sure I believed him, although I hoped it was true. Hannah used to drink at parties sometimes when we were younger, but I never did.

I went to parties to see people.

Leon hopped out of the car, hurried around the vehicle to open Hannah's door, and then opened mine. We thanked him in unison as we climbed out. A group of Youngie I didn't recognize stood in the doorway of the trailer, girls dressed in jeans and cropped shirts and boys in T-shirts and baseball caps.

I looked down at my dress and apron. Hannah and I used to dress Englisch for parties when we were younger. The truth was, I didn't miss it one bit. The jeans always felt uncomfortable on my hips, and I was forever wondering if the neckline of my shirt was too low, both things I never had to worry about in my dress and apron.

"Hey, Molly!" someone yelled from over by the oak tree.

"Hey," I called back, not sure who it was. Hannah and Timothy headed that way, but I stayed by the Bronco. I expected Leon to follow the others, but he waited with me, looking a bit nervous.

One of the girls on the porch, whom I didn't recognize either, said, "Sorry about your Dat."

"Denki," I answered, my voice wavering.

63

Samuel waved from the corner of the trailer, by a cooler. "Me too, Molly. How are you doing?"

"*Gut,*" I answered, but my voice cracked, giving me away. I took a deep breath and said, "Come on," to Leon. "I'll introduce you around." I started with Samuel, who offered Leon a beer. He politely declined. Next I led Leon to the tree, and introduced him to that group too, where Timothy had everyone laughing, except for Hannah, who stood off to the side.

When we arrived, the attention first shifted to Leon, whose blush I could see in the dim light as everyone told him hello, and then to me. The nice thing was, because this was the first party I'd been to since Dat passed, most people offered me their condolences. The bad thing was, the sweet sympathy kept pushing me to the brink of tears.

I thought I'd been hiding it until Leon said, "We can leave anytime."

"Jah," Hannah said. "This is a boring party."

I hoped Timothy hadn't heard, but he must have because he said, "I'd rather take you home now rather than later anyway."

I called out my good-byes, trying my best to be cheerful, but it had been a mistake to come. I hadn't expected grief to change me. But it had. I wondered if I'd ever enjoy the things I used to. But, no matter what, parties had lost their luster.

We were silent on the way home. As soon as Timothy stopped his Bronco, the three of us hopped out and thanked him.

"It was nothing," he answered.

But it was. He'd definitely gone out of his way for us. I waved and thanked him again as he drove off.

Hannah started up the steps to the porch while I hesitated just a moment.

"Good night," Leon called out to her. Then to me he said, "And to you, Miss Molly."

That made me smile.

Instead of continuing on to the barn, he stopped. "Do you mind if I ask you a question?"

I shook my head.

"How did your Dat die?"

"A heart attack." Standing there in the driveway, I spilled out the whole story to him. There was just enough moonlight for me to see the compassionate expression on his face.

"How sad," he said. "I'm so sorry."

"Denki," I whispered.

"Molly . . ." Hannah's voice surprised me. I thought she'd gone in the house. "We should get to bed."

"Jah." But I spoke to Leon, not to her.

"See you tomorrow," he said, starting toward the barn, but then he turned around and added, "Sweet dreams, Miss Molly."

I never dreamt—or at least remembered my *Drohms*—but I did that night. I wore Dat's green shirt over my dress and apron and stood in the middle of our field of lilies, all blooming at once. In the distance, I heard the beat of a horse's hooves—but I awoke before seeing the rider.

The next morning Leon wasn't at breakfast. "He's going to church in the district his Dat is from," Owen said.

"Where's that?" Hannah asked.

Owen shrugged. "I didn't ask."

"Did he take a buggy?"

"No, he rode Lightning." Owen stuffed a big bite of ham into his mouth.

"Wow," Hannah said.

Her Dat nodded. "That's what I told him." He grinned and

then kept chewing. No one *rode* a horse to church in Lancaster County.

After breakfast, Hannah and I cleaned up, but then I said I needed to get home. She helped me hitch up Daisy, and by the time I reached the lane to our farm, sweat was dripping down the back of my legs. It was going to be a scorcher—much hotter than the day before. Ahead, at the Mosiers' driveway, a group of men gathered around. I squinted. Mervin and Martin were both wearing their sunglasses. Next to them was their Dat. And someone on a horse. A palomino.

It was Lightning and Leon. Perhaps they'd gotten lost.

I urged Daisy forward. "Hallo," I called out as I neared the group. Everyone waved. Mervin took off his glasses and started toward me.

Leon turned Lightning toward me too. "Miss Molly," he said, tipping his hat.

"So you've all met?" I asked, my heart galloping again.

"Jah," Mervin said. "We all welcomed Leon to the area."

"Did you get lost?" I asked.

He grinned. "Ach, just about. But Mervin set me straight. If I hurry, I think I can still make it. Although I may be a little late." He ducked his head, as if embarrassed.

I didn't know where he was headed, but he was probably going to be a lot late.

"I'm glad you'll come back for the singing," Mervin said to Leon. Then he turned toward me. "You're coming, right?"

I nodded.

"What about Hannah?" Leon asked.

Mervin took off his glasses. "That's a great idea. Bring her too."

I pursed my lips together.

"Don't you think so?" Mervin asked me.

"Sure . . ." I answered, trying to think it through, not at all sure if it was best for her to come. But she'd probably planned to anyway.

"I'll see you tonight, then," Leon said, looking straight at me, and then bid us all farewell, flashing me a smile, and then galloping away.

"He's quite the dude," Martin said.

Mervin pushed his sunglasses atop his head and stepped out into the road, watching Leon and Lightning disappear around the curve.

Wanting to escape quickly, I called out, "I'll see you tonight," to the twins, swinging my buggy around.

"Jah," Martin answered but Mervin didn't say a thing.

I silently chanted, *Montana, Montana, Montana,* as I turned up our driveway, willing myself not to be interested in Leon Fisher. But I couldn't stop thinking about him.

I spotted Mamm standing on the front porch, gazing over our pasture, with Love at her side as I came over the rise. After I unhitched Daisy, I hurried around the house with my bag slung over my shoulder, hoping she was still there.

She was, although now she was sitting in the wicker chair, sipping a cup of coffee. The dog had sprawled out on the cool porch.

"How are you feeling?"

"Ach, Molly. Stop asking me that." She looked pale but otherwise all right. She pointed to the feeder hanging from the eaves of the porch. "We had a couple of ruby-throated hummingbirds this morning," she said. "And I saw a Cooper's hawk in the Mosiers' field this morning."

"Martin must have stirred up the mice, dragging the field."

She nodded.

"I haven't seen a mockingbird for a while though," she said. "Have you?"

I shook my head. But I couldn't be certain. I didn't have the interest in birds that my parents had shared.

"Your Dat always enjoyed the mockingbirds."

I pretended to be interested. They were just gray birds, with a bit of black and white on their wings. Quite plain, really.

She continued. "Did you know they can recognize people? Besides imitating sounds. Another bird. A person even . . ."

I knew all that. I sat down in the other chair, dropping my bag to the porch floor, saying, "I've been thinking . . ."

"Uh-oh," Mamm said and then chuckled.

I knew she was teasing. So I smiled and continued. "I've been thinking about other ways to make money besides . . ." I took a deep breath. "Your idea for me to marry Mervin isn't going to work. Hannah still really likes him." That was reason enough. There was no reason for me to mention Leon.

"Oh," she said.

"I can't do that to Hannah."

"Of course not," Mamm answered, reaching for my hand, filling me with relief. "But . . ." I tensed as she said, "Let's not give up hope. We never know what plans God might have."

I exhaled. "How about a pumpkin patch?"

She shook her head. "It's too late in the season."

"For next year."

"Maybe," she said.

I was brainstorming out loud, I knew. "We could change the house into a B&B."

"A what?"

"A bed-and-breakfast. We have three empty bedrooms." Four since Beatrice had moved in with me.

"And have strangers in our house? It's bad enough to have them in the pasture." She sounded like Beatrice. "It's easier for you, Molly," she said, her voice softening. "You like to be around people. It's not that your sister and I don't *like* others—we just don't thrive on being around them."

Mamm was right. Especially about Beatrice. She didn't have a friend like Hannah. She was content to be home. She didn't like singings. She'd never gone to a party.

I went stir-crazy if I didn't get out of the house.

"What about Martin?" Mamm asked.

I didn't respond.

"Molly?"

I looked at her. Her blue eyes watered. Perhaps from the warm wind. Her face had grown thinner. Probably because she hadn't been eating much. And her shoulders, usually square and straight, slumped.

I shook my head. It wasn't that I didn't like him. I did. But I couldn't imagine learning to love him, not at all.

"Back to those notions about marriage?" she asked. "Because commitment is what brings love."

The thing was, yesterday she could have convinced me of that, but after meeting Leon, I wasn't so sure.

"Partnering with someone is what matters. Weathering life's storms together—that's what counts," Mamm said.

I nodded. "But surely you felt something for Dat."

"Well, sure. I admired him. And I'd seen him with his first wife, and—"

"When?" I hadn't heard about that before.

"I came out here," she said. "Donna"—I'd forgotten that was her name. It was rare that anyone spoke it—"was from Ohio too. Our mothers were friends, although she was older than I was. Then she, your Dat, and I all ended up as part of the same circle letter."

I'd never heard any of this. "What kind of circle letter?"

"Birds."

I wanted to laugh.

"Jah," she said. "Donna and your Dat thought it would give them a hobby to share."

Amish people had all sorts of circle letters that they sent from person to person all across the country. Sometimes between relatives. Or people with a shared concern, such as a handicapped child, or between people who enjoyed hiking. I hadn't heard of one around birds, but I believed it.

"Donna and I struck up a friendship via the letters, plus we remembered each other because of our mothers' friendship. For some reason she invited me out to visit. She was quite sick by then—her cancer had returned—but she said she'd like to spend some time with me, so I came during the summer, when I was off from teaching school."

"And that's how you met Dat?"

She nodded, her face reddening. Perhaps it was the heat. Or maybe she was blushing.

"I hope this doesn't sound bad or put him in a bad light. He was devoted to Donna. He cared for her until the very end, keeping her at home, doing everything he could."

I nodded. I believed her.

"He never gave me a second glance."

I smiled. "It doesn't matter, Mamm. I know how Dat was. I'd never think otherwise. How did you two get together then, later?"

"We both continued on with the circle letter, after Donna died. Then a year later he wrote to me, and we started corresponding."

I enjoyed hearing the story, but I wasn't sure what it had to do with the situation I was in.

Perhaps she could tell I was growing impatient. "My point is," she said, "we already had a start, a shared experience."

"Over birds?"

Mamm chuckled, her eyes actually twinkling. I'd made it

clear through the years that I couldn't comprehend their intense interest in birds. "Oh, Molly," Mamm said. "Just listen to me. What counts is it gave your Dat and me a start. You already have that start with Mervin, but even more so. Don't give up on him. It could still work out."

Had she forgotten what I'd just said about Hannah?

I stood, slung my bag over my shoulder, and patted her shoulder. "Denki. It's nice to hear your stories." I opened the front door to the scent of cinnamon rolls. "This is how heaven must smell," I said, turning toward Mamm.

She had a pained look on her face.

Sure my use of the word *heaven* had hurt her, I said, "Sorry."

She shook her head as she stood, but she stumbled. I grabbed her arm. "Are you okay?"

She pressed her hand to the side of her Kapp. "Just a headache. I'll go rest. . . ."

I walked with her into the house. "How about in the sewing room?" I asked.

"No. Upstairs."

I followed her, realizing her room probably didn't seem as vacant to her as it did to me. Most likely, she found comfort resting in the bed she'd shared with Dat.

CHAPTER
5

Mamm came down for the meat loaf Edna fixed for our dinner and seemed to be feeling better. Afterward she sat on the porch again, probably looking for a mockingbird, while Beatrice curled up on the couch with her journal.

She'd kept one for years, insisting it was top secret. One time she'd left it on the table and I bumped it to the floor, hoping it would land open. It did. It looked like poetry from what I could see, but she flew into the kitchen as fast as anything and snatched it up.

I couldn't blame her. It had been a sisterly low for me.

I no longer tried to get a peek inside, but she acted as if I might as I sat down on the other end of the couch from her. She turned her head and the journal away from me and kept on writing.

The next thing I knew she was poking me with her foot.

"You've been asleep for over an hour," she said. "Are you all right?"

I never napped. Not even when I was a child.

"I'm fine," I said, although I felt out of sorts. I stretched, pulling away from the couch, my back damp from the heat. I'd dreamt again—except this dream had taken place at night. The *Shtanns* had shone like white carnations in the night sky while the lilies in the field glowed like fireflies. "Is Mamm still on the porch?"

She shook her head. "She's down for another nap. Edna's resting too."

"You should come to the singing tonight."

"Why would I?" She'd confided in me once that she planned to forever be a Maidel. I told her she'd change her mind. Who wouldn't want a husband and family? I couldn't imagine. How else would I use the gifts God had given me?

On the other hand I actually couldn't imagine Beatrice married. She probably would end up a Maidel.

I spent some time walking the property, making a mental list of what needed to be done the next day, but I did my best not to actually work on the Sabbath. We had a light supper of leftovers, and then the driver arrived to take Edna home. We thanked her for all she'd done as we walked her to the car. Edna hugged us all warmly and said to call if we needed her. "I'll be back before you know it," she said.

I think spending time on the farm did her as much good as it did us.

I waved until the car reached the bottom of the driveway and then took my cell phone to the office in the greenhouse, leaving it in the desk drawer—where I usually left it for the night—and walked over to Mervin and Martin's shop for the singing. A crowd had begun to gather outside, but I didn't see Hannah or Leon. Mervin, however, was front and center.

"Look who's here!" he said when he saw me. As he greeted me with a long hug, the group dispersed, revealing Hannah on the other side. I saw her over Mervin's shoulder. Saw her face fall. Saw her chin quiver.

Behind her stood Leon.

I pulled away from Mervin, but as I did, he grabbed my hand.

"Wait," I said, turning toward Hannah.

Mervin groaned as he saw her. "Ach, not now."

"Shh," I said to him. *Poor Hannah.*

But as she yelled, she didn't sound poor. Angry was more like it. "Molly Zook!"

Before I could pull away from Mervin, she was in front of me. "How could you?" She spoke at me but she swung her purse toward Mervin. He ducked.

Leon caught her arm.

She grabbed her purse with her other hand and swung at me. Leon grabbed her other hand and then wrapped his arms around her, standing behind her. "Whoa," he said.

"Don't 'whoa' me." She kicked her heel against his shin.

"What did I miss?" Leon asked.

"Ask her." Hannah spit out her words, lunging her head toward me.

"It's not how it looks," I said.

"Be honest," she said. "Timothy warned me."

"What did he say?"

"That Mervin said something about not coming to the party because you weren't."

I turned toward Mervin, flabbergasted that he would say something to Timothy, of all people, and that it would come out now, in front of Leon.

Hannah lunged toward me again.

"Stop," Mervin said. "Hannah, I should have told you sooner. I've known for a while."

"But you said you loved me," she practically snarled.

"I did. Months ago," he said. "But that changed when I started working for the Zooks. I love Molly now."

Instead of looking at him she glared at me. "How could you? If only Phillip hadn't dumped you."

75

"Hannah—"

"You think any man in the county would marry you if you wanted, but it's not true."

I gasped. "I never thought that." If I ever had, Phillip had proven me wrong. She'd just pointed that out herself.

"You're ruining my life." She lunged forward a third time, still restrained by Leon's strong arms.

"Could we talk?" I said to her. "Just you and me." I stepped toward her.

Her dark eyes narrowed.

"Please let her go," I said to Leon, trying to keep my voice even.

He complied. I braced myself for Hannah to hurl herself at me, but she didn't. Instead she clutched her purse with both hands. I straightened my Kapp and without saying anything more to Mervin, motioned for Hannah to follow me toward the Mosiers' barn. We passed a group of younger girls who all stared at us. By the time we reached the barn door, Hannah's shoulders shook.

I pushed up the latch and slipped into the dim interior. Hannah followed me.

I put my arm around her and she leaned against me, shaking. "I'm so sorry," I said. "I was told you two had stopped courting. I didn't know you still cared for him until yesterday. My Mamm was pushing me toward Mervin. . . ." Again I couldn't bear to tell her why—when she would never have a financial worry in her life. Besides, if she told her Aenti Nell that we might lose our farm, the whole county would know before morning. "But," I said, "I told Mamm today, as soon as I got home, I wouldn't consider courting Mervin because you still liked him."

It was as if I hadn't said a word. "How could you?" she blubbered.

"I know, I know. I wanted to talk with you about it yesterday."

She shook her head, as if she didn't remember my questions from the day before.

"After hearing you were still interested in Mervin . . . I knew it wasn't right. But I haven't had a chance to talk with Mervin." Actually, I probably could have this morning but it hadn't been on my mind then, especially after seeing Leon. Only talking with Mamm.

Hannah let out another sob.

"I'm sorry. It was all a series of misunderstandings, really. That's all."

"That's all? For you, sure. Not for me. Now Mervin loves you—"

"He only thinks he does. I'll talk him out of it."

"And into loving me?" Hannah hiccuped.

"Jah," I said.

"How?"

I pursed my lips. That was our dilemma. Maybe if Leon became interested in me, Mervin would see he didn't have a chance. But that wouldn't save our farm.

I sank down to the cool concrete floor.

"Molly?" Hannah knelt beside me. She wasn't used to me acting despondent. "What's the matter?"

"Nothing," I answered, holding on to the ties of my Kapp. *Everything.* "Just give me a minute."

She stepped toward the open door.

As long as I was nearly prostrate on the floor I decided I might as well pray, which honestly, I'd been having a hard time doing since Dat had died. I called out to God, silently of course. *Show me what to do. Bless our farm. Take care of Mamm. Preserve my friendship with Hannah. Make Mervin love her. And Leon love me.* And then, being only half aware of what I was thinking,

I prayed, *But only if he stays in Lancaster County instead of going back to Montana.* I found myself smiling, just a smidge. Maybe that was what God was up to.

When Hannah and I walked into the singing we both held our heads up high. Mervin frowned. But Leon smiled, straight at me.

I told Hannah I didn't feel well, which was true, and slipped out before the singing was over. I knew it was the coward's way out, but I couldn't bear to talk with Mervin in front of a crowd. I'd do it in the morning.

Just after I'd crossed over the plank of wood across the creek between the two properties, someone called my name. I turned back, peering into the dark night.

"It's me, Leon," the voice called out.

I reached the fence and put my hand on the top rail, trying to steady myself.

"May I walk you home?"

I managed to squeak, "Jah." And then flung one leg and then the other over the fence, determined to get the task done before Leon caught up with me. But as my second foot came down to the ground I tripped over a rock and stumbled forward, falling to my knees and the heels of my hands.

"Are you all right?" Leon must have vaulted the fence, because he was by my side, kneeling, before I collected myself.

"I'm fine." I brushed my hands together. "Just clumsy."

"It's awfully dark," he said.

It was. Clouds had blown in at dusk and now covered the moon and stars. And without my cell phone, I didn't have a flashlight. I should have taken the road instead of the shortcut.

"Let me help," he said, taking my arm.

My heart beat all the faster at the feel of his skin against mine. "Denki," I said, standing, sure he could hear the galloping inside my chest as clearly as I could.

We walked along in silence for a moment, me leading the way along the dark trail. But then a bark interrupted the quiet.

I called out, "It's okay, Love."

Leon chuckled. "Pardon?"

"Our dog." I was grateful he couldn't see me blush. "Her name is Love. Dat named her."

She crashed along the trail toward us, her tail waving. I put out my hand in greeting, and she licked it but then bumped Leon's leg with her nose.

He laughed. "She's not much of a watchdog, is she."

"No," I answered, although I was sure she could be if needed.

We continued walking along the field of lilies, Love staying close to Leon. Finally I asked him, "Why did you apply for a job in Lancaster?"

"It sounded like an adventure."

"Montana sounds like the adventure," I said.

"It is," he answered.

"So why did you come out here?"

"To see where my Dat grew up. And learn from someone who makes a living training horses."

"You don't train horses for a living back home?" I asked.

"No. We run cattle."

"Oh," I said, trying to imagine exactly what that meant. "I thought your Dat trained horses."

"He used to. I mostly learned from an old cowboy though."

"He must have taught you well."

"Denki," he said. "I'm going to start on Storm tomorrow. Owen says he's really a wild one."

"Well, no wonder, with a name like that," I said. "And Lightning too. Our horse's name is Daisy, and she's as gentle as can be."

He chuckled.

We'd reached the edge of our lawn and I stopped. Love stepped to my side. The only light on in our house was in my bedroom window—Beatrice was probably writing. I expected Mamm had been in bed for an hour or more.

Leon stepped to my side. "I'm not really sure what happened back there," he said. "Before the singing."

The clouds drifted, and a sliver of moonlight illuminated his face, showing his kind blue eyes. "But if it's true you and Mervin aren't courting . . . ." His voice trailed off. I realized he wanted me to confirm it.

"There's been some expectation that we would," I said.

"From your family?"

"My Mamm," I said. "And a little from Mervin."

"I see," Leon said.

I hurried to add, "But it's not what I want." Sure, I'd considered it yesterday for a few hours, but that was before I met Leon.

"Then," he said, speaking slowly, "could I call on you sometime?"

"Jah, I'd like that," I answered, turning back toward the house. The light went out. I was tempted to invite him in, but if Mamm wasn't asleep, it would be hard to explain what was going on, at least with Leon present.

"Can you come by tomorrow night?" I asked.

I'd talk to Mamm. She was a kind and compassionate person. She'd come around.

He nodded and said, "Good-bye, then."

I waved, not sure what to say. I'd never felt so self-conscious, so unlike myself. My bedroom window slammed shut. I frowned.

"Your Mamm?" Leon stared up at the window.

"No, my sister," I responded. "She's a little temperamental."

He raised his eyebrows but in fun. "I have a sister like that."

"Just one?" I teased.

"One in particular." He smiled again. "See you tomorrow."

Love started to take off after him, but I called her back and then waved, even though Leon couldn't see me, and turned toward the back door. Before I reached it I turned, placed my hand over my heart, and watched him as the clouds drifted even more, revealing the half moon shining down as Leon disappeared along the field. I hadn't asked him how long he planned to stay in Lancaster County—but I hoped for good.

The next morning at five, I sat up in bed feeling clammy, as if I might be ill. But then I remembered Leon. I'd never before felt anything close to how I felt about him. I nudged Beatrice, who'd drifted to the middle of my double bed, but she didn't stir.

I swung my feet out of bed and pulled the sheets and quilt tight, efficiently making my side of the bed. Then I dressed quickly, slipped my nightgown under my pillow when I'd finished, and leaned over to kiss Beatrice's forehead. "Rise and shine," I said.

She groaned. "I hate it when you say that."

I left her, stopping at the window to pull open the curtain. Rays of pink light were already starting to glow over the saplings in the far field. The rooster crowed as I hurried downstairs.

I'd made a point, long before Dat died, to be the first one up every morning. Over the years, both my parents had come to rely on me more and more. And now Mamm continued to. I liked the responsibility of being in charge, both with my circle of friends and at home.

I'd figure out another way, without marrying Mervin, to bring in more income. Perhaps if I came up with a solid business plan, Mamm would consider the bed-and-breakfast idea. True, we'd have to get permission from the bishop, but once he knew our situation I thought he'd agree it was a good idea. But I'd need to wait until we knew what, if anything, was wrong with Mamm.

Every morning at breakfast, she would ask me what jobs needed to be done as far as the nursery stock, the flowers, the garden, the orders, and the deliveries. I'd often hear her parrot what I'd said to Mervin. More and more often, I was the one who returned phone calls from landscapers—the few who still bought from us—and from retailers.

Once in the kitchen, I filled the kettle and lit the back burner of the stove. Next I grabbed the egg basket and hurried outside into the first light of the day. Love joined me.

As I pushed open the barn door, Love bolted inside, ignoring the cats that began rubbing against my legs. I'd timed every step of my routine, aiming for optimum efficiency. I cooed, "Good morning," and stepped into the first stall, quickly feeding the cats their allotment of dried food. That's all they'd get for the day—I wanted them good and hungry at night, when they did most of their mousing. That was how they earned their keep.

I grabbed the basket again and hurried out the back door of the barn to the watering trough, turning on the spigot for Daisy and the workhorses. While it ran, I rushed to the chicken coop, where Love stayed outside. The rooster crowed again as I entered. I ignored him and gathered the eggs quickly—all eleven of them. I'd added several more hens, hoping to begin selling eggs at the market too. At this rate, I'd start next Saturday.

After I left the coop, with Love at my heels, I returned to the trough and turned off the water, then walked as quickly as I could, without jostling the eggs, back to the house, leaving Love behind. I guessed she'd soon be in search of Mervin. As I entered the kitchen, the kettle began to whistle.

"Perfect," I said as I turned down the burner.

Mamm liked tea for breakfast, although I'd taken a liking to coffee. I frowned. I'd probably need to cut back on it to save money.

I heard footsteps upstairs as I placed three tea bags in the pot. Hopefully Beatrice was up. I poured the water, secured the lid, and then placed the kettle back on the stove.

Mamm told me once that Dat's older children had mellowed him. Neither of them had been a problem—not beyond the normal woes of child rearing, it seemed—so Dat, and my Mamm along with him, had been pretty lackadaisical when it came to rearing me. True, I'd socialized a lot, but I'd never gotten into trouble. They seemed relieved to let me work out my growing up on my own.

Unlike Hannah's parents, they'd never questioned me about spending the night with a friend or going to a party or a singing. They'd trusted me—and not only with my own life but with decisions that concerned us all. And Mamm had continued with that trust after my Dat's passing.

Part of the reason for my parents' reliance on me was probably my personality. Mamm had once told me I was a born matriarch. I'd smiled at that, acknowledging that I enjoyed being in charge.

Through the years, I'd given Bea chance after chance to take responsibility around the house and farm, but she hadn't. She seemed fine letting me lead.

Footsteps coming down the stairs signaled my mother's arrival. I took a mug from the cupboard and the milk from the fridge, sloshing in just enough to cover the bottom of the mug, just the way she liked it.

As she entered the kitchen, I handed her the tea. I had at least five minutes to talk with her about Leon—in some vague way to at least introduce the idea of him—before Beatrice appeared, if she was on schedule. Maybe more if she lingered.

But before Mamm could settle down at the table, a knock sounded against the side of the open back door.

"Whoever could that be at this early hour?" I said.

Mamm shrugged as she called out, "Come in."

Mervin entered, his sunglasses in his hand, looking lost. No wonder, after last night. Hopefully he and Hannah talked after the singing and sorted things out.

That didn't explain what he was doing in our kitchen at 5:35 a.m. though.

He looked at Mamm. "You told me to come before breakfast."

A puzzled expression settled on her face. "I did?"

"Jah," Mervin said. "On Saturday. Right before I quit for the day."

"Oh goodness," Mamm said. "That totally slipped my mind."

I grabbed three more eggs.

"How about a cup of tea?" Mamm nodded toward me.

"Denki," Mervin said.

I grabbed another mug, replanning my day as fast as I could.

Mervin usually went home for dinner. I could talk to Mamm then.

6

Mervin didn't go home for the noon meal; instead he ate with us in response to Mamm's invitation. She fixed sandwiches and didn't have any more memory lapses or headaches. In fact, she seemed perfectly normal.

Afterward, while Beatrice cleaned up, Mamm and Mervin went to look at the irrigation system, and I headed out to work in the flowers. Love followed me, stopping at the edge of the field. She seemed to be over her infatuation with Mervin.

I deadheaded the snapdragons, hoping for another round of blooms before the really hot weather set in, and then inspected the lily field. The Asiatic lilies would, depending on the weather, bloom in a couple of weeks. I hoped they'd be a big seller in the market. The first of the lavender had started to blossom. We'd sell those both as cut flowers and also transplant some into pots.

I made a mental note to ask Mervin to do that soon, so the plants had time to acclimate before Saturday. And to transplant the rest of the geraniums too. They'd been big sellers last Saturday.

After a while, I saw Mamm head back to the house, probably to take a nap. It was good for her not to overdo it. She'd seemed fine so far today. Maybe all she needed was the extra rest she'd been fitting in the last few days. More and more I agreed with her, that her episode on Friday was due to stress.

I stayed in the field, away from Mervin, determined not to have to talk about what happened the night before.

But just before supper, as I opened the back door to try to catch a breeze, there he was. Mamm had just come down from her room and heard me say hello to him, and she quickly invited him to eat with us. Beatrice had made chicken potpie, green beans, applesauce, and homemade bread. It seemed Edna had inspired us to get back to eating normally.

I kept the topic to business throughout the meal, bringing up what we needed to do the next day and the rest of the week to get ready for the market and keep up with all the chores. Mervin offered some suggestions, while Mamm asked a few questions, all of which made sense.

Just as we finished our meal, the sound of a horse's hooves came up our driveway.

"Who could that be?" Mamm asked, rising to her feet.

A shadow passed over Mervin's face. He and I knew perfectly well who it was, but neither of us said anything. I hadn't expected Leon so soon—or I would have said something to Mamm even with Mervin around.

Bea followed Mamm to the door but stopped on the stoop, although Mamm kept going.

"There's a guy out there," Beatrice said. "On a horse."

Mervin pursed his lips at me, but I sprang into action.

As I passed by her, Bea said, "He's really cute."

Love circled around Leon, happy to see him, as he stood at the edge of the lawn with Lightning's reins firmly in his hand. The horse wasn't happy to see Love, although the two looked like a matched set with their identical yellow coats.

Leon towered over my petite Mamm, and he was leaning toward her as if to hear her better—which was a funny thing for him to do, considering she was shaking her finger at him, something I'd never seen my Mamm do.

Leon chuckled, which only made Mamm more adamant about what she was saying.

I hurried toward them.

"Where did you say you're from?" she demanded.

"I didn't say—not yet," he said, his eyes dancing. "But now that you ask, from Montana."

"Montana. Oh goodness. No daughter of mine is going to court someone from that far away."

My face flushed. "Mamm," I called out. "Ask Leon in for dessert." I was pretty sure we had some ice cream in the freezer.

She turned toward me. Leon did too, a smile spreading across his face at the sight of me—and then a look of confusion at Mervin, who had fallen in step right behind me.

"He said he's come to call on you," Mamm said, stepping backward, unsteadily. I reached for her elbow. She added, "I told him you're not interested."

Years ago I'd heard a stupid song with words I couldn't entirely remember, probably at one of the big Englisch stores in town or in someone's car on the way to a party, but the lyrics went something like "Torn between two lovers . . . feeling like a fool." That was me, without a doubt. Of course, neither one was a lover—but I did feel like a fool.

And I had no idea what to do, except pretend nothing was wrong.

"I told Leon he could stop by, Mamm," I said as I released her elbow. I patted my leg for Love to sit before she sent Lightning bolting again. She obeyed, wedging herself against my leg. "He's working for Owen, training horses over at the Lapp place. I met him there."

Mamm's face lit up, her eyes lively again. "You're courting Hannah, then?"

He smiled. "Oh no, ma'am," Leon said. "I work for her Dat is all."

I jumped right in. "I meant to tell you about Leon today, earlier, but I didn't get a chance."

Mamm grimaced. "This is all wrong. It will not do."

I turned back toward Leon. He stood statue still even as Lightning nuzzled his hand, an agreeable expression still on his face even though what was going on was far from pleasant. "I'm sorry," I whispered. "It's my fault. I just didn't have a chance to . . . prepare her. She hasn't been herself." It seemed as if, again, Mamm's odd behavior was linked to more than stress.

He nodded. "I'll stop by tomorrow," he said. "To see how everyone is."

"Denki," I said. "Tell Hannah hello for me."

Mervin said he'd better get going. I agreed that was best. "We'll see you soon," I said, as I took Mamm's arm.

He told us good-night and headed for the shortcut to his farm. When Mamm and I stepped back in the house, Beatrice was collecting plates.

"Why don't you go sit in the living room," I said to Mamm, still holding on to her arm.

"Denki," she said. "I am feeling a little worn out." When we reached the couch, she said, "How about the porch?"

I agreed, walking to open the door. I worried we wouldn't be able to keep an eye on her though. One of our neighbors, who was close to ninety, had wandered off a few years ago. They'd finally found him in a neighbor's field after hours of searching. I didn't think Mamm would do that—she was, after all, only sixty-three—but at this point I wasn't sure.

"I'll send Beatrice out to sit with you," I said as Mamm stepped out onto the porch. She collapsed into one of the wicker chairs, her head in her hands.

After I told Beatrice I would do the dishes, that she should go sit with Mamm, I headed out the back door, pulling my phone

Cost-

from my pocket. I couldn't deny any longer something was going on with Mamm, something more than stress.

The last time I'd let denial get the best of me, I'd lost a parent. I'd call the doctor in the morning and try to move up her appointment for the CT scan. I considered leaving messages with Ivan and Edna to update them but then decided there wasn't anything more they could do. I'd call them after I spoke with the doctor. I did, however, call our bishop, leaving a message explaining Mamma's issues and asking for prayer.

Then, just in case Mamm's problems were only stress related, I did what I considered the first step in taking action to save our farm. I dialed Bob Miller's business number, listened to Cate's voice asking me to leave a message, and then left one—asking Bob to call me back because we were in dire need of good advice for our business.

As I ran the hot water, the phone buzzed in my pocket. I hadn't expected responses so soon. I dried my hands and answered as I darted out the back door. Cate's number popped up on my screen.

I answered with a quick "Molly speaking."

"Bob here. I just listened to your message."

I explained our problem to him, leaving out the part about Mamm wanting me to marry Mervin and me thinking I was falling for Leon, but I did mention Ivan's assessment and my worries about Mamm.

"I can come over tomorrow evening," Bob said.

"I know how busy you are, with the wedding coming up and all. . . ."

"Nonsense," Bob said. "I have plenty of time to help. I'll see you after supper."

I thanked him and hung up quickly. If we could figure out a way with Bob's help to save the farm, Mamm wouldn't feel it was necessary for me to marry Mervin. I couldn't tell Mamm I wouldn't marry Mervin because I thought I was falling for Leon. Especially now that she knew he was from Montana.

Before I went back in the house, I contemplated calling Hannah's number and leaving a message for Leon not to come the next evening until after eight, after Bob had left. But then I decided not to. Hannah's Dat would probably listen to the message. And then he would tell Hannah's Mamm, who would tell Nell. And then the whole county would know. And it would probably come back to Mamm.

No, it was better to take my chances that Leon would decide to wait until later to come anyway, especially after what had just happened. In Lancaster County most of our courting was done late in the evening, after dark. But maybe he didn't know.

The next day, after the nurse finally returned my call and assured me that we'd be fine waiting for Mamm's test, I told Beatrice to make a pie for our meeting with Bob. For some reason, even though we still had canned berries and apple filling from last summer, she made a sugar pie, something Mamm sometimes used to make in memory of her childhood. She'd grown up poor, and she often said vinegar pie or sugar pie was sometimes the only dessert they had.

I stood with my hands on my hips, in the middle of our kitchen, staring at the pie cooling on the counter.

"It's not that I want to impress Bob," I said. "But I do want him to know how much we appreciate his time." He was a successful businessman who also worked as a consultant, helping others improve their own businesses. His wisdom was invaluable. "I can't help but hope he'll have some ideas for us."

Beatrice shrugged. "You don't have to serve the pie. I just thought it would show how serious our situation is."

I pursed my lips, then remembered I'd come in the house for glasses of iced tea for both Mamm and Mervin. Mamm wouldn't come in for a nap. Taking some refreshment to her was the next best thing.

I filled the glasses and headed back outside, toward the greenhouse.

As I neared it, Mervin called out my name. I hurried, making the tea spill over onto my hand.

"Molly!" he called out again, this time with an edge of panic in his voice. I began to run, sending waves of tea onto my hands.

As I entered the greenhouse, the first thing I saw was Mamm sitting on a stool, her head down, with a panting Love right beside her. I put the tea on the potting bench beside the pots of geraniums and pulled out my phone, ready to call 9-1-1.

"Don't," Mamm said, glancing up at me.

I punched in the first number.

"I'm fine," she said.

She didn't look fine.

"Give me the tea," she said. "Then help me out of here. It's too hot for an old woman to be in a greenhouse. I have a headache is all, from the heat." It was the first time she'd ever referred to herself as old, maybe because she was nine years younger than Dat.

I gave her the tea, the phone still in my other hand. "I think I should call."

"And how will we pay the bill?" Mamm raised her head enough to look at me. "I'll go rest in the house." I understood she wanted to be responsible with our money, especially since she had an expensive CT scan coming up, but I still wondered if I should be calling the ambulance.

Dat had fallen out on the lawn, with Love at his side, and convinced us not to call for help. His back was sore, jah, and his arm. But probably from the fall. We got him inside to the couch, with Love staying at his side and pushing into the house for the first time in her life. By the time we realized he'd had a heart attack—and was having another—it was too late.

I helped Mamm from the stool and directed her to the door, with Love still beside her. Mervin followed us from the greenhouse. I turned to him and said, "You should go on home. Bob Miller is coming over to talk business after supper."

Mervin's voice was full of hurt. "And what about Leon?"

"I'm not sure. . . ." I answered.

"Oh" was all Mervin managed to say.

"Denki," I said. "I'll see you tomorrow." I stepped quickly to catch up with Mamm.

Mervin followed me. "Molly, I'm sorry. For all your troubles."

"Denki," I said again.

"I'll help in any way I can. You know that, right?"

"Jah," I answered again, wanting to tell him I didn't know what we would have done without him these past months but not wanting to lead him on any further. I kept quiet, shuffling alongside Mamm toward the house. I needed Mervin as a friend right now, for sure—I just didn't need the other complications.

Bob didn't arrive alone. Nan—his soon-to-be wife—came with him, sitting beside him in his posh buggy. Nan Byler had been raised Amish in New York, joined the church, and then left, intending to marry a Mennonite man. He died in a traffic accident. She joined the Mennonites anyway, drove one of the Lancaster County bookmobiles, and then said yes to courting Bob Miller.

In the last few months, she'd quit her job, given up her car, and joined the Amish, for a second time.

Soon they would be married.

Mamm stayed at the kitchen table while I went out to greet

the couple, Love falling in step beside me. Nan wore a Plain blue dress and a heart-shaped Kapp. I wondered if it had been hard for her to give up her print Mennonite dresses, not to mention her car. It never ceased to amaze me what people did for love.

"*Willkumm,*" I called out.

Bob hitched his horse to our railing by the barn and helped Nan out of the buggy. Under her Kapp and crown of blond hair with a bit of gray mixed in, Nan practically glowed, and Bob seemed as happy as I'd ever seen him, which said a lot. I'd never seen him the least bit down.

My heart lurched. I stood perfectly still as they walked side by side, not touching but as physically close as possible without doing so. Obviously they were in love—but they hadn't rushed into it. It had been a few years since they'd met. A year since they'd started courting. They'd taken it slower than most I knew would—her being Mennonite had surely complicated things.

"Beatrice has pie ready," I said, leading the way back to the house as Love greeted them.

I wished I could ask their advice about what to do concerning Leon, but I certainly couldn't ask that in front of Mamm. No, I needed to focus on making our business more viable. Once that was accomplished, Mamm would have no reason to want me to marry Mervin.

As I reached the back door, with Nan and Bob right behind me, the sound of horse's hooves fell on the driveway again, and Love took off at a run.

"Who is that?" Bob asked, turning.

I turned too, even though I knew. "Leon Fisher," I answered.

Leon rode a red roan, taller than Lightning and even wilder. "Hallo," he called out. Love ran alongside them.

"Is that the fellow staying over at Owen's place?" Bob asked. "The one training horses?"

"Jah," I answered.

"Invite him in for some pie," Bob said. "I'd love to hear about Montana. That's where he's from, right?"

I nodded. "Go on in," I said to Bob and Nan as I started toward Leon. "I'll be right there."

The horse snorted and pranced around, but Leon pulled up on the reins and settled him down. I approached tentatively, looking up at him. "Want to come in for some pie? A family friend, Bob Miller, and his fiancée, Nan, are here. They'd like to meet you."

"Are you sure?" he asked. "I don't want to interrupt anything."

"It would be good to have you come in. Bob would like to meet you. But then Mamm and I need to talk with Bob about our business."

"Sounds good," he said. "Mind if I put Storm in with Daisy?"

"He won't hurt her?" I hoped it sounded like I was joking. But I was serious.

"Jah." He patted the horse's neck. "He's a good sort. Just insecure."

"Is Love bothering him?"

Leon shook his head. "He does okay with dogs."

After he led the gelding to the pasture and secured the gate, we started back to the house with Love staying by his side. Leon smelled earthy, like sweat and dust and the scent of a horse but also a bit of spice. He swept off his straw hat, the western one again, and ran his hand through his dark hair as we neared the back door. "I take it this wouldn't be a good time to talk to your Mamm again about courting you."

I blushed. "No, not tonight. She and I . . ." I stammered. "We need to talk this all through first."

"Jah," he said. "That's what I gathered yesterday."

I led the way into the house. Everyone sat at the kitchen table—even Beatrice, which surprised me.

"We have another visitor," I said, using my cheeriest voice. "This is Leon Fisher, from Montana." I swept my hand toward him. "Leon, Bob Miller and Nan Byler."

Bob and Nan both rose and shook Leon's hand.

"Leon is going to join us for a piece of pie," I said, looking at Mamm. "Then he'll be on his way."

"Oh, the pie," Beatrice said, turning in her chair toward the counter.

"I'll get it," I said.

As I cut the pie, I noted that the consistency seemed off. Maybe the heat from the kitchen had kept it from cooling properly. I served it up on the plates without giving it another thought, listening to the conversation as I did.

Bob had asked Leon about Montana.

"Our farm is in the western part of the state," Leon said.

"Near the Bitterroot Mountains?"

"Not far from there," Leon answered. "My Dat raises cattle."

"That sounds like a commodity that would bring in money," Mamm said.

I turned toward her, surprised to hear her bring up the subject of finances in front of a stranger.

"Well," Leon said, "the price of beef fluctuates from year to year. It's not as profitable as it probably sounds."

I started around with the pie, serving Nan and Beatrice and Mamm first. Then the men.

"How many acres?" Bob took his plate of pie from me.

"Five hundred," Leon answered.

I stopped next to him.

Bob whistled.

Leon smiled. "It takes a lot of land to graze cattle."

"Of course," Bob said. "We can't compare acres in the west to acres here."

"Jah," Leon said. "Our ranch would be comparable, in profit and perhaps value, to a seventy-acre place here."

I doubted it. Maybe to a dairy farm, although milk wasn't the best moneymaker lately either, or one that grew soybeans or alfalfa, and maybe even corn. But not nursery stock and flowers.

I hurried back to pour the coffee I'd brewed.

"Let me help," Nan said. Before I could decline, she was out of her chair. I poured the cups and she delivered them. After I grabbed the cream from the fridge, I realized the rest were waiting on me and told them to get started on their pie—after all, Beatrice had made it.

As I sat down, Mamm took a bite. A funny look passed over her face.

I took a tiny taste and tried not to spit it out.

"Oh my," I said, reaching for my cup of coffee to wash away the taste of soda—at least that's what I thought it was. Did Beatrice accidentally put baking soda in the pie? I burned my tongue on the coffee, which still didn't take away the taste.

The others took bites and then stopped.

Beatrice took a bite—and held her fork in midair, an expression of realization settling on her face. It wasn't the end of the world, granted, but it had been a stupid mistake.

I pursed my lips as Leon said, "Delicious."

Beatrice smiled and took another bite.

So did Nan.

I took another, tiny, one. Heavy cream and sugar could save almost anything, I guessed, although the pie definitely had a baking-soda-biscuit flavor—minus the salt.

"Sugar pie is my favorite," Leon said. "This one is without eggs, right? The good old-fashioned kind."

Beatrice nodded. "Our Mamm calls it desperation pie. It's what her mother made when they were out of everything else—apples, berries, lemon juice, even eggs."

We did have eggs, but I wanted to sell them at the market.

"Desperation pie," Mamm said, her old sparkle back for a moment, "for hard times." She raised her fork toward Bob. "That's why you're here, right?"

We all smiled, even Beatrice.

After Leon finished his coffee, he said, "Thank you so much for inviting me in, but I need to be on my way."

I walked him to the door.

As we stepped outside he smiled at me, seeming in no way put out by another change of plans. In a low voice, he said, "How about if I come by tomorrow?"

"About that," I said. "Around here we do our courting later in the evening."

"How late?" he asked.

"Well, after dark."

He nodded. "I'll keep that in mind."

When I told him good-bye, he leaned toward me. I thought his lips brushed the top of my Kapp, but I couldn't be sure. Quickly he turned and strode toward the pasture. My heart pounded again, longing to be with him instead of going back inside. Still, there was work that had to be done. When I returned, Beatrice was nowhere in sight, which didn't surprise me. She hated business talk.

"Leon seems like a nice young man," Bob said as I sat back down at the table.

"Molly's courting Mervin Mosier," Mamm answered, looking down at her hands folded together on the table.

I decided it best not to respond.

"It doesn't look that way," Bob said.

I blushed. "The topic we need to discuss is how to save our farm." I put my hand on top of Mamm's.

Nan seemed as if she might say something but then didn't.

"What's going on?" Bob asked.

"Mervin Mosier would like to marry Molly," Mamm said. "She agreed to it a few days ago."

"Mamm, I said I'd think about courting him."

"And now?" Bob asked.

"It's complicated," I said, "but first of all, Hannah still cares for him."

"Marrying Mervin would save the farm," Mamm said.

I shook my head. "We don't know that."

Bob wrapped his hands around his mug of coffee. "When it comes to businesses, I've found that where there's a will there's a way," he said. "A way that works for all involved."

I nodded.

He turned toward Mamm. "Before we talk business though, Bishop Eicher talked with me about your upcoming CT scan."

Mamm wrinkled her nose. "I'm fine. A little forgetful recently, but the doctor thinks it's stress related, considering everything that's been going on."

Bob glanced at me.

I shrugged.

"Well," he said, "we can deal with that when you find out. In the meantime, let's look at your business."

An hour later, my head pounded as hard as my heart had earlier. Bob had suggested we expand the market and find a wider distribution for the nursery stock we grew.

My mother sighed. "I'm going to be praying that Molly will agree to marry Mervin so we can work with that wholesaler."

"Mamm," I said, "It would still take a few years to turn things around relying on that. We'd have to plant new inventory, wait for the trees and shrubs to grow." Flowers grew in a season, but nursery stock took several years. We needed something that would bring in income right away.

Nan caught my eye, giving me a sympathetic look.

Bob closed the small notebook he carried with him. He'd taken pages of notes. "I'll think this over," he said, "and get back to you with more ideas."

Mamm thanked him.

Nan and Bob stood and walked to the door. They said good-bye as Bea returned to the kitchen and settled down in the chair next to Mamm.

"I'll walk out with you," I said to Nan and Bob.

As I closed the back door behind us, Bob said, "You seem to have a handle on the business."

"Not really," I answered. "I had no idea how bad things had gotten."

"But you know the day-to-day operation," he said.

"So does Mamm. But I shadowed both my parents all these years, so I understand more of what Dat did."

"Well, you've certainly seen hard times lately," Bob said. "It's good to pull in resources and figure out what to do. Of course, once we know how your Mamm's health is we'll have a better idea of what the future looks like."

"Jah . . ." I said, hesitating.

"What is it?" Bob stopped at the edge of the lawn and turned toward me.

"I've been friends with Mervin for years—and for an afternoon I thought I might be able to marry him. . . ."

"But now?" Bob asked.

"I know I can't."

His eyes were kind as he looked at me. "Because?"

I cleared my throat, trying to speak.

Bob's voice was low but clear. "Leon?"

"Maybe," I whispered.

He smiled. "It's clear there's something between the two of you."

Nan shot Bob a look—subtle, to be sure. Then she said, "We're praying for all of you. It might take some time, but things will work out."

Tears stung my eyes, taking me by surprise. "Jah," I said, but I said it out of habit. For once I didn't feel it.

"Do you think your Mamm's urgency that you marry is part of her possible illness?" Nan touched my arm.

"I don't know," I answered. "She's never acted like this before. I know she's stressed, so it could be that. Or perhaps something else . . ."

"All the more reason for her to have the test done," Bob said. "All of you need to know what you're looking at."

I nodded.

"But keep in mind, the *Ordnung* doesn't sanction arranged marriages." He smiled.

"Jah, but it does require that we obey our parents."

"Your Mamm's upset right now. No one would expect you to marry someone you don't love," Nan said.

"Denki," I answered.

"In fact, you shouldn't marry a man if you're interested in another."

"Denki," I said again, appreciating Bob's affirmation.

We reached their buggy, and Bob took Nan's hand and helped her up with a tenderness that made my heart leap. A few minutes later they were headed back down the driveway. I watched until the buggy turned onto the highway.

I'd turned to head back toward the house as someone called out, "Miss Molly!" I hurried to where I had a better view of the road. Below me, Leon sat on Storm, waving his hat, his smile spreading across his face at the sight of me.

I ducked under the arbor, the clematis leaves tugging at my Kapp, and down the path to Leon, my flip-flops slipping on the loose dirt with Love trailing behind me. By the time I reached him, he was in the pasture at the end of the path, off the horse and waiting for me. Storm shied as I approached, but Leon tightened his grip on him and he came to a stop.

"Is everything all right?" Leon asked, touching my forearm with his free hand, sending a jolt through me. Love ran around the pasture, happy to explore where she was forbidden to tread most of the time.

I nodded. The truth was, being next to him had made everything at least better, if not all right.

"Want to go for a ride?" he asked.

For a split second I wanted nothing more than to be riding behind Leon, holding on to his waist, forgetting all my worries. But I hadn't been on a horse in well over a decade.

The gelding snorted and brushed up against my legs. I stepped away.

"I'm not dressed for it," I said. Hannah wore a pair of pants when she rode, but I didn't have anything like that. I'd never had a need. Until now. "Let's go for a walk instead." I pointed in the opposite direction of the Mosiers' farm. "That way."

"Sure," Leon said. "I'll lead Storm."

I sent Love back to the house, not wanting to risk her getting hit on the road. As Leon and I strolled toward the highway, Storm nipped at my back. Leon quickly moved him to the other side.

"So you really started riding as a small child?" I asked.

"Yes. One of my first memories is being on the back of a horse, giggling. I was two, maybe three. I was sure I was flying. I still feel that way."

I shuddered. All those years ago riding a horse had made me feel more like I was going to drown than fly.

He met my eyes. "I feel closest to God when I'm on a horse. It's when I pray the most." He smiled. "And praise the most."

"That's how I feel with my flowers," I said.

He nodded, as if thinking over what I'd said. "It's good to feel that harmony, jah? No matter what brings it."

I agreed. Although I hadn't been feeling it as much lately.

The sun hung low in the west. A flock of swallows swooped toward our barn. A cat darted across the highway. On the hill across the way, someone, perhaps Phillip, was walking the fence line of the field that had been plowed the week before.

When we reached the pavement we both started to speak at once.

"So, what—" I said.

Just as he said, "Hannah told me—"

We both laughed. "You go first," I said.

"No, you."

"Really, you," I insisted.

"She said the two of you are planning a camping trip with a group of Youngie."

"Maybe . . ." I thought she'd still be upset with me but maybe not. "It depends on how things go with my Mamm."

"Oh," he said. "Well, if you decide to go, I was hoping I could too. Owen thought it would be a good idea to take along a horse."

My voice brightened. "Really?" Having Leon come along on the trip seemed like a great idea. If bringing a horse meant he could come, I was all for it. Owen owned a truck and a trailer and had a driver he used all the time, so transportation wouldn't be a problem.

He grinned. "Hannah said you wouldn't be thrilled with a horse coming along."

I groaned. Here it came.

"That was all she said, I promise." His voice was kind. "Except that you're good at organizing events and the camping trip should be fun. She said everything you plan is fun."

My heart warmed. "That was sweet of her. And I think it would be great if you—and Lightning—came along." The camping trip had turned out to be a good idea after all.

"We don't do a lot of Youngie gatherings in Montana," Leon said.

"How come?"

"There aren't that many of us in our settlement. We spend most of our time with the grown-ups." He paused again and then said, "That's one of the reasons my parents agreed to me coming out east."

"So you could meet . . . other Youngie?"

"Jah." He blushed.

My heart began to gallop again.

He said, "I like you, Molly Zook."

I couldn't help but think that speaking so frankly was an effort for him—but he was braving his fears because he cared for me.

We stopped under a willow tree that hung over a wide spot in the road. A car zoomed by in the opposite lane.

I gazed up into his big blue eyes. They were like open doors, welcoming me inside. Sure he was a little shy, but in an inviting way.

Phillip Eicher had talked nonstop, never letting me get a word in. Plus, he was a perfectionist and judged everything, making subtle comments about a field that was plowed wrong or a buggy left unwashed or a horse not properly cared for. Half the time, when he was extra critical, I was afraid to say anything at all, afraid it would be "wrong." With Leon, I never felt that way. I felt accepted and that he welcomed what I had to say, but at the same time I didn't feel as if I had to carry the conversation. I never felt as if he were judging me.

"Your eyes are so beautiful," Leon said, placing his hands on my shoulders.

My face warmed. I'd thought my eyes were blue until I saw his. In comparison, mine were the color of pond water.

"And your smile," he said. "It's like you have everything figured out."

I wrinkled my nose. "Far from."

Leon continued, "Hannah tells me you're not the quiet type—but it's not as if you're a motormouth either."

"Hannah's right," I said. "I'm not the quiet type."

"But you've been quiet around me." His hands dropped from my shoulders to his side. "Is it Mervin?"

I shook my head, but then nodded. "It is and it isn't."

"You can be honest with me," he said. "I'd much rather have the truth than have you playing games with me."

"I don't play games," I said. Was that true? "Not with you anyway. I promise." I took a deep breath. He was too sweet and innocent to play games with. "What I'm going to tell you, I need you not to share. Not even with Hannah."

"Understood."

"I already told you our business is having financial problems . . ."

He nodded.

I went on to tell him just how desperate our situation was and that Mamm, quite out of character, had come up with a plan for Mervin and me to marry. "At first I said I'd consider it," I confessed. "But that was before I met you."

Leon's face was solemn. "You don't intend to marry for love?"

"No, I do." I put my hands to my warming face, surprised by my embarrassment, and turned away. "I can't talk about this."

He put his hands back on my shoulders, pulled me around, and then drew me close, pressing my burning cheek against his chest. I could feel his heart beating beneath his shirt, which comforted me, along with the lingering scent of homemade soap. He held me close and whispered, "So, if we can figure out what to do about your farm, you'll be free to court me?"

"I think so," I answered. "But you should know what else is going on with my family." I told him about Mamm's upcoming medical test. And then I told them about Beatrice. "I doubt she'll ever marry," I said. "I'll be responsible for her if anything happens to Mamm."

"Jah, of course," Leon said. He pulled me close again, and I turned my face up toward his. But instead of kissing me, he traced his finger down my nose, resting it on the tip.

"We should go back," he said. "I don't want your Mamm to think any less of me."

"She doesn't know I'm with you." I clung to him, felt his breath on my forehead. "So you're planning to stay in Lancaster?" I whispered. I didn't move as I spoke, hoping if I didn't he wouldn't either. I wanted to stay the way we were forever—until I heard the *clippity-clop* of a horse's hooves coming over the little hill on the highway.

I pulled away from him. Dusk was falling, but not enough to hide us under the willow tree.

The buggy's lantern was already lit, and its running lights were on. I expected a young couple—and almost laughed when I saw it wasn't. Nell Yoder and Joseph Koller sat side by side in his courting buggy.

She stared at first and then waved when she recognized me. A puzzled expression followed as they zipped on by. I doubted it would take her long to identify who was with me—and then one phone call to Hannah's mother, Pauline, would be all it would take for the whole county to know.

At the bottom of our driveway, I said, "I'll walk back up by myself."

"Is that best?" Leon asked. "Is that the way it's done?"

"Sometimes." It was best for now.

"Could I talk to your Mamm?" he asked. "Or both of us together?"

I shook my head. "Let's wait until after we know what's wrong with her."

Leon put his hand on my shoulder, and I reached up and squeezed it.

"I'll get going," he said.

"Be careful," I answered. Dusk had quickly turned to night.

"Storm's too ornery for anything to happen," he said. "We'll be fine."

I wasn't worried about Storm. I was worried about him.

He mounted the horse quickly and with a wave said, "Good night, Miss Molly."

I waited until he disappeared around the curve of the highway, and then I started my trudge up the hill. An owl hooted in the distance. Then a dog barked—but not Love—followed by our back door slamming.

When I reached the lawn, Beatrice called out to me from the chicken coop. "It wasn't locked," she said. "A dog took off with one of our hens."

"Which one?"

"The Leghorn."

"Oh no." A feeling of despondency washed over me. She was one of the new ones. "Where's Love?"

"I thought she was with you." Beatrice latched the door.

"Love!" I shouted. And then I called out her name again, this time even louder.

She came running up from the pasture. "Where were you?" I chided when she reached us.

She put her tail between her legs. It was Love's job to keep stray dogs away from the farm—especially the coop. "You belong here," I scolded, "not gallivanting after Leon."

Love bowed her head.

Beatrice frowned with me. "You're even bossy with the dog."

"I'm not bossy."

"You are," she said. "More now than ever."

I crossed my arms.

Beatrice gave me a pathetic look and then said, "So where were you?"

"On a walk."

"With?"

I shrugged.

She exhaled. "Leon."

I nodded.

Beatrice put one hand on her hip. "He's not your type."

"Why do you say that?"

"He's too . . ." She wrinkled her nose. "Thoughtful. Introspective. Caring."

I took a step backward. "What do you mean by that?"

She pursed her lips and then said, "Mervin's much more your type."

I shook my head, trying not to laugh. Was Beatrice interested in Leon?

Her eyes narrowed. "I hope you're not thinking that I'll marry Mervin if you don't."

I shook my head again, no longer amused. "I don't think any such thing," I said. "Hannah loves Mervin. She should marry him."

"Well, I'm not going to marry Martin either," Beatrice said.

"No one's asking you to," I said.

"Because I don't plan to marry anyone."

She'd said that before, said she'd devote her life to serving God. I'd responded that to serve God she'd need to serve His people—and that would mean actually interacting with them. That conversation hadn't gone well, so this time instead of going down that path again I changed the subject. "We need to figure out a way to save the farm ourselves," I said. "Without anyone having to get married."

She started toward the house, with me following. "I don't know what I can do to help."

"Be supportive of me," I offered.

"Then don't be so bossy," Bea answered. It was completely dark now, and I couldn't see the expression on her face.

I stopped walking.

She turned back toward me. "You'll figure out something," she said.

I froze on the grass, as if I'd been tagged in a childhood game of freeze tag, as she hurried on into the house. I usually wanted to be in charge—but this felt like too much responsibility. Sinking to my knees in the thick grass, I remembered my prayer in the Mosiers' barn a few nights before. Nothing had gotten any better. Only worse.

I could only hope Bob would come up with an idea to help us. And that Mamm would live another ten years at least, long after I was happily married—and maybe even Beatrice too, if she learned to be nicer.

Maybe Mamm would warm to my idea of a bed-and-breakfast. It wouldn't be a circus, as she feared. I'd do it very tastefully. The pumpkin patch too.

I squeezed my eyes against more tears, but then I thought of Leon. He liked me. He wanted to court me. He hadn't had a chance to answer my question about staying in Lancaster County, and I'd been too distracted by the sight of Nell to ask him again on the walk back, but I was sure he wanted to stay. Who wouldn't?

I swiped at my eyes and struggled to my feet. Why the double dose of both the good and the bad now? Why had I finally found love only to have us about to lose the farm?

I decided our house really was one of our best assets and set out the next day to explore my idea of opening a bed-and-breakfast, along with drumming up more business for our flowers.

Mamm and Mervin had gone back out to work on the irrigation system. I told Beatrice I had errands to run and she needed to see to the house chores.

"When you're done," I said, "weed the lilies."

She crossed her arms.

"Many hands make light work," I said.

"Jah," she said. "And a little sister's work is never done."

"No one's work is ever done," I said. "It's the way life is."

"It's the way life is with you," she retorted.

"Honestly, Bea. What do you expect to do? To sit around and write in your journal all day?"

"Of course not, but you think the housework doesn't take any time. It does."

"Well, work faster."

She scowled.

I left before I said anything worse.

I planned to visit bed-and-breakfasts in the area. My intentions were twofold. One, to offer to sell them our flowers and herbs. What could be more inviting to guests than beautiful blooms from a nearby Amish farm, delivered by me, along with fresh herbs for their food? My second motivation was to get a glimpse of the B&Bs, maybe even garner a tour, and see what we'd need to do to our house to accommodate guests.

First, I spent some time in the flower gardens, cutting snapdragons and lavender for bouquets and wishing the lilies had started to bloom. Next I headed to the herb garden, snipping a bucketful of rosemary, thyme, basil, coriander, and oregano. I made bouquets of the flowers and placed the herbs in paper cones and then put all of them in the ice chest.

Then I hitched Daisy to the buggy. By the time I was ready to leave it was midmorning. Breakfast would be done at the B&Bs, but hopefully guests would still be around. A few oohs and aahs would enhance my pitch to the owners.

Mervin stepped out of the greenhouse as I climbed into the buggy seat. "Where are you going?" He'd been avoiding me all morning, so I was surprised to see him.

"Errands," I said.

"Molly, tell me the truth."

"I am." I sighed. "I'm going to visit a few bed-and-breakfasts to see if they want to buy flowers or herbs."

He crossed his arms. "Your Mamm told me you had a wild idea about opening one of those up."

I shrugged.

"What shall I tell her if she asks where you are?"

"The truth," I answered as I pulled on the reins. "I have nothing to hide."

"I think you do," he answered.

Pretty sure he was talking about Leon, not any of my ideas for the farm, I made my escape, urging Daisy along.

The day was overcast, with clouds billowing on the horizon. A breeze urged us along, stirring a new hope inside of me. My feelings for Leon spurred me on. I'd no reason to be as pessimistic as I'd felt the day before. Troubles came to everyone at sometime or another.

The first bed-and-breakfast I stopped at was owned and operated by a Mennonite family. It was clear they weren't Old Order, not even close. But tourists seemed to like the fact that they were still somewhat Plain, even though they owned cars.

As I headed down their short driveway, I noticed a big garden to my right with flowers planted around the edges. Snapdragons and lavender. And a plot beyond it held herbs.

My confidence began to dim, but I chided myself. I might as well give it a try. Practicing on a Mennonite family would be good for me.

I spotted their hitching post, which I took as a good sign, tied Daisy, and then stepped to the back of my buggy. I'd attached our brochures to the cones and bouquets and took one of each out now. An older Englisch couple watched me from where they sat on the front porch. I decided to knock on the back door, hoping the proprietors were cleaning up after breakfast.

I knocked several times before a girl who looked to be around thirteen answered. She wore a print Mennonite dress, an apron, and a rounded Kapp.

"Are your parents home?" I asked.

She shook her head.

I could hardly believe they'd leave a child in charge. "I was hoping to talk with one of them."

She pointed toward the field. "My father's mowing and my mother went to town."

"Oh." I doubted her Dat would want to be interrupted. I handed her the flowers and herbs. "Could you give this to your Mamm? Tell her I have the farmers' market outside of Paradise. And I'd be happy to deliver anything she needs."

The girl pointed to their big garden. "We have our own."

"Jah," I said. "I saw that. But in case you need more . . ." As I spoke three strapping young men came around the side of the barn headed to the garden. It looked like the family had a work force too.

"Ellen," someone called out, "who's there?"

"An Amish girl," she called back over her shoulder. "I need to get back to work," she said to me.

I nodded. "Denki."

She handed me the bouquet and herbs.

Discouraged, I returned to my buggy. As I put the flowers and herbs back in the box, I realized the Englisch couple on the porch was staring at me. As I pulled Daisy around, the woman snapped a photo of me with her phone. I looked straight ahead, determined not to react. I imagined the photo being posted on the Internet along with a hundred other shots of Lancaster County.

The young men in the garden raised their heads as I passed by but didn't wave or say anything. As I passed the alfalfa field, the father shaded his eyes from the sun as he drove a fairly new tractor, most likely trying to determine who I was. He looked young—half the age my Dat had been.

Obviously the family had plenty of labor to manage a farm and a bed-and-breakfast. Plus the mother had a car she could drive to the grocery store and the Dat had a new tractor with rubber wheels, not an old one like we had with metal wheels that was continually breaking down.

Even if I did convince Mamm to let me open a bed-and-breakfast, how could I compete with a Mennonite family, let alone Englisch ones?

The sun burned the clouds away, and the day turned hot as Daisy pulled the buggy down the highway at a sluggish pace. The other bed-and-breakfasts were farther away, and soon, even though it was still morning, heat started coming up off the pavement. The warm day and the beat of the horse's hooves lulled me into a dazed state. My head had begun to nod when I heard a shout across the road.

"Miss Molly!"

It was Leon, of course, riding Storm. The horse snorted and turned his head away. Leon pulled him back.

"Where are you going?" Leon asked.

I pulled Daisy to a stop as he approached.

I told him about my visit to the first bed-and-breakfast and that I was headed to a second, and maybe another one or two after that.

"I could ride along," he said.

"How much time do you have?"

"All morning." He smiled. "I'm off on a long ride on Storm. Owen's orders."

The next bed-and-breakfast was off to the right, a few lanes down the highway. It wouldn't hurt to have Leon come along.

He rode ahead of the buggy until we reached the lane, but once we did, he fell back beside me.

"Hannah mentioned the camping trip again at breakfast," he said. "This time Owen asked if we could take both Lightning and Storm along."

"We?"

He laughed. "Hannah and me."

"Oh." Taking both Storm and Lightning on the trip sounded like an ordeal, but if it justified Leon's coming along all the more . . . "I think we could work that out." I inched forward on the buggy bench.

Leon smiled again. "Jah, that's what Owen said."

Owen had bought his truck a few years before. I was surprised the bishop allowed it, but it was less expensive, over time, for Owen to buy a truck and hire a driver than hire both to take his horses to sales. It was funny, to me, that he owned a vehicle he would never drive.

I mentioned to Leon that I appreciated how kind he'd been to Beatrice about the pie the night before, realizing I'd forgotten to thank him when we were out alone.

"She seemed a little out of sorts," he said.

"She's always been . . . unsettled," I said. "But more lately than before."

"With good reason," Leon said. "Besides, I know all about a sister being out of sorts."

He'd mentioned having a temperamental sister. I scooted to the very end of the bench, closest to him as he rode Storm. "Tell me about her."

"My second sister, she's five years younger than I am, has had some emotional problems." He quickly added. "I'm not saying Beatrice does."

I nodded.

"Anyway, no one knew what to do with Naomi. My Dat would tell her to snap out of it, but when she couldn't, my Mamm took her to the doctor and got some help."

"So she's better now?"

Leon took a deep breath. "Some. But not completely. She's worse in the winter. Better in the summer." He shrugged. "It's ongoing."

My heart lurched. "Do you miss home?" It sounded as if he did.

"A little," he answered.

"How about the cows? Do you miss them?"

He leaned forward and patted Storm's neck. "I'd rather train horses than run cattle. Nothing against cows, but horses are much smarter. There's more money in cows though."

Storm bobbed his head, which made me laugh.

"If I can't figure out a way to make a living working with horses, I can always go back to the ranch."

That wasn't what I'd wanted to hear, but it did seem he'd prefer to stay in Lancaster County and train horses than go home.

"Well," I said, "I appreciated your kindness to Beatrice. Her sticking around to hang out with Bob and Nan and you was a good thing. She tends to go off by herself and write in this book she has."

Leon smiled, shyly again.

"What?" I slowed Daisy as the bed-and-breakfast came into view.

"I have a book I draw in."

I remembered the leather book I saw beside his Bible. "Well, you don't go off by yourself."

"Actually, sometimes I do."

I wrinkled my nose. "You know what I mean."

His eyes twinkled as he said, "I'm not sure that I do." He

smiled wryly and seemed more amused than annoyed. I decided not to say anything more about writing—or drawing—in books. I'd already put my foot in my mouth.

When we reached the bed-and-breakfast, which I noted didn't have a garden nearby, not even any flower beds, just trees and shrubs, I parked the buggy. Leon said he'd stay with Daisy, so I grabbed the flowers and herbs from the back, along with a brochure. A car and a pickup were both in the driveway, along with a motorcycle.

The house was set back in a grove of trees, and I hurried along the brick path toward it, deciding I'd knock on the front door.

A middle-aged woman answered it immediately. Her face lit up when she saw me. "How can I help you?" she asked.

I explained who I was and why I was on her porch, at least as far as the flowers and herbs, not that I was hoping for a tour. She willingly took my bundles and the brochure.

She had a simple but elegant way about her. Her hair was shoulder length and a natural light brown, she didn't wear any makeup, and she carried herself with poise but exuded warmth. "This is our first year," she said. "We've talked about planting gardens next year, but I'd at least be interested in your flowers and herbs this summer."

"Thank you," I said, pointing to the brochure. "The first number is my phone—the second is our landline. Call me on my cell if you want something right away."

She smiled kindly.

"How is business?" I asked.

"Good. We're nearly booked for every weekend through the summer—and the weekdays are filling up too. We even have a wedding soon."

I hesitated, then found my courage, due to her kindness, and said, "I'm considering renting out a room at our place, occasionally to start with."

"Really?" She folded her arms around the flowers, herbs, and brochure.

I nodded.

"You know, I have people ask me sometimes if there's an Amish family they can stay with. Some for a night. Some for more than that. Could I give them your number?"

"Jah," I answered.

"And I have guests interested in having dinner with an Amish family. I have some homes lined up but could use more. The pay is actually pretty good."

I'd heard of Plain people hosting such dinners. "I'd be interested in that too." I couldn't imagine Mamm would be thrilled with the idea, but if it brought in a good amount of money, she might be.

"Would you like to look around?" the woman asked.

My heart fluttered at her generosity. "Please," I answered.

"Is he with you?" she asked, nodding toward Leon.

"He is," I said. I waved at him and then called out, "I'll be back soon."

She told me her name was Kristine and that the farm had been in her husband's family for a couple of generations. They'd inherited it a couple of years ago and decided to turn it into a bed-and-breakfast. "It took us that long to do all the work."

That sounded daunting. I certainly didn't have a couple of years.

Plush furniture filled the living room, with pillows and throws on the couches and chairs and lacy curtains covering the windows. Thick rugs covered most of the polished wood floors. In the dining room, rounded chairs encircled an elegant table that seated ten.

The kitchen was completely modernized with granite counters, new cabinets, and large appliances. The refrigerator was nearly as big as my buggy.

"Would you like to see one of the guest rooms?" Kristine pointed toward a staircase off the kitchen.

I nodded, following her but not knowing what to say. It was all so fancy. Light from the landing bounced down on the polished wood stairs. When we reached the top, I could see Leon out the window. He was holding Storm's reins while he stroked Daisy's neck. Storm held his head high as if he weren't happy about his competition.

"Is that your brother?" Kristine stopped, placed her hands on the windowsill, and then turned back to me.

My face grew warm, and I must have blushed.

"Oh, I see," she teased. "He's awfully handsome."

"He's from Montana," I said, which was a silly thing to say.

"Really?" she said. "I grew up in Idaho. What's he doing way out here?"

"Training horses."

She raised her eyebrows. "We had guests last week ask about riding horses. Their daughters both wanted to."

I didn't see where she was going.

"Does he do trail rides? Anything like that?"

I shook my head, but that was an idea.

"Too bad," Kristine said, heading down the hallway. "This room is vacant." She opened it wide and allowed me to step in first. The bed was huge, with a white coverlet and six plump pillows on it. I couldn't imagine anyone needing so many. I stepped closer to the bed and then noticed another door. It led to a bathroom. Of course Englisch people would expect their own. Why hadn't I thought of that?

"It's all so nice," I said.

"Thank you." Kristine headed back to the hallway and motioned for me to go first down the stairs. "You know, if you did rent out a room, no one would expect your place to look like this."

I didn't answer.

"They would just be thrilled to have a genuine Amish experience."

I hadn't thought about that.

"They would want to sleep in a bed like you do. Use a bathroom like you do. Eat a breakfast like you do."

"Denki," I said as I reached the kitchen.

"Pardon?"

"Thank you," I said quickly.

"Denki," she parroted. "I like that." She held my brochure up in her hand as she led the way through the dining room. "So you must be a pretty good gardener—or someone in your family is."

"We get by," I said.

"And modest too."

I tried not to smile.

"You know, what we could use help with is getting a garden started. Would you be willing to be our consultant?"

"Jah," I answered.

"We'd pay, of course."

I nodded. The truth was, I'd do it to be neighborly, but pay was good. Especially now.

"I'll call," she said. "About the flowers and herbs. Then in the fall about the garden, when things slow down."

I thanked her again.

"I like you, Molly Zook," she said as I followed her to the front door. "Mind if I meet your beau?"

"He's not really—"

She laughed.

"Sure," I said, following her outside.

Storm snorted and Leon held on tightly, keeping the horse's head up.

"This is Kristine," I said as we neared.

"Kristine Boyd," she said. "My husband and I own the B&B."

"Leon Fisher," he said before I had a chance to. He stuck out his hand and shook hers firmly.

"Molly says you're from Montana."

"That's right," he said. "In the northwest corner."

"I grew up over the state line in Idaho, near Sandpoint."

"I know the area," he said. "We delivered some horses up that way. It's beautiful."

They chatted for a moment, and then she broached the subject of the trail rides.

"I work for Owen Lapp," he said. "He boards and trains horses."

"No lessons? Or rides?" Kristine asked.

Leon shook his head.

"You never know," she said. "There might be a market for it among the tourists, and the locals too."

I couldn't imagine a bunch of Englisch girls at Hannah's place taking lessons from Leon.

"I'll mention it to Owen," Leon said, but I was pretty sure he was just being polite.

An hour later, Leon galloped beyond our driveway on the highway below as I stopped Daisy beside our barn. I unhitched the horse, led her to the pasture, and then pulled the ice chest from the back of the buggy and took it into the greenhouse. Love followed me.

"Your Mamm asked about you." Mervin stood at the planting

bench, his sleeves rolled up past his elbows, his sunglasses on against the glare coming through the windows. He had several of the large plastic rectangular planters lined up on one side and basil, oregano, and rosemary seedlings on the other.

I put the box against the wall, pulling out the leftover herbs to take in the house to use. "It's sweltering in here," I said to Mervin. "Can't that wait until later?"

He shook his head. "Your Mamm wanted more planters done up for Saturday."

They did sell really well. And the profit was good.

"You'd better go on in," he said. He had a concerned look on his face. "Edna's here."

"Oh. Do you know why?"

Mervin shook his head.

I hurried on to the house and through the back door. No one was in the kitchen. I put the herbs on the counter and called out, "Mamm?"

Her voice came from the front porch. "We're out here."

I stepped quickly into the living room. They'd left the front door wide open. I stepped over the threshold, closing the door behind me, and onto the worn planks of the porch. Beatrice and Mamm were sitting on the settee and Edna on the chair.

"Where were you?" Mamm asked.

"Running errands. I didn't know Edna was coming over."

"I didn't either," Mamm said. "She surprised us."

"I couldn't stay away," she said. "I kept thinking about Anna. So I hired a driver to bring me over for the day."

I was always happy to see Edna and for the extra help.

"Hannah stopped by, right when Edna arrived," Mamm said. "She was looking for you."

"To talk about the camping trip," Beatrice added.

"Oh," I said. "Jah, we've talked about that. But I was thinking we'd go in a month or so." Long after we knew how Mamm was. And besides, I'd need time to plan.

"No," Mamm said. "You should go as soon as possible. Invite your friends—your old gang, just the ones you've known all your life." Obviously she didn't want Leon going—and I wasn't about to tell her that he was already planning to, thanks to Owen. "And take Bea."

"We can't leave you," I said to Mamm as I knelt beside her. She placed her hand on my shoulder. Hopefully by the time we did go camping she would be fine—both physically and emotionally. Maybe she'd be over her opposition to Leon by then.

"You should go soon," Edna said. "I'll come to stay. And I'm sure Ivan will too. We'll do the chores. And watch over Anna."

"In fact," Mamm said, patting my shoulder, "I want you to leave next Monday and stay for two or three nights."

That meant we'd be gone on Tuesday, when she was scheduled to have the CT scan. I pulled away from her and stood. "Mamm . . . I'm going with you for your test."

She shook her head. "Remember that place we used to go to in the Poconos?"

I nodded. Years ago, Mamm and Dat used to take us camping. We all enjoyed it. But as the work of the farm grew, we began skipping years and then about ten years ago stopped going at all.

"Go there," she said. "You'd better get started on the planning right away."

I stared down at her. "Mamm, I—"

"Molly!" Her voice was as sharp as I'd ever heard it. "Mind me."

I stood tall, but a numbness started to spread through me. I couldn't understand why she didn't want me to go with her when she got her scan. In fact, I felt hurt that she seemed to prefer to have Edna, and even Ivan, with her instead.

Mamm stood. "I'll go talk to Mervin and ask him to arrange for a van."

"Shouldn't Mervin stay and help here?"

Mamm shook her head. "Molly, that's part of the reason for you to go on this trip. So you and Mervin—"

"I'll leave a message for Hannah," I said quickly. "And tell her what the plan is. I'll call for a van too, so don't say anything to Mervin yet. Let me figure out some things first."

Mamm reluctantly agreed.

As I steadied myself against the chair, Edna said she hadn't seen any mockingbirds lately.

"I don't know where they went off to," Mamm said. "I miss them. They're so smart, so perceptive."

"Dat sure loved them," Edna said. "Remember the one that would mimic him?"

Mamm nodded, and I headed into the house, thinking about Leon and the camping trip.

CHAPTER
9

Later in the day, I left a message for Hannah about camping, asking her to call me and not to mention the trip to Mervin until we'd talked, saying I just wanted to make sure we had all the details sorted out first. I added the last part more for her Dat, sure Owen would probably check the message and give it to her. I didn't want him to think I was scheming, even though I was.

Then I called and arranged for a van. While Mamm napped and Beatrice spent time on the porch with her journal, I sat with Edna at the table and had a cup of tea and one of her delicious buttermilk sugar cookies—rounded and chewy.

"Your Mamm told me there has been a young man coming to see you, besides Mervin."

I nodded as I swallowed.

"She's afraid you'll be going off to Montana."

"I'd never leave Lancaster County," I said, picking up my mug of tea. "I've had offers. Ohio. Indiana. Maryland. I wasn't interested."

"So he doesn't plan to go back?"

"It doesn't seem so."

"Do you know for sure?" She took another cookie from the plate.

I fought a feeling of unease. "Pretty sure."

"You shouldn't court anyone you wouldn't marry. And if you're not willing to move to Montana . . ." She took a bite of the cookie. "You know it's the woman who compromises on these things. Especially if his family has land—unless one of his brothers is going to get it." She took a sip of tea.

I shook my head. "He has a bunch of sisters, but he's the only boy."

Edna clucked her tongue, brushing her hands together as she did. "Sounds as if you should at least do some research about Montana, get an idea if it's a place you could stand. It's cold there, right? And it doesn't have much of a growing season. You might be able to raise Alaska daisies." She smiled as if she'd made a joke. "I'd miss you terribly. So would your Mamm. But then again, she left her family and came here."

That was true. But I got the idea she'd never been very fond of Ohio. On the other hand, I loved Lancaster County.

"And Dat, as much as he cared for Anna, never would have left the farm to move to Ohio. Of course I was still at home, but the land had been in his family for years. It was part of him."

Leon's land hadn't been in his family for years. His Dat had grown up somewhere near Paradise. Determined to change the subject, I said, "I've been thinking about your Mamm."

She leaned forward. "My Mamm?"

I nodded. "And how hard it must have been when she was so ill. I didn't really understand before, but this uncertainty about . . . Anyway, all that's gone on has made me think about it. And how young you were when she passed."

"Denki," Edna said. "That's kind of you. Jah, it was hard. But by the time she passed it was such a relief to have her out of pain, we were ready to have her suffering over. She'd gone through enough."

"Mamm told me she came and met all of you, while your mother was ill."

Edna took another sip of tea. "Jah. Wasn't that something? How they all got to know each other through the circle letter? Mamm wasn't even that interested, but Dat thought it might give her a hobby, to sit on the porch and watch for birds."

Edna was silent for a moment and then said, "I know my mother and Dat loved each other, but she never helped with the farm, not the way Anna always has. And they didn't have that spark Dat had with your Mamm."

I didn't know what to say, wondering if that made Edna feel bad. But then she said with a gracious tone, "It was such a blessing that Dat remarried. Anna was so good to me, to all of us, from the very start. Still is. And then for you and Beatrice to come along . . ." She sighed. "I'd prayed for years for a little sister. Then I got two." She smiled. "Of course you didn't act like a little sister for long. By the time you were two you wanted to run the house."

I grimaced. "Was I really that bad?"

"Oh, you weren't bad. It wasn't like you were disobedient—it was the opposite of that. You wanted to *do* everything. Chores. Dishes. Cooking. You'd follow your Mamm and me around, demanding that we let you work."

I'd forgotten how much I enjoyed talking with Edna. It warmed my heart. I realized with Dat gone, she was the one other person besides Mamm—and Ivan, but he didn't really count—who would always carry memories of me as a child.

Edna sighed. "Think long and hard about going to Montana. Your Mamm needs you."

It was my turn to lean forward. "I know," I said. "What I can't figure out, though, is why she doesn't want me to go with her when she gets her scan."

"She won't get any results that day."

"I know, but she—"

"She'll be in a tube for an hour. I think she's worried about that, but even more so about how you will feel, and she doesn't want to put any more stress on herself."

"I'd be fine."

"I know you would." Edna sighed. "She wants to be strong for you and for Beatrice. She doesn't have to be for Ivan and me."

I tilted my head, aware that maybe Edna and Mamm had a relationship deeper than I'd thought. It was no surprise. They'd known each other for nearly twenty-five years. Mamm had been there for Edna when she married, when she wasn't able to have children, when her husband died. Now Edna had a chance to "be there" for Mamm.

"Anna has always been so good to me," Edna said again. "It's a privilege for me to do something for her. And I think it's a relief for her to think of you and Beatrice off having fun at a place she enjoyed so much with Dat."

I understood. I was also sure that Mamm was much more worried about what the scan might show than she'd been letting on.

I thanked Edna for the cookies, grabbed a couple for Mervin along with a glass of ice water, and headed out to the greenhouse.

He was grateful to see me and for the snack.

"I'm going to go check on the lilies," I said. "I'll be back to help in here in a bit."

As I walked toward the field, I pulled out my cell to call Cate. I was pretty sure her husband, Pete, had traveled as far west as Montana. On second thought, I decided I didn't want to talk with him. He wasn't the gossipy type and neither was Cate, but still I didn't want to put them on alert.

Then I thought of a friend in Maryland who had a cousin

who'd been out west. I called her, and she went on and on about her cousin's impressions about Montana. "There are hardly any people—but lots of cows. Everything is a long ways away. Just going shopping is a really big deal. And winter lasts forever."

"What about growing things? Like flowers."

"Oh, she didn't say much about that. Montana definitely wasn't her thing—she likes Florida much better—but that's not to say you wouldn't like it."

I thanked her and hung up. I'd certainly never been to Florida, but from what my friend had said about Montana, I was pretty sure I'd like the southern state better too.

That evening, Mamm and Beatrice sat together on the settee on the front porch, most likely still anticipating the arrival of a mockingbird, while Edna and I cleaned the kitchen. She left just before Bob Miller arrived holding the manila folder in his hand, without Nan.

When I asked about her, he answered, "Betsy's over, along with Robbie and the baby." That was his youngest daughter, his grandson and namesake, and his granddaughter, Tamara. The little boy was not quite two now and the baby was a year. "Betsy says she came over to help with the wedding plans but when I left, Nan was taking care of the kids."

"I'd forgotten about your wedding," Mamm said.

I grimaced at another short-term memory lapse.

"I was going to ask if you and Nan could chaperone a Youngie camping trip," Mamm said. "But I don't suppose that would work."

"When?" Bob leaned against the porch railing.

"Next week. Monday through Thursday."

My face grew warm at Mamm asking such a thing of the

busiest man I knew—especially when he was just a couple of weeks away from getting married.

"I wish we could," Bob said, "but I have several appointments. What would you think of Pete and Cate going along?"

Mamm brightened. "Do you think they could?"

"Jah," Bob said, breaking into a smile. "They both work for me—there shouldn't be a problem."

Although I would have enjoyed having Bob and Nan along, Cate and Pete were preferable. Not because they wouldn't do a good job chaperoning us—they would. Not that we'd need it. But maybe Cate would have some advice for me about Leon.

Bob raised the folder in his hand. "I'll do more in the next week, but I worked up a plan that I'd like to explain."

"Of course," Mamm said. "Beatrice, you may join us if you'd like."

She shook her head and pulled her journal from where she'd tucked it along the side of the settee. "I'll stay here."

Once we were at the kitchen table, Bob assured Mamm that our district's mutual aid fund would cover the expenses for her doctor's appointments and the upcoming test. "We'll talk more once we know what the complete diagnosis is," Bob said.

The Amish rarely chose drastic measures to save a life. An elderly person with cancer or some other terminal disease didn't usually go through chemotherapy or radiation to extend life a few years. But Mamm wasn't elderly.

Bob opened the folder. "As far as your business, we need to figure out how much you need to produce per square foot of land to break even and then double that."

"That's what I was thinking," Mamm said. I knew she meant the Mosiers' farm.

"You may have to consider plowing up your lower pasture since you don't have much livestock," Bob said.

But that would mean giving up the farmers' market. Maybe another field of plants would bring in more money, but I couldn't imagine life without the market.

"Also," Bob said, "consider selling directly to florists. I thought we could brainstorm what other products or services you could offer. Anna, do you have any thoughts on that?"

Mamm shook her head, a frown settling on her face.

"Molly?"

I hadn't told Mamm what I'd been up to. "I have some ideas," I said. "One is selling our products to local bed-and-breakfasts."

"That sounds like a possibility," he said. "It wouldn't bring in a lot though."

"And I may have a job as a garden consultant," I said.

"I like your thinking," Bob said, "but again that's not going to bring in what's needed."

I quickly added, "How about hosting groups of Englisch people for dinners and renting out rooms for overnight guests? I have a lead on that."

Mamm crossed her arms. "Why would anyone want to eat here? Or stay here?"

"The bed-and-breakfast owner said they would," I answered.

"Both of those ideas would bring in more income," Bob said. "And a good profit."

"Would the bishop allow it?" Mamm leaned forward.

"You could ask," Bob said, tapping the eraser of his pencil on the table.

I nodded. "That was my plan."

Mamm exhaled.

I couldn't imagine how much she missed Dat. I know in the past they'd talk things through and then Dat would usually make a decision. But he always valued her opinion. Now it was up to her to decide.

Bob closed the folder and said to my mother, "I don't want you to make any decisions until after we know how your health is."

Mamm nodded, a faraway look in her eyes.

Bob said he needed to get going, to help Nan with the grand-children.

Mamm thanked him and then said, "Make sure and ask Pete and Cate. The Youngie need to make their plans."

"Will do," Bob said. "I'll tell Cate to give Molly a call."

That night, after the house was quiet, I took my lamp into one of our extra bedrooms. The double bed looked small, barely big enough for one person, let alone two. A scratch ran down the side of the bureau. And the curtains had yellowed. I stepped closer to the bed. But the quilt, a shadow pattern made a couple of years ago by Mamm, brightened the room, and the kerosene lamp on the table beside the bed was a bona fide antique that once belonged to my Dat's grandparents.

I tried to imagine an Englischer staying in the room. I couldn't—not quite. I could imagine Englischers staying in Hannah's house though. It was so much nicer than ours. And I hadn't thought before what an attraction horses would be— not surprising since they weren't to me—until talking with Kristine.

A flicker of jealousy of Hannah and all she had tempted me, but I shook my head at it. I wouldn't give in to that. I hadn't before—not during our entire friendship. I wasn't going to start now.

I'd figure out what needed to be done, what worked for my family, and do it. That was the only option I had.

After breakfast the next morning, as I walked toward the greenhouse with Love at my side, a buggy came tearing up our lane. I stopped, shading my eyes against the rising sun, unable to see who the driver was.

"Hallo," I called out.

"Guder Mariye!" It was Cate, shading her eyes from the rising sun. I should have guessed. She was known for her wild driving. And it was just like her to come over to see me instead of calling. She pulled her horse to stop by our hitching post.

"Do you have a minute?" She hopped down from the buggy, smoothing out her dress as she did.

"Jah."

"I'll walk with you, wherever you're going." Her blue eyes matched the bright morning sky.

I gestured toward the greenhouse, and she matched my stride along the side of the barn, the sun nearly blinding us as it bounced off the white paint. "Dat told me about your camping plans. Pete and I would love to go," she said.

"Denki." I hesitated to say any more.

"You don't sound very excited," she said.

"No, I am," I said. "Especially that you two are coming along."

"What's the matter, then?"

A robin hopped along the grass in front of us and then swooped upward, a worm in her mouth. We reached the greenhouse and I pushed the door open, motioning for Cate to go in first. It would be easier to talk inside, just in case Mamm came looking for me.

"Mamm's forcing us to go," I said, "because she wants Beatrice and me to be gone when she has her scan."

"Oh," Cate said, her voice grave. "But it will be good for the two of you to get away—especially Beatrice. She must be beside herself with worry. You've had double trouble with your Dat passing and now the concerns for your Mamm."

"Jah."

"Then let's aim to make this an adventure. For Beatrice. And for you." She smiled kindly.

I could see her reasoning. "And for Hannah too." I took my phone out of my pocket as I spoke, checking to see if Hannah had left me a message, responding to my call the day before. She hadn't. I'd expected to hear back from her about the camping trip by now.

"What's up with Hannah?" Cate asked.

"You know how she's been interested in Mervin all this time?"

"Jah. It seems like it's been forever."

I nodded. "Almost two years."

"Are they planning a wedding yet?"

"No," I said, dropping my voice to a whisper. "He's decided he's interested in me."

"You?" Cate stepped back in surprise and then said quickly, "I can see how he would be, honestly. It's just that he and Hannah seemed like a sure match."

"We all thought so. But then Mervin changed his mind, focusing on me instead once he started working here. And my Mamm thought it was a good idea, so we could combine the farms and save ours."

"Oh dear," Cate said, her face full of concern. "Any chance you have feelings for Mervin?"

I shook my head adamantly. "Not at all. In fact . . ." I hesitated again.

She stepped toward me, resting her hand on my arm. "I promise anything you tell me will be confidential."

"Have you met Leon? He's helping out at the Lapps' stables, training horses."

"No, but I've heard about him. From Nell. She stopped by with Addie yesterday."

"And she didn't say anything about me?"

Her eyes twinkled. "Now that you mention it . . ."

"Cate." I frowned. "Please be honest with me."

"She did say she saw the two of you under the willow tree."

I crossed my arms. So the rumor mill had begun.

"She also said he's awfully handsome. Tall. Dark. Muscular."

I couldn't help but smile.

"And Addie said he's a hard worker and a strong leader, that Owen's very pleased with him."

"What if we invite him along too?" Cate stepped to the other side of the bench, facing me.

"Owen already talked with him about coming along and bringing the horses."

"What's the problem, then?" Cate asked.

"Mamm doesn't know Leon's coming—in fact, she said we should keep the group to only our childhood friends."

"Oh goodness," Cate said.

"Her reason for wanting us to go camping is for Mervin and me to spend time together. . . ."

"With Hannah along?" Cate grimaced.

"Jah. But Mamm doesn't see how awkward that would be. I'd prefer Mervin not come along at all, and I asked Hannah not to talk with him about it—which I feel horrible about because that means Martin can't come either." I just couldn't bear the thought of Mervin following me around and Hannah lashing out at me again.

"Oh, Molly," Cate said. "I'm so thankful to be married. What a mess."

Neither of us said anything for a moment, and then Cate put her hands together, as if she were praying. "Things will work out," she said. "You'll see. I'll talk to Pete and see if he has any ideas."

"Denki," I said. "And I'll organize the food and all of that."

"Are you sure?"

"Of course." I'd also figure out a schedule for cooking and cleanup. "Let me know if you have any ideas of who else should come," I said to Cate. "Just a couple more people."

A voice behind me bellowed, "I have an idea."

I spun around to find Mervin standing by the barn, Love at his side, twenty feet from us, his sunglasses on his face so I couldn't see his eyes. He marched toward us but the dog stayed put. "Hannah came over last night. She told me all about the camping trip. She felt bad about you excluding me—and invited me. Martin too."

I stepped backward, bumping into Cate. I hadn't exactly said I wanted to exclude Mervin on the message I'd left. But she'd guessed it. Why hadn't she called me back so I could explain?

Cate glanced at me and I shrugged.

"It was all a misunderstanding," Cate said to Mervin. "We want you to come along. Martin too. I think we'll ask Ben also."

I groaned. "He and Beatrice don't get along." He was Betsy's youngest brother-in-law. He'd gone to our school, and he and Beatrice had bickered all through their years together.

Cate clucked her tongue. "Everyone will just have to work at getting along."

"I'm sure we will," Mervin said. "If Molly doesn't try to tear us all apart." He took off toward the greenhouse.

"Oh dear," Cate said, sounding as if she might laugh.

I groaned again.

She let go of my arm. "This will actually work to your advantage," she said.

"How's that?"

"You just need to figure out a way to get Mervin to fall back in love with Hannah. Then your Mamm won't keep trying to marry

138

you off to him. Jah," she said, the tips of her fingers pressed together, "you should thank Hannah for inviting Mervin. By the time we come back from our trip, that part of your worries will be over."

Her optimism was catching.

"We'll have fun. You'll see." She smiled broadly. "Do you have a place in mind?"

"Jah, a lake in the Poconos. We used to camp there when I was little." My throat tightened at the memory.

After we said good-bye, Cate hopped back in her buggy and took off, racing down the driveway.

I headed to the flower field. I wanted Mervin to stay my friend. I just wasn't sure how to make that happen—except to get him to fall back in love with Hannah.

Cate was right. That's what needed to happen.

Mamm kept Mervin potting herbs all morning, so I didn't see him until after our noon meal, when he climbed the fence from his farm to ours.

"Can you finish potting the geraniums?" I called out to him.

"Jah," he said, giving me a pathetic look, stopping at the edge of the flowers. "Your Mamm spoke with me about the landscaping business, about reviving it. She said Bob had some ideas." Mervin took his sunglasses off and twirled them around. "I think it's a great idea. And I want to be involved. I'd be happy to ask my Dat for a field on our property to plant more shrubs and trees."

"Oh dear," I said. "That seems like an unwarranted commitment."

"Not if . . ."

I started walking away from him.

Mervin followed me. "I know you don't see it right now, but, Molly . . ."

I walked faster.

His volume increased. "Leon's just a temporary problem. He'll return to Montana soon. You'll see what a good match you and I make—for our families and for us."

I began to speed walk. Mervin jogged after me and reached for my arm.

I pulled away and began to run.

"Molly!" he called out.

"We have a lot of work to do," I yelled.

"Come help me in the greenhouse."

I shook my head. "I'm going to go look at our camping supplies and see what we need." I ran the rest of the way to the house.

Dat had stored the gear down in the basement, tucked away past the wringer washing machine that was at least as old as Ivan. I'd been fighting with the beast my entire life. I washed my hands in the utility sink where the machine drained and then opened the storage room door.

I remembered when Dat had put all the equipment away for good. It had been a sad day for him. Sure, we still went on hikes where he and Mamm identified wild flowers and birds, but I knew he missed camping. We all did.

I opened the first box. On top was Dat's bird book. Then his native plants book. Like most people in our community, he was a nature lover. *"God's creation is the greatest cathedral there is,"* he'd often said.

I dug deeper into the box. There was a first-aid kit and out-dated bug repellent, and some old dish towels that we could have been using as rags.

I put the box to the side and grabbed two sleeping bags from the top of the stack. I'd need to air them out. Next was our tent. It would probably be a good idea to air it out too. As I pulled it from the pile, my cell vibrated in my pocket.

I eased the tent bag to the floor and checked my phone. Hannah's number. I headed outside, answering the call halfway up the stairs.

"Hallo," I said, keeping my voice sweet, just in case it was Leon calling, even though I was sure it wasn't.

"Molly." It was Hannah. "Before you talk to Mervin today, I wanted you to know—"

"I already talked to Mervin."

"Oh. He told you he's coming camping with us?"

"Jah."

"I couldn't bear to have him left out."

I tried to keep my voice even. "Even after the way he's treated you? You shouldn't go running after him like that."

"Jah, I know," she said. "But I still wanted to include him."

"I was just surprised you told him what I'd said." I noted the hint of a whine in my voice.

"Why wouldn't I?"

"Because it's not in your best interest."

"I was looking out for Mervin's best interest."

I threw my hand in the air, even though she couldn't see me. "You think he'll like you more if you tell on me?"

"But Mervin would have been upset."

Obviously she cared more about how Mervin felt than she cared about how I did. I guess I couldn't blame her for that. I sighed. "Cate is going to ask Ben along too."

"Cate's going?" Her voice held a hint of relief now.

"And Pete," I answered.

"That will be good."

"Just don't blame me if Mervin gets weird, like at the singing . . ."

Now she sounded hurt. "I won't."

I wasn't about to tell her what Cate had said about our getting Mervin to fall back in love with Hannah.

"No hard feelings?" she asked.

I sighed. "We've been friends too long to ruin it over Mervin Mosier going on a camping trip or not."

"Denki, Molly," Hannah said. "We'll have fun. You'll see. And you'll have three days with Leon." She giggled.

With Mervin trailing us.

"I need to go," I said. "I have a lot of work to do."

After ending the call, I slipped my phone back into my apron pocket and headed back toward the basement staircase, but Mamm called out to me from the slate pathway alongside the backyard. She wore a sweater and leather gloves.

I veered toward her.

"Mervin tells me he's going camping after all," she said.

"That's right." The less I said the better.

"*Gut*," Mamm said. "I told you everything would work out. Now come in the house and have a cup of tea."

I shook my head. "I have a million things to do." I clomped back down the basement stairs.

That evening I sat on the porch as the *clippity-clop* of a horse's hooves echoed along the road. Mamm had already gone to bed, and Beatrice was upstairs. I didn't think it best for Leon to come up to the house though, so I hurried toward the driveway, passing Love, who'd been asleep by the side of the house. She raised her head. "Stay," I said.

She kept her head up but obeyed.

I hadn't seen Leon in well over twenty-four hours.

Mamm's voice called to me out her open window, "Molly!"

I froze. "I'm just going for a walk."

She stood at the open window, wearing a white nightgown, her gray hair hanging down. "Don't be long," she finally said.

I felt as if the wind had just been knocked out of me as I continued on down the driveway toward Leon, who walked up it, leading Lightning. I put out my hand, gesturing for him to stop. He did.

When I reached him, he asked, "What's going on?"

"Mamm's awake. She's not happy with me."

"Did you tell her I'm going camping with your group?"

I winced. "Not yet. But I will . . ."

A sadness passed over his eyes. "I'm sorry," he said, taking my hand.

"It's not your fault," I answered.

"Molly!"

Leon jumped. Lightning snorted. I covered my face with my hand.

"I can see her in the window," Leon whispered.

I glanced over my shoulder. I wasn't sure she could see us, but she'd lit her lamp and now she appeared as a bright apparition.

"You'd better go," Leon said, releasing me.

"Jah."

"I won't come by in the next few days—I don't want to keep upsetting your Mamm."

Part of me wanted him to defy Mamm and stay. But mostly I appreciated his consideration. "All right."

"We'll have time when we're camping," he said. "Hopefully we can sort all of this out then."

I nodded. He swung back up on Lightning, turning her sharply, and headed back down to the highway. As he disappeared I tilted my head toward the sky. The first star shone brightly. Then another and another. I turned then, back toward the house.

Mamm's light was out and her window closed.

When I reached my bedroom, I saw Beatrice had moved back to her own. I tiptoed down the hall. Her light was out too. I opened the door. By the moonlight through her window, I could see she was asleep, clutching her writing book.

Overcome with loneliness, I headed back to my room, missing Leon.

That night I dreamt about Dat again. We were camping in the Poconos, hiking along the trail. Beatrice and I were little, and she rode on his shoulders while I ran on ahead.

Friday I worked long and hard, avoiding Mervin, doing my best not to think about Leon, and doing all I could to please

Mamm. It paid off. The day passed by peaceably, and that evening Mamm, Beatrice, and I all sat out on the porch, enjoying the cool breeze and watching the starlings feeding on bugs until dusk began to fall and they swooped above our heads toward the barn. There were things I should have been doing to get ready for the market, but I decided sitting with Mamm would ease her worries. I knew I needed to tell her about Leon going camping, but I also knew I didn't want to upset her. I decided to wait until Sunday after church. That would be soon enough.

Early Saturday morning I walked along the herb garden with Love trailing behind, finalizing my plan for the market. The vendors would start arriving soon to set up. I needed something catchy to draw attention to our flowers and herbs. Something tourists and locals would both like. Something to draw them in and make the sale.

I turned back toward the house, but a swallow darting out of the open barn door caught my attention. It didn't go far, landing on the bench of the wagon parked next to the barn. That was it! I'd fill the old wagon with flowers and herbs and haul the whole thing down to the pasture, to the market. The blooms and greens against the weathered boards would be sure to draw a crowd.

First I needed to cut the snapdragons, sweet peas, and the first of the lavender. I grabbed two cutting knives and my leather gloves from the workbench and a stack of buckets from the corner of the shed and headed to the flower field.

I'd only been working a few minutes when Mervin arrived. I pulled the second knife from my pocket and handed it to him without saying a word.

He began working parallel to me, in the next row over. "Hannah said Leon's pleased to be coming on the camping trip too."

I gave him a questioning look, unsure what his point was.

"Last night. Down at the river."

I turned my head toward him. "You went to the party?"

He nodded.

"Oh." So they'd all gone to a party without me. "Who else was there?" I regretted asking the question as soon as the words found their way out of my mouth.

"Martin went."

"Did anyone go with Hannah?" I rubbed my chin with the back of my hand.

"Like?" Mervin crossed his arms.

"Never mind." I bent back down to cut more stems. I doubted Leon had gone. He didn't seem to have much fun at the party last weekend.

"You can't fool me," Mervin said. "Or your Mamm."

I kept on cutting.

Mervin's voice grew louder. "I think she should know."

I continued cutting. "She will."

"Molly." Mervin's voice was sharp.

I stood straight again, waving the handful of sweet peas toward the lavender. "Could we talk about this later? We have a market to open in an hour. And I want to load the wagon with herbs and flowers."

"We won't talk about it," he mumbled.

He was right. I had no intention of talking with him later. I pointed toward the barn. "Help me load the wagon—then you can come back and cut more of these."

I grabbed the buckets and started walking, but Mervin caught up with me and took them from me. I marched on to the pasture to get Daisy and then hitched her to the wagon. As I led her to the loading dock, Mervin hauled the boxes of herbs and pots of geraniums out of the greenhouse. In no time we loaded the wagon with the table, buckets of flowers, the tarp, and poles.

"Go finish the flowers." I jumped up to the bench of the wagon.

"Don't you need help setting up the canopy?" I couldn't tell what his expression was under his sunglasses, but I guessed it was dejected.

"I'll manage." I had in all that time before we hired him—I certainly could now.

"Are you going to tell your Mamm or should I?" Mervin crossed his arms.

I ignored him as I urged Daisy forward. She didn't move. I tried again. This time she took a step and then another, and the wagon finally began to move. I hoped Cate was right that the camping trip would all work out. It was hard to imagine how.

Once I reached the pasture, I set up the canopy and table, greeting Joseph Koller across the way. When Nell arrived, she headed straight for his booth.

"Nell," I called out, motioning to the half of my table she usually used. "Over here."

"Hannah's going to share your table today," she answered.

As Joseph beamed at Nell, it became clear she was going to share his booth.

"Oh," I said. I couldn't help but smile, although I wished she'd told me sooner.

I positioned the wagon exactly where I wanted it and then unhitched Daisy, and ran her back to the upper pasture. By the time I returned to the market, with the four dozen eggs I'd set aside to sell, the first of the tourists had begun to arrive, but it was another hour before Hannah showed up, long after several of the boxes of herbs and the pots of geraniums had sold from the wagon, along with all the eggs.

"Late night?" I asked as Hannah slid her heavy box onto the table.

She nodded, yawned, and then started taking pint jars of jam from her box. "My Dat and Leon and I were talking at breakfast. We'll need to go to a place where there's a horse camp."

"There's one where we're going. Across the lake from the regular campsites."

She smiled. "I think we're going to have a lot of fun. Horses and all."

I took my small notebook from my apron pocket. "I've come up with meal schedules, that sort of thing."

Hannah smiled. "That's what I love about you. You enjoy the planning."

"Jah . . ." I could never understand why Hannah didn't.

"If it were left up to me, we'd have some sort of weird three-day potluck," Hannah said.

I wrinkled my nose. "That would be awful. Why would—"

An Englisch woman gushed, "Oh, look at the sweet peas. They remind me of my grandma's garden." The woman had to be a grandmother herself, so that would have been ages ago. "I'll take two bunches," she said.

Next she bought a couple jars of Hannah's jam. More customers gathered around our table and the conversation ended.

About an hour later, Hannah elbowed me. "Here he comes." Her face brightened.

Mervin walked toward us with a bucket of lavender in each hand.

"Hello," Hannah called out to him, followed by a broad smile that showed her dimples.

"Oh, hi," Mervin said to her, brushing by.

"We were talking about the camping trip earlier," Hannah said.

"Oh?" Mervin set the buckets down.

"About how much fun we're going to have." Hannah practically batted her lashes.

"Jah," Mervin said, his eyes falling on me. "I'm really looking forward to it." He pushed his glasses up on the bridge of his nose and then turned back to the hill. "I'll go cut more herbs." He headed to the trail.

We watched him for a long silent minute, until I said, "Hannah, can you watch my booth? I need to check on Mamm and Beatrice."

Before she could answer I hurried after Mervin. "Wait," I called out to him as I struggled up the hill. "I need to talk to you."

He stopped.

When I caught up, I took a moment to catch my breath and then said, "I'm glad Hannah told you about the trip—and that you're coming along."

He didn't respond.

"The more the merrier," I said, trying to lighten the mood.

We walked along with Mervin just ahead of me on the trail. I took a couple of long steps, ending up at his side. "You didn't say anything to my Mamm yet, did you, about Leon coming?"

He stopped and turned. I bumped into him, my head in his chest. I stepped back quickly, losing my balance just a little.

He caught my arm. "Why do you ask?"

"I don't want to stress her out any more than she already is."

"So you want to deceive her."

"I didn't say that—I want to tell her when the time is right."

"Why did you ask Leon, then?"

"I didn't," I said. "Hannah's Dat suggested it. She didn't tell you that?"

He shook his head.

"So you didn't tell my Mamm anything?"

"Actually . . . I did."

I groaned. "Did you tell her I invited him?"

"I might have implied that," he said.

I groaned again.

Mervin continued, "She called Ivan while I was still in the greenhouse."

I didn't bother to groan a third time. I guess it wasn't surprising that when Dat wasn't there to rely on she'd rely on his son.

"He decided to come over. 'To address the situation.'"

"Oh no."

"Oh jah," Mervin responded. "From hearing your Mamm's side of the conversation, I think Ivan is actually pleased. If you're interested in Leon, then you're not interested in me. Right?"

I kept my face as placid as I could.

"And then Ivan can buy the farm—at a good price, of course."

Again, I didn't respond. Mervin began marching across the lawn, veering to the right toward the herb garden. I fell back, letting him gain some distance. I'd check on Beatrice and then go back down to the market.

As I reached the open back door, I was surprised to hear Mamm talking loudly. It wasn't her way. "I just don't understand, not after I made it clear I didn't want her to court him—"

I opened the screen door in a hurry, stepping inside.

Ivan sat at the head of the table. "There she is," he said. "Ask her yourself."

I scanned the room. Beatrice wasn't in sight—thankfully.

Mamm took a deep breath and then said, "Mervin told me—"

I rarely interrupted my Mamm intentionally, but this time I couldn't help myself. "Hannah's Dat suggested Leon come along. To train the horses on the trail. I didn't invite him."

Ivan crossed his arms, resting them atop his belly. "You expect us to believe that?"

"I do." My eyes met his, and then, to change the subject, I asked if he was staying for the noon meal.

"Jah," he answered.

"And supper?"

He shook his head, to my relief.

"Ivan, wait for me here," Mamm said, standing slowly. She stepped toward me, taking my elbow. "I want to talk with you." She ushered me out the door and around the side of the house. "I believe you," she said. "But I also believe you're interested in Leon."

I didn't answer. I used to think a person could help whom they fell in love with, but I didn't anymore.

"If I can't figure out a way to keep the farm, I *will* sell it to Ivan," she said. "But that's not what I want to do."

"I know," I whispered. I'd never felt shamed by either one of my parents—until now. I knew I was going against my mother's wishes. Her disappointment weighed on me.

"So go ahead and go on the camping trip. And remember, I trust you."

I nodded. "I've never done anything to give you a reason not to trust me," I said. "And I don't plan to."

"Then you have my blessing as far as the camping trip," Mamm said. "But we still have some sorting out to do."

I nodded and then asked, "Where's Beatrice?"

"I think she's in the basement," she said.

"I thought she'd be getting dinner ready."

"I said I would today." Mamm turned toward the back door. "I guess I'd better get started."

My steps down the outside basement stairs fell heavy. I pushed open the door and squinted in the dim light.

"Beatrice?"

"In the storeroom."

She was holding one of the blue metal plates in her hand as I entered.

"I already sorted through all of that," I told her. "And aired out the sleeping bags and tent."

"Oh." She put the plate back in the plastic box.

"Jah, we just need to haul everything out. But not until Monday morning."

"Oh," she said again.

"Did you know Ivan is here?"

"That's why I came down here. I don't know why Mamm called him."

I wrinkled my nose. She must have heard something.

She didn't say what though. Instead she said, "I heard Ben's going on the camping trip too."

"Jah," I said, realizing I hadn't told her. I knew Cate had planned to ask him—I just didn't know if he'd accepted. "Is that going to be all right?"

She took a deep breath. "None of this feels all right. We don't know what's wrong with Mamm. You're sneaking around. Mervin's miserable. And Mamm's upset all the time." She looked straight at me. "I miss the way things used to be."

Sunday services were at the edge of our district at the Kemp farm. Leon came with Hannah's family and sat beside Owen. Mamm didn't leave my side the entire morning, except when Mervin approached me. He didn't talk about anything important. Just the hot weather.

Of course I watched Leon. I couldn't take my eyes off him. At one point, as he held Tinker, all of Hannah's little sisters gathered around him. As much as I appreciated Mervin, when he wasn't being obtuse, I couldn't understand why Hannah liked him over Leon. Not that I wasn't thankful for Hannah's choice, because there was a lot Leon could find attractive in her as a horsewoman, with a great family business. When Mamm, Beatrice, and I were leaving, Leon managed to get within a few feet of me. He tipped his hat and said, "Have a wonderful day, Miss Molly."

I slipped him a smile as Mamm linked her arm in mine and pulled me along.

On the way home, she said, "I'm afraid I'll regret letting you go on this camping trip. I don't know what Owen was thinking, wanting to send Leon along."

That was my saving grace. That it was Owen's idea. She felt if she said I couldn't go now, she'd be insulting him.

"It will all work out," I said, but she didn't respond.

Instead of going to the singing that evening, I cooked for the camping trip—stew, creamed chicken, and bean and bacon soup, while four loaves of bread, a big pan of corn bread, and berry cobbler baked in our double oven. I had bologna we'd made last fall for sandwiches and frozen packages of bratwurst for lunches, plus quarts of kraut, green beans, beets, and peaches, and a burlap bag of potatoes to bake in the coals of the campfire.

As I worked, my thoughts continually landed on Leon. I doubted he went to the singing either, which was also at the Kemp place. I wished he'd sneak over and ask me to go for a walk, but if Mamm found out it would only add to her stress. I'd be with Leon soon—although time seemed to be crawling along.

I packed our nonperishable food in cardboard boxes and then washed out the ice chest, readying it for the next day. After all the meals were prepared and while the bread and cobbler cooled, I went upstairs to pack a few last things in my bag. Mamm's light was off, but Beatrice's wasn't. I knocked on her door.

"Come in," she said.

I found her sitting on her bed, her journal in her hands, no bag or clothes in sight.

"Did you pack?"

Startled, she looked around her room.

"That's what you came up to do, remember?" That had been hours ago.

"And I will," she said, closing her journal and standing.

"You should do it now."

She gave me a scathing look. She was right—she was nineteen. It wasn't my business when she packed. I headed to my room to finish the chore and meal charts and the rest of my packing.

Monday morning, Mervin and I watered the flower fields and the herbs, while Beatrice was supposed to be fixing breakfast and filling the ice chest for the trip. When I hurried into the kitchen, along with Mervin, she was sitting at the table, a cup of tea in her hands, staring out the window.

"Bea?" I choked on the single syllable. "What are you doing?"

"Oh, just taking a break."

Nothing was on the stove, not one pan.

"What about breakfast?"

"I'll get to it," she said.

"Everyone's going to be here in an hour. We need to hurry."

Mervin said he'd see us later, adding, "I think breakfast is probably on the table at my house."

I nodded and asked Beatrice where Mamm was as Mervin let himself out the back door.

"She went outside."

"Let's get moving," I said, instructing Beatrice to fill the ice chests. "Put the milk in first, to keep it the coldest, along with the stew, sauce, and soup. Then put in the bologna." I put three slices of bread under the broiler in the oven. "Then go find Mamm. We'll eat right away."

She moved as slow as molasses. I pulled eggs from the fridge and a frying pan from the cupboard. "Go find Mamm now," I finally told Beatrice. "We can finish the ice chests after breakfast."

I started the eggs, then set the table and buttered the toast, turned the eggs, and had everything on the three plates as Mamm and Beatrice came through the back door.

"Wash up," I said. "Breakfast is ready."

We didn't talk much through the quick meal. Finally, after she took her last bite, Mamm said, "I want you two to have a wonderful time. No fretting, you hear?"

I nodded.

Beatrice didn't respond.

"We will have a good time. And don't you worry about us either," I said. "We will be thinking about you and praying."

"Denki," Mamm said. "God is in control—I certainly don't expect to live forever."

"We don't expect that either," I said quickly, "but a few more years would be a blessing to us." I'd meant what I said to sound humorous but it fell flat.

"You'd better get busy," Mamm said, "if you're going to be ready on time."

"Jah." I gave Beatrice a look. She turned away from me.

"Beatrice," Mamm said, "you need to be mindful of Molly."

My sister pushed back her chair and took her plate to the sink. I cleared the table in two swipes, and then packed the food, swept the floor, and made sandwiches for our lunch, including one for Mamm, in the time it took Bea to wash the dishes.

Mamm sat at the table, finishing her tea, as we worked. When I lifted the first ice chest and headed to the back door, she said, "Molly, you're more efficient than any machine."

I genuinely smiled, not in a prideful way but happy to know I was still appreciated by Mamm. I lugged the weight of all the food out to the lawn, managed to get the ice chest to the ground without landing it on my foot, and ran back for the second one. After stacking it atop the first ice chest, I headed to the basement by way of the backyard stairs, to haul the camping equipment up to the yard too, including our old folding lawn chairs. Love followed me back and forth, clearly hoping she was going with us.

By the time I finished, including grabbing the canopy I used on market days from the greenhouse, I was fifteen minutes ahead of schedule. I went back in the house, to the sewing room, and retrieved the box of Dat's shirts, along with a diamond pattern, a pencil, and the scissors. I'd have plenty of time to get started on the quilt for Bea while we were camping.

I knew Mamm wouldn't want any displays of emotion in front of the others when we said good-bye, and Beatrice must have sensed it too. Love, however, expected a hug, which I gave her. But then she tried to follow Beatrice and me into the van. Mamm called her back and held her collar. The dog whined as we waved from our seats, but then Pete slammed the door shut and both Mamm and Love stood looking forlorn as the driver pulled around the driveway. Edna and Ivan would arrive any time to spend the next few days.

Mervin and Martin sat in the very back, Pete sat in the front passenger seat, and Cate sat on the first bench, leaving the middle one for us. "Where's Ben?" I asked.

"We're going to pick him up," Mervin said. "At his folks' place."

"Oh." That hadn't been part of the plan.

"Along with Robbie," Cate added.

I couldn't help the surprise in my voice. "What?"

Mervin began to laugh.

"Jah," Cate said. "I'm afraid it's true. Betsy hasn't been feeling well. Nan is going to watch the baby, but with everything she still needs to do for the wedding, I said we'd take Robbie for the week."

"What about Betsy's mother-in-law?"

"She's off taking care of her aunt."

"Oh dear," I said, forming a long mental list of other people I thought could take care of Robbie, including Addie or her Mamm, but I knew it wasn't my business.

Pete directed the driver to the crossroads where we were to wait for Hannah and Leon. And we did wait . . . and wait. I called Owen's business phone and left a message.

Fifteen minutes later Owen returned the call, saying Hannah and Leon would be on their way soon. "They've had some problems getting the horses loaded," he explained.

I stifled a groan. Children and horses. What else could go wrong?

"Let's go pick up Robbie and Ben and then come back to meet them," Cate suggested. Betsy and Levi lived with his parents, along with Ben.

By the time we reached the Rupp place, we were all eager to get out. "Come inside," Cate said to Beatrice and me, while the boys greeted Ben. He'd grown taller since I'd seen him last and much more handsome. His hair, always a golden brown, had lightened in the sun and had more of a curl to it than I remembered. He carried a backpack in one hand and a Frisbee in the other that he lobbed off toward the field. Martin went tearing after it, while Ben turned his head toward Beatrice. She, however, hurried away from him, following Cate to the kitchen door.

As Cate pushed it open, she called out, "We're here."

No one answered.

Beatrice and I followed Cate into an enclosed porch.

"Betsy," Cate said.

We walked into a small kitchen with just one counter. Dishes filled the sink, and a greasy frying pan sat on the back burner.

Cate repeated her sister's name, but this time with more urgency. "Betsy!"

"Back here," came her reply.

Robbie came running through the dining room, wearing only a cloth diaper. "Aenti!" he squealed. His chubby arms twirled around his head of curly dark hair, and his brown eyes shone with mischief.

"Come back here!" Betsy shouted, appearing with a pair of rubber pants in one hand and the little boy's clothes in the other. Poor Betsy. She'd been so thin before becoming a mother. She definitely hadn't lost her weight since the last baby had been born.

Cate scooped her nephew up and headed toward her sister, taking the rubber pants and clothes. "I'll do it," she said.

"Denki," Betsy muttered. "The little trickster got away from me again." She placed a hand on the small of her back. The motion made her midsection appear bigger . . . Or maybe it was that big. My face grew warm. If Betsy was expecting again, enough to show so much, that meant she'd soon have three children. . . . Oh, goodness. Robbie wasn't quite two. The baby wasn't a year.

"Did Nan already pick up Tamara?" Cate had Robbie standing on the floor, stepping into the rubber pants.

"Jah," Betsy said. "She and Dat came over earlier."

"So you'll rest the whole time we're gone?" Cate slipped the shirt onto Robbie, fastening it quickly, and then the pants.

Betsy nodded. "The doctor said that will help get my blood pressure down. Otherwise he's going to put me on bed rest. Can you imagine? For the next few weeks?"

I couldn't imagine any of it. Especially not three babies in two years.

Cate let go of Robbie, and he darted toward the back door. "Not yet," she said. "Go get your bag."

He grinned, spun around, and headed for the back bedroom.

"It's not packed," Betsy said. "I'll go do it."

"I'll do your dishes," Cate said.

"Denki." Betsy turned to follow her son.

"We'll help tidy up," I said, glancing around. It looked as if a twister had touched down in the living room. A stack of folded diapers had fallen off the couch. A basket of laundry sat in the middle of the room, a toy wagon, probably made by Joseph Koller, was perched on its side next to it, a stack of newspapers lay scattered around a chair, and a baby doll was wedged underneath the end table.

It wasn't like the Betsy I had known to be so sloppy.

After I'd folded the clothes and straightened the diapers, I headed down the hall with both in the basket, the doll tucked under one arm, and the wagon under the other.

"Betsy?"

"In here," she said.

I stepped into a room with a double bed, a crib, and a bassinette. Stacks of diapers lined the bureau. The bed was made, a beautiful double ring quilt over the top, but that seemed to be all that was in order in the room.

Betsy was filling a bag with diapers, while Robbie sat on the bed, watching her. "Bye-bye," he said. "With Aenti Cate."

"Jah," I said. "And lots of others."

"Oh?" Then he smiled. "*Onkel* Ben too!"

I nodded as I put the basket on the bed and then the diapers on the dresser.

"You'll need to obey everyone," Betsy said to him. "Including Molly."

He nodded, peeking out from under the curls on his forehead. I had to admit he was cute, more so than most little kids anyway.

He lunged at me as if he wanted me to pick him up. I put

out my arms, but then he drew back, laughing, and scooted to the other end of the bed.

I'd never admitted it to anyone, but I was uncomfortable around kids. It wasn't that I didn't want to have children someday—I did.

And it wasn't that I was afraid of them, the way I was with horses. It was just that I didn't know what to do with them.

I kept it a secret, which wasn't hard considering I was hardly ever around them, and hoped for the best once I had children of my own. I'd heard women say "it was different" when they were your own. I could only hope it was true. I was so capable at everything else—other than horses—no one seemed to notice I avoided children. But I did.

As Robbie sat giggling at me, I waved at him. Again he came toward me as if he wanted me to pick him up and then darted away a second time, laughing.

Betsy turned her head. "Stop that, Robbie."

He did stop giggling, but then he grinned at me, his impish eyes lighting up. I waved again and then retreated to the living room to finish cleaning, something I felt competent to do.

By the time we finally left, after Betsy and Levi had both hugged Robbie, seeming sad to see him go, I wished we'd told Hannah and Leon to meet us at the Rupp place. They'd probably been waiting at the crossroads for nearly an hour.

But when we returned they still weren't there.

We waited and waited until my phone rang. It was Hannah. They'd gone to our farm when we hadn't been at the crossroads, thinking they'd misunderstood the plan. "Come back here," I said. "We'll wait."

Ten minutes later, they finally arrived. But by then everyone was hungry for lunch, so we pulled out the sandwiches and ate, sitting on the bumpers of the van, pickup, and trailer.

Leon, who wore his cowboy hat, cowboy boots, and jeans, sat on one side of me, and Hannah sat on the other, on the front of the pickup. They laughed about the mix-up. I wished I could share their humor. Cate faced us, sitting on the back bumper of the van. She kept Robbie with her as they ate, on the side closest to the field. Hannah and Leon chatted with the little boy, asking about what he wanted to do while we were camping.

"Fishing!" he said.

"Did anyone bring poles?" I asked.

"We did," Martin answered.

Hannah asked Robbie about his baby sister.

"I *wuv* her," the little boy said.

Robbie jumped toward me, grinning again, but then he veered off toward Hannah. She scooped him up in her arms.

Leon got up and tousled Robbie's hair. "You're adorable."

I wished I felt the way toward him that Hannah and Leon obviously did. But I didn't. I couldn't even fake it.

Beatrice's shrill voice interrupted my thoughts. "Ben Rupp, you'll be sorry."

Ben flashed her an impish grin and jogged backward, away from her, toward Mervin and Martin. Beatrice stepped forward, but then she stopped and stared at Leon as he made over the baby.

"We should get on the road," I said, hoping to stop my sister from any further theatrics. "We don't want to be setting up camp in the dark."

"That's not going to happen," Hannah said. "Isn't the campsite only three hours from here?"

"Jah," I said. "But we left two hours ago and have only made it five miles. At this rate, we'll get there about the time we have to leave."

As it turned out, I did exaggerate—but just a little.

Traveling with twelve people meant lots of restroom stops. And traveling with a horse trailer added two flat-tire stops. There was a spare in the trailer, so the first flat worked out just fine, except that the horses had to be taken out of the trailer. But the spare going flat meant there was no spare available. Leon said he would stay with the horses while the rest of us went to the next town to get the tire fixed. The men took the spare tire off too—it only made sense to get both tires fixed.

At the last minute I slipped out of the van, saying I would stay with Leon.

I didn't dare look back to see how Mervin responded, but Beatrice said, "Oh, brother. How about if I stay too?"

"There's no need," I said sweetly, as I walked away from the van.

Not surprisingly, Cate sent Pete to chaperone us. That was fine. Actually, out of anyone I preferred him, or Cate.

Soon after the van left, a car stopped and a middle-aged man rolled down his window, asking if we needed help. Pete stepped forward, thanked him, and sent him on his way.

Leon said he was going to take the horses for a walk and asked if I wanted to help.

I didn't—but of course I didn't say that, because regardless of the horses, I wanted to be with him. Lightning snickered and stomped her foot. Storm stepped forward.

"We can walk them up that side road a ways," he said.

"They seem unsettled."

He grinned, handing me Lightning's lead. "They'll behave, I promise."

The horse nudged me with her head. "Don't," I said.

She did it again.

I stepped back.

"Be firm with her," Leon said.

She butted up against me.

I skittered away. The only thing I liked about her, I was embarrassed to admit, was that she was the same color as Love.

"Don't let Lightning think you're afraid," Leon said.

Pete came around the side of the trailer. "Going for a walk?"

Leon nodded. "Want to come along?"

"I'll wait with the truck," Pete said. "Just in case anyone else stops to help."

Lightning butted me again. Pete smiled. I shot him a pleading look.

"Don't look at me," he said, tugging on his beard. "If it was a mule or a workhorse, I'd know what to do. But I don't know much about these fancy horses."

Leon chuckled. "These two aren't very fancy—more like unrefined."

"Well, have fun," Pete said, stepping onto the trailer ramp and sprawling out on it, his hands under his neck. "I'll just sunbathe for a while."

"Don't fry yourself," Leon said.

"Don't be long," Pete said. "The others should be back soon."

I doubted it, the way the day was going. At least I was with Leon. If only two horses weren't along with us.

I tried with Lightning, but she got the best of me, over and over, dragging me down to the ditch, then trying to run me into a tree. We finally made it to the side road, only to have Lightning take off ahead of me, dragging me along.

It was only Leon's yelling that stopped her. Even though the day was relatively mild, I began to sweat. Lightning waited for Leon to step ahead with Storm, and then she began nipping at my backside again. I swatted at her. She nipped again.

I ran ahead, nearly dropping the lead.

Leon turned around as Lightning went down on her front hooves.

"How about if we trade?" Leon asked.

I sized up Storm, who turned his head back toward me and bobbed it up and down. Surely he wasn't indicating his consent.

I handed Leon the lead for Lightning and then took Storm's. He immediately nudged me, hard.

"What's with these horses?" I asked, hoping my voice didn't sound as stressed as I felt.

Leon pursed his lips together. "Just keep going. He'll get the hang of it."

I started walking. The horse nudged me again.

Leon smiled.

"Don't," I said.

"I didn't mean to." He grinned. Even in my exasperation, my knees weakened.

But then the horse whopped my shoulder with his head. Startled, I dropped the lead. Storm hesitated for a split second and then took off at a gallop.

Without a word, Leon swung onto Lightning, bareback, his hands digging into the horse's mane, and took off after the gelding.

Pete whooped from the horse trailer ramp, standing up and waving his hat. I frowned, not wanting him to encourage Storm.

A cloud of dust blew up behind Lightning. Leon seemed to be bouncing around quite a bit on the back of the horse, but they were definitely gaining on Storm. Not knowing what else to do, I began jogging after them, feeling horrible for what I'd done.

A half hour later, with Leon leading both horses, we returned to the trailer just as the van stopped behind it. The pickup driver jumped out and opened the side door, grabbing both tires.

Cate held up an ice cream cone. "Sorry, we didn't get you guys any. We knew they'd melt." She turned to Robbie and gave him another bite.

"Ahh," Pete said, jumping down off the ramp and running over to the van, his mouth wide open. Cate smirked and held the cone up for him.

I shuddered at the thought of eating off the same cone as a two-year-old.

Pete swallowed the ice cream and said, "Yum, yum," making Robbie laugh, before hurrying to the truck driver's side, taking one of the tires from him.

Leon handed the leads to me. "I need to help with the tires."

I held up both hands. "Not a good idea."

"Come on, Molly," he said.

I shook my head. "I don't want us to waste more time because a horse got away from me again."

He turned back toward the van. "Hannah," he called out, "come give me a hand, would you?"

Robbie squealed—Hannah must have tickled him on the way out—and then she appeared with an ice cream cone in her hand. "What do you need?"

"Take the horses, please. Lead them away from the trailer."

She sashayed on over, her hips swaying a little bit. Mervin and Martin followed her out of the van and over to the trailer, as she took Storm's lead from Leon. He extended Lightning's lead to her too. She held up her strawberry ice cream cone and nodded at me. Leon shook his head.

An amused look crossed Hannah's face as she handed me her cone. She took the second lead and walked along the ditch side of the trailer and pickup. I followed, her ice cream dripping on my hand. I licked it, enjoying the taste of fresh berries.

She kept going, stopping about fifty feet up the road. When I reached her, Storm nuzzled her neck.

"Stop it," she said. And the horse did.

She transferred Lightning's lead to the same hand that was holding Storm's and reached for her ice cream cone. I handed it to her.

"How are things going with Leon?" She licked the melting ice cream.

"Good." Determined to change the subject, I asked, "How are things going with Mervin?"

She rolled her eyes. "At least Robbie likes me." She took another lick.

"We're really running late," I said.

She shrugged. "We'll get there when we get there."

I stepped closer to the road so I could get a view of the trailer. Leon positioned the tire while Pete held the iron. Mervin and Martin stood behind them while the two drivers leaned against the van.

I took a deep breath. If the drivers, who would be late getting back to Lancaster, weren't upset, I decided I shouldn't be either. All we had to do was set up camp.

In no time the tire was on, the spare stored, and the vehicles loaded and on their way again. In the van, Cate wiped Robbie's hands with a wet washcloth she pulled out of a plastic bag, and then he fell asleep. Pretty soon Cate's head rested against the seat and I assumed she'd fallen asleep too. Beatrice wiggled around as if trying to eke out more space for herself, at my expense. I sat straight, mentally going through my plans for when we got to camp.

"Molly," Mervin whispered, "want to walk around the lake tonight?"

I ignored him.

"Molly," he said again.

Martin poked me and snorted.

Ben chuckled.

"I heard you—all three of you," I answered.

"And?" Mervin's voice was louder.

"I can't think that far," I said. "Not until camp is set up and supper is served." I crossed my arms and closed my eyes. But I didn't sleep. I kept wishing I was in the pickup with Leon, with the horses safely in the trailer.

C H A P T E R

12

"How about this one?" Cate pointed out the window. We were on the horse-camp loop, where there were several campsites.

"I don't think that one's big enough," I said. "Let's go to the next one."

The van driver let out a sigh and accelerated. There weren't any other campers—one of the benefits of coming on a Monday. Through the trees, the blue of the lake sparkled in the late-afternoon light. A trail ran parallel to the road. From the entrance sign, it extended up the hill and into the forest. I imagined that's where Leon would ride.

Hopefully Hannah wouldn't go with him.

Why hadn't I gotten back on a horse way back when? If I'd only known Leon was in my future.

The van stopped. "How about this one?" Cate asked.

It was smaller than the previous one. "Let's look at one more site," I said.

The van driver sighed again and continued on. The pickup driver, who followed behind, honked his horn. I ignored it, but could hear Martin, Mervin, and Ben all turn around in the back seat.

"Molly." Beatrice nudged me. "What's the difference?"

I ignored her too.

The driver stopped at the next site. I peered out the window past Beatrice. It was definitely bigger. And closer to the lake. There were several flat areas for the tents. Two picnic tables. Lots of trees, both conifers and deciduous. Two fir trees stood the perfect distance apart to hang a clothesline.

"This is good," I said.

"Finally," the driver muttered, pulling ahead and then backing into the parking space. We all piled out into the cool mountain air as the pickup driver kept going and then backed the trailer into a low area at the far edge of the site.

"Leon wants to keep the horses away from the water," Hannah said.

"Oh. Why?"

She gave me one of her funny looks. "Sanitation reasons," she said, as if I should have known.

That got me looking for a restroom.

"Over there," Beatrice said, pointing to a little shed. "Pit toilets," she announced.

"No showers," Hannah added.

"It's only for three nights," I said.

"Only." Beatrice groaned.

"Come on." I started to the back of the van. "Let's get this unloaded so the drivers can get back on the road."

I'd expected the guys to start the process, but they didn't. Pete headed toward the horse trailer. Mervin, Martin, and Ben crossed the roadway to a grove of white pine trees and started picking up the slender cones from the ground and lobbing them at each other.

I cleared my throat.

They didn't respond.

170

"Mervin. Martin. Ben." My voice was loud—they still didn't respond.

"Hey!" I yelled.

Mervin froze, a pinecone in his hand.

"Help us," I said, nodding toward the van.

Cate crawled out of the side door with Robbie and his diaper bag. Hannah took the little boy, and he cuddled against her as she headed toward the horse trailer.

"If Leon doesn't need help, could you send Pete back?" Cate's voice was calm.

Hannah nodded her head and kept on walking.

"If Leon doesn't need help, could you come back here too?" I called after her.

She waved her hand at me without looking back.

The boys ran back over as the driver opened the back of the van, and we all worked together to unload the gear. "Put it on the picnic benches," I said. "Not on the tables." Everyone, mostly, complied.

The van driver said he'd see us midmorning Thursday and drove to the horse trailer, waiting for the pickup driver. Hannah held the horses' leads in one hand and Robbie in the other, while Pete and Leon unhooked the trailer. Together they pulled the green portable fencing from the bed of the pickup, and then bales of hay. No wonder Pete had gone to help. As soon as they were done, Pete headed back and the truck driver and the van driver took off, disappearing around the curve.

I organized the assembly of the tents, assigning Mervin and Ben to set up the boys' and Beatrice and Martin to set up the girls'.

"What are you going to do?" Beatrice asked, our old tent poles in her hands.

"Set up the kitchen," I answered as I opened the first box.

I'd probably need some help with the stove—but I planned to ask Leon for that once he returned from tending to the horses. And I'd definitely need help putting the canopy up over the kitchen table—although I had managed it alone a few times on market days.

I glanced down at Leon and Hannah. Storm sniffed Robbie's back, making the little boy giggle. Lightning stepped closer too, her ears forward. Hannah laughed and said something to Leon as he carried a section of fencing toward her. He answered and then easily placed the metal piece on the ground, as if it were plastic. I couldn't imagine the fencing would keep the horses contained, not after the way they'd taken off earlier.

I pulled two plastic tablecloths from the box and spread them over the tables. Next I pulled out the dishpans and rack, placing them on one end of the picnic table I'd decided to use as the kitchen.

Robbie began to fuss, and Hannah headed back to the campsite, the horses following along. Cate held a tent pole in her hand but started toward her nephew, meeting Hannah halfway. Pete trailed Cate, taking the pole from her before she collected Robbie in her hands.

"He's probably hungry," she said.

"We'll eat as soon as I can heat up the stew," I said.

"I'll get him a cracker." Cate headed toward his diaper bag on the picnic bench closest to her.

I stepped to where I had a clear view of Leon, sure I could see his biceps ripple under his blue work shirt. I felt as if butterflies were fluttering around in my chest—until Hannah returned with the horses, stopping in the clearing away from the trailer. Leon placed another section of fence behind them. I watched as he set up a third, guessing he was going to build the fence around the horses—and Hannah.

The butterflies stopped as my breath caught. I was jealous.

I took a raggedy breath and quickly turned toward the camp-stove box.

"Want some help?" Mervin asked, pushing his glasses to the top of his head. The sun was well hidden behind the trees now.

I glanced toward Leon again. Hannah laughed as he set up the fourth piece of fence. He'd be done soon.

"You could put the ice chests on the bench," I answered Mervin.

"Oh bother," Beatrice said. She was standing next to our half-raised tent, a broken pole in her hand.

"Get the duct tape," I said, "and fix it."

"We need it too," Ben said, pointing to the boys' sagging tent.

"Jah." Mervin eased the first ice chest onto the bench and then let go of it, resulting in a heavy thud. "Our tent has some problems."

Not only was it sagging, it tilted to the right too. "For sure," I answered.

Mervin laughed and then asked what else he could do.

I found it sweet that he was eager to help. I wanted to suggest he go finish the fence for Leon but knew that would never do. Mervin liked horses about as much as I did.

"Fill the jugs with water." I glanced around, looking for the water spigot.

He grinned. "I'll find it."

I smiled and then glanced down toward Leon, hoping he was almost done. He was placing another section of fence in place, his back toward me. But Hannah was looking straight at me. A frown on her face.

I posted the chore and meal charts on the tree closest to the picnic table, then called everyone to gather around for supper.

"Before Pete leads us in prayer," I said, "I wanted to explain how we'll be doing things." I pointed to the chart. "As you can see, I prepared dinner for tonight." Besides stew, I'd put out raw veggies, the homemade bread, and cobbler. "Everything is spelled out for the rest of the camping trip. Who has which meal. What's on the menu. Who's on cleanup."

Beatrice groaned.

"Who's in charge of collecting the firewood."

Martin groaned.

"Who's in charge of the fire."

Ben groaned and then muttered, "This is why I never plan to marry—"

"Denki," Cate said to me, "for seeing to all of this. It's necessary and a big help."

"You're all very welcome," I said, grateful for Cate's praise and a little miffed with Beatrice, Martin, and Ben. We were Amish raised, after all. We were used to hard work. And someone had to take charge. Like Cate, they should be thankful for what I'd done.

Hannah stepped toward the chart.

I smiled. "You and Mervin are in charge of cleanup tonight." Turning toward Pete, I said, "You can go ahead and lead us in the prayer now."

Hannah stopped next to me, brushing against my shoulder as Pete bowed his head for the silent prayer. Mervin narrowed his eyes and turned his head toward the lake, as if to remind me he'd suggested a walk after dinner. Jah, I did plan to go on a walk. But not with him.

Just before I closed my eyes, I noted that Beatrice was staring at Leon, who had his head bowed. She had a slight smile on her face, as much as I'd seen from her in the last couple of months.

I squeezed my eyes shut quickly, offering up a prayer that God would grant us peace and goodwill, that Beatrice would give up her affection for Leon, and that Mervin would gain back his for Hannah. *Please*, I pleaded, as Pete said amen.

Leon sat facing the horses during dinner, complimenting me a couple of times on the stew. The first time I replied that everything tasted better while camping. The second time I simply smiled.

I'd managed to sit across from him, and at first he seemed intent on me, but then I realized he was looking over my shoulder. Midconversation, as he complimented the cobbler, he struggled up from the bench and dashed around the table and across the campsite. I turned to watch him. Storm was pushing his forehead against the top railing of the fence.

"Can't he just hobble them?" I asked.

"No," Hannah responded. "Not for the entire time we're here."

I didn't respond.

Robbie threw a slice of bread toward me.

Hannah laughed.

"Don't encourage him." I stood, picking up my plate and Mervin's too. Next I picked up Martin's and Ben's. Then Hannah's.

"I thought Mervin and I were on cleanup," she said.

"You are," I answered. I put the dishes in the pan at the end of the table and watched Leon start back toward camp. The others stood and milled around. Ben picked up a pinecone and tossed it at Martin. He caught it and tossed it back.

I took a deep breath. "Who would like coffee?" I asked as Leon returned to the table.

"I'll take some," Pete answered.

I turned and reached for the pot simmering on the back of the stove. "Cate?"

"No, thank you," she said, picking up Robbie and heading toward the hand-washing station.

I poured the coffee in a blue enamel cup and handed it to Pete. "How about you, Leon?"

"Sure," he said, a bite of cobbler on his fork. "As long as you're going to have a cup too."

I poured us each a cup and sat across from him again.

Mervin, Martin, and Ben drifted across the road to the grove of pines.

"A walk sure would be nice," I said.

"Jah," Leon answered, his eyes drifting behind me again. "The horses could use some exercise. That's for sure."

"Oh," I said. That wasn't what I'd had in mind.

"There's a horse trail above the lake."

"Oh," I said again.

He took the last bite of his cobbler, followed by a drink of his coffee.

"But we should go soon. Before it gets dark." Leon stood, picking up his plate but leaving his coffee.

"We'll lead them, right? That's what you're saying."

"Unless you want to ride tonight," he said with a twinkle in his eyes as he put his plate in the dishpan.

I shook my head.

"You two should go ahead," Cate said.

Hannah had joined the guys across the road.

"Just make sure everyone does what they're supposed to," I said to Cate. "Don't do it for them."

"Of course not." She smiled at me.

After telling Leon I'd meet him by the horses, I slipped into my tent to grab my flashlight out of my bag. I took a moment to spread out my sleeping bag and place my duffle bag at the end. I also grabbed my sweatshirt.

When I crawled out of the tent, Beatrice was positioning kindling for a fire.

"That's Ben's job tonight," I said.

She stood straight and turned toward the guys. "Well, it doesn't look like he plans to make one anytime soon. And it's already getting cold."

As she spoke, Ben released a pinecone toward Martin.

"I rest my case," Beatrice said, returning to the kindling.

The lawn chairs were stacked to the side. I pointed to them. "Put those around in a circle. We can roast marshmallows when we get back."

She didn't respond.

"Beatrice."

"I heard," she barked.

"Goodness," I said softly, not wanting to make a scene.

"Go," she said, looking past me to Leon. Although the fire in the pit hadn't been started yet, one had already ignited in her brown eyes.

I gave her one last firm look, and then headed toward Leon, the flashlight in my hand.

He had both horses out of the fenced area by the time I arrived, and didn't offer me one of the leads this time. "This way," he said. "We can check out the trail for the ride tomorrow."

I stepped beside him, determined to keep ahead of the horses.

He glanced back at Pete and Cate. "Guess they decided we didn't need a chaperone."

I smiled. "I think they're too preoccupied with Robbie."

We walked along the road, side by side but not talking, until we came to the trail.

I stopped for a moment, breathing in the fresh mountain air, thinking of the camping trips with Dat. We'd camped on the other side of the lake, of course, but as much as being here made me miss him all the more, it felt good to be back at a place Dat had loved so much.

Leon seemed to sense my need to savor the moment and waited patiently. Finally I said, "Let's go."

At first the path was narrow, and Leon indicated for me to go first. The evening light dimmed as the canopy of leaves overhead grew thicker. In the shadows, mountain laurel bloomed—the white-and-pink blossoms shining like stars in the forest against the dark green leaves. After a few minutes of walking, the trail widened and Leon stepped beside me. The horses bobbed along behind us as obedient as could be.

A green bug with nearly transparent, fairy-like wings, landed on my arm. I held it up for Leon to see.

He grinned and then said, "We don't have bugs like that in Montana—at least not where I'm from."

A meadowlark sang above our heads, most likely his last song before bed. A moment later the sound of water stopped us. Leon pointed to the right. "Over there." We took off on a spur of a trail, the horses still behind us. After about fifty feet, we stopped. Ahead was a waterfall, tumbling down a rock wall and sending out a spray of water as it crashed into the creek below.

Moss covered the rocks along the creek. Trillium grew along the banks along with star of Bethlehem, the white flowers in full bloom. The creek wound its way into a ravine and then disappeared.

"How enchanting," I whispered.

Leon put his arm around me and pulled me close. The worries of the day fell away with the rush of the water. I was with Leon. In the Poconos. In the most romantic setting I could ever imagine.

Lightning nudged my back.

My face fell. With horses.

Leon pushed against the horse and then pulled me even closer, his lips brushing the top of my Kapp. I turned my face up to his, and his lips met mine, a hint of the berry cobbler still on them.

He wrapped me in his strong arms, the horse leads still wound around his hands as we kissed again.

Finally he pulled away. "Miss Molly," he whispered, his eyes dancing. "What have you done to me?"

"It's you that's—" Lightning nudged me again.

The horse whinnied. Leon laughed. "It's nearly the summer solstice," he said. "What better time of the year to be out in the forest with the girl I . . ."

I turned my head up toward him, my eyes searching his.

He blushed.

"Really?" I asked.

He stammered, "Is it too soon?"

"No," I answered, looking into his blue, blue eyes.

He took a deep breath, and I thought he was actually going to say the word, but his shyness must have gotten the best of him.

"I didn't mean to be too forward."

I shook my head.

He sighed and then said, "We should get back on the trail."

"Jah," I answered, growing aware that we were alone, without a chaperone, except for the horses. Full of feelings I hadn't experienced before.

I had to get Mervin interested in Hannah again. That was the only thing that would change Mamm's mind. Then she'd surely be fine with Leon. And if not . . .

What was I willing to do? Run off with him? All the way to Montana? Of course not.

He was staying in Lancaster County.

Once we reached the main trail, we continued up instead of heading back to camp. I asked Leon about his sisters. "Hannah's family definitely reminds me of mine," he said. "Except in mine the only boy—me—is the oldest, and in hers the only boy is the youngest."

"Jah," I said. "So in reverse."

"Exactly." He paused for a minute and then said, "I compared one of my sisters to Beatrice, but worse."

I nodded. I remembered.

"But I think she's more like Hannah."

"How's that?"

"Oh." It seemed he was looking for the right word. "Unstable."

"Hannah's much better than she used to be."

"Jah," he said. "That's what she told me."

For a moment, I wondered how much they'd talked. It seemed like more than I'd thought.

"I worry about her," Leon said. "She seems so taken with Mervin. It's miserable to love someone who doesn't love you back."

I wondered how much Hannah had told Leon about my experience with Phillip. She'd blurted out before the singing that he'd dumped me, but had she told Leon more?

A wild flower ahead caught Leon's attention. Orange and yellow, the bloom hung upside down. "Amazing," he said.

"It's columbine," I responded. "But it's late for it to be blooming."

"It's been fairly cool," Leon answered.

I bent down next to the flower, taking hold of the stem. I'd never seen an orange one before.

"I brought my pastels." Leon stood over me. "If I have time, I'll draw a picture."

"I'd like that," I said, straightening up.

We continued on.

"I'd like to see your art," I said.

"I'll show you, when we get back to camp."

I sighed. "I wish I had some sort of talent like that." It was a new wish. I'd never appreciated Beatrice's writing, but now I could see the value of expressing myself. Maybe I hadn't had anything worth expressing until now.

"Ach, Molly, you have all kinds of talent."

"I wasn't fishing for a compliment, really," I explained, embarrassed that what I'd said had probably sounded prideful. "But since you brought it up, what exactly are my talents?"

He laughed. "Well, you're a go-getter. And full of ideas. You take charge—a true leader. You're going to make a great wife—and mother."

I smiled and then said, as if it were a joke, "You haven't seen me with kids yet."

"How about today, with Robbie?" But then he cocked his head. "Actually, I don't think I did see you with   "

I interrupted him, plain and simple, keeping my voice light. "I am good with flowers though. They're much more predictable than children." Lightning nudged me for the . . . Actually I'd lost track of how many times she'd nudged me. "And horses."

"Except for drought, diseases, and storms."

"Well, sure. But it's not like a flower decides to bolt or throw their food across the table."

He laughed and then said, "I'm just teasing." He reached for my hand. We walked along in silence until we crested a hill. Ahead was a meadow, much brighter in the evening light than the forest had been. The horses slowed.

Ahead I saw a purple flower, actually several blossoms on a club-like shape atop a stem. I hurried my pace. "Do you know what this is?" I asked.

Leon shook his head.

"It looks like nettle," I said.

"It's similar, but I remember what nettle looks like"—he grimaced as if remembering the plant's sting—"really well."

"My Dat would have known." I'd left his book at home.

"I'll draw it too," Leon said. "Then we can find out."

"Denki." I knew far more about cultivated flowers than wild ones.

The horses stopped. Leon tugged on them. Their ears twitched and they wouldn't budge. He murmured, "Come on." They took a couple of steps and stopped again.

"What is it?" I asked, looking around the meadow.

"I don't know," Leon said. "Maybe a deer. They're so skittish, it could even be the scent of something else on the trail earlier in the day."

"What happened to make them so afraid?"

"I don't know. Owen bought them at auction in the spring. That's why he hired me, to train them—and another one he hopes to buy later in the summer."

He pulled again, leading the horses into the meadow, where we sat on a big rock. He took his cowboy hat from his head and placed it, gently, on top of my Kapp, grinning as he did.

Then he dropped the horses' leads on the ground and said, "There's no rushing when it comes to horses. If you're patient and win their trust, they'll eventually do what you ask them to."

Once we were headed back down the trail, Leon handed Storm's lead to me. I balked. "Give it a try," he said.

Reluctantly, I cooperated. Then Leon took my other hand. The feel of his calluses against my skin comforted me. We followed the trail as it wound down through the trees. He liked that I was a take-charge person. He appreciated it. We complemented each other that way. I was good with people—he was good with horses, a true leader in his own way.

"Where did you get your hat?" I asked, looking up at the brim.

"The old cowboy I worked for back home." He grinned at me again. "I only wear it for special occasions—and I only let very special people wear it."

I couldn't help but smile.

"He was one of my best friends ever. He was a crusty old geezer, but his mama had been a pioneer woman who loved the Lord. He cussed when riled, but he could recite Bible verses just as well. And he sent half his money to an Indian mission in North Dakota. And if anyone in the community had a need, he'd see to it—anonymously, of course. By the time he died—"

I gasped. "He died."

"Jah." Leon swallowed hard. "In March."

Just before Dat.

"Anyway, he had cancer. I stayed with him until the end. It was okay because he was so ready to see the Lord. That's all he talked about. I learned a lot about faith and love from him—not how to talk about it but how to live it."

"I'm sorry," I said.

Leon smiled, sadly. "He—Hank—paid my sister's hospital bills. There were some who didn't think the treatment she got was . . . right. He did."

"Wow."

Leon squeezed my hand. "Tell me about your Dat. Hannah said he was a good man."

"Jah." I swallowed hard, fighting the tears. "He was." Leon squeezed my hand again, and I could feel a current of understanding pass through me. "He would have liked you."

Leon's voice was tender. "More than your Mamm?"

"She'll like you, soon enough. I promise. Once my plan works."

He leaned toward me. "What exactly is your plan?"

My face warmed. I hesitated for a moment but then said, "When Dat died, my brother—half brother . . ."

Leon nodded. Hannah had probably told him about Ivan too.

"Anyway, he said it was God's will. Everyone who came to help in the days before his funeral said that too."

"Jah, that's what my parents said when Hank passed."

"I know, ultimately, it was," I said.

Leon's head bobbed.

"I just wasn't ready. . . ."

"Of course not." Leon let go of my hand, wrapping his arm around my shoulders and drawing me close.

"I have a lot of regrets when it comes to my Dat," I said. "I wish I would have stuck around home more. I wish I would have told him I loved him more. I wish I would have called 9-1-1 sooner." I shuddered. "I did the best I could—but it wasn't good enough."

Leon drew me even closer. "None of us is perfect."

"But that's why I don't want to put too much stress on Mamm."

"She'll be okay," Leon said.

There was no way he could know for sure, but his words comforted me.

"It makes our . . . relationship—yours and mine—complicated."

He looked off into the distance and then said, "So what is your plan?"

I shook my head. "I shouldn't have mentioned it, because I can't really do anything—not until we know what's wrong with my Mamm."

"I see."

"I'm sorry," I replied.

"It's all right." He tipped the cowboy hat back farther on my head. "I expect ruts in the road on the way to true love." He grinned, but not because he was teasing.

I exhaled slowly, appreciating his words. I pulled away and took his hat from my head, holding it up. "So what other special people—girls—have worn this?"

"Not many."

"How many?" I put the hat back on my head, and Leon reached for my hand again.

"Just one."

"Do tell." I nudged his bicep with my shoulder.

"Just a girl back home . . ."

"What happened?" I asked.

He paused a moment. "I guess you could say she dumped me."

I stopped in the middle of the trail. Why would anyone dump Leon? "I don't believe it," I said, mock horror in my voice. "Whyever for?"

Leon grinned. "Hard to believe, I know. Let's see. She said I didn't talk enough. I didn't express my feelings."

"Goodness." I gazed into his eyes. "But look at how you just opened up to me."

He smiled. "It was a conscious effort."

I smiled back, and then at a ridiculous attempt at humor, I asked, "But did she like horses?"

"Yep," he answered. "A lot."

I changed the subject, pointing to the wild phlox growing along the trail. "We grow phlox," I said.

"The tame kind," Leon joked.

"Jah, I train it," I answered, pleased that the mood had become more lighthearted.

The daylight was nearly gone, but I didn't want our time to end. Ahead was a log, covered with moss. I nodded toward it. "Just for a minute?" I asked.

Leon staked the horses beside the log and we sat. To our left was the spur we'd taken to the waterfall, and we listened to the water crashing and the other sounds—crickets, an owl hooting in the distance, a creature in the tree behind us.

A flickering out of the corner of my eye caught my attention.

Leon gasped.

I giggled.

Another firefly appeared.

"We don't have those back home." His voice was full of awe.

I stood and stepped toward them. "Will the horses be okay?"

He nodded. I took his hand and we started after the flickering lights, toward the waterfall. By the time we reached it, the forest was full of fireflies, dazzling us with their beauty against the dark green hues of the trees and the canopy of the almost-night sky.

My very being danced with their movement, as if Leon and I flew with them, our hearts as in sync as the light show before us. The sight was more beautiful than Englisch Christmas lights, snow falling in winter, and even shooting stars. I slipped off the cowboy hat and held it in my hand.

Enchanted, I took all of it in as a sign of a new start. True, my heart still weighed heavy with worry and grief, but I'd honestly never been happier in all my life.

Leon loved me. I loved him. Thank goodness I'd met him before I'd agreed to marry Mervin.

As we rounded the curve in the road, laughter rang out from our camp. Above, the stars were brighter and thicker even than back home, flooding the sky. When we reached the horse trailer, I took off the cowboy hat and handed it to Leon.

"Keep it," he said. "It looks better on you." I appreciated the small consolation to my dread of joining the others. I only wanted to be with Leon. But all good things, including walks in the forest, had to come to an end.

Leon led Lightning into the pen and then took Storm's lead from me and led him in too. Then he stepped into the trailer, going to the very back. A moment later he returned with his leather book and pencil box in his hands.

"What about your sleeping bag?" I shone the flashlight at his feet. "Don't you want to take it to your tent?"

"I'll sleep here," he said. "Close to the horses."

I stepped closer to the trailer. "In there?"

"Jah," he answered.

"But the floor is hard—and cold."

"I'll be fine."

I looked from Lightning to Storm, wishing there was another option.

"But you'll come up to the campfire now?"

"Jah," he said. "Of course."

Mervin was sitting by himself, with a hurt look on his face, while Ben and Martin talked about a softball game they'd played in the week before. Hannah and Beatrice listened. There wasn't enough light by the fire to see Leon's work, so we headed toward the table where Pete and Cate hovered over something, the lantern a few feet away. As I started to sit at the other end, I realized they had one of the plastic kitchen boxes on the table. I stopped. Robbie was sitting in the box, splashing around in the water.

Cate poured water over his curly hair, and the little boy giggled in delight.

"Grab the towel," Cate said to Pete.

"What's going on?" I asked.

"Bath time." Cate had a smile on her face. "Doesn't it look like fun?"

"But that's the kitchen box . . ." I turned toward the other table. The matches, the bowls, a few plates we hadn't used at dinner, a pan—all of it had been taken out of the box. That's when I noticed the dinner dishes hadn't been washed.

"Hannah!" I spun around toward the fire. "You and Mervin didn't do the dishes."

"We're waiting until Robbie has his bath," she answered. "Right, Mervin?"

He nodded, staring straight at me.

"We had to heat more water," Cate said as she lifted the little boy out of the box and into the towel Pete held. Pete wrapped the baby up tight, cradling him sweetly.

Leon stepped over and tickled Robbie's chin. The little boy shrieked. Hannah hurried from the fire and cooed over him too. Alarm filled me as Leon watched her, a look of admiration on his face.

Robbie shot me another impish grin.

Mervin, Martin, and Ben gathered around too.

"Don't get him all worked up," I said.

"You're the only one getting worked up." Beatrice was behind me, retrieving the bag of marshmallows from the end of the table.

I ignored her and turned the burner down under the kettle that had begun to whistle, and under the pan on the back burner too. Then I retrieved the pan from the table, filled it halfway at the water jug, and marched back to the stove.

Pete slipped Robbie into Cate's arms, and she headed to the tent with him—it seemed awfully late for such a little guy to be up—while Pete carried the box of water toward the waste area, dumping it with a swishing noise. Then he ran water from the jug into the box, swirled it around, and then dumped it again.

When he returned he dried it out with a hand towel.

Leon joined the others by the fire, taking a marshmallow from Beatrice and putting it on a stick.

I set up the drying rack, retrieved the dish soap and towels from the other table, and then poured the hot water, adding a little bleach to the rinse water. I doubted if Hannah would have thought to do that.

Mervin joined me. "I'll help you," he said.

"Denki," I said. Hannah needed to help too. Instead she was roasting a marshmallow, holding it awfully close to Leon's. Beatrice stepped around on the other side of him.

I swirled my hand in the dishwater as I added the soap. When I glanced at the fire again, Leon was eating his marshmallow. He held up the remaining half and called out, "I'll make you one."

"No thanks," I answered.

When I glanced up again, he was walking toward the horse

trailer, his book in his hands, the shadows of the night dancing in the flickering light around him.

Finally Hannah came to help with the dishes, ignoring both Mervin and me.

﹏

I slept fitfully. On one side, Hannah snored softly. On the other side, Beatrice kicked sharply.

A couple of times, an owl hooted. Several times one of the horses neighed, probably spooked by the owl. One time, I thought I heard Robbie cry—or perhaps that was a mountain lion after the horses. I thought of Leon unprotected in the trailer. What would he do?

After that there were no more hoots or cries, just Beatrice kicking me and Hannah drooling on her pillow. I drifted back to sleep, only to have Robbie wake me again—this time with laughter.

It was five o'clock, definitely time to get up at home, but maybe not on vacation. . . . I rolled over but couldn't get back to sleep. Hannah and Beatrice continued to sleep heavily, even when I crawled out of my sleeping bag and dressed, slipped on my jacket, unzipped the tent, and stepped out into the cold, overcast morning.

The fire was going, and so was the stove. Coffee was boiling on the back burner, sending a delicious smell my way. Pete was sitting in a lawn chair with Robbie on his lap, sharing a banana with the little boy.

"Good morning," I whispered, stopping to warm my hands by the fire.

Robbie squealed with delight, probably at seeing another person awake—certainly not at seeing me in particular. But then he reached out for me, and once again I responded, only to have him shrink back and shriek again.

"Ach, he's teasing," Pete said.

I forced a smile. Robbie didn't act that way with anyone but me. Maybe he could tell deep down I wasn't that crazy about children.

I headed to the chart, even though I had it memorized. I'd scheduled Cate and Pete to make breakfast and Leon and me to clean up. I turned toward the trailer. Robbie squealed again, probably thinking I was looking at him. I did give him a smile and a wave, then looked intently at the area around the trailer. The horses stood over a pile of hay that hadn't been there the night before. Leon was awake.

Perhaps he and I should make breakfast since it didn't appear Cate was up yet.

I poured myself a cup of coffee—thinking of Dat as I did because the blue enamel cups were his from all those years ago—and headed to the fire to ward off the chill.

Robbie held up his hands to me.

"Goodness," I said, catching sight of Leon out of the corner of my eye. I put my cup down on the stump by the woodpile and reached for Robbie. But again, he twisted around and dove against Pete's chest. I wasn't going to let a two-year-old hurt my feelings, but it was hard not to take it personally.

Leon called out a good morning. Pete responded. At their current volume, the rest of the group would be up in no time—and we could stick to my schedule.

I handed Leon my untouched coffee and filled another cup for myself as Mervin staggered out of the boys' tent, pulling on the canvas as he did, tugging the structure so it leaned even more. "I thought I heard your voice," he said, a smile on his face until he saw Leon. It turned into a frown.

Using my most pleasant tone, I offered him some coffee.

"Denki," he said, coming toward me. I poured the coffee

into another cup, handed it to him, and headed back to the fire. He followed.

Just as Mervin and I sat down, me in a chair next to Leon and Mervin next to me, Hannah stumbled from our tent, tying her apron as she did. She looked bleary-eyed but still as beautiful as ever, her dark hair tucked beneath her Kapp, her olive complexion glowing.

Robbie squealed in delight, far more than when he'd seen me.

Hannah's face lit up, and both Leon and Mervin laughed. Even the horses snickered behind us.

I got up, strode over to the kitchen box, and pulled out the frying pan.

"Come sit down," Pete said. "Cate and I'll do all that."

I wanted to ask when but bit my tongue.

Leon patted the chair beside him. "Come on," he said.

I cooperated, picking up my coffee cup and strolling over to the chair I had just vacated.

Robbie lunged for Hannah. She stood and took him from Pete. The little boy wrapped his arms around her neck. Mervin didn't take his eyes off Robbie—and Hannah.

I took a sip of my coffee. "Want to show me your artwork now?" I asked Leon.

"Sure. I'll be right back."

As Leon walked away, Pete stood up and headed to their tent, hopefully to wake Cate. Hannah and Mervin continued to play with Robbie. I downed half my coffee, wondering if Mamm, Edna, and Ivan had the chores done and were ready to go into town for the CT scan.

Soft murmurs came from Cate and Pete's tent, then laughter. Robbie looked toward the voices and clapped his hands.

Hannah said, in a baby-talk voice, "Cate will be out in a minute." I hated baby talk. I didn't see what the point was, not when the baby needed to learn how to speak normally sooner or later anyway.

Leon returned with his leather book again and his pencil box.

"What do you have there?" Mervin asked.

Leon held up both things, as if that explained it. Then he handed me the book to look through while he opened the box. He took out a smaller cardboard box.

"Oh, look at that," Mervin said, obviously insincere. "Pastels."

Hannah leaned closer, Robbie still on her lap. He started to fuss and reach toward me. I ignored the baby as I opened Leon's book. The artwork was good. There was a sketch of a horse to start with. Then a buttercup, done in pastels. Then a mountain range.

"Those are the Bitterroots," he said. "It's beautiful country and not too far from our ranch."

"Ranch, huh?" Martin said. "Not a farm?"

"Definitely a ranch." Leon took his pastels from the box.

"Color?" Robbie said.

Mervin's voice held a hint of mockery. "What exactly is the definition of a ranch?"

"We have five-hundred acres. Lots of cattle."

"So you really are a cowboy?"

"I drive cattle on a horse. If that makes me a cowboy, I guess so."

Mervin smirked, pointing to the book in my hand. "And an artist?"

"No, not an artist," Leon said.

It bordered on prideful to have Leon showing his work as it was; if he called himself an artist, we'd all be worried—even me.

I didn't tell Leon he was good, which he definitely was. Instead, I said, "I really like these."

Robbie squealed and then said, "Color!" again.

"What's with him?" I asked Hannah.

"He thinks they're crayons," she said. "He wants to color."

"Oh." Maybe Cate brought some coloring books.

"I'll do the columbine," Leon said to me, "later today."

"La-di-da," Mervin said. "Columbine. In color?"

"Knock it off," I said to Mervin.

Leon ignored him. "And the purple flower."

Mervin smirked. It wasn't like him to be so petty.

He crossed his arms and stared at me. Hannah pulled Robbie back against herself and looked at me too.

"What?" I said.

Robbie screamed.

I handed the book back to Leon. "I'll be back in a little while," I said. No one said a word as I walked away, but not in the direction of the horses. I headed toward the lake instead.

I stood with my hands in the pockets of my apron, my face turned toward the cool breeze wafting up from the water. On the opposite shore a hawk soared above the trees. Then he swerved and swooped down on the beach. I couldn't be sure, but it was likely he'd caught a mouse. Something dangled from his talons.

"Oh no." Beatrice stopped behind me.

"What?" I thought something had happened back at camp.

"That poor mouse, swooped away so unexpectedly."

"It's just a rodent," I said. The hawk flew beyond the trees, out of sight.

"It's one of God's creatures," she said.

"God designed it this way," I answered.

She crossed her arms and didn't say anything more.

"Did you want something?"

194

"The others sent me to find you."

"The others?"

"Well, Hannah did."

"Not Leon?"

She shook her head. "He's taking care of the horses."

That figured. "Why didn't Hannah come?"

Beatrice shrugged. "I think she's a little scared of you right now."

Her words fell like a landslide. "Beatrice, that's so unkind."

"It's true, Molly."

"Why would she be afraid of me?"

A pathetic expression settled on her face. "The schedule? The chart? Chastising her for not doing the dishes by the time you got back last night?"

"But I do so much—organize everything, call everyone. She could at least do her part."

She shook her head. "I'm just warning you. It's one thing to be bossy with me, but quite another to be rude to your friends."

"Beatrice, you—"

"It's true. Mervin and Hannah were going to clean up last night—just not exactly when you wanted them to or how you wanted them to."

"We are Plain," I answered. "With certain standards . . . and expectations. After all, 'cleanliness is next to godliness.'"

"That's just a saying," Beatrice said. "It's not like it's Scripture or anything."

I nodded. I knew that. Still, it served my purpose.

She continued, "But it does illustrate your false sense of what's important. You expect everyone to do things your way."

"We do have a certain conformity in our community," I said, doing my best not to roll my eyes. "If you haven't noticed."

"Jah, but your standards go beyond the norm. It's like you don't want anyone to have any fun."

"That's not true." I'd spent my entire *Rumschpringe* organizing fun. I was hurt, honestly. But maybe she was upset because Mamm had her scan in a couple of hours. Or she was feeling Dat's loss especially hard again. Maybe the same could be said for me. . . . Maybe I had been acting differently. I certainly didn't feel like my old self—the carefree girl who loved to organize events and gather everyone together. Instead I'd been feeling resentful and uptight.

Or maybe she was hurt because Leon was interested in me instead of her.

Beatrice pointed across the lake to a man and woman walking together. "Who is that?" They looked Amish. For a moment I feared it was Hannah and Leon.

"I don't know," I said, squinting. "I don't think it's anyone from our group though."

"It looks like Phillip," she said.

I shaded my eyes from the sun rising over the trees. "No," I said. "That's impossible."

"No, I'm sure it is," she said.

"Beatrice . . . let's go back to camp."

Halfway there, Leon met us, walking Storm.

"We'll go for our ride after breakfast," he said to me. "If that works with your schedule—after cleanup, of course." He winked.

"I'll have to double-check," I said, tugging on the ties of my Kapp and raising my eyebrows at him.

"Jah, you do that," he said as he walked away with Storm trailing behind. At least he could still joke.

I laughed, but my stomach lurched. I didn't see any way out of riding.

"Leon showed me his artwork," Beatrice said. "He's really good."

I nodded, hoping she didn't think he'd shown it to her first.

"He really *isn't* your type," Beatrice said.

I stopped in the middle of the trail. "What do you mean?" I spoke in the quietest of voices.

She stopped too. "He's sensitive and kind. And compassionate."

I didn't answer for a long moment. She'd said the same thing before. Finally I said, "I think you're jealous."

"Jealous?"

"Of Leon. And me."

She grimaced. "Don't be ridiculous."

"He's the only boy you've ever shown any interest in." I decided to take another approach and lighten the conversation a little. "Unless you're interested in Ben."

At that, she bent over as if she were sick. "Please," she said, "don't insult me like that." She straightened up and stepped ahead of me, looking back over her shoulder as she spoke. "Besides, he's as determined to stay single as I am."

I put my hand on my hip.

She turned around and arched her eyebrows. "Maybe Ben will change his mind, but I'm serious about staying single—and if I wasn't, he would be the last man on earth I'd ever consider joining in holy matrimony. True, Leon would be higher on the list, but I'd never move to Montana—never, ever, ever. Not even if my life—"

Before she could say any more, we were interrupted by a man calling out, "Molly!" At first I hoped it was Leon—but it wasn't. Familiar, jah, but not welcome. It sounded like Phillip Eicher.

I gawked until the man stepped out of the shadows and waved. "I wondered if your group was camping here!"

I groaned. It *was* Phillip. With his girlfriend.

At the same moment, Leon approached from the opposite direction, still leading Storm.

"Hi," Beatrice called out to him, her voice more cheerful than it had been in months.

I turned back toward Phillip, who waved wildly and headed toward us. It wasn't as if we hadn't seen him recently—although I hadn't actually talked with him when he'd been on the porch with Mervin the day we came home from Mamm's doctor's appointment.

"How's your mother?" he asked.

"Fine," I answered, and then quickly said, "Phillip, I'd like you to meet Leon Fisher." Motioning toward Leon, who had reached us too, I said, "Leon, this is Phillip Eicher."

Leon raised his eyebrows as he took off his straw hat—I still had his cowboy hat in my tent—and extended his hand. Clearly he remembered Hannah talking about Phillip jilting me.

As they shook hands, Phillip said, "You're not from these parts, are you?"

"That's right," Leon answered.

Phillip was much broader in the shoulders than Leon, and although both men were well over six feet, Phillip was a couple of inches taller. But Leon was much more handsome, with his blue eyes and his wide, open smile.

"I'm from Montana . . ." Leon's voice trailed off as if he weren't sure whether he should say more or not.

"Just passing through?" Phillip asked in his forceful way.

"Staying . . . for a while," Leon responded.

For a while? That wasn't the answer I'd expected. But then Leon winked at me, his face reddening as he did. He was only joking.

I expected Phillip to introduce his girlfriend, but he didn't.

I stepped toward her and said, "I'm Molly. Molly Zook. And this is my sister, Beatrice."

"Nice to meet both of you." She turned toward me. "I've heard all about you."

"Oh?" I glanced at Phillip, who'd asked Leon how old Storm was.

"Jah, not just from Phillip. I have friends who met you at a party last year."

"Really?"

She smiled broadly, showing her straight teeth. Her dark hair and brows framed her face. Her hazel eyes sparkled.

"I'm not sure I caught your name," I said.

"Jessie. Jessie Berg."

"Oh." There were many Berg families in the Lancaster area.

Jessie pointed across the lake. "We're camping with my family and decided to go for a quick walk."

"Why don't you come visit our campsite?" Beatrice asked.

I nudged her.

"Oh, we shouldn't," Jessie answered. "My parents will wonder where we are."

Leon put his hat back on his head. "We'd be happy to have—"

"We'll come back after a while," Phillip said. "How's that?"

"Great," Beatrice said.

I cleared my throat. "Leon and I are going riding this morning. If we're not at the campsite when you return, it was nice to meet you, Jessie."

Leon smiled. Storm snickered. I took a step away from Phillip.

Jessie reached for his arm and tugged on it. "My family will wonder where we are."

I'd heard Phillip's girlfriend wasn't allowed to go to parties or hardly out of her parents' sight. I was surprised one of her siblings hadn't been sent along to chaperone.

Phillip cooperated, waving as they left.

"Seems like a nice guy," Leon said.

Beatrice giggled.

"Stop it," I said.

"Molly thought so too," she sputtered. "Once upon a time."

Phillip's dumping me had amused both Beatrice and Hannah. The last thing I wanted was for everyone to sit around the campfire, remembering that I used to be interested in Phillip.

I'd rather die. Or ride a horse. Finally, that plan had some appeal.

CHAPTER

14

After breakfast I retreated to the girls' tent, hoping for some solitude to build my courage, but Hannah followed me.

I saw my opportunity to talk with her. "Beatrice said you're upset with me."

Hannah shrugged. "You've been a little bossy, but I get it. You're stressed about your Mamm."

I pursed my lips. "No, I'm really not." The fact was, my emotions felt all over the place. As happy as could be about Leon. Still grieving over Dat. Fretful about Mamm.

Maybe it was impacting me more than I realized.

Hannah leaned away from me, as if to get a wider view. "That's good to know."

"I'm fine. It's everyone else who is acting weird."

"How's that?"

"Throwing pinecones. Not keeping to a schedule."

She shrugged. "We're on vacation."

"We still need to be organized."

She took a deep breath and seemed as if she had more to say, but nothing came out. She shrugged again.

Last night Leon had said he expected ruts in the road when it came to love. That was true when it came to friendship too.

"Molly?" Beatrice called out.

And families. "Just a minute," I yelled back.

"What else are you trying to organize?" Hannah asked as she knelt down on her sleeping bag.

"What do you mean?"

"You're meddling."

"How's that?"

"Signing Mervin and me up for cleanup together. Bossing him around. You're trying to get us back together."

I started to shake my head but then stopped. Of course that was what I was doing, but she didn't need to make it sound so sinister.

"I can win Mervin back on my own—thank you very much." Her voice grew louder and her face reddened. "I don't need your help. And I don't want your help."

"All right," I said, concerned by her outburst. I hoped it wasn't a sign that she was growing unstable again.

She stared at me, her face still red, her eyes dark and brooding.

I couldn't help but remember visiting her when she was an inpatient a couple of years ago. I'd felt so helpless. I'd wanted to help her, but I'd had no idea what to do.

After a couple of days at the clinic, she'd gone through counseling. It took a while, but she got well. Her counselor encouraged her to get enough rest, eat right, talk about her feelings, and exercise, saying those were the things that could help her stay healthy. And it seemed to work for Hannah.

Still, I couldn't help but fear she might fall into depression again.

Hannah took a deep breath, turned away from me, and began digging in her bag. "So you're going to go riding?"

"Jah."

"Are you sure?"

"It means a lot to Leon. I need to give it a try."

When I'd fallen off the horse all those years ago and vowed to never get back on, it seemed reasonable. We were buggy people—not cowboys or fancy English riders. Sure some people, like Hannah's family, rode, but it wasn't all that common. I'd never dreamt I'd want to get back on a horse, until now.

She dug in her bag some more, pulling out a sweatshirt, her pajamas, a bottle of lotion, and a pair of socks, dropping them all around her. Finally she pulled out a pair of pants. "Wear these," she said, holding them up. "Under your dress." She shot me a sarcastic smile. "That way you can stay modest when you fall off."

She tossed them to me. I snapped them out of the air, exhaling as I did.

"Remember to use your knees," she said. "And ride Lightning."

I nodded. That's what I planned to do.

"Don't let her know you're scared."

"I'm not," I said.

She shook her head. "I know you are."

There was no point in trying to convince her she was wrong—not when she was right.

She crossed her arms. "Leon would still be interested in you, even if you refused to ride."

"I want to do this. Face my fears. All of that."

Hannah crawled toward the flap, leaving her things strewn around, but then turned to face me. "Just don't get yourself injured again."

After she left, I zipped the tent, even though I was only pulling the pants on underneath my dress. I slumped down on my sleeping bag. I wasn't going to have Leon thinking that Hannah, with her love of horses and children, would be a better match than me.

Footsteps approached the tent. "Molly," Beatrice said. "Phillip and his girlfriend are headed this way."

"Denki." I wondered what Phillip had told Jessie about me. I sighed. Who was I kidding? Everyone knew what a fool I'd made of myself. Even Leon. I kicked off my flip-flops, pulled on the pants and my socks, and slipped on my tennis shoes, tying them tightly. Boots would have been better—but the tennis shoes would have to do.

I grabbed Leon's cowboy hat, unzipped the tent, and stepped through the open door, coming face-to-face with Phillip. I froze for a second but then said, "Hallo again."

He looked around. "I need to talk with you, Molly."

"Why?" I started toward the others.

He reached for my arm. "I just wanted to tell you I meant no harm, before."

I pulled away and hurried around him, sure he'd stop talking if only I could put some distance between us.

"Molly," he called out. "I was so hurt by Addie, I wasn't ready for a relationship again."

Mervin and Martin, who were standing around the fire, both turned to stare.

"I didn't mean to hurt you," he said.

Hannah and Jessie, who were standing by the stove, also turned toward us.

I kept walking, swinging my arms and Leon's hat as I did, my face growing warmer with each step.

"I know you're not used to people saying no to you." Phillip kept coming toward me.

"What?" I turned.

"People usually do what you want." Even though he was standing right next to me, his voice remained loud.

"I am going on a horseback ride," I whispered. "If for some

reason you feel compelled to talk with me about the past, we can. Later. In private. But not now."

I turned back around, this time to face Leon.

"Everything all right?" he asked.

"Jah," I said, rushing past him, bumping his arm with his hat. "Everything's fine."

But of course it wasn't. Phillip had shown up out of the blue. Mamm was having a CT scan in another hour. Our farm might not be ours for much longer. Hannah and Beatrice were both miffed with me. Mervin wouldn't leave me alone and wasn't falling back in love with Hannah. Even if he did, making me free to court Leon, I still had to figure out how to increase our revenue to save the farm—because increasing our acreage by using the Mosiers' fields wouldn't be an option.

But more immediate than all that, I was off to ride a horse. One of those humongous equestrian beasts that I'd sworn I'd never be caught dead on again.

"Molly!" Phillip caught up with me.

I turned around, I was sure with a frantic look on my face. Jessie had started toward Phillip, weaving her way around the lawn chairs spread around the fire. "Phil," she called out, "how about a cup of coffee?"

In that moment, although I couldn't say I liked her, I could say I appreciated her. She was young, but she was no doubt astute—far more than Phillip Eicher would ever be.

I continued walking as fast as I could, but Leon caught up with me. "What was that about?" he asked.

"Nothing."

"I'd say it was something."

Having to explain it all would only worsen the humiliation. What had Phillip said? That I wasn't used to people telling me no?

"Molly." Leon caught my arm. "How long did you and Phillip court?"

"Not long," I answered.

"Were you serious about him?"

I shook my head.

"But he broke up with you?"

I ducked my head and walked faster. "Let's talk about this later," I said, glancing over my shoulder. Cate, Pete, and Robbie had come out of their tent and were watching us, along with everyone else.

As we neared the horses, I noticed they were already saddled.

"Can we walk them up the trail a ways?" I couldn't bear to have everyone watch me struggle up to the saddle.

"Sure," Leon said. "We can walk them all the way to the meadow if you'd like."

"Denki," I said, pulling his hat on my head.

Leon opened the makeshift gate and told me to wait and then led both horses out of the fence. I fell into step with him as we made our way to the trailhead. I didn't dare look back. I could imagine all of them sitting around talking about me—but at least Leon wouldn't be around to hear it. When the trail narrowed, I took the lead.

"Is now later enough?" he asked.

"For?" I was blond, jah, but I didn't play dumb—except for now.

"To tell me about Phillip."

"Oh," I answered. But I didn't say anything else.

The trail widened and Leon stepped to my side. "I told you about the girl I courted in Montana," he said.

I didn't answer.

"Hannah mentioned Phillip that night at the singing and

later too, but I didn't follow everything she said. Was he part of your group?"

I shook my head. "I only saw him at singings. I thought I had feelings for him." And told him so once.

"But he didn't for you?"

"Ach, do you have to be so blunt?" I tried to laugh but couldn't. My pride stopped me.

"Do you still have feelings for him?" Leon's voice was filled with concern.

"Of course not," I answered. But I wasn't sure he believed me.

A small creature rustled in the undergrowth, and Storm stepped backward. Leon stopped a moment, coaxing the horse to continue. I marched ahead, leaving Leon behind, dumbfounded at how everything had changed since last night. The enchantment was gone.

Jah, it hurt to have him questioning me like that, but it hurt even more to know Hannah had been talking about me behind my back. It seemed to me as if Leon and Hannah had a lot of time on their hands—to talk about me.

Leon must have stopped for something else concerning the horses, because by the time I reached the meadow, I couldn't see him on the trail. I sat down on the rock in the middle of the meadow, waiting, looking up at the sky. The sun had burned away the gray clouds from earlier. The day promised to be warm—at least for the mountains. In a few minutes I heard the horses and then Leon whistling, sounding as if he didn't have a care in the world.

"Ready to ride?" he called out as he rounded the corner. He flashed that sweet smile. My heart warmed a little. Then it began to thaw. Maybe he hadn't been judging me.

I stood and walked toward him, meeting them at the edge of the trail. Leon put his arm around me and pulled me close. "You're right," he said. "None of this is a big deal. I was just trying to understand."

The weight of his arm across my shoulders comforted me.

"As far as the horses, just remember they're just a bunch of nerves connected to a relatively small brain. Sure, they're smarter than cows, but that's not saying a lot. Keep in mind, horses don't act out on purpose. They just haven't learned how to cope yet. It's our job to help them learn they can trust us, that we have their best interests in mind."

I smiled. Actually, I had my best interests in mind, but I didn't need to tell Leon that.

"Which horse do you want to ride?" he asked.

"Lightning." I tipped back the cowboy hat and looked into his eyes.

"Good choice." He led Lightning forward and handed me the reins. "Do you need some help?"

I shook my head as I eyed the stirrups, grateful Hannah had given me the pants to wear. I lifted my skirt to my thighs, grabbed the saddle horn with my hand that held the reins, stepped into the stirrup, hoisted myself up, and swung my other leg over the horse.

"Great!" Leon beamed at me, obviously encouraged that I could at least get on a horse.

I smiled back as I settled into the saddle. Maybe I hadn't forgotten everything I'd learned from the one time I'd ridden with Hannah way back when.

With no visible effort, Leon landed in the saddle on Storm. We rode side by side. I jostled more than I should have, I knew, but it wasn't bad. I took a few deep breaths, willing myself to relax. And I did, a little.

The brilliance of the morning warmed me. The feel of the horse—her muscles flexing with each step, her even breathing, the thud of her hooves—actually brought me a small measure of comfort.

"Having fun?" Leon rode as naturally as he breathed, one hand on the horn, turned toward me.

I didn't actually respond, but my jostling up and down probably looked like an affirmative nod.

As we left the meadow the trees grew thick again, and Leon led the way. Lightning stopped once, drifting toward the grass in the underbrush. I had a moment of panic, thinking I might need to call out to Leon for help, but pulling on the reins, up and to the left, I got her going again.

On we went. The rhythm of Lightning's steps lulled me further away from panic. A goldfinch sang from high in the branches of a tree. A fern grown halfway over the path caused Lightning to shy a little, but I assured her she was all right and she continued on.

Grateful I'd been brave enough to face my fears, I urged the horse to go faster. Leon and Storm had gotten ahead of us. Lightning complied. The increased bouncing brought a new measure of anxiety, but I squeezed my knees together more and settled down. In a few minutes, the feeling of harmony returned.

The slope of the trail increased, and I slid back in the saddle, causing me to grow tense again, but the back of the saddle stopped me. I exhaled. I was fine.

Leon waited for me at the summit of the hill. When I reached him, he pointed ahead, over a plateau of grassland. "See the willows in the distance?"

I nodded.

"There's probably a creek. Let's ride to there. Then we'll turn back." Storm took off at a trot, and Lightning followed, with no prodding from me. Soon both were galloping. My only consolation to my body being jerked up and down was that Leon couldn't see me. In no time we reached the willows, and he slid off Storm, again without any effort, and then took Lightning's reins from me, holding them as I struggled down.

I took a step away from the horse. I'd definitely be sore tomorrow, probably even today. Leon led the horses down to the creek. I stayed on the bank and watched the horses drink. When they were done, Leon pulled three apples from his saddlebag. He gave one to each of the horses and then led them back up the bank, where he gave the third apple to me.

"What about you?" I asked.

"I thought we'd share."

I took a bite and handed it back to him.

He took a bite, chewed, swallowed, and then said, "You're doing really well. I can't believe it's been years since you've ridden." He handed the apple back to me.

It had been thirteen years, to be exact. "I'm surprised it stayed with me." I took a bite of apple right next to where his mouth had been. I couldn't help but be pleased with myself, even though I shouldn't have been.

We shared the apple back and forth until it was gone. I fed the core to Lightning and giggled at the feel of her mouth against my palm.

Leon took my hand.

"I'm so glad you're not going back to Montana," I said, tipping my face toward his, expecting a kiss.

"Whoa," he said, stepping backward. "Why wouldn't I go back to Montana?"

"Why would you? If . . . I mean . . . if you had the opportunity—"

"To stay in Lancaster?" His voice fell flat.

I nodded. Who wouldn't want to stay in Lancaster? My heart began to race even faster.

He continued, "My job with Owen is temporary. He only hired me to train a select group of horses."

"But you could get another job," I said. "You said you'd prefer to stay in Lancaster County."

"I don't remember saying that." He gazed down at me, his eyes intent. "I love Montana. It's home. I'm far more comfortable there than . . . in Lancaster." He looked west as he spoke.

I shook my head. "That night, when we were under the willow, when I said I felt responsible to care for Bea and Mamm—"

"And you said your farm is failing."

"Jah, which means I need to stay in Lancaster. How else can I save our farm and provide for my family?"

He stepped away from me and took off his hat, swiping his hand through his damp hair. "I thought you could sell your farm and your Mamm and Bea could come with us, to Montana— if . . . that's how things worked out."

I may have jutted out my lower lip a little at that.

Neither of us spoke for a long, long moment.

Finally, Leon said, tenderly, his voice low, "Miss Molly, we can trust God to lead us. It's not something we need to figure out right now."

I felt my eyes widen, but somehow I managed to control my tongue. I'd trust God to change Leon's mind—that was for sure. "Jah, let's give it some time," I managed to say. Turning toward the horses, I said, "We should head back."

In a daze, I managed to get myself back onto Lightning. I was in good shape from all the physical work I did, but still my legs were shaking. I waited for Leon to lead and then I blindly followed. By the time we reached the forest again, I was choking on my tears, thankful Leon couldn't see me. *Why, God? Why did you finally bring along someone like Leon only to have him want to go back to Montana? Please make him want to stay in Lancaster.* I prayed that last part over and over, silently.

By the time we reached the meadow, Storm had picked up speed. Lightning followed, this time keeping up. My fear of riding horses had been replaced by a new fear. *Montana.*

There was no way I, let alone Beatrice and Mamm, could tolerate living so far from Lancaster.

I finally saw things from Mamm's perspective. I felt her grief. No wonder she'd been opposed to my courting Leon. I thought of her now, in the tube of the CT scan, holding perfectly still, thinking about me, whether I'd choose Mervin or Leon, Lancaster County or Montana. She hadn't been behaving like a foolish old woman. Her concern was well founded. I'd been the ignorant fool, living in denial, seeing the situation the way I wanted it to be.

In my dazed state, I thought the creature rushing toward us was a deer, even though I knew that was absurd. It wasn't until the fawn-colored Great Dane barked that I realized what it was. Lightning reared and then landed hard as I screamed. Leon yelled at the dog as he pulled back on Storm's reins. Storm sidestepped.

Lightning reared a second time. This time I was too terrified to scream.

The dog barked again. Lightning stepped off the trail as she landed, hitting a rock. The dog barked a third time. Lightning began to buck, sending me forward in the saddle. I screamed again.

Leon spun around on Storm. "Pull back on the reins!"

I did, as I hard as I could, which forced Lightning to stop bucking, but made her rear. I squeezed my knees together, doing my best to stay on the horse, as I slid back on the saddle, sure I was going to go over the back.

The dog ran up the trail.

Lightning spun around and then bucked again.

The dog was gone, but the horse didn't stop. I managed to get one foot out of the stirrup, then the other. I pulled on the reins sharply, stopping the bucking once again, but like before, she reared. I grabbed the horn, dropped the reins, slid my left leg over the saddle, and jumped for my life, landing to the side of the trail—first on my feet, but then I fell backward, onto my behind. Leon's hat flew off my head.

By then Lightning was pointed the way we'd come. She took off, in the opposite direction of the dog, bucking as she fled.

Leon jumped off Storm to my side. "Are you all right?"

I nodded my head, unable to speak, as I struggled to a sitting position and then to my knees. But I was shaking so badly I fell back down.

"Does anything hurt?"

I shook my head.

"Wait here then," he said, jumping back on Storm and taking off after Lightning.

I don't know how long I stayed there, all alone, but finally I struggled to my feet, still trembling. I shook each arm. Kicked each leg. I truly seemed unhurt except for my sore backside. I rubbed it, pulling down my dress as I did, thankful again for Hannah's pants. Then I rubbed my hands together, brushing off the dirt and little pebbles.

What made me think I could ride a horse? At least this time I hadn't broken my arm. But I could have. Or my head.

And all Leon was concerned about was the horse. I grabbed his hat and turned toward the camp. There was no reason for me to wait. I continued on down the trail.

I hoped that when I limped into camp no one would be there. But as I neared, I knew I'd be faced with yet another challenge for the day. They were all sitting around the now-extinguished fire, laughing—and to make matters worse, Phillip and Jessie were still there.

Hannah stood holding Robbie, waltzing around with him. The little boy waved his arms. Mervin beckoned the baby to him, but Robbie clung to Hannah. She grinned at Mervin, and he stepped closer to her, taking her arm. They took a couple of steps together, with the baby between them. Clearly, Mervin was transferring his affection from me to Hannah.

She pulled away from Mervin and he stepped after her.

Everyone laughed even more. At least that part of my plan was working. I tossed Leon's hat into the trailer and continued on to face my next ordeal.

Hannah froze when she saw me, and the laughter stopped. "Molly! What happened?"

"Lightning bucked me off," I said.

Her eyes widened. "Where's Leon?"

"Going after Lightning."

"On foot?"

"No, on Storm."

The volume of her voice increased. "Why didn't you stay to help him?"

I wanted to laugh. "How could I help him?"

Hannah stepped toward Cate and slipped Robbie into his aunt's arms. "Which trail were you on?"

I pointed to the one at the end of the road.

Hannah took off running right past me, a crazed look in her eyes, as Mervin called after her. "Want me to come along?"

"No," she called back. I watched until she was out of sight. Before, when she'd grown unstable, she'd shut down. She wasn't doing that now. It seemed to be the opposite, as if she were winding up.

Then I reeled back around to the others. "It's not like she's going to be able to do anything to help."

"Two sets of hands are a good idea," Martin said.

"Jah. That Lightning has to be worth a lot of money," Mervin added, his voice harsh.

"Come sit down," Cate said.

"I need to wash up," I responded.

But before I took more than a step, Beatrice said, "We were just talking about you."

I grimaced.

"Jah." Phillip smiled.

I could imagine what he'd been saying. When I spent time with him, he'd talked about Addie obsessively. When he and Addie had been courting, he'd gone on and on about the farm he hoped to buy, which he never did. It wouldn't surprise me if I was the topic of his obsessive talking now.

Jessie rose to her feet, her face red.

Phillip leaned back in the lawn chair, looking as if he were about to tip over.

I headed to the wash station. When I was done I went to the tent. After I changed my clothes, I started to sit down on my sleeping bag, but that hurt, so I reclined on my side.

There was more laughter from the group around the campfire as tears stung my eyes. I'd never felt so alone in all my life.

Far worse than Lightning bucking me off was knowing that Leon intended to go back to Montana.

Why hadn't he made that clear before I'd fallen in love with him? He'd said true love wasn't smooth, but I hadn't expected this. But the truth was I was in love with him. I couldn't stop how I felt—not any more than I could fathom moving to Montana.

Hannah's and Leon's voices woke me. The tent had grown hot as the sun rose to midday. I rolled off my sleeping bag. I hadn't meant to fall asleep.

Leon asked, "Where is she?"

"Who?" Mervin asked and then laughed. Maybe that part of my plan was working. But his insincerity stung a little.

Cate's voice held a hint of exasperation. "She's in her tent."

I stood, willing myself to be brave. It wasn't as if Leon had chosen the horse over me—not really. He'd asked if I was all right before he took off. And Mervin was correct. Lightning was worth a lot of money—and Leon was responsible for her.

And I was sure he hadn't purposely misled me about Montana. He just didn't understand why I'd never be able to go.

I unzipped the door and climbed out, determined to put on a positive front. "Here I am."

Leon was already halfway to me. "Are you okay?"

I nodded.

"Thank goodness Hannah came along," he said. "I had no idea where you went."

"I'm sorry," I said. "I didn't know how long you'd be."

"It didn't take me long to stop Lightning. But then I searched and searched for you."

I was touched with his concern. I hadn't thought what it would be like for him to return and have me gone.

He jerked his thumb toward the horses. "You need to get back on," he said. "The sooner the better."

I shook my head. Jah, I loved him, but I wasn't crazy.

"You were doing so well. That was a fluke to have the dog come through like that. Lightning had a relapse is all. Honestly."

"It's time to get dinner started," I said.

"If I remember right, it's Ben and Beatrice's turn."

I frowned.

He reached for my hand. Over his shoulder I could see everyone watching us, including Phillip and Jessie, who obviously had nowhere better to be. At least for once Phillip wasn't talking.

"Come down to the horses," Leon said. "It will be good for you—and Lightning."

"All right."

I followed him, only to find Hannah brushing Lightning in the little corral.

"Going to get back on?" Hannah asked. She seemed fine now. Maybe her crazed look was simply from worry over the horse.

I shook my head.

Hannah gave a little smirk. I bristled. Maybe she wasn't fine.

"Don't you think Molly should?" Leon said to Hannah.

"Oh jah, sure," she answered. "But it took her all these years since the last time she fell off. Don't get your hopes up."

I wanted to tell Hannah not to talk in front of me that way, but I was afraid of sounding catty in front of Leon. And I didn't want to set her off again. Instead I reached out to stroke Lightning's neck, but the horse sidestepped, bumping against Hannah, who pushed back.

I attempted to stroke the horse again, more tentatively, but this time she stepped backward.

Hannah popped up from beside the horse. "Could you wait until I'm done?"

"Of course," I answered, leaving the corral quickly and heading back to the camp. I'd get the meal started—that was something I could do.

"Build the fire up," I said to Ben as I pulled the bratwurst out of the first ice chest. "Everyone can do their own grilling." We'd brought kraut and pickled beets, and I would put out the leftover veggies from the night before too. "Come on, Beatrice."

"You'd better hurry up," Ben said to her. "If you don't work you don't eat."

"Guess you'll go hungry today," she said with a smirk. "Oh, wait, you should be nearly starved by now."

He patted his nonexistent belly and said, "Vacations don't count."

Bea stood and said to Ben, "Well, we're in charge of this meal so you'd better reconsider."

He stood and began poking at the fire to stir up a spark as Bea put her hands on her hips and turned to me. "You need to go sit down."

"Ach, Beatrice . . ."

"We don't need your help." She started toward the ice chests.

"Come on," Cate called out to me, patting the chair beside her.

I hesitated a moment but then complied, calling over my shoulder, "Scrub the potatoes and wrap them in the foil—then put them in the coals." We used to do that when we camped as children.

Beatrice put her hands over her ears and mouthed, "*I know how to fix potatoes!*"

She might think she knew, but chances were she wouldn't do

it right. I settled down next to Cate. Robbie sat on her lap and didn't turn toward me.

"Why don't you go help Hannah," I said to Mervin. Maybe Leon would come back then.

Apparently Mervin was so used to taking orders from me on the farm that he obeyed. Or perhaps the chance to spend time with Hannah was all the motivation he needed.

Phillip sat on the other side of the fire with Jessie. She stood and took his hand and said, probably because of me, "We should get going."

"Come around to our campsite after lunch," Phillip said. "It's a nice walk around the lake."

"Jah," Jessie said. "I'd like to introduce all of you to my family."

"We'd like that," Beatrice said from where she stood behind the picnic table. I imagined she was being unusually friendly, for her, just to annoy me.

"We were planning to take a hike," Martin said.

"We were?" I leaned forward in my chair.

"Ach, it's true it's not on the schedule, but I think we can pencil it in." Martin stood quickly and walked with Phillip and Jessie to the edge of the camp.

I hadn't meant it as a challenge. I just hadn't heard the plan. They headed over to where Mervin, Hannah, and Leon were tending the horses.

I slumped farther down in my chair.

"Bad day?" Cate asked.

I nodded.

"I've had a few of those," she said, patting my shoulder. "It'll get better."

Ben knelt down to build the fire up. Robbie squirmed to get down.

"I'll take him," Pete said as he reached for the little one, swung him onto his shoulders, and then walked away from the circle of chairs.

Beatrice yelped. She'd dropped the sausages in the dirt. I started to stand, but Cate grabbed my hand. "She'll figure it out. You made that schedule for a reason. Right?"

I leaned back. I actually wasn't sure why I'd made that schedule. I couldn't sit still. It didn't feel natural. I started to stand, to go get the box of Dat's shirts to begin cutting up for the quilt for Bea, but Cate put her hand on my arm and pulled me back down.

"Relax," she said. "This is supposed to be a vacation."

Ben poured something on the fire—kerosene, probably—and it burst into flames. Cate and I scooted our chairs back. Then Ben strolled over to help Beatrice, but soon they were bickering as if they were still in school together.

I couldn't stand it any longer. Rather than humiliate Beatrice by yelling across the campsite, I stood and marched over to them. "Stop it," I whispered.

"What?" Beatrice asked, a dumbfounded look on her face.

"We were just teasing each other," Ben said.

"Really? That's not what it sounded like."

"Molly." It was Cate, patting my chair.

I returned. "Isn't their bickering getting on your nerves?"

Cate smiled. "They haven't figured out how to communicate with each other yet," she said. "But they're working on it."

"Communicate what?"

She smiled, knowingly.

I leaned forward and turned toward her, whispering, "You think they *like* each other?"

"Jah."

"Stop!" Ben put his hands over his ears, turning away from

Beatrice. "You talk faster than"—he nodded toward the trailer—
"a runaway horse."

Cate laughed. "Isn't it obvious?"

"At least I make sense," Beatrice said. "Robbie has a better
vocabulary than you do."

"Ouch," Ben said, staggering backward. Beatrice gave him
a two-handed push, and he fell against the table.

I couldn't help but smile. "Maybe you're right."

"Of course I am," Cate answered. "Beatrice reminds me of
me. She'll come around. So will Ben. In the meantime, try to
stay out of it."

That's easier said than done, I thought as I tried to sit still.
In another minute, though, I was up gathering roasting sticks
from the night before and began burning the marshmallow off
of them so they'd be ready for the sausages. Martin came back
from walking Phillip and Jessie to the trail that wound around
the lake, but then he wandered down to the horses.

Pete was down there too, with Robbie, letting him run around
the outside of the corral. Lightning stuck her nose over the
railing and sniffed the little boy, who let out a wild laugh. The
horse wasn't spooked at all by the outburst.

After a few minutes, Cate retreated to her tent, probably to
read a book. Beatrice and Ben were now arguing about what
sausages were made from.

Beatrice pointed at the meat. "Well, these came straight from
our butcher."

"That doesn't mean it doesn't have all sorts of stuff in it,"
Ben said.

"But it's all from our pig. It's not like it's from some animal
we didn't know. Stop being so persnickety."

Ben rolled his eyes and retreated to the fire. Beatrice followed
him. I drifted over to the kitchen table and finished putting

lunch together, calling everyone to gather around when I'd
finished.

After lunch, I knew Leon and I needed to talk things through,
so I told him I'd stay with him and the horses while the others
walked around the lake.

"And go for another ride?" he asked.

I shook my head.

"I'm going to stay and read a book," Cate said. "I'll keep an
eye on the horses."

"Oh no," I said. "We don't expect you to do that." The
thought of Cate chasing the horses through the campground
was humorous—but not if it really happened.

"No, let's go with the others," Leon said.

Maybe he didn't want to talk. Or be alone with me.

He started down to the trailer and I followed. "They'll be fine.
As long as someone's here—just in case a passerby got the wild
idea to ride them or something." When we reached the horses,
Leon checked the leads that were tied to the trailer. "Then we
can ride again afterward."

"About that," I said. "I really don't—"

Beatrice, her journal in her hand, called out from the path
to the lake. "Are you two coming or not?"

"Coming!" I called out.

When we reached the others, Robbie held a stick in his hand,
waving it around as he walked. No one seemed concerned about it.

"Shouldn't he stay and take a nap?" I asked Pete.

"He'll take one when we get back," he said. "A walk will
help wear him out."

Ben and Martin led the way, with Beatrice trailing behind
them, carrying her notebook. An Englisch couple ahead on

the beach turned to stare at us for a moment and then returned to talking. A dog, not the one responsible for my flight off the horse—this one was small and yippy—darted out toward us. A woman sitting on a picnic table in the trees called him back.

Robbie trailed behind, waving his stick around and around. Pete and Hannah stayed back with him. Mervin caught up with Leon and me, gluing himself to my side. I turned around, taking a few steps backward. Perhaps I'd gotten my hopes up too soon. "Hannah is so good with Robbie," I said. "Look at her." Both Leon and Mervin turned around.

She was holding the little boy's hand, the one not clinging to the stick, and then scooped him up into her arms. Robbie waved the stick our way. Hannah started reciting, "'Ring around the rosie,'" spinning him around as she did. Somehow she managed to get the stick out of his hand and launched it away without him noticing. Then she smiled at him, her dimples flashing, which sent him into peels of laughter.

She started chanting the nursery rhyme again, this time louder, as if soliciting attention. It worked.

Mervin stopped and waited for them. Robbie fell backwards, secure in Hannah's arms, his head now upside down, and laughed some more. She laughed, loudly, with him.

Leon and I continued. I glanced over my shoulder. Robbie was walking now with Mervin holding one hand and Hannah the other, talking over the little boy's head as they strolled along. I smiled. My plan seemed to be working after all. But Hannah concerned me. She seemed on edge. And growing more so.

By the time we reached the halfway point, Robbie had started to fuss. I turned around again. I hoped Pete would take him back for a nap, but he trailed behind, gazing out over the lake at a canoe, with two figures—one large and one small—wearing orange life jackets, heading toward the shore opposite ours.

Hannah scooped Robbie up again, but he started to cry anyway.

"Ach, poor little guy," Leon said, stopping. "He's probably missing his Mamm." I stopped too. When Hannah and Mervin caught up with us, Leon put out his hands for Robbie, who fell into them. Leon put the tyke on his shoulders, holding him firmly around the ankles. Hannah started jogging alongside them, making faces at Robbie as she did. Leon began trotting, following Hannah. Mervin took off after both of them, leaving me behind. Robbie looked over his shoulder at me for a moment, his curly hair a mop atop his head, his mouth stretched in a wide grin.

In our communities, children were valued but not catered to. Except, apparently, Robbie.

I increased my pace, just enough to catch up with Beatrice, who was jotting something down in her journal as she walked. After a moment she looked up, smiled at the sight of the group now galloping in front of us, and then turned toward me. "Having fun?"

I took a deep breath. "Jah . . ."

"I keep thinking about Mamm," she said. "The test is over, right?"

I nodded.

"Does your phone work out here?"

I shook my head. I didn't have service so I'd turned my phone off. "They won't know anything yet anyway."

Beatrice said, a little sharply, "I know that." She opened her journal again and jotted something down.

She and I walked in silence, rounding the corner of the lake. To our right were the campsites where we'd stayed as children. The canoe Pete had been watching neared the dock we used to fish off with our Dat long ago. A man in a life vest climbed out,

225

tied the canoe to the dock, and then reached down and lifted a girl out. The child was at least seven or eight—much too old to be carried.

Another man, Phillip, I was sure, walked from one of the campsites toward them. The two men spoke for a moment, and then Phillip reached down into the canoe, retrieved the paddles, and followed the man and girl. I guessed she was Jessie's sister and that something was wrong with her.

We continued on. When we arrived at the edge of their camp, Jessie called out a welcome to us and invited us to sit around their fire. The little girl now sat in a wheelchair. Her head was small and tilted to the side. She had the same dark hair as Jessie. Her left hand was rigid and the rest of her seemed stiff too, except for her smile. Her whole face lit up at the sight of guests.

Jessie introduced us to her parents, Bill and Becky Berg, and then to her siblings—eight in all, five brothers and three sisters. Her parents looked too young to have so many, especially one as old as Jessie, who was the firstborn. The youngest, also a girl, was probably two or so. She pointed to Robbie, who ducked behind Pete's leg and laughed.

"Molly's the girl I was talking about," Jessie told her parents. "The one who used to be friends with Phillip." *Friends*. The word was definitely coded.

"Oh," her mother said. "I see." She sized me up and then looked at Jessie. As far as looks, her daughter had me beat by a long shot. As far as capturing Phillip's fancy, she'd won there too. And I was happy about that, truly. So why did it all feel so awkward?

I was determined not to let it bother me and instead tried to recall all of the kids' names—which I couldn't, but I did register the name of the girl in the chair. *Bella*. I knew it meant beautiful.

I tried not to stare. Her mouth moved as if she were trying to say something. She probably had a metabolic disorder—a genetic condition, that was hereditary and unfortunately all too common among us Plain people. I couldn't help but wonder what Phillip, with his need for perfection, thought of the possibility of having a disabled child. True, most of us were raised to accept everyone—but I thought it would be a bigger challenge for Phillip than for most.

Jessie stepped to her sister's side and leaned close. "Jah," Jessie said. "They're staying for a while." Then she undid the brakes on the wheelchair and pushed Bella between two lawn chairs.

"How about some lemonade?" Jessie's Mamm, who seriously looked young enough to be the big sister of the family, grabbed a stack of plastic cups and stepped toward an insulated jug. She had the same dark hair as her daughters, and the same dark brows and striking hazel eyes.

Jessie passed out the lemonade to all of us guests first and then to her family members. She handed Phillip a cup with a lid. He gave her a questioning look and she nodded toward Bella. Phillip sat beside the girl and helped her tip the cup. She gave him a wide smile after she swallowed, and he patted her arm, a little awkwardly, as if he didn't quite know how to behave. So instead he started to talk, describing Bill Berg's farm in detail. It seemed the family was quite wealthy. Jessie gave him a wilting look, but Phillip kept on talking. Finally she said, "Phil, no one wants to hear about our farm."

"Sure they do," Phillip said.

She shook her head and said, "So what are your plans for the rest of the afternoon?"

Martin mentioned fishing, but as he spoke Robbie grew fussy again. Pete said he'd head back with him. Mervin, Hannah, and Leon volunteered to go too. I glanced at Bea. She was sitting next to Jessie, seemingly enjoying herself for once. Martin and Ben looked awfully comfortable too.

"I'll head back to camp also," I said.

"Me too," Beatrice said, jumping to her feet, holding up her book. "I want to get some writing done."

We thanked the Bergs, leaving Ben and Martin to weather another of Phillip's stories, this one about the farm he worked on, and left quickly.

Robbie started out in Pete's arms but soon ended up in Hannah's. Leon and Mervin fell in behind her.

I walked a few steps back, my muscles stiffening more.

"You know . . ." Beatrice said, catching up with me. I expected some sort of commentary about Leon. Instead she said, "You're really lucky Phillip broke up with you."

"Ach," I whispered. "I don't need your thoughts on this. Especially not now."

"No really. He's the kind of man you were bound to marry. Someone shallow and full of himself. You're lucky he was in such a sorry state after Addie dumped him—otherwise you two would probably be married by now."

I shook my head and slowed down even more, not wanting the others, especially Leon, to hear Beatrice. "I have no idea what you mean."

"Phillip never would have appreciated the real you—I don't know if you would have even been able to be the real you. It would have been all about him. You need someone as strong as you are—but caring. Someone who will rein you in." She laughed at her joke, drawing both Leon's and Mervin's attention.

But not for long. In a split second they'd both migrated to Hannah's side as she put a sleeping Robbie over her shoulder with the grace of a woman who loved children.

"Actually, the issue at hand may no longer be who will rein

you in. . . ." She looked from me to Leon to Hannah and nodded her head in a knowing way. "And to think I thought I might
have a chance with him."

"What does that mean?" I practically hissed.

But she skipped ahead, away from me without answering. I
was sure she never really thought she had a chance with Leon.
It was more of a competitive reaction toward me.

However, I could see why she thought Hannah had a chance
with him.

I fell even farther behind, fighting off the despair growing
inside of me.

Leon didn't ask me to ride again that day. He took Storm up
the trail while Hannah and Mervin led Lightning around the
campground, talking as they did. I was horrified when Hannah
asked Cate if she could give Robbie a ride on Lightning, fearing
a dog might come tearing through camp. "I'll put him in front
of me," she said.

Cate actually seemed to consider it but then said, "No, not this
trip. Let's wait until he's older. Or Betsy and Levi are around."

The afternoon air hung warm and heavy. I pulled the box of
Dat's shirts from our tent and took it to the picnic table, pulling
out the diamond pattern and my scissors. The others came and
went, but no one asked me what I was up to. I felt melancholy
thinking about Dat as I cut the fabric, about our camping trips
all those years ago, and then about Leon off riding Storm by
himself. If only I were braver.

Before it was time to start supper, I put the diamonds I'd cut
on top of the shirts and then stowed the box away in the tent.

After bean and bacon soup and corn bread for supper, prepared by me—all alone, since Leon didn't return until just before

we ate—Martin and Ben went fishing while the rest of us sat around the fire. The weather had cooled some, and the heat of the fire felt good. Leon and I sat side by side on a stump. I'm not sure which one of us scooted over—maybe both of us—but soon our legs were touching. All was well. I'd been foolish to think otherwise.

Except for the question of Montana . . .

Mervin glowered at me for a moment, but then turned toward Hannah. As darkness fell, though, the horses started stomping around, and Leon said it was time for him to turn in.

He leaned toward me, his shoulder touching mine, and looked me in the eyes. "See you in the morning."

I nodded. After he left I decided to go to bed too, and Cate, Pete, and Robbie soon followed. The others, however, stayed up and laughed long into the night.

Consequently, the others slept in the next morning. This time I didn't mind. I enjoyed the time around the campfire drinking coffee with Pete and Leon while Cate tended to Robbie.

I'd put Mervin and Hannah down on the chart for break-fast—which meant we ended up eating late.

Afterward, we all walked around the lake except for Cate, who stayed back to read, and Martin, who went fishing. The others stopped in and said hello to Phillip and Jessie, but I kept on walk-ing. The day was already warmer than the day before and muggy.

I waited for the others to catch up at a trailhead and we continued on, walking away from the lake and getting in a good hike before it was time to go back and start the noon meal. But when we arrived back at camp, Cate had everything out for sandwiches.

After lunch I headed over to the horses, and Leon. I still

wasn't going to ride, but I did want to try to pet Lightning again. But when I arrived, Hannah was already there, putting a saddle on Lightning.

"Leon said you're going riding again," she said, looking up at me, flashing her cute dimples. "I told him I'd saddle Lightning for you."

I shook my head.

"Oh, come on," she said. "It will be good for you." She bent down to fasten the saddle.

I squatted, peering at her from under the horse, and lowered my voice. "Hannah, please. I can't."

She popped back up. "Then I'll go." Her dimples flashed.

I stood. That wasn't exactly what I wanted.

Leon's deep voice came from the other side of the trailer. "Molly, the sooner you get back on the better."

Hannah met my gaze and then, speaking about me again, said, "She's too sore." Then she mouthed *"Right?"* to me.

I shrugged. I actually hadn't felt that bad, but now that she mentioned it . . .

She whispered, "Do you mind if I go?"

Of course I minded! But I answered, "No. Not at all."

I headed around the trailer to Leon. He was holding Storm's reins in his hands, looking into the horse's eyes. "Later then?" he asked.

I nodded. Although I had no idea when that would be. "Anything I can do to help?" I kept my voice cheery.

"No," he answered. "We might be gone awhile."

I felt my eyes narrow—I forced them wide. I wasn't going to be clingy—it was just a ride. They probably rode together all the time back at Paradise Stables.

"Well, have fun." I turned away from Leon. "I'll see you when you get back."

Perhaps Leon acknowledged what I said, but I didn't hear him. I stepped around the trailer. Hannah was standing with her nose to Lightning's. Both of them had their eyes closed, as if they were kissing. If I were allowed a camera, I'd have taken a photo. If I knew how to draw, I would have gone back to my tent to sketch it. But as it was, I blinked, committing the image to memory. As much as Hannah was driving me crazy at the moment, she was still my best friend.

And she loved horses.

Something I never would.

But that didn't mean I'd lose Leon to her, did it?

Hannah stepped into the trailer for a moment and came back out wearing Leon's cowboy hat. The gall of her! I willed myself not to react. Then she stepped to the side of Lightning and hoisted herself up in one graceful movement. She looked as if she were the queen of the world on top of Lightning, who, perhaps because of Hannah's confidence, held her head high.

I marched around the trailer, where I watched her and Leon meet up as they headed toward the trail. Hannah nodded toward Leon, her profile toward me, her dimple flashing as she smiled. She was flirting with him, I was sure. He smiled back, causing my heart to fall, and then they took off at a trot in unison. Neither jostled in their saddles. Both held their horse's reins in a relaxed manner. Lightning and Storm both seemed at ease—and eager to get going.

"How come you're not riding with him?" Mervin poked my arm.

"I'm a little sore," I answered.

"So?"

"Leon wanted to go on a long ride."

"Great," Mervin groaned. "Just when I come to my senses, Hannah rides off with the cowboy—someone who shares her interests, someone much taller than me." He pulled his sunglasses from atop his head and put them on his face. "Someone much better looking."

"That's not true," I said, even though it was.

He sighed. "They make a good couple. She's so beautiful. He's so handsome."

I nudged him. "So you're over me, then?" I felt relieved, but also a bit rejected.

"Jah," he answered, pushing his glasses up on his nose. "Sorry about that. I lost my senses for a time. But being with Hannah, seeing her with Robbie, knowing what a great Mamm she'll be . . ." He shrugged. "I don't know what I was thinking to stop courting her."

I nodded and then swallowed hard. "You two are sweet together."

"Denki," he said. "And doubly so for being so understanding. Something will work out with your farm, right?"

I smiled.

"Ivan buying it wouldn't be so bad," Mervin said. "Maybe he'll let you live there for a while longer at least."

"Mervin," I snapped. "Don't say such a thing."

He shrugged. "Hopefully things will work out with you and Leon." He smiled. "Maybe you'll end up in Montana, if Hannah doesn't—"

I couldn't bear to hear another word, so I interrupted him. "Beatrice brought a set of dominoes." Causing her bag to weigh a ton. "Let's go play."

He shook his head and started toward the trail.

"Where are you going?" I called out.

"After Hannah."

"You'll never catch them."

"I'll do my best." He took off at a run.

I shuffled back to camp. Pete and Robbie were sleeping on a quilt spread in the shade of their tent. Martin and Ben had returned and they were sitting at the picnic table with Beatrice, who had pulled out her ten-pound set of dominoes. She had her back to the fire pit.

Cate looked up from where she sat in a lawn chair, her feet propped on the stump, a book her hands. "Ach, Molly. What's the matter?"

I slumped down in the chair beside her and said, "Nothing."

"Where's Leon?" she asked, turning her head toward the horse trailer.

"He and Hannah went for a ride—because I didn't want to."

"Of course you didn't," she murmured.

"And Mervin took off after them."

"On foot?"

I nodded.

She looked as if she might laugh but didn't. "It sounds as if everything is working out."

"I'm not so sure."

"Ach," she said. "Hannah's crazy about Mervin. And Leon's crazy about you."

Beatrice responded from where she sat at the table with a "Harrumph."

I lowered my voice more. "Beatrice doesn't think I'm good enough for Leon." I sighed. "It's funny, because when Hannah first met him she thought he was a country bumpkin. Now she probably doesn't think I'm good enough for him either."

"That's ridiculous," Cate said. "Mervin likes Hannah and Leon likes you. What's not to work out?"

I shook my head. "They're both crazy about Hannah."

"Why do you say that?"

"They both want to be with her."

"Ach, I'm sorry." Cate closed her book. "As far as Leon, it's probably a misunderstanding." She chuckled. "Pete and I had a few of those."

I shifted in the chair. "But you two adore each other."

"Jah, that's true," she admitted. "I've been blessed in marrying my soul mate. But it wasn't that way at first, let me assure you. I felt horrible about myself."

I grimaced. I knew they'd had some problems.

"Which doesn't mean I think you feel horrible about yourself," she quickly said. "You don't. Just about not having a knack with horses and children. But that's not enough to scare Leon away."

My sister turned around on the bench, away from Ben and Martin. "But your bossiness is," she said looking straight at me. "It's enough to scare anyone away."

"Bea," I snapped.

Cate patted my arm again.

"Denki for trying to help," I said. I stood and, without addressing my sister, turned around and left the campsite. I started along the pathway to the lake but feared I might bump into Phillip and Jessie.

If I started up the trail I might meet Mervin coming down. Or Hannah and Leon. But perhaps, if Cate was right, Leon would let Mervin ride and Leon would walk with me. I wasn't going to run after them the way Mervin had, but I wasn't going to give up either.

I stopped halfway to the meadow to catch my breath. The day had grown hot and muggy, the cool mountain air long gone. Through the trees a doe stood statue still, watching me. When she finally turned away, a fawn followed her deeper into the forest.

As I started walking again, I noted more columbine, Queen Anne's lace, and then the purple flower I couldn't identify. I thought of Dat when I spotted trillium in the distance—but I didn't go off the trail to get a closer look. Not today. Not in the emotional state I was in.

A hot breeze began to blow, stirring the treetops above my head, sending down a shower of pine needles onto my Kapp. I brushed them off and tilted my head back. An especially tall red pine caught my attention. I remembered when Dat turned seventy he said, "I'm not old—for a tree." We'd all laughed. The tree above me was much older than seventy, anchored by deep roots in the same place all these years, only seeing—if trees could see—what came by it. Hikers. A dog. Wildlife. A man and a woman on horses.

I kept walking. Next I noted a half-dozen seedlings that had sprouted on a log, now partly rotted and covered with moss. That made me think of Dat too, and Mamm, of what they wanted for Beatrice and me. For us to follow the Lord, join the church, and then marry men who loved God. And have families of our own. That was the Plain way.

In keeping with his feelings about nature, besides saying the forest was more beautiful than any cathedral, Dat also said it was far more holy. I believed him. I'd been drained dry since Dat's passing, but for a moment I felt God's presence as I walked along, felt him beside me. But then my thoughts drifted back to whether Leon might be falling for Hannah.

It wasn't as if Hannah and Leon hadn't spent time together before the camping trip. They lived on the same property. If they were interested in each other, why hadn't they figured it out before?

But maybe that had been Leon's plan. To pretend he wasn't interested in her. To use me. And then win Hannah over.

And why not? Perhaps he thought it would be a way into the family business, into training and raising horses for a living. After all, what did I have to offer him? Nothing but a flower farm—and a failing one at that.

Or maybe he'd realized in the last day that Hannah was far more likely to follow him to Montana than I was. She wasn't attached to her family's land, and she didn't have a parent and sibling she was responsible for.

I felt like Job in the Bible as I walked on, rubbing my backside. My Dat was dead, my Mamm possibly gravely ill. The man who'd jilted me just happened to turn up in the same campground—with his new girlfriend. My sister had turned against me, as had my best friend. The man I loved suddenly didn't seem all that interested in me. And the land I loved would probably soon be sold—to my half brother.

Overhead, in the patch of sky visible above the trail, gray clouds gathered. A bead of sweat trickled down the side of my face. I swiped it away.

Though I hadn't admitted it to myself, I was out in the forest looking for Leon and Hannah, hoping to stop what I feared was happening between them. It wasn't like me to grovel—but that's what I was doing, coming after them.

As much as I hated to admit it, Beatrice had been right. I'd been more controlling than usual lately. Perhaps with all that had happened—all that I hadn't been able to control—I was grasping to take charge of all I could. I did have high expectations about how things should be done. And I'd been projecting—a term I'd learned from Cate—those expectations onto everyone else. What did it matter if the dishes were done an hour later, or bleach wasn't used in the rinse water?

The hot breeze picked up more as I neared the meadow. I stopped and leaned against the bark of a silver maple tree, its umbrella of leaves shimmering above my head. *Lord, what am I doing?*

Not trusting, that was for sure.

In a moment of conviction I started to turn around. But then I heard a yelp, a man's voice. *Mervin's?* Curiosity got the best of me, and against my better judgment, I continued up the trail.

When I reached the meadow, I didn't see Mervin, but Hannah and Leon were sitting on the rock—where he'd sat with me two evenings before—side by side, the horses grazing untethered nearby. I froze on the path, willing myself to turn around, to flee, to not subject myself to any more embarrassment.

But before I could move, Mervin came through the trees to the left of me, marching into the meadow, his dark glasses pushed on top of his head.

Hannah saw him too. She stood, calling out his name.

"How could you?" Mervin asked her. "After all we've gone through."

Hannah looked toward Leon and then back at Mervin. "What are you talking about?" She planted both hands on her hips and started walking toward the trail, looking back and forth as she did. Finally she yelled, "Molly! Where are you?"

When I didn't answer, she bellowed, "I know you're out there. You wouldn't miss this! Why would you do this to me?"

Confused, I stepped backward on the trail, tripping over a tree root. To keep from landing on my backside again, I lurched forward, accidentally falling to my knees, where I stayed.

Leon's voice, full of surprise, called my name next, but as a question.

I didn't answer.

"She didn't put me up to anything—honest," Mervin said.

"Molly!" Hannah shouted again.

"She's right there." Mervin pointed at me. "On the trail."

I stood quickly and turned around, tears stinging my eyes.

"Come back here," Mervin yelled at me.

I froze. He'd never spoken to me that way before.

"Please," he pled. "Tell Hannah the truth." He sounded as if his heart was breaking—the exact way I felt.

I turned back around. He motioned to me. I obliged. When I came out of the trees, Hannah and Leon were standing apart, staring at me.

How could they treat Mervin and me so badly?

"Hannah," Mervin belted out, sounding as if he was emboldened with me close by. "How could you do this to me? Don't you know I love you?"

She broke out into a grin, until Leon stepped forward and asked, "Is Mervin who you want, Hannah?"

Her face fell as she looked from Mervin to Leon and then to me.

"Because," Leon said, "you don't have to—"

Hannah's expression contorted. "I'm finally catching on." She sneered. "Mervin doesn't really want me." She marched toward me. "Molly, how could you?"

I stepped behind Mervin. "How could I *what*?" I tried to keep my voice calm. Hannah was closer to the brink than I'd feared.

"Set them up to make a fool out of me!" She started around one side of Mervin.

I darted to the other. "I didn't."

"You did." She grabbed Mervin's arm, spinning him around as she tried to grab me from the other side.

I pointed to Mervin. "Look at him, Hannah. He loves you. Don't you?" I clutched his other arm.

Hannah screamed again, this time without words, and stomped into the forest. The three of us didn't move for a moment, but then I followed her, leaving Mervin with Leon and the horses.

"Hannah," I called out. "Wait!"

I never would have guessed Hannah could be so agile traipsing through the forest. While I crashed through, snagging my dress on twigs and tripping over roots, she seemed to glide. In no time she was far ahead of me. Maybe she wasn't as despondent as I'd feared. She certainly seemed to have a lot of energy. When she was depressed before, she shut down. She never would have fled through a forest. Maybe she was just angry this time. But her emotions were unfounded. If she'd only listened to Mervin and me.

And Leon—except he actually hadn't said anything in my defense. In fact, he'd come to Hannah's defense, saying she didn't have to . . . Have to what? Marry Mervin? When she could marry Leon instead?

My heart fell—hard.

Once I caught a view of the lake below, I decided to keep going toward it. When the slope of the hill grew steeper, I carefully made my way, taking sideways steps. Halfway down, I stopped and rested, taking in the view below. Hannah was nowhere to be seen, but I thought the smoke coming from the other side of the lake was from Jessie's family's campsite.

I couldn't make out any activity from where I thought our camp should be, not even two horses heading down the road, but two canoes were in the middle of the lake. The four orange life jackets were hard to miss. Each canoe had a man—probably Phillip and Jessie's Dat—and two boys, most likely Jessie's brothers. Phillip was the youngest of a big family and his parents were as old as my Dat had been. It was probably a good thing for him to spend time with Jessie and her family. Maybe he would learn how to be a good husband and father from Mr. Berg. If not, perhaps Jessie would train him all on her own. She seemed like the kind of girl who could accomplish that.

One thing I knew, even though we were Plain, we were all very different. Including Hannah. I sighed again.

She would find her way, when she wanted to.

The day grew even stickier. On the horizon storm clouds billowed, a storm brewing in the distance.

I continued on, finally coming out of the brush and trees above the lake. I crossed over the road, deciding to follow the shoreline back to camp.

But as I passed through the trees between the road and the water, I saw a figure sitting at a picnic table, writing in a book. "Beatrice?"

She looked up, a dazed look on her face. "What are you doing here?" Before I could answer, she struggled to her feet. "Are you all right?"

I hadn't noticed until she asked that dirt and moss stained my apron. Scratches covered my arms and legs. And I'd torn the hem of my dress. I looked back up at my sister. "On the inside or the outside?"

"Both?" she said, stepping away from the table, leaving her journal.

I nodded. But the truth was, I hurt badly. For the first time ever, I was sure, she reached out to hug me.

"I'm sorry about what I said yesterday—about you being controlling."

"Ach, that's okay. You were right." I sat down at the table as she returned to where she'd been sitting, and spilled out the short version of what had just happened.

"Oh, Molly," she said. "So Hannah thinks you put Mervin and Leon up to acting like they love her, just to hurt her?"

"I . . . think so."

"And you think Hannah stole Leon from you?"

I nodded again.

"You're both moronic," she said.

"What?"

"Jah. You've been friends since you were tiny. Why would you treat each other this way?"

"I didn't do anything."

"Except you believe she stole Leon."

"But she did."

"You don't know that."

I glared at my sister. I needed her to sympathize with me, not chide me.

"They were sitting together."

"On a rock, you said."

I nodded.

Beatrice squinted. "So was it a really big rock? Were they sitting far away from each other?"

"No, side by side."

"Did you or Mervin ask for an explanation?"

"No." Actually, I hadn't thought to. And there certainly hadn't been time.

Beatrice sighed. "I apologized for what I said about you being controlling—but part of it is true. First you wanted to go on this trip for fun. Then you didn't because of Mamm. Then you did when Leon wanted to go. But you didn't want to invite Mervin. Then when it seemed getting Mervin to fall back in love with Hannah would work to your advantage, you were okay with it."

I chose not to react to Beatrice's accusations.

"I know you, Molly. Remember, I've been watching you my entire life."

I exhaled slowly.

"So you had a plan and it backfired. Don't punish Hannah for it."

"Punish her. I can't even find her."

Beatrice seemed a little alarmed. "She's lost?"

"No. I'm sure she knows exactly where she is." She was the one who had been riding horses her entire life. She probably had a built-in compass. Or the horse did. But she wasn't riding a horse . . .

I pushed the thought out of my mind. "She doesn't want to be found," I said. "She purposefully evaded me." I stood. "I'm going back to camp, where I can count the minutes until we can go home." *Home.* At this rate, it wouldn't be ours for long.

"That's it?" Beatrice stood too.

"What do you mean?"

"Your best friend is lost in the woods."

I shook my head. "She's not lost."

"And the man you love—"

"Stop!" My heart lurched.

She crossed her arms. "It's your pride," she said. "You hate to be wrong. And you hate even more for someone to tell you you're wrong."

"That's not true."

She sat back down at the table and opened her journal. I could only imagine what she was going to write. "Have fun writing about me."

She didn't bother to look up. "Believe me, I have better things to write about."

I knew I needed to do something. I just wasn't sure my going back into the forest was it. Besides, Leon and Mervin were more likely to find Hannah—when she was ready to be found—than I.

I limped back to camp. Cate would know what I should do.

When I returned to the campsite, Cate was curled up on the blanket outside their tent next to Pete, with Robbie between the two of them, covered by his blanket. They were all asleep, or so I thought. I didn't mean to be spying—and I didn't feel as if I was, until Pete placed his hand on Cate's stomach. She smiled, her eyes still closed, and wrapped her hand around his.

It was such an intimate gesture that my face grew warm. According to Hannah, who'd heard it from Addie, Cate had lost a baby two years before. We'd all been hoping she'd have another chance soon.

Now it looked as if that hope had come true. Tears stung my eyes again—both out of joy for Cate and Pete and fear for myself. Would I ever experience the love they shared? My heart lurched again.

Martin and Ben must have gone hiking—or maybe fishing—because they weren't around. I changed my dress and apron, then did my best to scrub my legs and arms. Beatrice came back to camp and went straight to our tent. Cate and Pete were scheduled to fix dinner, but I hated to rouse them from their rest.

Deciding I'd watch the storm roll in over the mountains, I

headed back down to the lake but stopped at the shore when I saw Phillip and the rest of their group. The canoes were both at the dock, and Jessie's Dat was climbing out of his. The boys climbed out too, but Phillip stayed put. A few minutes later, his Dat returned, carrying Bella, who was wearing her life jacket, followed by Jessie, carrying a life jacket, and her Mamm. Mr. Berg placed Bella in the canoe, in front of Phillip, and then after Jessie had cinched her jacket she climbed into the second one. One of the older brothers climbed in behind her and then one of the younger brothers climbed in the middle. The Mamm bent down and kissed Bella, and the parents waved and headed back to the trail. It looked as if they were going off on a hike, all alone, something they probably didn't do often.

Clearly they were trusting Phillip with Bella. Perhaps they saw more in him than I did.

Both Jessie and one of her brothers paddled their canoe, but of course Phillip was alone in paddling his. He kept up with them easily though. The sound of their voices carried across the lake. Although I couldn't make out their words, I could tell they were having fun. A peal of laughter—Bella's, I was sure—lifted my spirits, just a bit.

The warm breeze turned into a wind as I watched, standing in the shadows of the trees. Farther up the shore from me, Martin and Ben fished. They called out to Jessie and Phillip, and the canoes, gliding side by side, just a couple of oar lengths apart, made their way across the lake.

When they reached the middle, they stopped, and the boy in the middle of Jessie's canoe stood. He called out to Phillip, who shook his head, but as he did the boy leapt out of the canoe. I was sure he'd land in the water, but the canoes had drifted closer together, and he managed to make it—almost—to Phillip's canoe.

What happened next took only a split second. He must have grabbed the side and tried to climb in but instead he pulled the canoe over. As Phillip and Bella spilled out, the other brother, still in the canoe with Jessie, stood in horror.

Jessie's voice surged over the lake as they capsized too. I ran along the shore, aiming to get to the dock, fearing Bella was trapped beneath the canoe. There were no other boats in sight, but I hoped someone in one of the nearby campsites had a raft or a rowboat or another canoe.

Phillip's head popped up out of the water, frantically looking around. In a split second he disappeared to the other side of the canoe and then a moment later reappeared with Bella.

"Bring her to the dock," I yelled. That would be faster than me sending a boat after them. Thank God they all had life jackets on. "Boys," I yelled. "You bring in the canoes."

Jessie helped her youngest brother get one while the older boy got the other. Phillip made good progress, holding Bella's head out of the water. Martin and Ben ran along the far shore, their fishing poles bobbing up and down.

I reached the dock first, but Phillip wasn't far away—only fifty yards or so. I had no idea he'd do so well in the water. Martin and Ben rounded the curve of the lake as I got down on my knees at the end of the dock.

"You're doing great, Bella," I called out. "Phillip almost has you to the shore."

By the time he reached the dock, I could tell he was exhausted. He reached for the dock's edge, pulling himself and Bella as close as possible. I leaned down, extending my arms. "I can take her," I said.

Phillip's hand shook a little as he pulled Bella around, with her back toward me. I grabbed her under her armpits and lifted, dragging her up to the dock.

"Are you hurt?" I asked, hoisting her into my arms. She shook her head, taking a raggedy breath, followed by a shudder. Her face was wet, but she didn't seem to be crying. Her Kapp was soaked and her bun had come undone, her wet hair plastered to her face.

She began to shiver uncontrollably as the wind whipped around her body. Phillip hoisted himself onto the dock and looked back over the lake. Jessie and the boys with the canoes were still far from the dock but making good progress.

"Take her back to camp," Jessie called out. "Get her out of her wet clothes."

"Are you all right?" Phillip asked Jessie, positioned as if he might jump back in.

"We're fine," she shouted.

I started for their camp. Bella felt light in my arms. Phillip said he'd take her, but I told him to go on ahead and get a towel.

Before I reached camp, two of the other brothers came running from the woods, one with their baby sister in his arms. The other one took Bella from me. By the time they led me to their parents' tent, Phillip had a towel ready. I took it from him.

I followed the boys into the tent, and the brother carrying Bella placed her on a cot with side rails. The brother carrying the baby put her in a portable crib at the far end.

"Is this Bella's suitcase?" I pointed to a zippered bag at the end of the cot.

He nodded, taking off her Kapp as he did and then her apron. But then he looked at me and said, "Can you do the rest?"

"Of course," I answered.

By then the baby was crying, and both boys went to her, taking her out of the tent.

"Is she okay?" Phillip asked from outside the tent.

"Jah," I answered, not realizing he'd stuck around. "You should go help Jessie."

"Denki, Molly," he said, his voice cracking a little.

"No problem," I responded. "Now go."

His hurried footsteps fell away from the tent.

Bella seemed fine with my undressing her, drying her, and then redressing her. I worked gently and efficiently, surprised that it came so easily to me, considering how little childcare I'd done. She was able to move her right arm easily enough and helped me as best she could. I chatted away, telling her Jessie and the boys would soon be to the dock with the canoes, that they probably were already, and how thankful I was that Phillip was strong and a good swimmer.

She nodded her head, and her eyes pooled with tears.

I told her that her Mamm and Dat would be back soon, but that made her mouth turn down, so I changed the subject, asking how she liked her little sister. She smiled at that. Caring for Bella was easy—but she was predictable, unlike most children. She couldn't even talk, let alone run away.

What did that say about me? Disappointed with my thoughts, I tied her apron, grabbed a blanket from the bed, wrapping her in it, and then scooped her up, trying to hold her away from my damp dress. It was easy to love Bella simply for who she was. Was that something I could learn to do for all of God's creatures—including my friends and family?

As I carried her out of the tent, we heard Jessie's voice, and Bella smiled again.

"Look at you," Jessie said, strolling toward us as if nothing had happened. "Out of your wet things already. That's what I'm going to do."

As I put Bella in her chair, Jessie turned back toward me. "Denki," she said. "You saved the day."

I shook my head. Martin and Ben would have been there soon enough. Or Phillip would have rolled Bella onto the dock.

But I was thankful I'd been there to help, to make things a little easier.

I left then, passing Phillip and the boys on the trail back to the lake a minute later. He smiled and thanked me again. The boys smiled too but didn't say anything.

The Berg family was good for Phillip—and he was good for them.

I was genuinely grateful for what God had planned for Phillip Eicher. But I couldn't help but wonder what his plan for me might be. Perhaps he'd forgotten I was in need of one.

As I neared our camp, I didn't hear or smell horses. Leon and Mervin hadn't returned yet. Maybe they, going against everything the Amish believed in, had attacked each other up the trail over Hannah. Maybe one of them was badly injured. I shook my head at the ridiculous thought.

As I neared the tents, Cate woke up, or maybe Robbie woke her. She shuffled over to the fire, carrying him. "I didn't mean to sleep so long," she said with a yawn.

Then she sniffed . . . and smiled. "Guess I'll go change him first." She headed back toward the tent, Robbie high in her arms, his head resting on her shoulder and his bottom up in the air. He stared at me with his big brown eyes, his curly hair a tangle on his forehead.

I asked Bea, who sat at the picnic table, if Hannah had returned. "I haven't seen her," she said. "What happened out on the lake? I heard yelling."

I told her and then went to our tent to change my clothes, putting on my last clean dress. There was no sign that Hannah had been in the tent.

As I climbed out, I heard hooves on the road. Leon and Mervin rode the horses down the lane, stopping at the trailer and dismounting. I started toward them, hoping Hannah was with them, as Leon led Storm to the other side of the trailer.

"Did you find her?" I called out.

Mervin turned toward me, his hand on Lightning's bridle. "We thought she was with you."

"You weren't looking for her this whole time?" I asked.

"Of course not," Mervin said. "Why would we? Didn't you catch up with her?"

My face flushed as I shook my head. "What were you doing all that time, then?"

"Leon was teaching me to ride."

"Oh," I said. "I thought you hated horses."

He shrugged. "Hannah's been asking me to learn to ride for a couple of years. I thought today was as good a day as any."

"So after what happened in the meadow you and Leon are friends?"

Mervin shrugged again. "We aren't enemies." He nodded toward the west. "I hope she beats the storm."

"Jah, me too."

"What if she's lost?"

"She isn't," I said. "If I could find my way back, she can."

Mervin shook his head at me. "I didn't take you to be so coldhearted."

I tilted my head. "Coldhearted? Really?"

"She's your best friend."

"Jah, it's not that I'm not worried about her. I think she's staying away on purpose . . . but I guess that isn't reason to be any less concerned." A sense of panic grew inside of me.

He took his sunglasses off his face. "What do you mean?"

"I'm afraid she's not doing well."

Mervin's face grew pale, and then, still holding on to Lightning, he called out, "Hannah's missing!"

Leon poked his head around the trailer, followed by Storm. "We'd better go look for her."

Pete started down from the campsite. "How long has she been gone?"

"A couple of hours," Mervin answered.

Martin and Ben approached, still carrying their fishing poles, followed by Pete, who asked, "Where was she last seen?"

"Up in the forest, off the trail," I answered.

A worried expression settled on Pete's face. "Who was she with?"

"Well," Mervin said, "she was with Leon, until Molly insulted her and then chased her through the forest."

"Mervin!"

He turned back toward me.

"That's not what happened," I said.

"Why didn't you tell us sooner?" Pete asked, looking straight at me.

"Because she was saving little Bella Berg from drowning in the lake," Ben answered.

"What?" Mervin asked.

"That's not exactly true," I said. "I just helped get her out of the lake. And into dry clothes." Which may have distracted me from being as worried as I should have been about Hannah. I should have alerted the others sooner.

"Let's go find her," Leon said, leading Storm all the way around the trailer. Then he looked up at the sky. "I hope that's not an electrical storm on the way."

Pete and Leon took off on the horses. Mervin and Martin headed toward the lake, determined to backtrack the route I'd taken down the hill, in case she'd hurt herself and wasn't able to make it back to camp on her own.

Ben and Beatrice headed out past the trailhead, thinking Hannah might have become disoriented and ended up on the road. That seemed unlikely, unless she'd decided to hitchhike home, which I was sure she wouldn't, no matter how despondent she felt.

"You can go ahead and join the search," Cate said. "I know you're worried about her." She held up the whistle around her neck. "I'll blow as hard as I can if she comes back to camp."

I looked toward the road.

"I'll feed Robbie," she said.

"What about dinner? I made creamed chicken. The noodles are in the box."

"Oh." She glanced toward the schedule and then said, "I'll work on that too. But hurry," she said. "You can catch up with Beatrice and Ben."

"Denki." I grabbed my sweatshirt and flashlight from our tent and hurried after my sister. But from about fifty feet away, I could hear her bickering with Ben.

"We should go up the trail," he said.

"Why would we do that? Leon and Pete have that covered."

"We might be able to see her in the trees from foot, where they'd miss her from the horses."

"Not if she doesn't want to be found," Beatrice said. "We're going on the road."

I stopped, unable to bear the squabbling. If they were going up the road then I'd go up the trail.

The air had cooled with the coming storm but the wind had stopped. I wiggled into my sweatshirt, slipped the flashlight in the pocket, and marched up the trail once again.

The overhead clouds darkened what was left of the day, as did the towering trees above me. I zipped my sweatshirt and increased my stride. I was certain Hannah could have found her way out of the forest, if she'd wanted to.

Unless she'd been injured.

I doubted any animals would have hurt her. Most of the wildlife around would be far more afraid of her than she of them. Honestly, I couldn't imagine Hannah being afraid of much. But she might have fallen. Or twisted her ankle. Or hit her head on a limb.

Or perhaps she was trying to stir up more drama, trying to get everyone to feel sorry for her.

But what I most feared was that she'd had an episode like she'd had a couple of years ago and couldn't function.

An owl hooted deeper in the forest. A slight breeze picked up through the treetops. Needles, pinecones, and twigs fell around me. I brushed the top of my Kapp and continued on.

When I reached the meadow, I searched the edges of the forest, but couldn't see anything—except for trees. Even though it wasn't sunset yet, I began to feel ill at ease being by myself.

A shiver ran through me.

What if someone had taken Hannah?

I exhaled slowly. That was ridiculous.

Maybe the dog that scared Lightning the day before had attacked her.

I shook my head. No. The dog had startled the horses, but it didn't seem like a ferocious creature. In fact, under normal circumstances I was sure I'd really like the dog—much more than the horses.

The owl hooted again. In the distance, thunder crashed.

I hurried away from the middle of the meadow to the edge of the trees. A minute later thunder crashed again. It wasn't any louder, and because I hadn't seen the strike, I had no idea how close it was.

"Hannah!" I yelled, turning to the place where she'd left the trail that afternoon. "Where are you?" I didn't really expect that she was close by, but with an electrical storm on the way, the situation had turned dire. Not just for Hannah but for everyone out looking for her too.

I stepped off the trail and into the underbrush, squinting in the dim light, trying to track Hannah's earlier flight—but it was useless. After a few minutes, I decided finding my way to the hill over the lake had been more of a fluke than it had been based on my own skills. Maybe getting lost was easier than I'd thought. I decided to go back to the trail.

When I reached the meadow again, more thunder, this time louder, rolled out from the west. A moment later the sky lit up with a flash of lightning. I counted out loud to five, then the thunder crashed. I started back down the trail.

The storm could be on top of me in no time.

The next strike wasn't any closer, but the one after that was— only two miles. The ionized scent of electricity charged the air.

I wondered how the horses were doing and expected Leon

and Pete to come racing down the path at any time, but they didn't.

The next strike flashed about two miles away. As the thunder crashed again, the rain began to pour. I pulled the hood of my sweatshirt over my Kapp and hurried even faster. A couple of times I tripped over tree roots in the trail. The third time, I fell to my hands and knees. Only the top layer of dirt had been pelted by the rain, making just a bit of mud. I brushed my hands together and flicked my skirt, attempting to dislodge the mud. When that didn't work, I brushed it as best I could and hurried on.

The next crash of thunder came from east of me. The storm had passed over the top—directly toward where Hannah most likely was. Perhaps Leon and Pete had headed that way too. And Mervin and Martin.

I froze on the trail for a moment. It had already passed over Beatrice and Ben, on the road. Surely they'd known not to stay out in the open. I couldn't bear it if anything happened to Ben or Beatrice.

Tears stung my eyes. Or to Hannah.

Or Leon.

Or Pete—with a baby on the way and all.

Poor Cate must have been worried sick back at camp. I began running. It was nearly dark by the time I reached the end of the trail, so I took my flashlight out and turned it on.

I heard voices in the distance, above the rain.

"Hannah!" I yelled.

"It's Beatrice" came the reply.

"And Ben."

I waved my flashlight in that direction, illuminating the falling rain. A moment later, my sister stepped into the beam of light and then Ben did too. They were both drenched.

"We were nearly struck!" Ben called out.

"We were not," Beatrice countered. "It was a mile away, at least."

I turned back toward the camp and kept walking, having no desire to listen to them. Hopefully the storm had forced Hannah back to camp too—maybe I just hadn't heard Cate's whistle.

When I reached the trailer, I waved the flashlight toward the makeshift corral. It was empty. Then I shone it toward camp.

"Is that you, Molly?"

"Jah," I answered.

Cate stood under the canopy with Robbie in her arms, the lit lantern hanging in the middle.

"Is Hannah back?" I asked.

"No." Cate held her nephew close.

"Anyone else?"

She shook her head.

As Beatrice and Ben came up behind me, the rain slowed, but we all crowded under the canopy. A few minutes later the rain stopped, leaving a fresh, clean scent.

"I'll see if I can find some dry wood to get a fire going," Ben said.

"Denki," I said. "Let's go change out of our wet dresses," I said to Beatrice. "Although I'll have to change back into one of my dirty ones—I only brought three."

"You can wear one of mine." Beatrice shivered. "Then what should we do?"

"Get help from the authorities," I said. I'd wait until the others returned, to see if they'd found her, but before it got much later, I needed to contact someone and ask for more help.

As Beatrice and I finished changing, we heard voices and then the neighing of a horse.

"We couldn't find her!" Leon called out.

"We couldn't either," Mervin, sounding farther away, shouted back.

I stepped out of the tent. Pete had dismounted and held Lightning's reins in his hand. "Are you two doing okay?" he asked Cate. Robbie reached for him.

"Jah," she answered. "But you're soaked."

"It was a warm rain though," Pete said.

Storm pranced around, and Leon pulled hard on the reins and headed toward the trailer.

"We need to call for help," I said.

"Do you have service?" Mervin asked.

I shook my head. "I'll go find the camp ranger." Stepping back into the tent, I grabbed my flashlight and a dry sweatshirt.

Beatrice followed me out of the tent.

Everyone had gathered around the fire, except for Leon and Pete, who were tending to the horses.

"I'll go with you," Mervin said.

"Denki."

I headed toward the road, with Mervin a few steps behind, but then I veered toward the horse trailer, feeling as if I should let Pete know, out of respect, considering he was the oldest of all of us. Both men were taking the saddles off the horses.

"I'm going to find the ranger," I called out. "Mervin's going with me."

"Good idea," Leon responded.

"Jah," Pete said. "You're doing the right thing."

At that Mervin and I headed to the road, to backtrack to the entrance to the camp. But after we'd taken only a few steps, someone called out, "Wait."

It was Hannah, her voice coming from between the trailer and the lake.

"I'm here," she said. "Safe and sound."

I questioned "sound" but didn't say it. "Are you all right?" I hurried toward her. "We were just going for help."

"I'm fine," Hannah said. "I fell asleep on the hillside and woke when it started raining."

I shone my flashlight toward her. She didn't look fine. Scratches covered her arms. Streaks of mud had dried on her face. She held her Kapp in her hand, her hair falling out of her bun around her face.

Mervin stepped toward her, but she shied away from him.

"Can we talk?" he asked.

"Not now." She crossed her arms over her sopping-wet dress and apron.

It dawned on me that she might be embarrassed, although she probably didn't have any idea how worried we all had been.

"Let's go to the tent, then," I said, shooing Mervin away. Leon and Pete saw my gesture too and stayed back.

The rain had soaked her to the bone, but thankfully she had her riding pants on.

I led the way to the tent, calling out to the others, "Everything's fine. Hannah's here."

Bea stepped forward but then stopped. They all must have sensed it wouldn't do any good to overwhelm Hannah.

"We're going to our tent," I said calmly. "We can all talk in the morning."

After Hannah entered, I went to the washbasin and wet a cloth for her, then hurried back. I sat on my sleeping bag while Hannah scrubbed her face, arms, and hands, and then changed into her nightgown. She brushed her long dark hair out and then braided it quickly.

"Did you get lost?" I asked.

"Not really," she answered. "I got distracted—thinking."

"About?"

She slipped into her sleeping bag. "Why you'd turn both Leon and Mervin against me."

"Hannah, I swear to you I didn't. They both, on their own . . ." I couldn't say it, couldn't say it out loud that they both . . .

I couldn't even think it.

She pulled the flap of the sleeping bag over her head.

I whispered, "Why did you pursue Leon when you know I'm interested in him?"

She moaned. "I was hoping to make Mervin jealous. But Leon doesn't like me, honest."

"Then why did he ask whether it was Mervin that you wanted?" I whispered.

"Leon has been like a brother to me. That's all," she answered, her voice weary. "You and Mervin totally blew things out of proportion."

I hoped she was right—but I didn't believe her.

By the campfire, Martin said something I couldn't make out, and then the others all laughed, including Leon. I couldn't help but feel jealous of all of them conversing and having a good time.

I decided to put my nightgown on too and go ahead and get in bed, but sleep wouldn't come. After a while I asked Hannah if she was awake. She didn't answer. But by the sound of her breathing, I suspected she was. A long time later, it seemed, Beatrice came into the tent.

Then the others must have gone to bed too because someone extinguished the lantern and there was no more talking.

I kept thinking about Leon, interrupted now and then by Hannah's sighing. After a while she got out of her sleeping bed and grabbed her jacket. Then she unzipped the tent, which seemed incredibly loud in the stillness, and slipped out into the night.

I waited a moment, trying to hear which way she went. Perhaps she was hungry. But then I heard one of the horses whinny. She hadn't gone to the ice chests. She'd gone to Leon.

Of course I followed her, slipping my sweatshirt over my nightgown, hoping I wouldn't be seen. The fire had died down to embers. Someone had pulled all the lawn chairs under the canopy, plus the food boxes, the stoves, and everything else that might get rained on.

I looked up at the sky. It was an inky black, but to the west the clouds parted some and a few stars shone through. If I didn't feel such angst, I'd have thought the night beautiful. Then I remembered it was the summer solstice and wondered if Leon had thought about it. Earlier in the week I'd imagined us out on another hike on the longest day of the year, like the first night we'd arrived. But now it was the middle of the night. That, like so many things, hadn't turned out the way I'd imagined.

I swung wide, away from the guys' tent and Pete and Cate's, following the tree line down to the trailer.

Robbie cried out, hopefully in his sleep. One of the horses whinnied again. I tensed as I stumbled over a rock, but I grabbed a tree, stopping my fall. I hadn't brought my flashlight—it would have only given me away.

The clouds parted a little more. I could make out a shadow of a figure by the trailer, then the pale figure of Lightning. I stepped carefully, not wanting to give myself away.

I stepped behind a tree and poked my head around. I had a profile view of Hannah with her face pressed against Lightning's nose, her arms wrapped around the horse's neck. Hannah didn't say a word, just stood quietly. I guessed her eyes were closed.

Storm stood a few feet away, shaking his head as if he wanted a turn. He whinnied again. Hannah waited a long moment and then pulled her arms from Lightning and walked over to Storm, embracing him the same way. I directed my attention to the trailer, expecting to see Leon at the opening. I squinted. No one was there.

But then the trailer swayed a little. The clouds drifted more, and the moon appeared, riding high in the sky. By the light of it I saw Leon poke his head out of the back of the trailer.

"Are you okay?" he asked.

He was speaking to Hannah, and I didn't think he saw me. She nodded.

"You should get some sleep."

"Jah," she answered. "I will."

He retreated, the trailer swayed a little more, and I stepped back, puzzled. I picked my way back through the trees to the tent and had just settled into my sleeping bag when Hannah returned and climbed back into her bed. A few minutes later her breathing slowed.

But I still couldn't fall asleep. When we were girls Hannah and I had spent every chance we could together. School, church, and weekends at each other's house. It wasn't that we got along perfectly. We argued. Competed with each other, even though it went against what we were taught. Criticized each other some. But still we got along, mostly.

It was funny how horses brought out the best in her but the worst in me.

When we were girls I finally agreed, after years of her begging me, to go riding. It was a big deal for me to even get up on a horse, but that went okay. Hannah led the way on her horse, and mine followed without me having to do anything except to try to keep from bouncing out of the saddle. Hannah told me to move with the horse, that there was nothing to fear. And after a bit, even though I kept jostling, I started to relax.

As we neared the creek, though, Hannah's horse took off. Mine followed. I slid all over the saddle, yelling for Hannah to stop.

She did, on the other side of the creek, which made my horse stop abruptly in the water. With a jolt, I fell sideways, the saddle going with me. I fell fast and hard, landing on a rock, my arm tucked underneath me.

Right away, even in the icy water, I knew I'd broken it. I also knew I had to get out of the creek, but it was hard to balance with my arm limp beneath me.

Hannah jumped off her horse and grabbed a branch along the bank. She extended it so I could grab it, and I was able to make it to the bank.

My parents met us at the doctor's office, where I was X-rayed, casted, and sent home. I didn't see Hannah until Monday morning at school, and when everyone gathered around to sign my cast she burst into tears. I thought she was jealous of all the attention I was getting.

We didn't spend much time together for a few weeks until one Saturday afternoon when Mamm told me she'd invited Hannah over to spend the night. My parents didn't meddle much in my life, not even back then, so I was surprised.

That night Hannah cried again. Finally she told me she thought I'd been killed when I fell into the creek and it was her fault. I liked that she thought it was her fault, for a moment, until she started sobbing.

"That's silly," I said.

Once she quit crying, she told me I needed get back on a horse soon or else I'd be afraid to ride for the rest of my life.

"That's silly too," I said.

When Hannah went home the next day, Mamm asked me to help her in the garden. My arm was still in a cast, and there wasn't much I could do, but she insisted. I held the string while she tied the beans to the pole. "You know," she said, "when we're hurt, how we react to that hurt is often more important than how we were hurt in the first place."

I didn't understand what she was saying.

She sighed. "It's important, Molly, that you don't hurt someone else just because you've been hurt."

I insisted I'd done nothing to hurt Hannah.

But she was right. I had. It hadn't been her fault I'd fallen. And I had been ignoring her—worse, I'd been punishing her.

In the dark tent, with Hannah breathing deeply on one side of me and Beatrice on the other, I choked back a sob. I missed Mamm. I wasn't ready for her to die too. What would I do without her?

She'd been right back then, when I was a girl. I wonder what she'd say to me now. Had I hurt Hannah again? Because I was scared? Because I was hurting? Because I wasn't in control?

The smell of coffee and the clatter of pans woke me the next morning. Hannah rolled toward me. Beatrice was wedged against my back. They'd sandwiched me. I closed my eyes and fell back to sleep.

"Do you three plan to sleep all day?" It was Ben, right outside our tent.

"Leave them alone," Cate said, her voice farther away. "They're probably exhausted."

"Hanner." Robbie sounded as if he was right outside our tent too, along with an aviary of finches tweeting their little hearts out.

"Come on," Ben said. Maybe he came to retrieve his nephew. I nudged Beatrice. "Roll over," I said. "We need to get up." She groaned out loud.

Then gently, I said, "Hannah."

She turned toward me, opening her eyes. "Time to get up?" I nodded.

She sat up, her wavy hair loose and fuzzy. I searched her face, trying not to be too obvious. She seemed okay.

Hannah and I climbed out of our sleeping bags and got dressed. I had to poke Beatrice again to get her moving. As I crawled toward the tent door, Hannah held up the tear-down-camp chart. "Forgetting something?"

Beatrice groaned, out loud. "Don't," she said, a straight pin between her lips bobbing up and down, the other in her hand, headed for her Kapp. "No one needs you taking control. Everyone knows what to do."

I took the paper from Hannah. "I decided not to post it." It must have fallen out of my bag and been dragged over by our moving around in the dark.

Beatrice knelt as she pinned the front of her dress, her head down. "It's insulting," she said. "The way you treat everyone."

"No one's insulted," I said, still holding the paper.

Beatrice looked up at me. "That's not true." Her disloyalty stung.

I folded the paper in half and stuck it back in the folder in my bag. "Beatrice, I already said I'm not posting it."

I hurried from the tent, but on the way out caught Hannah shrugging her shoulders at Beatrice. Everyone—even Ben and Martin—was up, although I didn't see Leon anywhere. Last night I'd felt like a villain for not sounding the alarm earlier about Hannah being missing. This morning everyone acted as if nothing had happened.

Cate asked Hannah how she slept.

"Fine," Hannah answered.

Lightning was tied to the outside of the trailer, but Storm was gone. Leon must have gone on a morning ride. Cate and Pete were preparing breakfast, but everyone else was sitting around the fire.

I thought of suggesting everyone do something to pack up the campsite but instead poured myself a cup of coffee and sat down too. Hannah scooped up Robbie. Immediately Mervin stepped to her side.

A few minutes later, Leon appeared in camp, his western hat pushed back on his head. He sauntered over to Hannah's side too and tickled Robbie's bare feet. The little boy squealed. I turned my attention to the fire.

"Time to eat," Cate called out. The others quickly rose to wash up and then help with getting the meal on the table. By the time Pete was ready to pray, everyone had gathered around.

I hadn't had to say a word to hurry them along.

After breakfast, even though I feared offending everyone, I asked Mervin, Martin, and Ben to do the dishes while Hannah, Beatrice, and I made sandwiches to pack for our lunch on the ride home. The boys did what they were told, with a break for a pinecone fight. I bit my tongue and didn't chastise them.

When they finished, I wanted to tell them to pack up their tent, but I knew it was obvious. They could figure it out. Instead I said, "The drivers will be here in an hour or so."

I turned to Hannah. "You and Beatrice tear down our tent and pack it." I searched for Pete and Cate but couldn't find them. Their tent was still standing.

"What are you going to do?" Beatrice asked.

"Pack up the kitchen boxes."

As I worked, Pete and Cate returned to camp, each holding one of Robbie's hands. They put the little boy in the tent and followed him inside. I assumed they were packing their things.

"You need to roll up your bag," Beatrice said to me.

"Please do it for me," I answered, as nicely as I could. "And get the box of Dat's shirts too." I'd gotten some work done on the project, but not as much as I'd intended.

The clank of metal reverberated from the horse camp. I imagined Leon was tearing down the corral. He hadn't asked for anyone to help him. Hannah must have heard him too because she urged Beatrice to hurry. "Then we can go help Leon," she said.

"First you two need to fold up the lawn chairs and pick up the garbage," I said. Scraps of paper littered the ground near the fire.

The two exchanged a look. "You just can't stop, can you?" Beatrice muttered.

I cringed. And I'd been trying so hard not to be bossy.

Minutes later, Pete carried bags from their tent to the edge of the parking space, lining them up on the curb. Then Cate came out and the two began taking down the tent on top of Robbie, who laughed and laughed inside. It seemed everyone in camp enjoyed his peels of glee, except for me.

Beatrice pulled my sleeping bag and duffle bag from our tent, dropping them on one of the lawn chairs. Next she carefully placed her things on another chair, as did Hannah. After they quickly dismantled and packed our tent, Beatrice grabbed the paper bag of garbage from breakfast and headed toward the dumpster on the other side of the road as Hannah headed down to the horse trailer.

The boys hadn't started on their tent yet. They were back across the road, lobbing pinecones at each other. Considering how long it was taking for Beatrice to return, I guessed she'd joined them.

I closed the first kitchen box and began packing the dishes as Leon came up the little hill with one of the blue metal cups in his hand. He held it high. "Any coffee left?"

"Just a little." I lifted the pot. "And it's barely warm."

"Good enough." He poured himself some, then turned toward Cate and Pete's collapsed tent. Robbie had his head out of the door, grinning. Pete stooped to pick him up, but the little one scrambled back inside.

Leon laughed. "The great thing about little kids is that it's all about the moment."

For a second, as I stopped and watched the tent wiggle with

Robbie scooting around inside, I envied the little boy, but then I thought how far behind schedule we were. "But we don't have time for that right now."

Leon laughed again. "That's why it's so hard to hurry kids. They're not thinking about what happened yesterday or what has to happen later today. They just want to enjoy now."

I went back to envying Robbie. I'd enjoyed being with Leon in the forest at the waterfall and then when the fireflies came out. And on our horse ride, before he told me he might end up going back to Montana. But besides that, I hadn't lived in the moment on this trip. I'd been worrying about Mamm, the farm, if Leon loved me, and about Hannah.

Now I worried about getting packed up on time.

I turned back to the box, but Leon reached for my hand and pulled me to his side. "Ach, Molly, I know you're fretting over things. And I know you and I have something to talk through. But we came up here to have fun, jah?"

I didn't respond.

He continued. "You've been so serious."

I pursed my lips together. "Well, someone needs to be."

"I see your point," he said. "And that's one of the things I admire about you. Being in charge. Getting things done. But all of us, except for Robbie, are adults. Everyone might not do things exactly the way you want them done—but they'll do them, eventually."

I narrowed my eyes. "Did Beatrice put you up to this? Or maybe Hannah?"

He put the cup down on the table. "As a matter of fact . . ." He met my eyes. "No." Then he walked away.

I stood stunned for a short moment and then yelled, "Who do you think is going to wash your cup? Because if you think there's someone in charge of that, you're wrong."

He came back, took the bottle of dishwashing detergent from the table, and picked up the cup, taking both over to the hand-washing station. He brought the cup back wet, picked up a dish towel from the table, and quickly dried the cup. "Done," he said, leaving it beside the box.

My face grew warm as he walked away. Was that the way to treat someone I loved? I thought of my parents, of how they'd served each other. Their road to true love, I was sure, had never looked like this.

My face burned with embarrassment as I finished up the packing, folding the tablecloths last and putting them with the dish towels and bath towels into a plastic garbage bag, placing it by Pete and Cate's things. I'd thought of Phillip as a perfectionist, but what about me?

I lugged the kitchen boxes over to the end of the parking space, stacking them on top of each other. Was that part of my aversion to horses? And to children? I couldn't control them, so I didn't want any part of them?

I moved my bags on top of the kitchen boxes, along with Beatrice's and Hannah's, and then folded up the lawn chairs. Next I dismantled the stove and packed it.

The van drivers were scheduled to arrive at any time, so I sat down on the picnic table bench to wait, wishing I had time to go tell Bella good-bye. And Phillip and Jessie. Pete slid Robbie into Cate's arms, and she started toward me. "Want to hold him while we fold up the tent?"

"I'll help Pete," I said. She shrugged and continued across the road. Immediately the others stopped throwing pinecones and gathered around the baby. It only took Pete and me a few minutes to finish up their tent. When we were done, I went back to the table to stare at the guys' tent while I waited for the drivers.

"Uh-oh!" It was Mervin's voice. "Here comes the van. We'd

better hurry." He, along with Martin and Ben, tore into camp, running straight for their tent. Mervin flipped the door open and all three dove inside as the whole thing sagged down on top of them.

I couldn't help but smile as they laughed. They had no problem living in the moment. One of them stood, holding up the middle. First one bag came flying out, then two more. Next their sleeping bags sailed out the door. All landed in the dirt.

I stood and walked to meet the van driver, who had backed the vehicle into the parking place. He and Pete loaded everything that was ready to go. By the time they were done, Ben shuffled their sleeping bags and duffle bags over, while Mervin and Martin crammed their tent into its bag. Then Mervin ran it to the van, tossed it on top of the rest of the load, and then brushed his hands together in satisfaction, a grin spreading across his face.

"Made it," he said. Then he looked around and asked, "Where's the truck?"

"It'll be here in just a minute," the van driver said. "They stopped for gas."

"They?"

He nodded. "Owen came along too."

Hannah ended up riding in the truck with her Dat and Leon, which had Mervin pouting in the back seat and me feeling more insecure than ever.

As we pulled onto the highway, Ben leaned over the seat and grabbed Beatrice's journal from her hands. She turned around, grabbed it back, and beaned him on the head.

"Ouch!" he yelled.

Beatrice leaned forward. "Why don't you—"

"Stop it," I shouted.

For a moment everyone was quiet, but then Robbie began to wail and Cate tried to soothe him. Beatrice said to me, "This is the last trip I'm ever going on with you."

After that, everyone stayed silent—for the next hour. When we stopped to eat our sandwiches at a rest area, I walked away from the group—they could figure out lunch on their own—and pulled out my cell phone. When I was well out of hearing distance from the rest, I called our business phone. Of course no one answered. And I didn't expect anyone to. I left a message saying we wondered how Mamm was and that we'd be home in two hours or so.

As I returned to the group, who had the ice chests out of the truck but not opened, my cell jingled. I pulled it from my apron pocket. It was Mamm—or at least our number. I turned away from the group and answered quickly.

It was Ivan. "Did you have a good time?"

"Jah," I answered. He didn't press me, although I knew my voice didn't sound very convincing. "What are you doing in the greenhouse?"

"Just going through some paperwork."

I could imagine. "How's Mamm?"

"Resting."

I bit my tongue to keep myself from pointing out I hadn't asked what she was doing. "What did the tests show?"

"It's not dementia."

I sighed with relief.

"It's a tumor."

"Oh no." My heart fell.

"But they don't know if it's benign or malignant. They need to do more tests for that."

"When?"

"Monday."

"Where?"

"Lancaster again. I'll take her," Ivan said. "I've already arranged it with your driver."

"Denki," I said, although I didn't mean it. I felt more and more pushed away. "May Beatrice and I go too?"

"There's no need."

When I didn't answer him, he added, "Anna will have to spend the night. It would only complicate it to have you girls around."

"We can talk more when I get home," I said, ready to end the call.

"There's one more thing."

My heart sank. "What?"

"She fell yesterday, on the walkway. Maybe because a stone had dislodged. Or perhaps she lost her balance."

I gasped. "Is she all right?"

"Jah, just a little sore. We found an old cane in the attic. She's using that."

"Denki," I answered.

As I hung up. I remembered Beatrice had told me I was a female version of Ivan, just last Christmas. I couldn't think of a worse insult, but I was sure, especially after this trip, that she hadn't changed her mind. Even though I felt pushed aside, I was thankful for his take-charge attitude. He was doing what he thought best for my Mamm.

Hannah and Mervin were standing by the horse trailer, away from the others. Leon and Owen had joined the rest of the group by the van and were chatting with Pete. After a minute Pete grabbed the ice chest and lugged it over to a picnic table. Cate followed with Robbie, but then she gave him to Ben and opened the box, taking the sandwiches out and then the carrots and celery. She sent Pete back to the van for something.

Robbie fell from Ben's arms into Leon's. Then he lunged toward me. I ignored him, knowing he'd just twist away if I came too close. He'd been playing tricks with me the entire trip.

I continued on to the van, hoping for a moment of peace, arriving as Pete pulled the chips from a box in the back. As I climbed through the open side door, I overheard Mervin saying to Hannah, "But I love you. I always have."

Hannah was clearly upset. "What about Molly?"

"I was a fool," he said. "I've always loved you."

"I don't believe you." She turned toward the others. I followed her gaze, sure it had landed on Leon, who had Robbie on his shoulders now. The little boy squealed in delight.

"Hannah, don't hold my stupidity against me," Mervin begged.

My face grew warm again and I slammed the van door. I had no desire to eat with the others.

When we reached Lancaster County, the driver of the truck took the direct route to Hannah's home. I hadn't told her or Leon good-bye. I doubted I'd have been able to patch things over with either in a short interaction—but still, my heart ached and lurched and ached some more. I'd never felt so out of sorts in all my life.

When our driver pulled into the Rupps' driveway, Betsy and Levi walked out to meet us. Robbie squealed at the sight of his parents and began shaking his arms and legs in his car seat. Pete opened the side door, and Cate unbuckled her nephew and then passed him to Pete, who passed him to Levi. From his Dat's arms, Robbie lunged for his Mamm. Betsy laughed, took him, and propped him on top of her belly.

"How are you feeling?" Cate asked.

"Much better. The rest did me good."

"Is Tamara back?"

Betsy shook her head. "Nan will bring her tomorrow."

"There's only a week until the wedding."

"I know," Betsy said. "It wasn't my idea for her to keep the baby longer. It was hers."

Ben crawled out from the back seat, saying to Beatrice as he did, "It's been fun—not."

"Good R-I-D-D-A-N-C-E," she responded.

He grinned. "See you next week."

Beatrice answered. "Maybe—not." I hadn't told her about Mamm's situation yet. Perhaps she would be too ill for us to attend the wedding.

Next the driver dropped off Mervin and Martin, and from their lane I could see the lilies beginning to bloom in our field.

I kept my eye on them, happy to be home. The van turned up our driveway, and Love romped toward us from the yard. Mamm came out of the house, a smile on her face, limping along with the cane.

"What happened?" Beatrice gasped, jumping out of the van.

"Just a fall," Mamm said. "I'm fine."

Pete and Cate climbed out to greet her as Beatrice and I retrieved our things, and Love ran circles around all of us. I placed everything in an orderly line on the edge of the lawn. Before I could stop her, Mamm lifted one of our bags. "Mamm!" I called out.

"Here," Pete said, taking it from Mamm. "Let me carry that inside."

I protested, insisting I could do it. Pete ignored me and grabbed several other bags, piling them on one ice chest, while the driver grabbed the other one.

"Where's Ivan?" I asked Mamm.

"Out in the greenhouse," she said.

He'd probably been going through years of our business accounts.

"Edna's still here. She's in the house," Mamm added.

I expected that—and was very grateful.

Beatrice put her arm around Mamm. "How are you?"

"Just fine."

"Mamm . . ." I said. "Ivan told me what's going on, but I didn't have a chance to tell Beatrice." I should have pulled her away from the others and told her. I shuddered a little. I didn't want everyone else to know our business—to know how vulnerable we were. I was too afraid what Mamm's coming diagnosis might mean for our family. All these years I'd been the one in our group of friends without any problems, but not anymore.

Mamm leaned against her cane and put her arm around Bea. "Of course one test leads to another. I have to have some more on Monday. Ivan and Edna will take me again."

"Are you past the worst of it though?" Beatrice asked.

"Probably . . ." Mamm answered and quickly changed the subject. "I thought I heard a mockingbird this morning, but by the time I got downstairs, it was gone."

"Maybe we'll hear it this evening," Beatrice said. "Let's sit out on the porch after supper."

I grabbed a kitchen box. "I'm going to take this to the basement."

Pete and the driver returned from the kitchen. "Where do you want the rest of it?" Pete asked.

"We can do it—honestly," I said. "Denki for your help." I turned to Cate. "You too."

"Thank you," she said. "You're the one who worked so hard."

Pete waved as he climbed into the van and I called out a thank-you to the driver too. I hoisted the first of the plastic boxes and headed toward the basement, put it in its exact place, and took the other ones down too. Then, with Love at my side, I walked to the greenhouse office to say hello to Ivan.

He sat at the desk, files stacked around, and papers strewn here and there. I hoped he was keeping everything straight.

I cleared my throat at the open door.

He turned, taking his glasses from his face. "When did you get home?"

"Just now," I said, stepping into the room, leaving Love at the door.

Ivan had never been one for outside work, at least as long as I'd known him. He seemed as happy as could be digging through our accounts.

"How was the camping trip?" he asked.

"Fine."

His eyes twinkled. "Any closer to marrying Mervin Mosier?"

Showing just how out of control I was, tears welled up in my eyes and then spilled down my cheeks. Love began to whine. Clearly Ivan didn't know what to do, but he tried, standing awkwardly, putting an arm around me, but holding it rather stiffly with a good distance between us.

"It's nothing," I said, pulling my apron to my face. "I'm just tired."

"Jah, camping can do that. I remember how much I hated it as a boy."

Behind my apron, I smiled through my tears. I could just imagine Dat dragging Ivan off to the mountains. "Can we talk later?" I asked, peeking above the fabric. "About Mamm? And the farm? And all of this." Except for Mervin Mosier. There was no reason to talk about that now. I just hoped, in the near future, there would still be reason to talk about Leon.

"Sure," Ivan said. "Go get some rest."

Love licked my hand on the way back to the house. At least she still wanted to be near me. Instead of resting, I took the tent and sleeping bags down to the basement. Then I grabbed the box with Dat's shirts, deciding after I'd stashed it in the sewing room I'd put away the food, but Edna already had it all done.

Mamm and Beatrice were sitting at the kitchen table, drinking tea.

Edna gave me a hug and said, "I'm fixing a treat. Sit down."

I did, watching Beatrice and Mamm out of the corner of my eye. Beatrice told her all about the trip, about the golden eagle we'd seen, and the meadowlarks and finches.

"Did you see any columbine?" Mamm asked.

"Jah," Beatrice answered. "I saw some on the road, the evening . . ." She paused. "Anyway, it was orange and yellow. I've never seen anything like it."

Mamm beamed. "I remember seeing those with your Dat and you girls, all those years ago."

I took a deep breath. I hadn't remembered. "There was a purple flower," I said. "Like nettle. A cluster of blossoms on a stem."

"Ach," Mamm said. "Heal-all."

I tilted my head. I'd never heard of it.

"People used to make a tea from it. It's supposed to be good for everything from a sore throat to a weak heart."

I put my hand to my own heart as it lurched inside my chest.

Mamm noticed, putting her hand on my arm. "Are you all right?"

"I'm fine," I said.

"She had a rough time," Beatrice said.

I shook my head slightly.

"What is it?" Mamm asked. "Did things not go well with Mervin?"

"Mamm," I said, "that was never meant to be." I stood as Edna started toward us with two bowls of strawberries and cream in her hands.

"Ach, Edna," I said, taking the bowls from her. "You're too good to us."

She beamed at me and returned to the counter.

I breathed in the sweet scent of the berries and the richness of the cream as I served my Mamm and sister. Usually strawberries and cream brought me great comfort, but today the halved red shapes made me think of my own broken heart.

My only comfort was in Mamm not knowing the true reason for my angst.

As Beatrice told Mamm about the grove of white pines, I realized Beatrice's ignorance probably brought Mamm comfort too. It was one less thing she needed to worry about.

I sighed as Edna served me, saying, "Denki," but thinking Beatrice would soon know—we all would—what Mamm's prognosis was.

In the morning, as I finished making the tea, Love barked outside, and I went to see who was there. Mervin and Martin stood on the stoop, ready to knock. They backed up when I opened the door. Love ran a circle around them.

"Your Mamm left a message," Martin said, putting his sunglasses on his face even though the sun was barely over the hill. "She said she needed another hand."

We did have the lilies to cut, so jah, there was work for Martin for the day, but I couldn't imagine there would be work all the time for him too.

Ivan came out of the house with his cup of coffee, squinting when he saw Martin. "Am I seeing double?" He laughed and then extended his free hand to shake Martin's. "I haven't seen you for a while."

Ivan turned to me and said, "So Anna figured if things didn't work out between you and Mervin—"

"Ivan," I interrupted, "did you notice the lilies?" I grabbed his arm and pulled him around to the corner of the house, pointing him toward the field.

As it turned out, both Edna and Ivan helped us cut the lilies—and so did Mamm. She insisted—although she mostly sat in the lawn chair on the edge of the field and watched with Love sprawled out at her feet.

"Oh, it's just beautiful," Edna said, surveying the field. Beyond the lilies, the lavender bloomed. In another few weeks, at the far end of the field, the tiger lilies would begin to blossom. The orange of those flowers against the purple lavender would be even more striking than the pink and white of the Asiatic lilies. "You've done a good job," Edna said. "I know it's a lot of work."

"Jah," I answered. "But there's nothing else I'd rather do." I took a small knife from my apron pocket and handed it to her.

We each took a row of the lilies that had started to bloom, working our way down it. In no time I was in the lead, with Mervin not far behind me. Beatrice and Ivan were tied for last. Around nine, I convinced Mamm to go in the house with Beatrice for a cup of tea. Love followed them—she'd been sticking close to Mamm now.

"Go ahead," I said to Ivan. "The truck will be here in a half hour, but we're nearly done. We'll be ready." Thankfully the wholesaler had arranged for the transport.

"It was this way when we were growing up too," Edna said as she and I stood together, looking over the flowers. "He was always gifted at getting out of work." She grinned. "I guess I'm soon to be getting out of the work myself. I need to get back home this afternoon."

"Denki for your help," I said. I truly meant it. The last couple of months would have been unbearable without her.

"I feel for you and Beatrice," she said. "It's a lot for you to deal with."

"We'll be okay," I said. She'd lost her mother when she was younger than I was now, but she'd had her Dat for a long time after that. Hopefully we'd have Mamm for years to come too.

She gestured toward the twins. Martin had nearly caught up with Mervin in their side-by-side rows. "Which one is interested in you?"

"Was," I whispered. "The one in the lead."

"And why did your Mamm hire the other one?"

"She's hoping maybe we'll turn out to be compatible."

"The other one wasn't?"

"Not really," I said. "Besides, he's in love with Hannah, my best friend."

"Jah, I remember her." She paused. "And Ivan said you were interested in someone else?"

"Am." I sighed. "I've never felt the way about anyone else the way I do about Leon. Ever. I didn't even know I could feel this way."

Edna grinned. "That's the one Ivan is pulling for, jah? So you'll move to Montana?"

I grimaced. "Ivan wants me to move to Montana?"

She smiled and patted my arm. "Of course not. But if Anna needs to sell, he'd like to buy the place."

"That's what I'm afraid of."

She cocked her head. "What do you mean?"

"That he'll do the same thing with this place that he did with yours."

The questioning look stayed on her face.

"Sell it," I said.

"Jah, sure. What's wrong with that?"

I frowned.

"He's not sentimental," Edna said. "Don't hold that against him. And as far as my place, he did me a big favor. He gave me as good a price as anyone would have at the time and saved me a lot of trouble. I needed all of my time to be with Frank, not . . ." Her voice broke a little, but then she took a deep breath and said, "I don't know what I would have done without Ivan's help."

"Oh," I managed to say, realizing I'd misjudged the situation.

"And," she said, "I hope you're *not* thinking of *not* marrying this Leon and *not* going to Montana just because of this farm. Dat wouldn't have wanted that."

I kept my voice low and even. "Mamm does."

"Maybe she thinks she does, but she came here from Ohio. I'm sure she wants you to follow the Lord's leading." Edna's brown eyes, so much like my father's had been, were the brightest I'd ever seen them. "She hasn't been herself. Tell her how you feel about Leon. She'll understand."

"But what about the farm?"

Edna smiled tenderly. "You have to trust God about that. Believe me," she said. "There's a whole lot worse things than losing a piece of property. Losing love? Jah, that's what really hurts."

She turned away quickly as tears pooled in my eyes for her. "You should go in the house with Mamm and Beatrice," I said, my heart contracting. "I'll be in after a while."

Edna turned back toward me. "Don't get me wrong. I'd miss you like crazy if you moved to Montana."

I gave her a hug. "Denki for being so open," I said. "But I don't see that ever happening." Not now.

I walked back down my row and got back to work, finishing just behind Mervin. He locked eyes with mine, but he didn't say anything.

"What's next, boss?" Martin called out, a few steps behind.

"We finish the other rows," I answered. It didn't take us long, and then we hauled the buckets of flowers out to the loading dock, adding more water as the truck turned up the driveway. Mervin and Martin did the lifting while I talked to the driver.

It felt good to be back on the farm, filling my competent and confident role, where people did what I asked them to and everything ran like clockwork. After the driver left, I sent Mervin and Martin to irrigate the shrubs and ventured back into the house. Edna had joined Mamm and Beatrice at the table, but Ivan was nowhere in sight.

"He's back in the office," Mamm said, without my even asking where he'd gone. I hadn't thought to check when I was by the greenhouse.

I headed that way, but Ivan wasn't in the office. Instead he was standing at the doorway to the barn, peering inside.

"What do you need?" I asked as I approached.

He turned toward me. "Why do you always make me feel as if I'm trespassing?" He pushed his glasses up on his nose.

"Goodness, I was just wondering if you were looking for something, if I could help you find whatever it is."

He shook his head. "I don't need anything. I'm just taking in the view."

I crossed my arms. "Why are you still going through Dat's accounts?"

"Just curious . . ."

"But I thought you did that last time you were here," I said.

He shook his head. "Just the last few years. Now I'm looking at how things were before the building boom stopped."

I took a deep breath, hoping Bob Miller would still come through with recommendations for us that could turn things around, but what I said to Ivan was, "Well, you must have determined by now it's not a very good investment."

"Oh, I'm not looking for an investment," he said and then chuckled. "More likely a tax write-off."

"So you might keep it if you buy it from Mamm?"

He wrinkled his nose. "Probably not."

The next morning, after cutting flowers and herbs for a couple of hours, Mervin, Martin, and I stopped by the house for a cup of coffee before the market opened.

"See how hard she works," Mamm said to Ivan as I entered. "You'd think we could turn things around. If we only had more land." She gave Mervin a pleading look.

I ignored her comment, grabbing three mugs at once from the cupboard, setting them down on the counter with a bit of a clatter.

I poured the coffee and motioned for Mervin and Martin to come get their cups. Then I pried three sticky buns from the pan, put them one by one on paper napkins, and motioned to the boys to get those too. As they did, I glanced at Mamm. "Don't come down today," I said, nodding at the cane. "I'll come up and check on you when I get a chance."

"We'll be fine," Beatrice said.

"I'm sticking around for the day too," Ivan said, putting down the paper and picking up his coffee cup.

"Let's go," I said to Mervin and Martin after we'd finished our snack.

Love followed along. I told the twins to transfer the planters from the greenhouse onto the wagon while I went to get Daisy.

They loaded the wagon, and I hitched the horse. "You two can take the wagon down," I said, grabbing a bucket and heading to the lavender. Once I had it filled, I headed down the hill. The twins had parked the wagon, arranging the pots of flowers and herbs in a pleasing display. One of them must have taken Daisy back up the hill.

Nell had already arrived, and instead of setting up next to me, she had once again spread her potholders out on a table under Joseph Koller's canopy. I don't know why I didn't expect it—but then I took a deep breath, chastising myself. Who was I to begrudge a middle-aged woman love after all these years?

Nell stepped around from Joseph's table. "Hannah's going to share your space again today."

"Oh?" That surprised me.

"Jah. She put up quite a bit of strawberries yesterday—said she might as well sell jam today."

I smiled, trying to appear cheerful about the arrangement but wishing Hannah had called me. I patted my apron pocket. I hadn't been checking my messages very often since we'd returned from camping—plus I had the ringer off because I knew Ivan didn't approve of my having a cell, especially not in the house.

I had five messages. My heart raced, hoping at least one was from Leon. Two from Hannah, left yesterday afternoon. And three from other vendors, left yesterday evening—all who wouldn't be able to make it today for one reason or the other. That would cut into my profits.

I listened to Hannah's messages last. The second was all about her coming to sell her jam, how she'd already talked to Nell and knew the other half of my table would be available. The first one simply said, "Call me."

There was nothing from Leon.

Hannah showed up late, a little frazzled. Mervin must have spotted her buggy because he came down the slope and helped her unload her jars while I waited on customers.

One bought all of the potted geraniums in the wagon. "Bring down more," I said to Mervin.

He practically had to tear himself away from Hannah. She

looked at me, but that was all. I was fine with avoiding the conversation we still needed to have. For all I knew she and Leon were now courting.

The next customer bought all of my rosemary and half of the thyme. After I'd finished the transaction, I said, "Hannah, would you keep an eye on things? I'll be right back."

I hurried up the hill to grab what the twins had cut and ask them to cut more. Beatrice stood at the clothesline, taking down the wash. I didn't bother to ask her to stop.

The twins came out of the greenhouse, each carrying two pots of geraniums. "Are there more herbs?" I asked.

Mervin nodded toward a bucket by the garden. I hurried over and grabbed it. Mervin had just finished cutting another bucket of rosemary. "Keep going," I said, grabbing one bucket and then the other. "They're selling like hot cakes." My stomach growled at the thought. The sticky roll wasn't going to be enough to tide me over until lunch. When I reached the back of the house, I put the buckets down and hurried through the door into the kitchen, leaving it open.

Mamm wasn't at the table, but Ivan was, still reading his newspaper. "How's it going down there?" he asked without looking up.

"Great," I answered. "The twins can hardly keep up with replacing what we're selling." I opened the refrigerator. I took out a hunk of cheese and sliced a few pieces off, and then grabbed a loaf of bread from the box, cutting off the heel and taking it.

As I turned around, Ivan folded the newspaper. "You'll never turn the farm around with the market."

I nodded. "I know. I have other plans."

Ivan chuckled. "I bet you do."

I knew he was teasing, but I felt too sensitive about what was going on to join in any kind of banter. I headed to the door and Ivan followed me onto the stoop. Martin came around the corner of the house just as Ivan said, "Has your friend from Montana shown up today?"

I grabbed the two buckets by the handles, pretending I didn't hear him.

"I didn't think so," Ivan said, his back to Martin. "If Mervin is set on Hannah, then it looks like you'll have to get the second twin to marry you if you want to save the farm. Otherwise I'll go ahead and make an offer."

I don't think he had any idea how he sounded. He thought he was making fun, but his words cut deep. I put down the buckets. "Stop. We haven't even missed a payment yet. There's lots of other things we'll try first."

Ivan shrugged and headed back into the house.

Martin stood frozen a few feet from me. "Don't mind him," I said, sure my face was as red as the geraniums in the pot in his hands. "Let's head on down."

"Listen . . ." Martin said, following me, his breathing funny.

"Are you all right?" I asked.

He nodded. "Just nervous."

"Martin," I said, "Ivan was just being stupid." I ducked under the arbor.

"You don't have to cover for him," he said. "My Dat told me your family's finances are bad. I just want you to know, I'd marry you in a heartbeat—especially if it meant saving your farm." Now his face was red too.

"Martin, that's no—"

"That's not the only reason," he said. "I've always admired you. I've always thought you'd make a good wife." He glanced over his shoulder, up at our house. "And joining our two properties is all the more reason."

"Denki," I said. "Really." I was touched by his willingness. "But you don't love me."

"I could. I'm certain of it," he answered, as sincerely as could be.

I shook my head gently. "Something will work out. For all of us." I stopped then.

Martin bumped into me. "Sorry," he said.

"No, I'm sorry. I haven't been trusting God—not at all— since Dat died. I've been frantic and controlling. And I've made everyone else uptight too." I smiled at him. "He has a plan for all of us. The right one."

He exhaled, seemingly relieved. I laughed. "I appreciate your offer, Martin, but promise me you'll only marry for love."

He nodded.

"Come on," I said, leading the way down the trail. I preferred that Leon would reach out to me to work things out. But if he didn't, I'd find out a way to go to him.

I loved him.

Once Martin put the geraniums on the wagon, he hurried back up the hill for more, and I headed toward my booth. I lowered the bucket of rosemary to adjust my grip, and as I rose back up, the *clippity-clop* of a horse's hooves on the pavement, unaccompanied by the whir of wheels, caught my attention.

I stepped to where I could see through the booths to the highway, and sure enough, Leon was trotting Lightning down the pavement toward us.

20

When I reached our booth, Hannah was wrapping the last of the lilies for a customer. I busied myself arranging the new flowers, doing my best to ignore Leon as he tethered Lightning between the first row of stalls and the buggies and wagons the vendors drove to the market.

My stomach lurched. Then it flipped. He hadn't called or tried to contact me since the trip. I didn't want to appear too eager, but I wasn't ready to give up on him either.

As Leon approached our booth, he tipped his hat to Hannah first and then to me.

"Hello," I said, as calmly as I could.

He picked up one of Hannah's jars of jam.

She laughed. "You don't need to buy that. There's plenty at the house."

"Jah, I'm not shopping for myself. I was thinking about putting a box together for my Mamm. Her birthday's coming up." He pointed to my bucket of lilies and lavender. "Wish I could send her flowers."

"You could send her one of your drawings," Hannah said.

I took a deep breath, imagining him showing Hannah his book.

"Ach," he said, blushing a little. "She has plenty of my drawings, I'm afraid."

"My Aenti Nell is selling potholders. Your Mamm might like one of those. And they'd pack well." Hannah stepped away from the table and then without looking at me said, "Molly, would you keep an eye on things for me. I'm going to introduce Leon to Nell and Joseph."

As the two strolled away from me, Hannah said, "Nell and Joseph are courting. Isn't that sweet? After so many years of being single, she's finally found someone to love her."

My stomach lurched again, this time sending a wave of nausea through me. I had thought I'd found someone to love me too. Maybe I'd end up being old and alone someday after all.

"And someone for her to love?" Leon said.

"Of course," Hannah responded. "That's how it works, jah?"

Leon nodded. "Most of the time."

My face grew even warmer than it had been from running up and down the hill. Did he think I hadn't acted in a loving way to him?

A few minutes later, Mervin delivered two more buckets of flowers. He paused when he saw Hannah and Leon chatting with Nell and Joseph. Then he wandered over and joined in on the conversation, but as soon as he did, Hannah hightailed it back to our booth.

A group of customers congregated around, and we kept busy taking care of all of them, but once Mervin realized where Hannah had gone, he came back over too.

"More lavender," I said to him. "And rosemary." He left, a little reluctantly it seemed.

"Denki," Hannah said. "I don't want him following me around."

"Oh look, lilies!" an Englisch woman about my age exclaimed, turning to the older woman beside her. "They're the right color. What do you think?"

I quoted the price for a bouquet as Leon drifted back toward my booth.

"Oh, we're not looking to buy today," the older woman said. "We're looking for flowers for a wedding. For next Friday."

"Really?" I didn't know the Englisch planned weddings in such a short time.

"The florist we'd ordered our flowers through just went out of business," the younger woman said. "So we decided to do it ourselves. We were going to go to a wholesaler . . ."

"We can do it," I said. "We have more lilies coming on. We can have them ready for you on Friday morning. At seven."

"Perfect," the older woman said, as Leon continued on to the next booth.

As we talked out the details, I thought through the logistics. Bob and Nan's wedding was Friday morning. Even though the wedding would begin at nine, I'd have plenty of time to cut the flowers early that morning.

The bride, whose name I learned was Jennifer, ordered lavender and baby's breath in addition to the lilies.

After they left, I scanned the market for Leon. He'd stopped at a produce booth. I waited on more customers, including Kristine from the bed-and-breakfast I'd visited. "I wanted more of your herbs," she said.

We chatted as I wrapped rosemary, thyme, and basil for her. "You have a wonderful place here," she said, pointing up toward the house.

"It's a little shabby," I said.

"No, not at all. It's authentic. People would love to stay here."

I told her I wasn't sure if I was going to be able to open up that sort of business or not.

"Well," she said, "I'm sure whatever you decide to do, you'll succeed at it." She took the herbs from me. "But if you do decide to take in guests, I'd love to be a resource for you."

"Denki," I said.

She glanced around. "Where's that handsome boyfriend of yours?"

My face grew warmer. "That's not going as planned either."

"Give it time," she said as she walked away, giving me a wave as she did. "You two make such a sweet couple."

Thankfully, Hannah was busy with her own customer and didn't overhear my conversation—at least I didn't think she did.

When Mervin returned to our booth, Hannah scurried over to Nell's side. "Why does she do that?" Mervin asked me. "Why can't she believe that I love her?"

I shrugged, and Mervin took off after her. Hannah darted back over to me, and Mervin followed after her.

"Leave me alone," she hissed.

"Hannah—"

"Stop it," she said. "You've humiliated me enough."

Nell hurried over. "Hannah," she cooed.

Hannah's face had grown disturbed. "I'm going home," she said, bending down to grab her box.

"No, wait." Mervin grabbed her arm, but she yanked it away.

Leon appeared, asking, "What's the problem?"

"Stay out of it," Mervin said. "You've done enough already."

"Mervin, go get more herbs," I said. "The bed-and-breakfast lady nearly cleared us out."

He glared at me and then at Leon but turned toward the hillside and walked away.

As Hannah put the last of her jars in the box, Leon stepped forward and picked up her box. "I'll ride alongside you," he said.

Then he turned to me and said, as politely as could be, "Good-bye, Miss Molly."

"Bye," I managed to chirp, my heart contracting again. Was that it? A final good-bye. Was this how it was all going to end?

I swallowed hard, willing myself not to cry. I needed to talk with him but I couldn't now. Not with Hannah in the state she was in.

"Hannah, wait," I said. She turned. "I'm worried about you. Have you thought about seeing your counselor again?"

Tears filled her big brown eyes. "Do you think I should?"

I nodded, walking beside her.

"I have been feeling stressed." She took a deep breath and then exhaled slowly. "I'll think about it."

When I returned, Nell had moved her potholders over to my booth. I sent Mervin home to eat, and then whispered to Nell, "What's going on?"

She pursed her lips, her round face bunching up, and said, "Nothing. Absolutely nothing."

"What happened?"

She turned to face the hill, and I followed her example. "Joseph just told me he started courting someone else this week," she said, speaking in a normal tone. "A widow his oldest daughter introduced him to. A little older than me. She has ten kids of her own. He said he has more in common with her. It took him all morning to work up the nerve to tell me." Nell lowered her voice a little. "I think he's afraid if he married me, we might have a baby. The old fool." She sounded tough, but I could tell by her voice she was hurt.

I put my arm around her. "I'm sorry."

"I'm not," she answered. She took a raggedy breath. "Not about Joseph. Obviously he's not the right one. But I am sorry for me. That I got my hopes up again . . ." She swiped at her eyes.

I took a good look at her out of the corner of my eye. She

wasn't that old, probably around the age Mamm was when Beatrice was born. Nell probably could have a baby. And she had a sweet face with her dark hair and clear brown eyes. The truth was she looked a lot like Hannah. I could easily imagine how beautiful Nell had been when she was a girl.

My heart welled with love for her. I felt like my old self for a moment. Worried about someone else. Wondering what I could do to help.

My mind whirred with ideas, and then I put my arm around her and whispered in her ear. "Don't be surprised if God doesn't have someone else planned for you. Joseph was probably just the warm-up." A plan began to brew inside my head.

Not wanting to seem too obvious, I waited a few minutes and then asked Nell to see to my sales for a few minutes. I jogged up the hill. Martin had a couple of buckets ready to go, lined up along the lawn. I hurried into the house. "Ivan," I called out. "I need your help."

He stepped into the kitchen from the living room, his glasses in his hand.

"Could you carry some flowers down for me?"

He seemed a little put out, but did what I asked. I led the way, carrying one of the buckets while he carried the other. When we got to our booth, I put my bucket down first and then took his. Then, as if it were an afterthought, I said, "Oh, have you two met?"

"If we have," Ivan said, "it's been years."

"Nell, my brother, Ivan. Ivan, Nell Yoder."

"As a matter of fact," he said, "I do remember you from when we were young, although I think I'm quite a bit older."

"Oh, I don't know about that," Nell answered, followed by a sweet smile.

I left them to chat and wandered over to Joseph Koller's booth. "Want to trade some flowers for a toy?"

His face lit up, confirming every word Nell had said.

I pointed to the wooden toy I had in mind—a carved horse. Robbie would be thrilled. The little boy had teased me relentlessly, but the next time I saw him, I planned to win him over. That's what the old Molly would have done. I was going to try my best to lighten up.

The next morning, Mamm said she wanted us to go to Edna's church. That surprised me, considering early Monday she'd be off to the hospital, but then it dawned on me—maybe that was why she wanted to be in church, and since it was our district's Sunday off it made sense to go to Edna's.

After breakfast, while Beatrice cleaned up, I hitched Daisy to the buggy, and once everyone was ready, off we went to the other side of Paradise.

Edna was overjoyed to see us. Mamm sat between Edna and me while Beatrice sat on the other side of Edna.

We sang the usual songs from the *Ausbund,* and then one I'd never heard before called "The Love of God Is Greater Far." As everyone else sang, and we listened, Beatrice pulled out a small pad and pen from her apron pocket.

"'O love of God, how rich and pure! How measureless and strong!'" Edna's district sang with joy on their faces. The song must have been a favorite with this group. The last verse started with

> "Could we with ink the ocean fill,
> And were the skies of parchment made . . ."

And then ended with

> "To write the love of God above
> Would drain the ocean dry;

Nor could the scroll contain the whole,
Though stretched from sky to sky."

Beatrice scribbled furiously as Mamm and I joined in singing the chorus. Generally speaking, we weren't to be so bold as to assume that we or anyone else was going to heaven. That was up to God. We were to live our lives as if we were—but only God could know our hearts. But I was pretty sure Dat was in heaven and experiencing the love of God in a way we could only imagine.

At the end of the song, an elder walked up to the front and began reading about Mary and Martha. I had to admit, it wasn't one of my favorite stories. I always felt sorry for Martha. She worked so hard and did so much but then got chastised for it by Jesus. But as the elder read, I realized that Jesus only chastised her after she'd complained to him. She hadn't been doing the work for him, or trusting him. She'd been doing the work for herself, which caused her to resent her sister.

"Mary sat still, worshiping the Lord," the elder said, "while Martha worked frantically to get everything done." He went on to explain that it's not wrong to work. A few people laughed. "What's wrong is to not trust God while we work. Just as it would have been wrong for Mary not to trust as she sat still."

He kept talking, but I didn't hear much after that. After he finished, another elder came up and read 1 Corinthians 13. It had been my Dat's favorite passage, and Mamm squeezed my hand, her bony fingers digging into mine. The elder read from the King James Version instead of High German. "'Charity suffereth long, and is kind; charity envieth not; charity vaunteth not itself . . . Doth not behave itself unseemly, seeketh not her own, is not easily provoked . . .'"

I thought of the word for *love* in Pennsylvania Dutch—*Leeva.*

And then the word for *Christlike—Grishtlich*. Loving others meant not wanting my own way.

What did that mean, exactly? Letting go of Leon to court Hannah if that's what he wanted? If not, being willing to go to Montana with him? Did it mean selling the farm to Ivan without a fight?

I took a deep breath. It meant something—I just wasn't sure what.

At the end of the service, the first elder came back up and said he had a verse from Psalms for us to remember through the next two weeks. He recited, "'Make thy face to shine upon thy servant: save me for thy mercies' sake.'" He smiled and then said, "Let that be our prayer."

That's what I needed—God's saving mercy. In my grief, I'd ignored it the last few months. Dat had died—not God.

We stayed for the meal afterward and then gave Edna a ride to her place. Ivan would take Mamm to the hospital tomorrow, and Edna would come over to help us care for Mamm once she came home. She hugged Mamm extra long as she said good-bye.

Monday morning, Ivan arrived to take Mamm a few minutes earlier than we'd expected. "I'll go grab your bag," I said to Mamm, heading toward the staircase, not wanting her to attempt to carry it herself using her cane.

The room was in its usual meticulous order. I hadn't been back in since I'd boxed up Dat's things, and it looked exactly the same, including the blue notebook on the little table. It seemed everyone but me—at least Beatrice, Leon, and Mamm—had a book they wrote in.

This time curiosity got the best of me, and I went around the bed and opened the book. The pages weren't lined, so it was more like a drawing book. There was a sketch of two birds—mockingbirds—on the first page, their wings both shaded in until they looked as gray as they were in real life, contrasting with the white feathers. I flipped to the next. There was a strike, a barred owl, a swift, and then a ruby-throated hummingbird. All were identified, in Mamm's handwriting, but I wasn't sure who'd drawn them.

"Molly?"

I jumped.

"What are you doing?"

I turned around, the book still in my hand.

"That's private," she said. She leaned against the doorjamb, no cane in sight.

I put it back on the table. "It's just drawings of birds."

"No," she answered. "It's more than that." She shuffled over to her bureau, took her brush out of the top drawer, and put it in her bag.

I picked up her satchel and, feeling like a child, followed her down the stairs.

When we reached the kitchen, Beatrice asked for at least the third time how long Mamm would be gone.

"Until Wednesday, if all goes well," Ivan said. "They'll put Anna completely out for the biopsy—and then they'll want to keep an eye on her."

Beatrice hunched over the table. "What if it doesn't go well?"

"Bea . . ." I stepped around the table and put my arm around her. She surprised me by grabbing my hand and squeezing it.

Mamm patted Beatrice's shoulder. "It will be fine, child. Don't worry."

Ivan stood, his coffee mug in hand, and walked to the kitchen sink, where he gazed out the window. "Here comes the driver," he said. He took a last drink of his coffee and then dumped the rest in the sink. He turned toward Mamm. "Ready?"

She nodded.

Mamm hugged me and said, "Take care of things around here."

She seemed to have forgiven me for snooping. I hugged her back. "Everything will be fine—you'll see—here and at the hospital too."

After she hugged Beatrice, we all walked out to the car. Doris waved at us as Mamm climbed into the front seat.

Ivan hesitated a moment and said quietly, just to me, "Are you sure you two will be all right here alone?"

"Jah," I answered. "Why wouldn't we be?"

"It worries me, is all."

"I'm plenty capable," I answered.

He nodded, as if he'd heard it before, and climbed into the back seat. He would stay at his own place the next two nights. Doris would drive him back and forth to the hospital.

I watched as the car disappeared down the driveway. When they returned on Wednesday, they wouldn't know the results of the biopsy. Ivan had said that would take a couple more days. But we would be that much closer to knowing what the future, for all of us, held.

I'd prepared myself, being the pragmatic person I was, for my parents to die while I was still young. I'd taken a rational approach. Chances were, they would. They had been as old as most of my friends' grandparents. Still, when Dat had died, it caught me off guard.

And no matter how realistic I could be, I could think of no practical way to deal with the possible death of my mother.

Tears pooled in my eyes again, and I swallowed hard. The only way to get through the next two days was to work hard and put it out of my mind. I grabbed a hoe from the tool shed and headed out to the lavender. Two identical heads, both covered with straw hats, bobbed along above the purple blooms. Mervin and Martin were already hard at work.

At least I had that to be thankful for.

In the early afternoon, Ivan called my cell phone. He said the biopsy had gone well and Mamm was in recovery.

"I'll call before I leave the hospital," he said.

A few minutes later, a landscaper called to place an order, explaining Mamm had given him my number last week. The man had gotten a job when another contractor had a family emergency and couldn't finish it. He needed sixty shrubs for a parking lot project—all by tomorrow. He'd send a truck in the morning.

I gladly accepted the order, and the twins and I got busy. Late in the afternoon, I pulled Beatrice from the house to help. She wasn't pleased but pitched in. By suppertime we had the shrubs pulled, wrapped in burlap, and transported to the loading dock.

I sent Mervin and Martin home and Beatrice to the house to fix a simple supper. Then I headed to the office to write up the invoice. After that was done, I sprayed down the shrubs, soaking the burlap. Then I headed toward the lily field to see how the blooms were coming along.

As I passed the house, Beatrice was sitting on the front porch, her journal in her lap, staring off toward the lowering sun.

"Want to walk with me?" I asked.

She shook her head.

"Come on, Beatrice. It's not good for you to spend so much time by yourself."

She held up her journal as if to indicate she wasn't alone.

"Suit yourself." The truth was, I needed to be with someone. It was too quiet with Mamm gone. A wave of loneliness swept through me. I missed my Dat. I missed the group of Youngie I'd hung out with for so many years.

I missed Hannah.

And I missed Leon, most of all.

The next morning, the landscaper was pleased with the shrubs and that we were able to fill his order in such a short time. As Mervin and Martin loaded his truck, he asked to talk with Mamm about what else we had.

"She's not available right now," I said. "But I can show you."

Love stayed at my side as I led the way to the back field. She was friendly enough to the man but also protective of me. I showed him the trees, shrubs, and decorative grasses. It wasn't a huge collection, but it was definitely adequate, especially for what it seemed this landscaper needed. He followed me down a row and then back up, commenting on the selection and the health of the plants.

"I'll definitely be in touch," he said as we walked back to the truck. "I have a project in a new subdivision next month. I'll figure out what I need and let you know."

After the man left, Mervin approached me. "Would you talk to Hannah?" He took his sunglasses off, showing his sad puppy-dog eyes. "Tell her how much I love her. She won't believe me. She still thinks I'm teasing her."

"She's not really listening to me either," I said.

"I'm afraid she's falling for Leon."

My heart sank, but I didn't say anything.

"Well, if you get the chance to talk with her . . ."

I nodded. *Chance* was a disappointing word. If I got the *chance* to talk to Hannah . . . If I got the *chance* to talk to Leon . . . Mervin headed back into the greenhouse.

Lord, I prayed, *how about an opportunity instead of a chance? To talk to both Hannah and Leon.*

Ivan called my cell just after supper and said Mamm was doing well. "We'll be home tomorrow," he said.

"Edna's coming to help us," I said. "I know you shouldn't be away from your work for much longer."

"I'm bringing a stack of it with me. I'll stay until the weekend at least."

We would have been fine without him, but it might help Mamm to have Ivan stay. She'd been used to Dat's support all these years. Ivan was definitely competent. As much as I'd—at first—felt as if it should have been my role to be with Mamm, I could see that he probably dealt with the doctors better than I would have been able to. He'd have a better idea of what questions to ask, both of the doctors and the business office.

After he said good-bye, I headed out to the front porch, leaving Beatrice to clear the table. Instead of doing it, though, she followed me out.

"You should call someone and go have some fun," she said.

I shook my head as I leaned against the porch rail, focusing on the field across the road.

"No, really. You're making me nervous hanging around so much. Go over to Hannah's." She stood behind me. "Or see if Martin wants to go to the party down by the river."

I turned toward her. "There's a party?"

"I'm guessing there is. If there isn't, you could organize one."

I shook my head. I had no desire to go anywhere—and certainly not to organize anything—but she was right. I *was* restless.

Mamm, Ivan, and Edna arrived at eleven on Wednesday morning. Mamm was pale and using the cane. She said her head ached but otherwise was fine. They'd used a needle to do the biopsy and hadn't even shaved a patch of hair, which surprised me. We put her on the sickbed in the sewing room and then finished up dinner.

Ivan took over the desk in the living room, and when I went to call him to the table, he asked me to wait a minute.

"I just want you to know," he said, twirling his glasses in his hand, "that if I buy this place I'll never turn all of you out. If I resell it, you girls can stay with me, until you marry. Then Anna can live with one of you—or with me if that suits her better."

I wasn't going to bother saying I didn't think Beatrice would ever marry, but I did ask, "What if I never marry?"

"Oh, you will." Ivan put his glasses back on his face. "Perhaps not one of the Mosiers . . . or the Montanan. But someone will turn up." He turned his attention back to his paperwork. *"Someone will turn up."* He made it sound so devoid of love and emotion and everything I felt for Leon.

For the rest of the day Beatrice waited on Mamm, Edna saw to the housework and cooking, and Ivan did his accounting, while I saw to the outside work, ordering Mervin and Martin around, a role I was enjoying less and less.

Midafternoon, I went in for a drink of water, and Edna offered me a piece of strawberry pie. How could I refuse?

She sat with me while I ate. "Do you remember us talking about the circle letter? The one that introduced my Mamm and yours?"

I nodded.

"And how your Mamm came out to visit?"

I nodded again.

"I thought of something else that happened when she did."

"Oh," I said, between bites.

"Your Mamm took over the kitchen while she was here, saying

it was the least she could do. I was fifteen and Ivan was already out on his own. I'd been doing all of the cooking and cleaning, so it was nice to have some help. One night before dinner, your Mamm was cooking and mine was sitting at the table. She was bald from her treatments—with her Kapp on, of course—and in pain. We knew she wasn't going to live much longer, although no one would talk about it.

"Your Mamm spilled something on her apron and took it off to rinse it right away. She said she'd run up to her room to get another, but my Mamm told her not to bother. My mother stood, a little shaky, and untied her own, and then handed it to your mother, saying, 'I want you to have this. I don't need it anymore.'"

I put down my fork and exhaled slowly.

"Jah," Edna said. "I didn't really think much about it at the time, but now . . . I think it was as if she chose your Mamm—for Dat, for all of us."

I shivered, my eyes filling with tears. That was love. Suddenly my view of Dat's first wife took a 180-degree turn.

That evening, Ivan borrowed our buggy to go somewhere— although, even when I asked him point-blank, he didn't answer. My guess was over to see Nell Yoder. That made me smile. Maybe there was hope for Ivan yet. I couldn't wait to see how love might change him.

Maybe there was hope for me too.

Thursday we all continued with our routines, but after our noon meal a car I didn't recognize turned into our driveway. I guessed it was a tourist who noticed our flower fields and wanted to buy some or perhaps was hoping for a tour. That happened every once in a while.

Thankful I was the one outside and not Beatrice or Ivan, I put a smile on my face. But as the car came closer, I saw the passenger was an Amish man—Bob Miller. I squinted, wondering why he'd come by our house the day before his wedding.

I headed to the car, meeting him as he climbed out. He had a folder in his hands. "How is your Mamm doing?" he asked.

"Good," I responded. "Do you have time to come in?" I shaded my eyes with my hand.

"I'd love to," he said. "But I'm on my way to the hospital. Betsy's in labor."

"Oh dear," I said. "She's a few weeks early, right?"

"Jah. She was late with the first two. We didn't think she'd be early with this one."

I nodded, understanding he and Nan wouldn't have scheduled their wedding when they did if they'd suspected Betsy would be having a baby.

"I've come up with some more ideas for your business." He handed the folder to me. "Give this to your Mamm when she feels up to it. Then, in a week or two, we can talk."

I took it from him. "Denki."

"You can look at it too," he said. "Not that you need my permission."

My face grew warm as I glanced toward the car. The only other person in it was the driver. "Is Nan at your house?" I asked.

He shook his head and then climbed into the passenger seat, leaving the door open. "She's already at the hospital."

"What about Cate?"

"She's home." He pulled the door shut but quickly opened the window. "Actually," he said, "she could use some help getting ready for the wedding. Is there any chance . . . ?" He grimaced. "What am I thinking? You have plenty going on."

"No, I can help. Ivan and Edna are both here," I said.

307

He smiled. "Her Aenti Laurel is over—she's the organizer for the wedding." I nodded, not surprised. For most Amish weddings, a close relative handled that job. "And Nell and Addie are over too, but Laurel isn't feeling well. I told her she should go on home, but she hadn't when I left. Could you give Cate a call? I think she could use your help. She and Pete are finishing an order for me, so she's in her office." He smiled again. "Denki."

"See you at the wedding," I said.

He smiled again. "God willing."

I waved as the driver maneuvered the car around and then pulled out my cell phone and called Cate.

CHAPTER

21

That evening after supper, I waited for Cate out on the porch with Love at my feet. Cate couldn't get away as early as she had hoped and ended up spending most of the afternoon helping Nell and Addie. A hummingbird flew in and fed at the feeder, seemingly unaware of me. Across the highway the faint sound of a woodpecker reverberated against our house. The redheaded woodpecker had always been my favorite. I thought of them as a hardworking bird.

I stood, thinking Cate should have arrived by now, and headed down the steps. Under the oak tree two birds pecked in the thin grass. Gray-and-white birds. I stopped. The mockingbirds had returned. Thinking of the first page in Mamm's book, I started back up the steps to tell Mamm but then heard a buggy coming up the drive. I'd tell her later.

Love ran out ahead of me toward the birds, and I called her back. She didn't obey, and I shouted again, "Love!"

She came, settling down by the back door. The mockingbirds flew up into the tree.

Much to my surprise, Cate had Robbie with her. The little boy was sitting next to her, a frown on his face.

"He's been out of sorts," she said. "He wouldn't go to Pete

or Addie. He only wanted me, so I decided to bring him along. They both have so much to do. I figured he'd be fine riding with us. Robbie scooted closer to Cate.

"Hold on just a second," I said and ran back to the house and up the stairs to my room, grabbing the carved horse.

When I returned I handed the toy to Robbie. He clutched it but didn't smile.

"Ach, how sweet of you," Cate said. "Denki." She lifted her nephew's chin. "What do you say?"

He shook his head solemnly, his curls bouncing back and forth.

"Robbie."

"It's okay," I answered. Poor guy. He seemed awfully out of sorts. "I can drive," I said. I was a little leery of Cate's horse, but I figured with her along he wouldn't misbehave. She handed me the reins, and Robbie crawled up on her lap, the toy in his fist. As her horse sped down the highway, she said, "Thank you so much for calling. I needed to get away from there. Don't get me wrong, I appreciate Laurel and Nell, and especially Addie, I really do . . ."

We were headed to the next district over to borrow a third church wagon for the wedding. These wagons were moved from home to home with everything needed for Sunday services . . . and weddings.

"Sounds like there's going to be a huge crowd," I said.

"Jah, which we expected. But we didn't anticipate Betsy going into labor early." She sighed. "We'll just have to trust God to work it all out."

"How are you feeling?" I asked.

"Oh, fine . . ." She glanced my way and then asked, "Why?"

"Oh . . ."

She smiled and then said, "Dat didn't say anything, did he?"

"No." My face grew warm. "I shouldn't have said that. There

was just a moment, while we were camping, that I wondered . . . if . . . you know . . ." I stumbled over my words.

"I might be pregnant?"

"Jah . . ." Overcome with embarrassment, I feared she wasn't. She didn't answer for a long moment, but then said, "You guessed right. I am. But we're not telling anyone. Well, Nan guessed it too, and she told Dat."

"I won't say a thing," I said. "Except that I'm really happy for the two of you."

"Denki." Cate beamed brighter than I'd ever seen her, snuggling closer to Robbie. "So are we, God willing that this one is meant to be."

I didn't pry. "Well, he certainly has blessed you so far."

"Ach, Molly, you'll be where I am in a few years. Married. Settled in a home. Pregnant."

I felt the tears starting again and turned my head toward the field of knee-high corn to my right.

"What is it?" she asked.

"Everything's ruined," I said.

"Between you and Leon?"

I nodded, my head still turned.

"But Mervin likes Hannah again, right?"

"Jah, but Hannah thinks Mervin is teasing her. I told him I'd try to talk with her, but I haven't seen her. Mervin's afraid she's falling for Leon since they spend so much time together." I pulled back on the reins to slow Cate's horse as we rounded a curve. "Who in their right mind would choose Mervin over Leon?"

Cate laughed but then stopped abruptly. "I'm sorry," she said. "Hasn't Hannah liked Mervin for a long time?"

"Jah."

"They make a good couple. Leon is definitely more your type."

"But I'm not his," I said.

"How so?"

"I'm not good with horses, for one thing."

She urged hers to go faster again, even though I was driving. "You can learn."

I made a face.

"Or not," she quickly said.

"Besides, I'm not that good with kids. And he's crazy about them."

"Oh, that's what that was all about—Hannah holding Robbie so much." She rested her chin on top of her nephew's head.

"Jah, but she wasn't doing it to attract attention. She really likes kids."

"Most girls do," Cate said with a nod. "Personally, I didn't. It wasn't until I got married, well, until Pete and I really came to love each other, that I started wanting to have a baby. Once Robbie came around I was smitten, but before that I was exactly like you." She smiled. "Leon probably didn't even notice."

"I doubt that."

"Did he say anything?"

I shook my head.

I pulled the reins to the left, turning Cate's horse across the highway and onto a side road. Then she looked at me again, an expression of sympathy on her face. "Things really will get better," she said. "I promise. If Leon isn't the one for you, then God has someone else."

"That's just it. I don't want anyone else. I want Leon."

"Then don't give up."

I nodded, although I had no idea what that meant right now.

Cate added, "Don't be so hard on yourself. Your Dat's passing was so recent. Now your Mamm has all these health concerns, not to mention the business problems. If you don't feel your usual self, don't despair. You will again. It takes time."

We rode in silence for a few minutes as I mulled over her words.

Then, as I pulled into the next driveway, she said, "Something that took me a long time to learn was to extend grace to myself too. Up until then . . ." She shook her head. "Well, let's just say I'm not sure how others put up with me at all."

An old man started to step down from the porch when he saw us, pointing toward the church wagon by the barn. Robbie stirred as I stopped the buggy. He'd fallen asleep and clung to Cate.

"Could you take him?" Cate asked me.

"I can try." I wasn't optimistic at all. But, perhaps because he was so tired, he allowed his aunt to slip him into my arms, the toy still in his hand. Cate hopped down from the buggy, and I slowly stepped to the ground.

The man helped unhitch Cate's horse from the buggy and hitch it to the church wagon.

"I—or someone—will be back with it on Saturday," she said. "And to pick up my buggy."

As we climbed onto the bench, me still holding Robbie, the man's wife came out of the house carrying a stack of bowls. "Don't forget these," she said.

"There's no more room in the back," her husband said.

I scooted closer to Cate, and she put them on the floor of the wagon, in front of the bench.

Then the man said, "I forgot the chairs." He headed into his barn and returned with six folding chairs. "I told your Dat I'd send these along."

He moved the bowls to the bench and then wedged the chairs onto the floor, forcing me even closer to Cate with my feet turned toward hers at an angle. We both giggled. Robbie stirred a little and then settled back against me.

Cate thanked the man, and we were soon back on the road.

313

Robbie's warm body molded against mine. I sniffed the top of his sweaty head, but it wasn't a bad smell. There was a sweetness mixed in with the sweat from his curly hair.

Cate asked, "Mind if I stop at the park to use the restroom?"

"Of course not," I said. It wasn't much out of the way, and the evening was beautiful.

There was a crowd in the park, maybe as many as two hundred people, and obviously some sort of production going on. Performers, dressed in a variety of costumes—Englisch clothes from a few decades before, wide skirts and narrow ties, and then what looked like some kind of primitive people—milled about on the amphitheater stage.

"Oh good," Cate said, scooting forward on the bench. "I know we can't stay to watch it, but I hoped they were doing a play tonight." She pointed toward the restrooms. "I just need a quick stop. Then we'll be on our way."

As she drove the church wagon through the parking lot, heads turned toward us, mostly tourists I was sure, and I wished I'd brought the fliers for our farmers' market.

Cate stopped the wagon in the no-parking zone along the restrooms and then handed me the reins. "I'll be right back," she whispered.

Robbie stirred but didn't wake.

I scanned the crowd, not surprised we were the only Plain people in sight. Then I watched the production. An Englisch girl chased another Englisch girl across the stage. Then a man, barely dressed, hopped out from behind a cardboard tree. I squinted, trying to make sense of it all.

A movement in the real trees, along the edge of the park, caught my attention, distracting me from the performance.

A Plain man rode a horse, followed by someone else on a

horse. I groaned out loud. It was Leon and Hannah, riding along the pathway, coming toward us, but then they stopped by an oak tree and Hannah slid off Lightning. She staggered a little and then leaned against the tree. Leon jumped off Storm and took the reins from Hannah.

The sight of them made my heart hurt, but it looked as if Hannah was ill, and that worried me. I waved, but Leon didn't respond.

When Cate came out of the restroom, I pointed toward the tree. "I'll go check," she said.

By the time she was halfway to the tree, Leon had seen us. He said something to Hannah, and she looked up, but then put her hands on her knees and leaned forward, as if she might faint.

Cate talked with them for a few minutes and then, holding Hannah's arm, started back toward the wagon. Leon followed, leading the two horses.

"What's the matter?" I asked when they'd nearly reached us, keeping my voice low.

"Vertigo," Cate answered.

"Uh-oh," I responded. Hannah used to get it a few years ago—some sort of inner ear problem.

"It came on really suddenly," Cate said. "She almost fell off Lightning."

"I can't ride home," Hannah groaned.

"Of course not," Cate said. "I'll take you home."

Hannah nodded, grateful for the offer. I glanced at the chairs on the bench. We'd have to leave some of this behind to make room.

I gave Cate a searching look. She nodded toward Leon and the horses. "Would you consider riding Lightning back?"

"Of course not," I answered.

Leon was close enough to hear and flashed me a smile. "Lightning's cured of her fear of dogs. I worked on it all week."

"You can lead her," I said. "I'd rather walk." We weren't too far from Hannah's farm. I scooted off the bench with Robbie, holding him tightly. Once I was on the pavement, I told Hannah, "I'll hand him to you when you get up there."

She shook her head and pulled away from Cate. "I feel like I'm going to be sick."

We all waited for a long minute until the danger seemed to have passed, and Hannah climbed up on the bench. "I can't hold him," she said.

"I'll take him," Cate said.

I started to pass him up to her but he began to whimper and cling to me. Cate took him anyway, but he began to scream.

Several people watching the play turned their heads. I quickly took Robbie back. "I'll walk with him," I said.

"It's too far," Cate whispered.

"I'll take the shortcut and meet you at Hannah's house."

"I'll go with her," Leon said.

Cate hesitated a moment and then agreed. Hannah closed her eyes and tipped her head back against the seat. Cate pulled the wagon around and headed for the road. I watched the performance as I followed Leon toward the trail. Two girls were back on stage, along with two men.

The taller woman said, "'Good Hermia, do not be so bitter with me. I evermore did love you, Hermia. . . .'"

The actress continued, "'Save that, in love unto Demetrius, I told him of your stealth unto this wood. He followed you. For love I followed him.'"

I stopped, patting Robbie's back to keep him quiet as I did, and missed a few of the woman's words, but then she said, "'And follow you no further. Let me go.'"

Leon looked back at me.

The taller woman, who had been talking, appeared mad. She

spoke again, saying, "'Oh, when she's angry, she is keen and shrewd! She was a vixen when she went to school. And though she be but little, she is fierce.'"

My face grew warm. I couldn't help but think of Hannah and me, thinking I had been the one acting like a fierce vixen.

Leon motioned for me to come along as an Englisch woman, probably a grandma, stopped beside me coming back from the restroom for a peek at Robbie.

"What's the play?" I whispered to her.

"A Midsummer Night's Dream."

I gave her a questioning look.

"Shakespeare," she added.

"Oh," I said, although that didn't give me much more of an explanation. I'd heard of him, but that was all.

"Cute baby," she said.

"Denki," I answered, still watching the stage—until she smiled at Leon. That I caught. I guessed she thought we were married and Robbie was ours.

"'Love looks not with the eyes but with the mind,'" the woman whispered.

"What?"

"It's from the play. Seeing you and your husband together with the horses and the baby made me think of that."

My face grew even warmer, but I didn't say a word, and after a moment she continued on, sitting back down on the edge of the crowd, and my eyes fell back on the stage. The half-clothed young man waited along the side, ready to go back on the stage.

The shortcut was a trail through a wooded area along a creek. It came out close to Hannah's house but was at least two miles, maybe farther. It had been years since I'd been on it. After I refused to ride horses with Hannah we would hike it sometimes with Mervin and Martin and some of the other Youngie in the summer. That was before we started going to parties and running around more.

By the time we neared the creek, my arms felt almost numb from carrying Robbie. I shifted his weight a little, and he snuggled even closer to me. I stopped and leaned against a tree, resting my back.

"You should get up on Lightning," Leon said, stopping beside me. Storm snorted, but Leon pulled him closer and he stopped.

"I can't ride at all—let alone ride and hold Robbie."

"You wouldn't have to ride. I'll lead the horse."

"How would I get up?" I asked.

"I'll hold Robbie while you do," he answered.

I shook my head and started walking again. What had I been thinking to offer to carry Robbie the whole way back? Asleep he was as heavy as a sack of seed.

The path widened, and Leon stepped to my side. We walked in silence for a while. I wanted to talk with him, about what went wrong, about how he felt about me, about how I felt about him. I asked God if I should bring it all up—but I didn't feel a peace about it. I did feel an acute ache between my shoulder blades though.

Leon stopped. "Want me to take a turn with Robbie?"

I nodded. It was worth a try.

"You lead the horses," he said. As I transferred Robbie into his arms, my hands brushed against Leon's forearms and a shiver shot up my spine. He leaned back a little, trying to settle Robbie against his chest, but the little boy began to scream and dropped his toy horse. I retrieved the horse in a hurry and gave it back while Leon patted his back, but Robbie became more unsettled.

"Get up on Lightning," Leon whispered. "Let's just give it a try."

"What about my dress?"

He turned around as he spoke. "I won't watch. Get all situated and then let me know. Chances are we won't see anyone along the way."

I grabbed the saddle horn and pulled myself up. Once I yanked my dress down as well as I could, I told Leon and he stepped to the side of the horse and handed Robbie up to me. He continued to cry, but as I pulled him close, his head on my shoulder, and leaned back against the saddle, he stopped fussing, wedging the toy between us. Leon led Lightning, along with Storm, and soon the rocking of the horse's steps seemed to lull Robbie back to sleep. My back and arms still hurt, but not like they had.

Leon turned toward us, walking backward. "You look really nice up there."

I couldn't help but smile.

As the horse ambled along, I found myself lulled into a quiet state. Had I never taken the time to just hold a little one and enjoy it?

Above, the breeze played with the leaves of the treetops high above the trail. A bird called out. A dog barked—and I cringed, braced for the horse to rear—but Lightning didn't react. I closed my eyes, moving with the sway of the horse, my heart beating along with Robbie's, listening to Leon's soft footsteps on the trail and his occasional murmurs to the horses.

A half hour later, he stopped and reached up for Robbie. Then I slid off the horse, as modestly as I could, and a minute later I led the way off the trail to the road near the Paradise Stables sign.

I grew more anxious as I walked beside Leon. My opportunity to talk with him was quickly vanishing. As we neared the house, he said, "You know I told you I'm not very good at talking about things. And asking questions."

I nodded. I remembered.

"But there's something I need to ask you. . . ." He took a deep breath. "That's the real reason I came over on Saturday to the market—to talk."

"But then you left with Hannah . . ."

"Jah, I was worried about her. She's been having a hard time lately."

"Do you care for her?" I asked.

"Of course. She's a friend. Besides being my boss's daughter." He stopped and turned toward me, his face reddening. "Molly, what are you asking?"

I shrugged.

"She's a friend. That's all," he said. "Mervin cares for her, right? You're hoping they get back together."

"That's what I'd hoped," I said. "I guess now I just want to leave it up to God."

"*Gut*," he answered. "That's what I've been thinking. My friend Hank's favorite Bible verse was from Psalm 139."

I knew that passage. It was all about being fearfully and wonderfully made.

Leon quoted, "'For thou hast possessed my reins.'" He stopped.

"That was his favorite verse?" I nearly burst out laughing.

He nodded, a smile spreading across his face as he jiggled both pairs of reins in his hands.

"That figures—for a horse person," I added.

"But it's so true. God does hold our reins."

I couldn't disagree. "What were you going to ask me?" We only had a couple of more minutes. Perhaps we could still talk things through, although to what outcome now I couldn't imagine.

"Does our relationship depend on me staying in Lancaster? Or would you be willing to go with me to Montana?"

I nearly choked on my words. "Are you going back soon?"

He nodded. "I've had an offer on a job. Training horses, not too far from my folks' place. It turns out Owen isn't going to buy the third horse he hoped for me to train after all. So I'll be out of a job here soon."

The screen on the front door banged, and Cate appeared before I could answer. "Molly!" She'd parked the church wagon in front of the house. "Ready to go?"

Leon groaned.

I answered, "Jah."

Leon brightened. "Were you talking to me?"

"No, to Cate." My heart lurched as I walked. In a daze I climbed into the church wagon, sliding up against the chairs, balancing Robbie as I did.

Cate climbed up next and then said to Leon, "Thank you so much for your help with Robbie and Molly." She took the reins up and then almost as an afterthought asked, "Will we see you tomorrow?"

"I'm not sure," he said.

A burst of panic sent my heart racing. Did he plan to go back to Montana soon? For a moment, I wished I'd told him I would be willing to go with him. But by the time Cate turned onto the highway, I came to my senses.

I couldn't leave Mamm and Bea.

CHAPTER
22

Once I got home, I headed straight for the greenhouse office and retrieved the folder Bob had given me.

As long as I was there, I checked for messages. I had one, from Mervin, saying he wouldn't be coming to work in the morning before the wedding. "Bob called—Betsy had her baby, everything is fine. Another girl. But he asked me to help set up in the morning. He's worried about Cate doing too much. So Martin and I are going to go over there and help out. We figured you and Beatrice could get the flowers cut. I knew you'd understand. See you tomorrow."

I shook my head as I hung up the phone. He left a message on the landline instead of calling my cell because he didn't want to talk with me in person. But the truth was Bob and Nan and Pete and Cate really could use the help. If I didn't have the flower order to fill, I'd go too.

I grabbed the file and headed toward the house. There was no use lighting the lamp in the office when Beatrice would have already lit the one in the kitchen.

But when I walked in the back door, all was dark and quiet. Mamm called for me from the sewing room.

I stepped into the hall. The door was open and a lamp lit. She sat in the chair at the sewing table, one of Dat's shirts in her lap.

"What are you doing?" I asked.

She held up a blue diamond. "Beatrice said you're making a quilt from these," she said. "I think that's a great idea. I'll help."

"We could make two," I said. I hoped there was enough fabric for two. "One for Bea and one for you."

"Oh no. If there's enough, I want them both to be for you girls."

"Well, good night, then," I said, but then remembered the birds. "Oh, I forgot. The mockingbirds are back."

Mamm's face brightened.

"I saw them before I left with Cate."

"Oh, I'm so glad," she said.

I headed toward the door.

"Molly."

I turned back toward her.

"I want to apologize for snapping at you about looking at the notebook before I went to the hospital."

I shook my head. "I shouldn't have."

"You may look at it if you'd like." She folded her small hands in her lap. "Your Dat and I started it the day we were married. The mockingbirds were the first birds we saw together that day. He drew them."

I smiled. I hadn't even known Dat could draw, but it made sense considering how creative he was.

"And then I'd write the name. We kept lots of notebooks over the years. That was the first."

"But I never saw any of the notebooks around the house."

"We kept them in our room. We wanted something to share, just between us."

"That's so sweet, Mamm," I said.

She smiled.

324

"The mockingbirds are the reason your Dat named the dog Love."

I shook my head in confusion.

"He named our first puppy Love too, but she got hit by a car when you were a baby."

I still didn't get it and my face must have shown it.

"Your Dat would yell for the dog, and then the mockingbirds would mimic him, calling out, 'Love! Love!' He wanted to try it again with this dog. It worked."

I laughed. "I never picked up on that."

She nodded. "It was our secret."

I walked across the room and hugged her. "Denki," I said, ready to go to bed.

"Sit down for a moment, Molly," she said, nodding toward the bed. "There's something I wasn't completely honest about."

I obeyed her, alarm rising inside of me. I'd never known my mother not to be honest.

"I told you I didn't love your Dat when we first married, but that wasn't true. I did love him. I loved him the first time I set eyes on him, when he was still married to Donna. But I felt so guilty about it, so ashamed, that the story I told myself was that I didn't love him when I married him—that I grew to love him. And then that's what I told you."

"Oh, Mamm."

"Even though I felt as if I'd done something wrong, I wasn't going to let that shame keep me from the only man I'd ever loved."

"But you didn't do anything wrong." I leaned forward. "Did you? Like telling him how you felt when he was married to Donna."

"Of course not. The exact opposite, in fact—I focused on her, cared for her as best I could."

"Edna told me how good you were to her Mamm. How good you were to all of them."

Mamm blushed.

"And she told me how much Dat loved you, which I saw too. What a great relationship you had. Edna was so thankful for that."

Mamm put her hand to her face as she inhaled.

"And she told me something else. Do you remember when Donna handed you her apron?"

Mamm tilted her head. "I'd spilled something on mine . . ."

"That's what Edna said. She thinks her Mamm chose you— wanted you to be Dat's next wife. That's why she invited you out. It probably was a comfort to her to think he might want to marry you, that you would be a stepmother to her children."

"Oh goodness, Molly. Do you think so?"

"It makes sense to me." I stood.

"Wait," she said. "There's one more thing I want to talk with you about."

I couldn't help but yawn. I had to get up by four in the morning. "Mamm, we both need to get to sleep."

She shook her head. "I'll be fast. When I woke up after the biopsy, the first thing I thought of was you. And what I'd asked of you, as far as marrying Mervin. That was wrong of me."

"Denki," I whispered. Even though the whole sorry mess was over, it still helped to have her apologize.

"If you love this Leon, you—"

"He's going back to Montana."

"Then go with him," she said.

I sank back on the bed as if the wind had been knocked out of me. "It's over between us."

Her face fell.

"Besides, what about the farm?"

Mamm inhaled deeply. "That's it. Sure your Dat and I worked

together and shared everything, but he carried the burden of the business side of all of this. I panicked when I realized how bad things were and that I was responsible for all of it. I didn't have your Dat to trust, so you'd think I would have trusted God, but I did the exact opposite. I tried to solve it on my own, and the easiest way seemed for you to marry Mervin, which was ridiculous of me and even more so when it was obvious you were interested in Leon."

I stood again. "It doesn't matter. I wouldn't want to go to Montana, even if Leon and I were courting . . . until we know how you are."

"But that's just it," Mamm said. "If you love him, you should be willing to do that no matter what. I moved here from Ohio."

I narrowed my eyes. "But you didn't like Ohio."

"True." She smiled. "At least be willing to do what God wants of you. Love is full of challenges—that's why you need God's guidance."

I nodded. "I think God has been teaching me the same thing he's been teaching you." I kissed the top of her Kapp. "I forgive you. Now go to sleep. We want you rested enough to go to the wedding."

As I headed through the dark living room to the staircase, I saw the front door was open. Thinking someone had forgotten to shut it, I stepped toward it, only to find Ivan sitting on the porch.

"You're up late," I said.

He nodded toward the chair. "Want to join me?"

"I can't," I answered, tucking the folder from Bob under my arm. "I have an early morning tomorrow."

He spoke, as if he hadn't heard me, "Don't do like I did."

"What's that?"

"Let marriage pass you by." He sighed. "I was busy building my business. And I was a perfectionist. And I was afraid of

327

emotions. There were several women I could have married, but I always found something wrong with them."

My face grew warm.

"Don't you do that too. You don't want to end up a lonely old person like me."

"You're not old," I said.

"Jah, I am."

"Well, God still might come up with something for you."

Ivan chuckled a little.

"Do you want to move back home?" I asked, my face growing warmer as I spoke. "Not because we're going to sell you the farm. We're still going to try to make it work."

"So you've come to your senses." He leaned forward.

"What do you mean?"

"That it's not right for you three to be living alone."

"We're fine living alone."

He shook his head. "I worry about you. Living in town would be safer."

Had I misjudged him again? "Is that why you wanted to buy the farm?"

He nodded.

"Not to make money off of it?"

He frowned. "How coldhearted do you think I am?"

"I'm sorry," I whispered. Then, in a normal voice, I said, "Really, the three of us are fine. Hopefully we can turn things around. If not, you'll be the first to know." I took a deep breath and exhaled slowly. "But if you wanted to move in with us, we'd be pleased."

Now he smiled. "You don't need an old bachelor set in his ways around."

He was probably right. Still, I would have been willing to give it a try. I gave him a quick hug and I told him good-night.

As I turned to go he said, "Hopefully you'll have a man in the house again soon."

I chose to ignore his comment. I didn't want to tell him I'd ruined everything on the camping trip.

I tiptoed up the stairs. Jah, I had forgiven Mamm, but I couldn't help but wonder how things would be with Leon if she hadn't interfered. Maybe not any different.

After lighting the lamp in my room, I leafed through Bob's proposal. He commented on several things we were doing right, including the farmers' market, the cut flowers, and supplying contractors. Among his suggestions were to add more early crops next year—sunflowers, zinnias, and more lilies—and to offer them to other local markets to expand our sales. He also suggested adding more deciduous shrubs to meet the expanding landscaping market and growing more woody branches, such as dogwoods and bittersweet, and marketing those to floral suppliers, along with berried branches too. He had a section on time management, saying that more seasonal workers would pay off in the long run.

At the end of his notes, he wrote that we needed a solid business plan—and he'd be willing to help us draft one at no cost. He believed with our continued hard work, the growing need for landscaping plants, and clear direction, our business should turn around in two to three years.

I closed the folder. I'd definitely be around to make it happen—I just hoped Mamm would be too.

After changing into my nightgown, I extinguished the lamp and crawled into bed. I tossed and turned. I know I slept, because I dreamt about the fireflies in the forest. Instead of watching them, Leon and I flew with them, something I absolutely believed possible in my dream state. I awoke feeling cheated.

At three forty-five I slipped into a work dress and sweatshirt, stepped into Beatrice's room, and tried to wake her, but she only snapped at me and rolled over. She wouldn't be any use out in the field anyway. Next I checked on Mamm in the sewing room, where she was sleeping peacefully.

Love greeted me as I headed to the work shed to collect buckets for the flowers, my gloves, and two knives, in case the first one became dull, trying to imagine what the Englischer wedding would look like with so many flowers. Then I lit a lantern. Sunrise was well over an hour away.

I walked to the row we hadn't cut, setting down the lantern and buckets. Love waited at the edge of the field for me as I began cutting, quickly and efficiently, pulling off the anthers when needed so Jennifer wouldn't have yellow pollen blowing through her wedding.

I'd worked for about a half hour when I heard the *clippity-clop* of hooves on the pavement, reverberating in the quiet of the morning. Of course in my dreams it would have been Leon coming to confess his love to me. But he'd had the chance last night. Why would he come out now? Someone else was out for an early morning ride.

Regardless, I straightened my back to look but couldn't see who it was. I returned to cutting the lilies, losing myself in my work.

A few minutes later, Leon's deep voice interrupted me. "Howdy, Miss Molly."

Startled, I looked up. Love hadn't barked. Instead she was licking his hand.

He stood at the end of the row wearing his cowboy hat. "Would you like some help?"

I straightened my back again, placing my hand on my hip. "This is farm work. I thought you only did ranch work."

"Would you give me a chance?"

"What do you know about cutting flowers?"

"Only that I'm willing to learn," he said.

I took a deep breath.

He grinned.

My heart melted a little. I took the second knife from my apron pocket and held it up. "I'll show you what to do," I said.

He made his way down the row. I demonstrated the cut, at a slant and quick, and then handed him the knife. He grasped it and cut a flower, a little clumsily, but it worked.

"Good," I said, pulling a bucket from the bottom of the stack. "Start at the beginning of this next row."

He took the bucket and the knife and followed my instructions. When my bucket was nearly full, I carried it to him and took what he'd cut and then headed to the spigot and filled the bottom with water.

Leon and I worked alongside each other in silence as the sun came peeking over the hill, casting a pinkish hue over the flowers. Even as light flooded the field, neither of us talked. I started to—but realized I had no idea what might come out of my mouth—so I stopped.

Leon and I carried the buckets of flowers to the loading dock as a pickup turned up our driveway.

I hopped down from the dock to direct the driver to back up the pickup for easier loading. I'd expected Jennifer's mother, but it was Kristine, the owner of the bed-and-breakfast. "Good morning," she called out.

I waved.

She smiled and began to back into the space without my instructions. When she climbed out of the pickup, she looked up at Leon and called out, "How are you?"

He grinned and then greeted her.

"Such a sweet young man," she whispered to me. "You two must have made up."

I grimaced, but perhaps it didn't look that way to her. She smiled and then said, loudly, "When Jennifer said she'd purchased the flowers from you, I volunteered to pick them up."

"How do you know Jennifer?" I asked.

"She's getting married at our place today."

"Oh." I'd imagined a big church wedding.

Leon started to load the buckets.

"I have a few other weddings booked. I thought I'd pass on your business information to them."

"Thank you," I answered.

"Well, let me know if you have any questions about the bed-and-breakfast business. I'd be happy to give you advice."

"I will. I'm not sure what we'll decide. . . . My Mamm is having some health issues."

"Oh, I'm sorry," she said.

I thanked her for her concern. "Hopefully we'll find out today how bad it is." I gave her the invoice, and she said Jennifer's mom would get a check in the mail.

After she left, Leon told me he had something for me. "It's in my saddlebag." I walked over to the hitching post with him, Love wedging herself between the two of us. He pulled two papers from his bag. "Here," he said, handing them to me.

They were the pastel drawings of the columbine and the purple flowers.

"It's heal-all," I said. "My Mamm identified it."

"That's what Hannah's grandma said too. It heals broken hearts."

Touched, I said, "Really?"

He nodded.

Mamm had said it healed weak hearts. I liked broken hearts better.

"Will I see you at the wedding?" I asked.

"Jah," he said as he unwound Lightning's reins from the post. "I told Owen I'd go with their family."

If I didn't speak to him now I might not have another chance.

"I have something I wanted to tell you," we both said at once and then laughed.

"You first," Leon said, tipping his hat at me. For a moment I wanted nothing more than for him to put it on my head again.

"You asked me if I would have gone to Montana with you," I said. "I wasn't sure at first—and it took me a long time to think this through. But now I can't, not with Mamm ill. Not when we don't know what's wrong. Not until she's back to right."

"I understand." He slipped up onto Lightning, his blue eyes still on me.

I whispered, "What were you going to ask?"

He shook his head. "It wasn't important." He turned Lightning around. "See you soon."

As he rode away, Love followed him.

"Love, come back!" I yelled. "Love!"

"Love! Love!"

I whirled around toward the oak tree. The mockingbirds were calling for Love too. My heart lurched as I hurried to the house, Love loping along behind me.

Ivan was waiting at the back door, his coffee cup in hand. "Was that the Montanan?"

"Jah," I said.

"Did he come a-courting?"

"No," I answered. "He came a-helping."

Ivan hitched up the buggy as I quickly washed and changed into my nicest dress, and then hurried Beatrice along. Mamm was quiet on the ride to the wedding, and I was afraid she was overtired from staying up late the night before. Ivan chatted away about the crops we passed, guessing at how much each would bring in that year. I stopped listening by the time we were halfway there, and I was pretty sure Beatrice hadn't been listening at all.

Betsy wasn't at the wedding, of course, but it seemed most of the rest of the county had shown up. There were well over six hundred people, which wasn't usually the case for a second wedding, but it was Nan's first, and Bob knew everyone—not only in the county but all over the country—Amish and Englisch alike, it seemed. The Millers had cleared out the shop for the event and had hired two kitchen wagons.

Cate was standing out by the shop with Robbie on her hip when we arrived. He fell into my arms, still clinging to his toy horse.

"Goodness, what changed?" Beatrice asked me. I smiled as Robbie gave her an impish grin.

"We need your help," Cate said to me. "Aenti Laurel fell ill about a half hour ago and had to go home, and Addie isn't here yet. Could you take over as the wedding organizer?"

I'd been to a hundred weddings. I thought I could do it. "Jah," I answered. "I'd be happy to."

Cate gave me a rundown of who was working on each crew.

"I'll go check on everyone," I said, still holding Robbie. On the wedding day, the organizer made sure everyone was doing their job—the cooks, the servers, and the clean-up crew—and that they were timely. There were very clear expectations. No one would accuse me of having too high of a standard.

Both Beatrice and Cate followed me into the shed. Nan had relatives from New York who were helping set up the benches, including a niece named Hope. Cate introduced her to Beatrice right away, saying Hope enjoyed writing too, and the two seemed to hit it off—as much as Beatrice did with anyone. I was thankful she seemed willing to do Cate the favor of befriending Nan's niece, which would be one less worry for Cate during the day. Beatrice stayed to help Hope, although the project was almost done.

I spoke with Nan's brother, who assured me he would lead the crew to set up the tables for the meal as soon as the service was over.

Next, still carrying Robbie, I checked on the cooks in the kitchen wagon, breathing in the homey scent of roasting chickens, stuffing, and gravy. The potato crew had the peeled potatoes soaking, ready to be boiled. The truth was, it looked as if Laurel had done such a good job getting everyone organized that the day probably would have run like clockwork without her—or me. But I was happy to help.

I'd started to the house to check if Nan was ready, when Hannah arrived with her family. Her face was pale but she seemed steadier on her feet than she had the night before, although she didn't carry Tinker—her next younger sister did. Hannah smiled when she saw Robbie with me but didn't say anything. I searched behind her for Leon, but he was nowhere in sight.

Instead I saw the Bergs coming from the parking lot in front of Bob's showroom. They'd hired a driver, and Phillip had come with them. I watched as he quickly retrieved Bella's wheelchair from the back of the van, expertly popping it open. A moment later he returned, with Jessie at his side, carrying Bella. He carefully put her in the chair and then pushed it toward me. Bella grinned when she saw me, and I stepped forward to greet them. Phillip lifted the tips of his fingers in a wave and said hello. Jessie smiled warmly as the family all passed by. When Mr. and Mrs. Berg came along, she reached out and squeezed my hand.

I watched as they all filed into the shed. Even in my sorrow, I couldn't have been happier for Phillip Eicher.

I continued on to the house. Nell was in the kitchen and it took me a minute to realize that she was standing up with Nan. That made me smile. Nan was still in the back bedroom, so I didn't see her, but Cate stepped out and I told her to watch out the window and I'd wave when all the guests were seated in the shop.

As the last of the guests filed in, Leon showed up on Storm. I couldn't help but think he cleaned up good—even though he looked good to me all the time. He tipped his straw hat to me—no sign of his cowboy hat now—as he approached and then took it off as he entered.

I waved at Cate, and then she, Nell, and Nan, wearing a deep purple dress, hurried over, followed by Bob. Cate took Robbie from me, and she and I entered the shop. I didn't follow her to the front but instead slipped into the last row on the women's side, by Beatrice, Mamm, and Edna, who had met us there. Then the wedding party filed in.

When it came time for the actual ceremony part of the service, after the singing and preaching, it felt as if the entire congregation scooted to the edges of the benches and collectively held its breath. I know I did. Not because we expected anyone to object or for there to be any great revelation or even any unusual words—an Amish wedding was as predictable as the rest of our lives. No, we all held our breath in honor of true love. Of two people finding each other after losing love, living faithfully, and working through the obstacles that faced them, slowly but surely.

Nan appeared radiant. Her blond hair, what was visible under her Kapp, was definitely streaked with gray, but her face looked young for her age. Bob also had a few streaks of gray in his dark hair and beard, but he hardly looked to be the father of grown daughters and now the grandfather of three, with Cate's baby on the way.

He was definitely younger than my Dat was when he married for the second time. I smiled as the preacher took the couple's hands. I guessed Nan was in her early forties, just a little older than my Mamm was when she married. Bob and Nan, theoretically, could have children. I smiled a little at that. Betsy's three children and Cate's too could have an aunt or uncle younger than them.

As the preacher placed Bob's hand on top of Nan's, I was thankful to be a witness to God's goodness, regardless of the plans he had for me.

I scooted back on the bench, and as I did, caught sight of Leon sitting next to Ivan. That surprised me some—I'd expected him to sit by Owen, but perhaps as late as Leon was, the only place left for him to sit was by Ivan.

CHAPTER

23

After the service, the guests milled around outside while the set-up crew put up the tables in the shed. I made sure all the servers were ready to go, and had them line up outside the kitchen wagons. Addie and Jonathan led the crew and Nell helped too. I wasn't surprised when Ivan stepped to her side and asked how he could assist. That made me smile.

My phone vibrating in my pocket caught my attention, and I quickly stepped away from the shed, fearing perhaps I'd gotten Jennifer's order wrong. But when I answered it, a man asked to talk with Mamm.

I didn't bother to ask who was calling. I guessed it had to do with her test results. It seemed she was giving everyone my cell number these days.

I turned toward the crowd of people. The first group was going in for the meal, but Mamm was standing, leaning slightly on her cane, by Edna under the oak tree. I hurried toward her, passing off the phone. "It's for you," I said.

She took it, but instead of talking immediately she started to make her way past the crowd. I followed.

When she reached the driveway she stopped and said, "Hello. This is Anna Zook."

Then she listened for what seemed an hour but was only a few minutes.

Finally she said, "Thank you. I'll call to make that next appointment later this afternoon."

My heart fell.

She ended the call and handed the phone to me.

"Mamm?"

She smiled. "It's benign."

Tears of relief sprang into my eyes.

"I'll still need treatment—maybe surgery but more likely radiation. I have a specialist I'll consult with. But it's not nearly as dire as they feared. The doctor's optimistic that it will respond to treatment and that I have many years of living ahead of me. Once the tumor shrinks, my balance should be good again. And my memory."

I was grateful she didn't bring up the matter of money. I'd talk to the bishop about the mutual aid fund. She took my arm and said, "Walk with me, would you?" We did, along the edge of the driveway, up the lane.

"I'm not sure what this means for us—for the farm," she said.

"Can't we keep going the way we have been? Bob thinks we can turn things around in a couple of years."

"Ivan doesn't." She sighed.

"Listen, if you want to sell it to Ivan, that's fine with me. I have to trust God with this. I'm driving myself—and everyone else—crazy trying to make all of this work." I couldn't stop the tears.

"Did you talk to Leon about how you really feel?" she asked. "Ivan said he was over this morning."

I shook my head.

"You have to," Mamm said. "If you don't, I will."

"Promise me you won't," I said, mortified by the idea.

She smiled. "You have until the time we go home." Then she said, "I'm still going to try to save the farm. I'll go over Bob's ideas. I'm going to tell Ivan to give us a year. If we can't make it by then, we'll entertain an offer."

Up by the rose garden, Hannah and Mervin stood shoulder to shoulder next to Phillip and Jessie. Beatrice and Hope chatted, maybe even flirted, with Ben and Martin. Leon stood a few feet away.

"Go have some fun," Mamm said. "You've been acting as if you're as old as I am since your Dat died."

Edna stepped to Mamm's side. "Let's go eat," she said.

I headed up the little hill toward Hannah, asking her when I reached her if she was feeling all right. "Jah," she answered. "It was the weirdest thing. I was better by this morning." Then she whispered. "Mervin and I are officially back together." She reached for my hand. "I'm going to go see my counselor. I called her this morning before we came. She said it sounded as if a few maintenance sessions were in order."

I squeezed Hannah's hand. "It's *gut* to take care of yourself, jah?"

She nodded and then said, "The same is true for you."

My face flushed, but then Robbie came running up the hill, distracting both of us. I expected him to go to Hannah, but he reached up to me. I scooped him up. He laughed, but not at me. I followed his eyes. Leon was making faces at the toddler, but when his eyes met mine, Leon grinned.

"Go talk to him," Hannah said, nudging me.

I handed her the little boy. This time he didn't cry.

Leon saw me moving toward him and met me halfway. "Miss Molly," he said, tipping his hat.

Without even saying hello, I blurted out, "I didn't say what I needed to this morning."

"Neither did I." He nodded toward the edge of the property.

I walked beside him. I'd need to go check on the servers in a little while, but I had some time.

We stopped by the fence line, under the leaves of a silver maple.

"I should have said more this morning," Leon said. "I guess I was . . ." He smiled, but his blue eyes appeared sad. "I hate to admit it, but I've been fearful. After you fell off Lightning, I was afraid of being rejected again. Afraid you'd never trust me."

I shook my head. "It's not your fault I'm not good with horses. And as long as I'm being honest, I'm not very good with children either. It's not that I don't want to be a Mamm—I do. I'm just afraid I won't be a very good one."

"You seemed to have charmed Robbie."

I smiled. "No, he charmed me."

"I think he charmed us all," Leon answered, "and I don't care if you're good with horses or not. Sure, I thought it would be fun to ride together." His eyes twinkled. "And after last night, I hope you'll give it another try. . . . But that's not what I want to say to you."

He stepped back toward the tree and leaned his hand against it. "I wanted to say that I think I offended you, and I'm sorry. I care about you. I understand why you can't leave your Mamm and sister." He took a deep breath. "I'll stay here instead of returning to Montana. That's what I wanted to say this morning." He took another deep breath.

I stepped toward him, and he wrapped his arms around me. I put my head on his chest, and we stayed that way, the leaves of the trees winking above our heads.

"I do have one question," I said, looking up into his eyes.

"Anything."

"When you and Hannah were in the meadow and Mervin came across the two of you and then I arrived . . ."

He groaned.

"What did you mean when you told Hannah she didn't have to put up with him. Because," I said quickly, "it seemed to me you were about to declare your love to her."

He shook his head. "I told you I worried about her, that she reminds me of my sister."

"What were you saying then?"

"That she didn't have to put up with Mervin going back and forth. That she should wait until he figured things out, for sure." He leaned back and looked me in the eyes.

I managed to squeak, "Oh."

After a long pause he said, "What did you want to tell me?"

"I wasn't willing to leave Lancaster County, not even for you, but I was wrong. I am now. Mamm's going to be okay, but last night—when we didn't know—she told me I should go with you anyway. And she was right. I didn't see that until today."

"This love," he said, "is a lot of work."

"Maybe that's why God commanded us to love one another. Maybe he knew how hard it would be," I said. "And that we might give up."

Leon's face brightened. "Jah."

I pulled away and looked up into his eyes. "Could we start over?"

He didn't answer, not with words. Instead he kissed my forehead. Then the tip of my nose. And finally my mouth.

We did start all over, courting every Sunday night.

And so did Ivan and Nell, officially. Ivan sold his house, but he didn't move in with us. Instead he bought a small acreage outside of Paradise and remodeled the house for his bride-to-be.

Mamm took a series of radiation treatments, which shrank the tumor enough that she regained her balance and her memory. Every once in a while she seemed moody, but I wasn't sure if that was the tumor or the grief that still accompanied her, day in and day out.

Sadly, Cate lost her baby soon after Nan and Bob wed. Addie told me. Cate never mentioned her loss, but I knew she grieved too.

By August, I'd started hosting meals for Englisch tourists, and by September, the bishop gave his approval for us to take in overnight guests too. Bob was right, mostly, about our business. We did turn things around—but it was the help of Leon's labor through the summer and fall in the evenings that eventually made the difference.

He and I soon came to the conclusion that our barn would be perfect to board horses. And with a little work, the corrals would work to train them. Thankfully we hadn't plowed up the pasture to plant more flowers.

By our wedding day in November, we knew Lancaster County would be our home. Leon's parents came from Montana for the wedding, and we hoped to go to Montana the next year—for a visit.

We were well supported at the wedding by family and friends. Beatrice, on the other hand, continued to be out of sorts at times, but I think Dat's death had come at a harder age for her than it had for me. I trusted, in time, she'd find her footing.

Robbie sat quietly with his parents, two little sisters, and Cate and Pete through the service but afterwards giggled and laughed, happy to have his group of grown-ups together, bouncing from one of us to the next to the next, charming us as always but sticking closest to Hannah and Mervin, who still hadn't set a date for their wedding.

Before our wedding meal was served, Leon and I went out on the porch for a breath of fresh air. Love came around the side of the house and up the steps, wagging her tail, slapping first Leon and then me. It may have been my imagination, but I was nearly certain I heard the mockingbirds sing out, "Love! Love!" I couldn't help but think how pleased Dat would have been to have them call on my wedding day.

Mamm and Bea, who held a quilt in her arms, followed us out. "Here," she said, extending it toward me. "Mamm and I made it for you."

Tears filled my eyes as I realized it had been made from Dat's shirts. I'd been too busy to give making one for Bea another thought. They'd kept their work a secret all this time. I ran my hand over a green diamond and then swiped at my eyes. "Denki," I whispered. "Is there enough fabric left for another one?"

Bea nodded. "For a lap quilt. We'll keep it in the living room— for all of us to use."

I hugged them both, and then Mamm took the quilt from me. "I'll put it in your room," she said, motioning for Bea to follow her back into the house.

Leon and I stood alone for a long moment, and then he wrapped his arms around me, saying, "Miss Molly, I love you."

The mockingbirds called out again, for certain, and then Leon reached for my hand, locking my fingers between his, and led me back into the living room to our table. As we waited for the meal to be served, he leaned over and whispered in my ear, "The road of true love—for the moment—is running smooth."

"Jah," I whispered. "Enjoy it. You never know when we might hit a rut."

My husband still longed for Montana, and even though we were now able to make a livelihood in Lancaster, I knew God might direct us to go west someday.

As we laughed together, Bea, followed by Ben, plowed through the room, a scowl on her face. For a moment I wondered what I'd had against moving after all, but then Ivan announced it was time for the prayer. We all bowed our heads in silence. I said a prayer of thanks, for my family, for my friends, for Leon.

And for all the love around us, today and forever.

Acknowledgments

Many thanks to my husband, Peter, and our children—-Kaleb, Taylor, Hana, and Thao—for inspiring me and encouraging me on this amazing writing journey. I'm also grateful to Laurie Snyder and Tina Bustamante for reading early drafts of this story and for their expertise. I'm indebted to those in the Plain community who have shared their stories with me. Any mistakes are mine alone. My gratitude also goes to Aunt Sparkie and Uncle Wally Walker, who once had a farm dog named Love. You and your family have ben an inspiration to me through all these years.

I can't thank Bethany House Publishers enough for their support. My editor, Karen Schurrer, is essential to my writing process, and it's an ongoing delight to partner with everyone at Bethany on THE COURTSHIPS OF LANCASTER COUNTY series.

This novel and the others in the series have all been inspired by Shakespeare's plays. It's been my privilege to study his work and mull over his themes, plots, and characters as I write these novels.

Most of all, I praise God for the opportunity to tell stories that reflect a long literary tradition of beauty, hope, and redemption.

Leslie Gould is the coauthor, with Mindy Starns Clark, of the #1 CBA bestseller *The Amish Midwife*, a 2012 Christy Award winner; CBA bestseller *Courting Cate*, first in the COURTSHIPS OF LANCASTER COUNTY series; and *Beyond the Blue*, winner of the Romantic Times Reviewers' Choice for Best Inspirational Novel, 2006. She holds an MFA in creative writing from Portland State University and has taught fiction writing at Multnomah University as an adjunct professor. She and her husband and four children live in Portland, Oregon.

Learn more about Leslie at www.lesliegould.com.